"SAY NO"

To Brad, Sam, & Beth
With Best Wishes
Graeme
Whatley

"SAY NO"

A Short Story

BY

GEORGE WHATLEY

authorHOUSE®

AuthorHouse™ UK Ltd.
1663 Liberty Drive
Bloomington, IN 47403 USA
www.authorhouse.co.uk
Phone: 0800.197.4150

© 2013 by George Whatley. All rights reserved.

No part of this book may be reproduced, stored in a retrieval system, or transmitted by any means without the written permission of the author.

Published by AuthorHouse 10/01/2013

ISBN: 978-1-4918-7988-7 (sc)
ISBN: 978-1-4918-7989-4 (e)

Any people depicted in stock imagery provided by Thinkstock are models, and such images are being used for illustrative purposes only. Certain stock imagery © Thinkstock.

This book is printed on acid-free paper.

Because of the dynamic nature of the Internet, any web addresses or links contained in this book may have changed since publication and may no longer be valid. The views expressed in this work are solely those of the author and do not necessarily reflect the views of the publisher, and the publisher hereby disclaims any responsibility for them.

Dedication

I would like give as special thank you to my wife Shirley for all her support, without it, this book would not have seen the light of day, my daughter Sharon for all her help in checking my bad punctuation and layout of the story, I would also liked to thank Margery who helped me collate this book together

George Whatley

"I swore never to be silent whenever and wherever human beings endure suffering and humiliation. We must always take sides. Neutrality helps the oppressor, never the victim. Silence encourages the tormentor, never the tormented"

By Elie Wiesel

"To sin by silence when they should protest makes cowards of men"

By Abraham Lincoln

CHAPTER 1

Just as it had done every fortnight during the previous two years, the NATGAS 2, a gigantic 100,000 ton gas ship, gently slipped its moorings at the port of Rabat in Morocco. Fully loaded, its cargo consisted of 180,000 cubic meters of Liquid Natural Gas (LNG).

Its departure led by tugs, and assisted out of the port by an on board Pilot, the giant ship cleared the harbour and got under way. The Pilot transferred to a pilot ship and watched as the behemoth cleared the port. Her gargantuan size dominated the evening skyline with its six giant double-skinned, sphere-shaped storage tanks, another leviathan of the seas setting sail with a valuable and deadly cargo of cryogenically cold Liquid Natural Gas intended for sale to various industries, power plants and domestic fuel suppliers.

The cargo of LNG was sometimes sold on the open stock market whilst ships were in transit and on occasion even the gas ship itself changed ownership before it had even reached its destination. That was, however, the nature of the energy world and its markets. Some energy companies were a law unto themselves and were so powerful that they controlled whole countries, with owners and top directors powerful enough to be above the law, influencing on a major scale world governments as they controlled the world markets in energy and in the distribution of oil and gas.

For Captain Don Williams this was to be his last trip for a while as he was due to have some time at home with his wife and daughter before his daughter went off to university. He had become very familiar with this particular voyage and was looking forward to a break. He was, of course, under no illusions as to how lethal and hazardous the cargo was which was contained in his vessel, however, he had no concerns regarding his crew. It was nothing unusual for ships to be crewed by seamen of many different nationalities and he had sailed with Abdul as his First Mate on the last three trips. He had come to value and relies on Abdul's experience as a seaman even though he did feel that Abdul possessed a much darker side to his nature. He knew better than most captains that it did not pay to delve too deeply into another sailor's life as they all had reasons to be where they were and doing the particular job they did on the NATGAS 2.

Captain Don Williams had no idea that as he commenced his last voyage, under cover of darkness at the Port of Agadir in southern Morocco, a very large and powerful ocean-going luxury speedboat called the Fast Lady had been stolen. Now the same Ocean-going luxury beauty was heading at speed out into the ocean with a crew of heavily armed and determined terrorists on board under the leadership of a man known as Parvis.

Parvis and his crew of eight handpicked men had loaded the Fast Lady with an arsenal of hand-held rocket launchers, guns, mortars, explosives, detonators, fuses and specialist climbing equipment.

Parvis was a well-known terrorist and was wanted for acts of terrorism and running terrorist cells and carrying out terrorist bombings in nine separate countries. Over the last few months he and his fellow terrorists had enhanced and honed their skills at the training camps in the foothills of Afghanistan. They had also learned their latest trade well from Somalian pirates off of the Horn of Africa.

As the crew had prepared their weapons, they had spoken of their determination to strike at the heart of the West once and for all and to strike terror in the western world.

After a day at sea, the NATGAS 2 was a hundred miles off of the Islands of Madeira. It was there, that under cover of darkness the Fast Lady approached the NATGAS 2 unseen. As early morning dawned, the Fast Lady was manoeuvred very close to the stern of the ship where she hove to under the lee of NATGAS 2, bouncing around in the wash created by the giant ship. It was then Parvis ordered four of his men to board the gas ship.

The four men proceeded to fire grappling hooks with special adapted lines out of hand-held launchers, up and over the railings of the lower deck. They then pulled on the lines to make the grappling hooks grip. The wire lines opened up to make wire ladders and two of the men lifted themselves swiftly and silently off the deck of the speedboat and swung outwards, gripping the wire ladders and scrambling upwards, clearing the boiling wash of the ship and attempting to board via the stern. As one of the men reached halfway up the ladder, he slipped and fell and disappeared into the boiling sea. The hook on the other man's ladder slipped from its anchor point and the man was left flaying around in the air as the ladder fell away, eventually dropping him also to his death into the wash of the great ship. The rest of the group of terrorists looked on in horror.

"Now we have fewer men to work with" Parvis stated angrily and ordered another man to take the place of the second man on the third ladder.

"You have ice in your veins, he was your friend" the man commented.

Parvis offered the man a cold, dead stare "Be careful my friend that you do not join him" he said threateningly "now move".

All three men knew of Parvis' reputation and were perfectly aware that he could and would kill without compunction. They also knew that if they slipped from the wire ladders like their comrades, they would fall to certain death into the churning cauldron of foam, but this was what they had been trained for.

So, with some trepidation, the men swung out one at a time, out over the boiling wash and climbed slowly up the wire ladders. On reaching the lower deck, they climbed from the ladders and slipped safely over the railing onto the deck.

One of the men commented "You've got to give it to those Somalian pirates, they do this using bamboo poles".

All three of the men then set off silently towards the Radio Room before they were seen and an alarm sounded.

The Fast Lady swung about and stood off to the lee of the gas ship to wait for full daylight.

Once at the Radio Room, the three terrorists secured it and left one terrorist on guard whilst the other two terrorists firstly lowered the gangway ladders at the side of the ship down to where Parvis and the other men waited on board the Fast Lady. The remaining terrorists then stormed their way to the Engine Room where they took it at gun point. They again left one terrorist on guard whilst the other terrorist made his way to the Bridge where he burst in taking the Bridge crew completely by surprise.

Abdul the First Mate was at the wheel. He was pushed to one side as the terrorist took control of the Bridge.

"Prepare to be boarded" the terrorist said to Abdul "or be blown out of the water. With this cargo, you will all die and we will all see Allah together". The terrorist's eyes shone with a fanatical gleam "there is a speedboat out there with hand-held missiles levelled at this ship, ready to blow us all to Kingdom Come. It is up to you to decide whether you are ready to meet with your Maker" then suddenly screaming an order "stop this ship now!"

With the terrorist aiming the gun menacingly at Abdul, Abdul took back the wheel and was forced to slow the ship down and heave to. The Fast Lady immediately came alongside and the remaining men aboard her rushed up the gangway ladder and boarded the NATGAS 2. One terrorist was left on board the Fast Lady whilst Parvis and the other terrorists made their way to the Bridge.

As they entered, tension on the Bridge increased markedly.

"Welcome aboard" Abdul said sarcastically to Parvis as he greeted the terrorist leader "that was like taking candy from a baby. May the fleas of a thousand camels infest your armpits".

"Very expensive candy" Parvis rejoined and thereafter ignored Abdul, obviously treating his remark with the contempt that he thought it deserved. A few moments later, as if something suddenly crossed his mind, Parvis approached Abdul and pointed his gun at Abdul's head.

Everybody on the Bridge seemed to freeze and hold their breath. Time seemed to stand still and the air became frigid with tension. Parvis suddenly broke into a huge grin, lowered his weapon and enveloping Abdul in a bear hug, kissed him on both cheeks. "Well done my friend. How are you? This has been a long time in the planning. Now the fun and games can really begin". He paused for effect and added "We have a lot to do in a short time before the world wakes up to what we are doing. This is better than playing with toy boats by the river where we dreamt of taking over the world when we were children".

"That was a long time ago my friend" Abdul replied "what are we going to do with the crew? We can't trust any of them".

"What do pirates do with unwanted guests aboard their ship?" Parvis asked, a broad grin on his swarthy features "they make them walk the plank of course—firstly, we need to get the Fast Lady on board, we may need her later, besides, I could become accustomed to the pirate's share of having my own sea-going luxury speedboat. If I remember correctly you sank the last boat I had with a well-aimed rock".

Abdul laughed "That was after you pushed me into the river if you remember, and I nearly drowned" Abdul said and slapped Parvis on the back.

"I got you out though didn't I?" Parvis said "besides we both got a good hiding from our parents for getting our best clothes muddy and wet".

"If you remember further it was two days after that when you and I were at school that our village was bombed by the Americans. Both our parents were killed in that raid. The infidel Americans said their apologies and that it was a case of accidental friendly fire".

Parvis and Abdul hugged one another in friendship.

"For that act my friend it is now payback time" Parvis said.

Abdul made the crew of the NATGAS 2 haul the Fast Lady onto the deck of the ship at gun point. This was carried out by using the ship's derrick. They positioned the speedboat so it could be launched quite easily in the event of an emergency.

After the Fast Lady had been secured, Parvis turned to Abdul and said "Now we need to get rid of the excess baggage before they become troublesome".

Captain Williams and the crew of the ship were herded at gun point by the terrorists to the stern of the NATGAS 2 where a long plank had been lashed to the stern, overhanging the turbulent sea below. Below them, unseen and forgotten were the three ladders still attached to the ship by their grappling hooks. The ends of the ladders were bouncing around in the white frothing waves.

Captain Williams protested vehemently about the way he and his crew were being treated. For his protests he was shot and wounded by Parvis and then flung unceremoniously screaming over the side. Three other crew members attempted to rush the terrorists but were shot for their efforts.

Abdul rushed up screaming "Stop firing you imbeciles. Do you want to blow us all to Kingdom Come? Do you not realise we are sitting on a time bomb? If you puncture any one of those gas tanks we will be freeze dried by the cryogenically cold liquid gas, then blown sky high if that escaping gas finds an ignition source".

The terrorists picked up the bodies of the three dead crew members and slung them unceremoniously overboard, treating the bodies like so many sacks of meat. The rest of the crew huddled together, scared and unsure of what was going to happen next.

Parvis appeared holding a steam hose line. The rest of the crew who had been rounded up were forced to the end of the plank by Parvis, who used the steam hose to prod them like so much cattle in an abattoir. Parvis was laughing as he sprayed scalding steam at them until they either fell screaming into the sea or jumped to avoid being scalded.

"This way is safer and it saves bullets" Parvis stated dispassionately "now that's the first phase completed".

Parvis turned to Abdul, shut off the steam hose and said "Now we prepare for the next phase. We need to set a course to rendezvous with our friends. Lay on a course so we should be able to catch up with them by dawn tomorrow, then it is payback time. We can take our little trip to New York together and hit the Americans where it hurts. It is a pity we cannot fly the Jolly Rodger. I fancy myself as Blackbeard the pirate".

CHAPTER 2

Three months earlier, Jeff Baker had decided to make it up to his wife Karen for all the time he had spent away from home and in the office. He was going to take her on the holiday he had always promised her and that she deserved. Now that he had gotten his department in some semblance of order, they were going on an extended luxury cruise so they could spend some quality time together.

Jeff was big built. He stood just over 6 foot tall, was very stubborn and had very strong principles. Karen had always said he would die by his principles. He believed with every fibre of his being that people came before profit or politics.

Karen was a brunette, very shapely and about 5'6" tall. She loved Jeff for what he was although sometimes he tried her patience with his profound beliefs and causes.

Jeff had seen Cyril and Jen recently. They were a couple he and his wife had grown very fond of during an incident in the Estuary. Cyril was a wiry built man, very intelligent and one of the best jewellery thieves Jeff had known. Jen was a nicely proportioned lady who did not suffer fools lightly. Jen and Cyril had settled down to recent married life and were very happy.

At the same time, Jeff had met Derek and Sandra who had also recently arrived back from their extended honeymoon.

Sandra was a slightly built brunette who had been a military nurse and had nursed Derek through the injuries he had sustained during the Estuary incident.

Derek was a mild mannered, gentle giant of a man, big built and very powerful. Sandra had insisted that Derek heal from his injuries before he took on anything else.

The double wedding of Jen and Cyril and Sandra and Derek had been a wonderful occasion. Jeff had given both brides away and Karen had been matron of honour.

With all the publicity created from the Estuary incident, Cyril said he was so well known now he would have to give up being a tea leaf. Jen had retorted that she could think of other things he could do.

Jeff had suggested that if he was bored doing nothing, he could consider specialising in the security of buildings such as galleries or museums as he thought the phrase 'it could take a thief to catch a thief' was very apt in Cyril's case, and with Cyril's knowledge he would be the ideal candidate to prevent a theft.

Jeff had mentioned the cruise to Cyril and Jen and invited them along to join him and Karen as the women had become good friends, plus, it would be a way of getting some peace away from the media for a while.

"I have never been on a posh holiday before" Jen had said "I'd be out of place".

"Don't be silly" Karen had responded "you can hold your head up with the rest of them. Anyway, most of the people that go on cruises have a champagne lifestyle but lemonade money, which does not apply to you two".

"It would be nice to dress for dinner" Jen had mused then added "I'd need a new wardrobe though" with a side long look at Cyril.

Cyril had melted "Anything for you" he had responded with a smile.

"Do you mean it?" Jen had asked excitedly then had hugged him once she realised the truth of his statement.

"I suppose we had better do some shopping then" Karen had said in a bemused tone and looked at Jen "don't forget, Cyril will need a dress suit and a tuxedo for the formal evenings".

"I'm not dressing up in a penguin suit" had come Cyril's rejoinder.

"How about doing it just for me" Jen had said in a persuasive tone of voice looking at him lovingly "I am sure you will look very handsome and I'll make it up to you!"

"Oh alright! I can't refuse you anything" Cyril had said smiling.

"It was lovely to see them together" Karen had said, it made her heart soar.

"Is John married, or does he have a lady in his life?" Jen had asked "I've never heard him mention anyone".

Jeff had also met John during the Estuary incident. He was a personal agent to the Prime Minister.

Jeff had answered "I believe he does have somebody but he keeps himself to himself. He said that his orders are to keep me safe and they come direct from the Prime Minister but I always have the feeling that there is something else on the agenda but I can't quite put my finger on it".

Unbeknown to Jeff, at the time when Jeff had been discussing the cruise with his wife and friends, John had been in a meeting with the Prime Minister and other Cabinet ministers. As the meeting had finished and they were going out of the door, John had overheard one of the Ministers talking to the Prime Minister about the Estuary incident " . . . . a bit fortunate that Wilson exposed himself when he did at that press conference, otherwise you could have been diving out of his way for years to come. Knowing how good a reputation that man has for being a professional killer, it was a good job your man here was better" he said tapping John on the shoulder. The Cabinet Minister had then left the meeting.

When all the Cabinet ministers had gone, John had started mulling over the comments he had overheard, in his mind. A few things did not add up. He had confronted the Prime Minister. "How come Wilson knew of, and was prepared for that press conference in advance? He couldn't have got a camera gun at that short notice without alarm bells ringing somewhere?" The realisation had then hit him like a sledgehammer. "You were the one to call that press conference and you chose the venue!" With unbelievable comprehension dawning inside his head John had said "It was you that let Wilson know about that press conference so you could bring him out of hiding, hoping I would kill him in a shootout".

"Well, you did, didn't you?" the Prime Minister had retorted calmly.

"What would have happened if I had missed?" John had asked astounded "and what other papers were found in Councillor Randle's safe?"

"Well, instead of being beholden to Jeff" the Prime Minister had explained "I would have been beholden to Wilson. Do you know how they used to trap and kill tigers in India years ago?"

"What's that got to do with the situation?" John had asked puzzled at the turn of the conversation.

"Well" continued the Prime Minister "when they trap tigers, they leave a goat tethered to a tree and lie in wait for the tiger to attack the goat and then they kill the tiger if they can. Sometimes the tiger wins and gets the goat and sometimes it doesn't".

"How could you do something like that?" John had asked the Prime Minister, horrified.

"Wilson forgot the basic rules in your profession" the Prime Minister had stated "don't get emotionally involved with your target, so I counted on Wilson's hate of Jeff to override his professionalism and go for the kill with such a passion that he would expose himself enough so you could take him down".

"What about Jeff and the others? Did they know you had set them up?" John had asked.

"They don't have to know, it would spoil their sense of adventure in the life of politics" the Prime Minister had replied "by the way, I understand Jeff is planning to go on a cruise. Be on the same cruise with your wife Rose, make it look as though it's a coincidence. I need to find out the whereabouts of anymore papers from Councillor Randle's safe".

John had walked away, disgusted, with the parting shot "Thank Christ I am not a politician!"

Meanwhile, Jeff had said to Cyril "How about contacting Michael".

"I know Michael is visiting his cousin in America who I believe is someone quite high up in the American Naval Intelligence" Cyril had said.

Michael was a retired professional boxer. He was a slightly built man but very fast. He had been a friend of Jen's for years. Jeff had met him and got to like the man a lot during the Estuary incident.

It was then that Cyril had mentioned "I believe he's also going to see his relations in Canada. They are well to do and pretty high up in the Canadian Mounted Police. I think Michael is a bit of a dark horse. I didn't know he knew so many influential people. By the way, he did leave me a contact number in case of an emergency. Do you want me to ask Derek and Sandra? I know Derek is away at the moment on holiday. He has been at a loose end and bored with nothing constructive to do. He said he wanted to get back into wrestling but with the injuries he received and he really is too old to put in all the training required. Mind you, I wouldn't tell him that to his face!"

"With all his experience he has gained from being in the ring I would have thought he would have set up a wrestling school for youngsters" Jeff had said.

"Did you know he could have been a contender for the Olympics if it hadn't been for that bad fall he took?" Cyril had volunteered "and I reckon he could have been a medal winner".

"He never said, what a dark horse. You would not believe it of such a big man" Jeff had replied.

"So it could be the four of us for the cruise?" Jen had queried, looking expectantly at Karen then had added "with lots of clothes shopping beforehand that's going to be wonderful. When do we start going to the shops? I feel like I could do with some retail therapy".

Both Jen and Karen had gone into a huddle to discuss which stores they would visit and what days they would be able to go together to shop.

"When are we going to decide on where we are going on this cruise?" Jen had asked "as that will determine what clothes we need to get".

"Decide whenever you want" Jeff had replied "all we have to decide is which cruise and where we want to go. We had better get together and decide, so if you come to us this Sunday for dinner we can discuss it then. I will be able to tie up all loose ends in 3 months. Let's plan it for then. I've always wanted to go around the world and we can start with America and pick up Michael on the way. In the meantime, we can get some brochures and see what's out there".

"Oh no, what a terrible pun" Jen had laughed "I hope we don't have to put up with them on this cruise".

"What" Jeff had asked frowning "what do you mean what a terrible pun?"

"Look, he doesn't even know he's doing it. How do you put up with him Karen?" Jen had laughed as she glanced teasingly at Karen.

Both Karen and Jen had laughed as they shared their excitement about the shopping they were going to be doing together.

"What pun?" Jeff had continued to ask, confused.

"Going on a cruise and see what's out there?" Jen had finally put him out of his confusion "see as in looking or sea as in sailing?"

They all laughed.

"You've spent too long in business meetings, you're losing your sense of humour Jeff. The best cure for that is to go on a long cruise with friends and have a good time" Cyril had said, slapping Jeff on the shoulder "you need to recharge your batteries".

CHAPTER 3

So, three months later, on the day that the NATGAS 2 had set sail, Jeff, Karen, Cyril and Jen arrived at Harwich Port where the magnificent white cruise liner Baroness of the Sea dwarfed the harbour, you could hear the plaintive cry of the ever opportunist seagulls as they soared back and forth, the smell of the ozone of the sea, the very busy hub-bub of the port as the ship was prepared to sail, The ship resembled a huge majestic lady ready to welcome them into her bosom, to then whisk them off on the luxurious holiday they so badly needed.

Once they had boarded, they were given a champagne reception in the opulent VIP lounge and welcomed aboard by the senior crew. They were then escorted to the dining room where a magnificent lunch was served.

At lunch, they spotted Derek and Sandra across the dining room and joined them.

"How come you are on this cruise?" Jeff had asked in surprise.

Sandra explained that their presence had been a surprise for Jeff, that Cyril, Jen and Karen had put together the plan. Sandra went on to explain that Derek had been getting bored so she had persuaded him into going.

"By the way" Sandra said "did you know John and his wife Rose are on board as well? I saw him at the boarding gate. He was in deep conversation with the Chief Security Officer".

"I wonder why he is here" Jeff queried.

After the lavish lunch, they were shown to their cabins.

"What a civilised way to holiday" Jen said "no queuing like at the airport and because we are travelling from an English port we can take as much luggage as we want. I was able to bring all my new clothes with no weight restrictions".

"What you mean is" Cyril said "that whilst we had a weight limit of 200 pounds each, you had 350 pounds and I had 50 pounds".

"You want me to look lovely for you, don't you?" Jen pouted, rising above Cyril's banter.

"You look lovely to me with no clothes on" Cyril had rejoined.

"Cyril! Don't, you are making me blush" Jen retorted shyly, her cheeks colouring a bright pink.

They all laughed with her.

As the crew escorted them to their cabins they were advised that their luggage was waiting them ready for them to unpack.

Jen said as an aside to Cyril "Wait until I get you in there" and then turning to her friends "shall we see you for drinks before dinner?"

"We'll call your cabin and set up a time for cocktails" Jeff said.

Their cabins were identical and consisted of a balcony, en-suite bathroom, queen size double bed, table and chairs, dressing table and two large wardrobes. There was even a small fridge with a mini bar attached. All the cabins were situated next to one another on the port side of the ship.

A young man and woman knocked on Jeff's cabin door. They introduced themselves as their personal cabin crew and were informed that either one or the other would be on duty at any time.

There were apparently other crew, such as someone to clean the cabin every day, put out fresh towels and if either Jeff or Karen wanted anything like tea every morning or the mini bar refreshed or even wanted a meal served in their cabin, they were only to let them know and it would be brought to their cabin.

The cabin crew moved on to John and Rose's cabin next door, Karen said "What a civilised way to travel. I could really get used to this". She then spontaneously hugged Jeff who responded by kissing her very passionately.

Karen wriggled out of Jeff's arms and said, laughing "Let me unpack first, then you can finish what I just started. In the meantime, you can pour me a nice gin and tonic. Do yourself a brandy whilst you're at it then we can find a way to celebrate the start of our holiday".

Jeff walked out onto the balcony with a brandy in his hand to be out of her way as he knew she liked to be organised. Leaning against the railing, he watched the other passengers boarding. There was a brass band playing the song Sailing. When the brass band took a break, a Scottish pipe band played reels and laments in its stead.

"This is a lovely way to travel" he called over his shoulder to Karen. Karen answered back that it was a gorgeous cabin.

When Karen had finished unpacking she told Jeff where she had put everything and then joined him on the balcony.

"Where's my drink?" she asked.

Jeff handed her the drink he had made her and said "Just as you like it with ice".

They watched the last people boarding the liner. The harbour crew then hastened to prepare the ship for departure.

The ship's horn sounded and as the cruise liner slowly left the harbour jetty, the beginning of the cruise was accompanied by the sound of the brass band and Scottish bag pipes playing together.

Jeff made two more drinks to say Bon voyage.

Karen took her drink from Jeff, took a couple of sips then kissed him very passionately.

"That big bed looks inviting? I hope I don't get lost in it" she said.

"I'll find you and hold you safe" Jeff responded.

They both giggled like school children and fell on the bed wrapped in each other's arms. The distant sound of Scottish pipes playing a lament drifted into the cabin as he looked lovingly into Karen's eyes. He kissed her passionately.

Later in the cocktail bar, all eight of them met up to drink cocktails made especially by a cocktail waiter to celebrate the start of the cruise.

John introduced Rose to them all. Rose was slim built and very pretty and she seemed used to John introducing her to new people. She said that John had wanted to give her a good holiday to make up for all the long hours his job kept him away from home.

The Captain and his staff circulated amongst the other guests, introducing themselves and encouraging the guests to meet one another.

The Captain then introduced himself to Jeff and the rest of the group and then introduced them to a Middle Eastern gentleman and his wife.

The man said his name was Mustafa Ali and his wife's name was Asar. He said he could not join them in drinking cocktails but would drink orange juice with them as he was a Muslim and drinking alcohol was against his religion. He explained that he was Ambassador to a very rich sheik who had joined the cruise with his entourage.

Mustafa seemed very intelligent and a gentle caring man, willing to hear the other side of the issue at hand before expressing his own very distinctly and in a pleasant way. Mustafa was eager to talk to Jeff about the Estuary incident but it was not the time or the place.

Conversation was polite small talk as others joined them. Most of the conversation was with the officers and senior crew members asking them questions about different aspects of the Baroness of the Sea.

Eventually, they all went in to dinner. As they parted, Mustafa ventured that he hoped to see more of Jeff but added that he would be very busy looking after the Sheik and his entourage.

Jeff's party were escorted to their table by the Head Waiter who explained that this would be the table allocated to them for the duration of the cruise. He also stated that John and Rose would also be sat at the same table. He introduced the crew that would be looking after them and then introduced himself as William. The second waiter introduced himself as Michael, and the Wine Semillon introduced herself as Shirley.

Jen whispered to Sandra and Karen "We could get used to being pampered like this couldn't we ladies?" Sandra and Karen agreed.

"Yes, and we deserve to be" Rose added, and then they glanced at one another and promptly burst out laughing.

"Shall I choose which red and white wine we'll be having?" Cyril asked. They all nodded so he went into a huddle with the Wine Semillon who eventually nodded in agreement and went off to get the chosen wines.

"What have you ordered?" Sandra asked.

"You'll enjoy the wine, I can guarantee it" said Cyril "I used to run an off licence for years in my mis-spent youth. I picked up a bit of knowledge on wines".

They all enjoyed a wonderful lavish 7 course evening meal before taking a romantic stroll on deck before retiring to their cabins.

CHAPTER 4

The following day, Karen, Jen, Sandra and Rose decided to have a manicure and pedicure.

Cyril and Derek had gone swimming and Jeff said he would watch them from the upper lounge area. John was in the gym keeping fit.

Jeff was sitting in the lounge overlooking the pool watching Derek and Cyril mess about in the pool like two children when Mustafa joined him holding two coffees.

"I took the liberty of getting you a coffee if you want one" Mustafa said "I wanted to talk to you alone about the Estuary incident—if you don't mind. I did ask the Captain to introduce us as the Sheik and I had heard of you and we wanted to meet you".

"The people that you met with last night who I am travelling with were there as well" Jeff said reticently "they can tell you just as much as I can".

"Yes they can" Mustafa replied "but they cannot tell me about your ideals, what makes a man like you tick, why you have bucked the system and how you have won through in the end. You have won through over impossible odds and you are admired for that throughout the world. There are not many men like you around that will follow an impossible dream. The Sheik and I wanted to understand the principles that you live by".

Jeff's mind flooded back to what had been the start of what was now known as the Estuary incident. The memory of the incident was still very painful to him.

It had been late in the evening. He had been at home when the telephone had rang. He had answered it, had spoken for a while and had then put the telephone down.

"That was Bob" he had told Karen "he's changed the meeting for tomorrow. He can't make the meeting in the Estuary, we will have to meet on the mainland. He said something about a major breakthrough and meeting someone important after the meeting".

Jeff had frowned and said "He also asked me to bring that list of names that we have been working on as he thinks it might be important. He was quite mysterious about it. He also said something strange. He couldn't tell me about it over the phone as it wasn't a secure line".

Karen had said "Perhaps it might be a breakthrough on the investigation of that spill they had two years ago".

"I still believe that was a big cover up" Jeff had replied "for those findings to have come out someone very powerful must have sat on the results of that investigation".

They were both referring to a major spill of liquid gas at a gas terminal two years previously when Jeff believed that the company in question had tried to cover up the major spill by not reporting it to the authorities so that their safety record would not compromised.

Jeff had commented at the time of the spill that had there had been an ignition source present when the cloud of gas had escaped. It would have been the biggest peace time disaster ever known. He had been ridiculed by the company, been called a sensationalistic scaremonger and an activist who had only been trying to frighten people. He had been assured that everything had been under control and the fact there had been no explosion proved that the terminal was safe.

Jeff had realised that it was going to be a late night as he needed to prepare the list he had been working on. He had only heard with half an ear his wife speak to him as he was so engrossed in the paperwork he was preparing when she went to bed.

He had been angry that the cover up of the spill had worked and the company had gotten away with a small fine. He had felt that the Whitehall mandarins had struck again by pulling the power strings to safeguard the energy companies, and he had known that as much as he tried to expose the situation he was being buried by powerful people. One of his fellow campaigners had even commented "If you carry on the way you are in trying to find and expose the corruption, you could find yourself in a concrete slab propping up a motorway". The man's name had been Doug and he had died whilst in police custody. The police had said that it had been a heart attack at the time. There had been an investigation but nothing untoward had been found or brought to light.

Little did Jeff know how close to the truth he was going to be and that the principles that he held so dear were going to be stretched to breaking point over the next few days.

The meeting with Bob had been about the forthcoming public inquiry they had been trying to get started to look into the conflagration of high fire risk industries being planned all along the Estuary. Jeff had been representing the local residents as Chairman of a group called 'People Must Come First'. The group was a non-political and non-violent group that were concerned with the dangers of the conflagration of the energy industry being sited close to residential areas.

A short and stocky man, Bob had been Chairman of another group of legal brains called 'Legal Help for People' who assisted environmental groups with putting forward their cases at public inquiries.

As Jeff and Bob had met in the car park, Bob had welcomed him and said "We had better hurry. I think they may have started". He had then slipped some papers to Jeff and had said "We will look at those later and compare the names to yours". They then hurried inside and joined the meeting.

Neither of them had noticed that they were being followed into the building by a man in a dark suit.

Bob and Jeff had sat down at the meeting. It had just started and Jeff had risen from his chair to get himself a cup of coffee from the tray by the wall. Without warning there had suddenly been a massive explosion. The windows had crashed inwards and the building had shaken violently. A large piece of masonry had fallen from the ceiling and had plummeted down onto where Bob and his group had been sitting. Jeff had been thrown into an alcove by the blast, where he had hit his head against a wall with a heavy crack and had been stunned. He had been covered by a cloud of dust and debris and sharp pieces of plaster and wood.

Dazed and with his head ringing, choking back the dust Jeff had looked around, trying to make sense out of what had happened and had tried to peer through the shifting cloud of dust settling over everything and hanging cloyingly in the air. He had gazed somewhat dazed at what had been the inside of a beautiful listed building with walls draped in large ornately coloured tapestries, old pictures, stained glass windows and plaques on the walls all of which had been torn, broken or totally destroyed and in pieces. It had been so sad that this sort of damage had been done to something that had looked as though it had lasted hundreds of years.

Jeff's head had hurt badly and his mind had been spinning as he had tried to make sense of the situation. His first thought had been whether it had been a terrorist bomb that had exploded nearby at the Central Command Building.

What had made him first think of terrorism was that for most of his working life Jeff had been involved in security. He had worked his way up to be the head of security of a major bank and had been highly respected.

He had been caught up in a bomb attack in London many years before and had been lucky to survive. Whilst others around him had died or been badly injured he had escaped with hardly a scratch, but the memory of that day had been ingrained on his mind and he would never forget it.

Jeff had been coming to an opinion from one or two things that had happened in connection with Bob quite recently that Bob had known more than he was letting on. As the saying went 'his coat buttoned up over more than one layer'. Jeff had been going to ask Bob for his opinion on it after the meeting but events had overtaken the situation.

As the dust had started to settle and his head had started to clear, Jeff had looked across to where he had been sitting prior to the explosion and had seen a large pile of masonry and rubble and the twisted and broken bodies of his friends and of some he had only just met. He had managed to get to his feet and had staggered over to them to see if he could help but he had been too late. He had frantically scrambled through the debris to find Bob but his friend had been pinned under a large piece of concrete.

He had cleared the dust from Bob's face. Bob had looked at him and had whispered "Why?" and then the light had gone from his eyes.

Dazed and confused as to what had happened, Jeff had glanced around him and at first had perceived only an eerie silence, then, after a few seconds the ominous creaking of masonry crumbling and creaking wood had impacted on his hearing. Glancing upwards Jeff had seen the top parts of the wall of the building begin to tilt inwards. He had dived for the safety of the alcove into which the initial blast had thrown him, just as the top part of the wall had crashed down onto where he had been standing. A large lump of concrete had flown through the air and had caught Jeff a glancing blow to the side of his head and everything had gone black.

A throbbing pain to his head had greeted Jeff as he had slowly regained consciousness. How long he had been unconscious he did not know, but had guessed by glancing at the hands on his watch that it could not have been more than a couple of hours.

He had looked around to see the building in ruins. The alcove where he had lain covered in dust had protected him from the collapse of the building. Where his friends had been seated was a large pile of rubble.

Jeff had realised with a sense of shock that he had been the only one to survive the explosion.

Unbeknown to Jeff, he had been unconscious for 24 hours and it had been the following day when he had regained consciousness. He had scrambled out of the alcove covered in pulverised concrete and masonry and with dried dusty blood staining his hair and the side of his face.

Looking around at the ruins of what had once been a beautiful building, now its tapestries in rags and with the building creaking ominously, Jeff had stumbled his way across the rubble and had staggered out onto the street.

As Jeff had climbed from the rubble of the collapsed building he had tried to brush himself down as best he could, blinking away the dust from his eyes. As he had glanced up, the scene before him had reminded him so much of when he had been a small child during the blitz in south London where he had grown up and where his playground had been a bomb site.

Jeff had been born in St James' Hospital in south London during the Second World War. He had been the youngest of 4 children, his siblings being a sister and two brothers. He, like everybody else at that time, had been a latchkey kid but he had had a hard but good childhood. In those days nobody had had money so everybody had been in the same boat. If you had wanted money for sweets (that were still on ration as was everything else) or had wanted to go to Saturday morning pictures you had to go out and earn it. You had to do things such as chopping wood for kindling and selling it, or taking old beer or lemonade bottles back and getting the money on them. In those days kids were never indoors and the local street and bomb sites were the playgrounds.

As Jeff had climbed from the ruins of the building he had come out of his reverie and had staggered into the arms of a soldier.

The soldier had said abruptly "You gave me a fright. That building has been searched already so I never expected to see anyone alive, let alone walking out of there. Are there any more survivors we missed?"

Jeff had turned round shaking his head and had looked at the collapsed building he had just come from. He had not believed how he had survived.

The soldier had asked him his name and Jeff had told him. The soldier had then introduced himself as John and had explained to Jeff that he had just come from his unit to report to his commanding officer at Central Command. John had advised Jeff of first aid units being erected to take care of any casualties and had pointed down the street "There's a makeshift first aid post starting up over there, you'd better go and get yourself checked out then report to the police station. What's left of my unit is over there". John had pointed to some smouldering ruins "I must get to my mates, it looks like we have our work cut out. Why is it always up to us squaddies? The bloody politicians create the problems and we have to pull them out of the shit when it all goes wrong". He had marched off looking bemused but determined.

Jeff had staggered to the makeshift first aid unit that John had directed him to. A young nurse had spotted him and had said "Hey, you'd better come over here and let me clean you up. That looks like a bad cut you have there".

Considering the utter chaos that had been all around them it had seemed so surreal that Jeff should have been sitting having his head dressed and bandaged and talking to a young nurse who had been very sweet. She had let him know that her name had been Mary. She had told him that she had been drafted in from the local hospital to set up a new first aid unit because she had had a sister who had lived nearby who she could stay with.

Jeff had asked her if she knew what was going on.

Mary had replied that all she knew was that there had been a large explosion from the direction of the Estuary and that there had been many casualties. As she had chatted to him, she had told him that she was sweet on the very soldier who had sent him to the first aid unit. She had seemed so proud that he was due for promotion to sergeant quite soon.

As she had been finishing dressing his wound, a medical officer had come into the first aid tent and had said "Leave off doing minor injuries. We have hundreds of seriously injured people coming in soon and minor injuries will have to wait. Enforce a triage system from now on".

Mary had slipped Jeff some pain killers for his headache and had said "I must go. It looks as though we are going to be very busy. If you see John please could you tell him I care and I will be staying at my sisters and I will see him as and when I can".

Jeff had thanked her and had then replied that if he saw her soldier boy John he would pass on her regards and then he walked out of the makeshift first aid post and what passed for civilisation.

CHAPTER 5

"Look Mustafa" Jeff said coming out of his reverie "I just have a code of principles that I am prepared to live by and die for, it's that simple. If I believe something is fundamentally wrong . . ." Jeff paused and then continued "There comes a time in someone's life when you have to say no and mean it. Whatever the issues that are involved, all a person has are the principles that they live and die by.

Jeff had said these words so many times recently, little did he know that they were going to haunt him over the next few days when the deadly arm of The Senate would reach out again and try to snare him in a deadly cat and mouse game set in the middle of the Atlantic that would be a political nightmare with biblical disaster consequences.

"Even if by saying no it would lead to your death?" Mustafa asked with incredulity.

"Even then" Jeff answered "I happen to believe that all a man has in this world is his word of honour no matter how rich or poor he is. That is all there is. I happen to be a man of my word and I will not break my word for anyone or anything, and that is the code that I live by, and will probably die by. Anyway" he finished with a wry smile "when I die there will only be two pall bearers carrying my coffin as there are only two handles on a dustbin". He laughed.

"You English have a strange sense of humour. You joke about your death, and you do not take life seriously, even though you have been close to death. I saw the news bulletin that showed when you were attacked by a man called Wilson I believe? Yet you still maintain your sense of humour" Mustafa commented, then he added "you English have always laughed in the face of adversity, I find that strange and I have never understood it. We have men in my country that have said they are men of their word, but they change when they get into a position of power".

"I also believe and understand that power corrupts and that is normally through greed" Jeff replied "but absolute power corrupts absolutely, that's what happens when fanatics try to take control through fanaticism and lead normally peaceful people to do unspeakable atrocities in the name of the fanatic's ideals. I believe that this is wrong and that is when you have to say no!"

"What do you mean by that?" Mustafa asked.

"I have always understood" Jeff continued "that if we look back in history it tells us of lessons we should have learned, but we never learn them. It also tells us of atrocities that we should not have let happen but we did, and we still do let them happen, generally through apathy which I happen to believe is the biggest killer of freedom and truth in peaceful people".

"Can you expand on that?" Mustafa asked, a look of puzzlement on his swarthy features, but fascinated by the insight into the mind of a man he and the Sheik had much admired for a long time.

"For example" Jeff obliged "if you consider what happened in Communist Russia. It consisted of Russians who wanted to live in peace yet Russian Communism was responsible for the murder of about 20 million people, so it would seem the peaceful majority were irrelevant. Chinese Communists managed to kill a staggering 70 million but China's population is and was very peaceful as well. In

Germany, only a very few people were Nazis, but before the peaceful people knew it the majority sat back and let it happen and we were plunged into World War II. You have the same in the Middle East where the silent majority of peaceful loving people are being plunged into a holy war by fanatics. The victims in any war are the ordinary peaceful loving people. Very few are politicians or religious zealots. I have said before and will probably be saying it until the day I die—I believe the world politics can be interpreted by poli as in many and tics as in parasites so I translate politics as many parasites and when you look at the different countries and their religious leaders and their leaders in political fields there are many parasites with no consideration for the peaceful people they are representing who want to live in peace.

There are fanatics in the Western part of the world, the far Eastern part of the world and also in the Middle Eastern part of the world and they are the enemy of peace loving people.

It is not class, creed, nationality or religion that divides people as they are all acceptable to one another, but it is because some people believe it's nice to be important, but they forget it's more important to be nice.

Nice people like nice people no matter what part of the world you come from or what religion you follow and it will make no difference whether you are rich or poor.

I have come to believe that religion is manmade as it is like a mountain. Your view of the mountain is your view of religion. Every religion has a higher being which can be translated as the top of a mountain, so your view of religion is the view you see at the time of looking at the mountain. It is the same mountain but you don't see the whole mountain".

Jeff checked himself, smiled wryly and apologised to Mustafa for getting on his soap box and boring Mustafa with his philosophy of life.

"Not at all" Mustafa answered "on the contrary, I find what you have to say very deep and thought provoking and it is worth thinking deeper on. I must say I was not expecting that from a political member of the British Government".

"I am not a political member of the British Government" Jeff replied "I am only a loose cannon that the Government want to tie down. I have no interest in the politics of politicians, as I said before, they are parasites. It's people I care about.

There are very well meaning people that can and do a lot for their community, but it seems when they themselves get bogged down in politics they can very easily lose their way and quite often march to the much larger sound of the fanatic's drum instead of the beat of the drum they started with. Do you understand the analogy I am trying very badly to express?"

"I have heard that you have a saying in your country" Mustafa mused "empty vessels make the most noise, so the fanatic's drum might not be making a good noise but it is making a loud noise and that is what gets the attention, but a drum you are playing has a lovely tune but is not always heard".

"Something similar to that" Jeff agreed "but that's enough philosophy for one day. We are on holiday, so let's relax and enjoy ourselves with one another's good company".

"Thank you for your time" Mustafa said with a slight bow and added "the Sheik would like you and your party to join him at a reception before dinner tonight if you have nothing better to do. I hope we meet again soon so we can carry on our little talk. I am fascinated by your views and I find them very interesting. You have left me with a lot to think about. I hope I did not disturb you too much" and then he left.

Jeff had a feeling that it was not the last he would see of Mustafa.

At that moment, John joined him. "Was that Mustafa you were speaking too just then as I came on deck?" he asked.

"Yes, why?" Jeff asked "we were talking about philosophy and politics. He seemed a nice guy. Don't tell me you find that sinister?" He glanced sideways at his companion.

John said "There's something about him I can't put my finger on and until I do find out what it is I suggest you avoid him".

"You're telling me I can't speak to someone because you think they are suspicious?" Jeff asked, annoyance in his tone.

"My job is to keep you alive even when we are on holiday" John replied flatly.

"Are those your orders from the PM?" Jeff asked in an irritated tone of voice.

John remained silent.

"I know you mean well" Jeff said "but you also know I will not be put in a cage so don't start now. Let's enjoy the cruise and the good company of friends and I do include you and Rose in that statement".

"You make it so difficult for me as your bodyguard to do my job" John groaned "one of the first rules are don't get emotionally involved with your client or his family".

"I won't tell if you won't tell" Jeff rejoined jokingly and smiled at John.

They were eventually joined by Derek and Cyril who were laughing.

Derek said "You should have had a swim with us. I managed to duck Cyril a few times".

"What do you mean" Cyril said "the pool emptied when you jumped in you big galumph?"

"You might be fast" Derek said "but even a big man like me can catch you. You must be slowing down in your old age".

Cyril turned to Jeff. "I think I could get used to holidays like this. Cruising certainly spoils you for other holidays and I know Jen is having a marvellous time. By the way, when are the women going to be finished getting pampered?"

"About now I think. Perhaps we should join them for lunch before they go into the duty free shops and spend a fortune" Jeff answered "by the way, we have all been invited to a reception to meet the Sheik tonight before dinner".

"What! Rubbing shoulders with a Sheik?" Cyril gasped "how come?"

"Mustafa just invited us all to the Sheik's reception tonight".

"Jen will want to wear her posh frock" Cyril said "as will all the women".

"Have we got to dress posh as well?" Derek asked.

"Full bib and tucker" John replied "we can't let the girls down can we?"

All four of them went off together to find their wives and get some lunch and tell them about the invite.

CHAPTER 6

It seemed that the Sheik and his party occupied half a deck of cabins and the ship was a hive of activity that seemed to be fussing around him like bees round a honey pot.

The suite of cabins had been dressed with drapes so as to look like a palatial Arabian tent and was very rich and ornate.

Jeff's party was met by Mustafa and taken to the Sheik to be introduced.

"Ladies and gentlemen, may I please present Sheik Ali Mustafa".

The young man in front of them was dressed in robes of pure white with a vivid red sash in which was tucked an ornate jewel encrusted dagger. The pin which clipped his robes together was also encrusted with diamonds.

"Welcome to my humble abode" the Sheik said in perfect English.

Jeff raised his eyebrows at the Sheik's excellent command of English.

"I see that you are surprised by my command of English Mr Jeff" the Sheik said "I was educated at Oxford University".

"You speak English better than I do" Jeff complemented.

"That is a very nice compliment coming from a man whose views I respect" the Sheik said, inclining his head in a small bow "I understand now when you explained to Mustafa the saying whilst it is nice to be important it is even more important to be nice".

Jeff realised that he must have been the subject of their conversations before tonight. He bowed slightly to the Sheik and responded "I have always believed it is harder for a poor man to be generous than a rich one so when a poor man gives he will always give more than a rich man".

"Your thinking interests me deeply" the Sheik answered "you do not think like most Westerners. There is depth to your thoughts that I find fascinating. But, let us not bore our other guests with the philosophy and ways of different cultures. You are here to be entertained as my guests".

Captain Williams and his First Officers had also been invited to the reception as had been some other important passengers.

The food served was delicious, even though half of what they ate was unknown to them.

The evening was a success and it was late when they made their way back to their cabins. Jeff asked them all to join him and Karen for a nightcap in his cabin, however, Derek said he had had enough for one night and that himself and Sandra would take a rain check but would maybe join them tomorrow night.

Cyril, Jen, John and Rose agreed and went back to Jeff's and Karen's cabin for a nightcap. Once they were inside the cabin, as soon as the door was closed, Cyril said "If he's a rich Sheik then I'm a Dutchman".

"What do you mean by that remark?" John asked "he appeared to be all that he said he was, it was a very nice evening".

"I know quality when I see it" Cyril replied "and he did not have quality. Everything about him was false. Oh yeah, he spun a good yarn about his father and his uncles owning oil wells and how rich they were but he himself was false. He might have gone to university in England but he's certainly not who he says he is".

"How can you tell that?" Jeff asked.

"That robe was not silk as he inferred for a start. The jewels in the pin that held it together and in the dagger were just paste".

"Get out of it, paste? They looked real to me" John exclaimed disbelievingly.

"Believe me, I know jewellery. I've lifted enough to know the difference between paste and the real thing. What puzzles me, is why the entire charade?" Cyril continued "what can he gain from it? He must have some money because he paid for the top cabins for all his staff as well as all the elaborate entertainment. I am very curious. Perhaps if you get this Mustafa on his own you might be able to find out". Cyril turned to Jeff "he seems to like your company—although I don't know why". Cyril paused for a moment. "I don't know what it is but it don't hang together quite right. And he seems to have a lot of bodyguards, but they always seem to be taking their orders from somebody else".

Mustafa was so busy with the Sheik Jeff saw very little of him over the next day although he did keep an eye out for him.

They had been at sea for only a couple of days when their dream holiday cruise turned into a horrific nightmare.

CHAPTER 7

It all began when Jeff looked out of the cabin window early in the morning. Dawn was just breaking and he could see a very large vessel heading towards them. It appeared to be overtaking them very closely and then began changing its course so it would fall in very close to and behind the cruise liner. Jeff went out onto the balcony for a closer look. The nightmare began to unfold as Jeff realised that the newcomer which had been heading for them was a very large gas container ship. He could just make out the name on the bow of the giant gas ship as the NATGAS 2.

At first, Jeff thought the NATGAS 2 had a problem and that the Baroness of the Sea was on a mercy mission. Perhaps a crew member on board the NATGAS 2 had been taken ill and the Baroness of the Sea was offering assistance.

As the giant gas tanker pulled up close behind the Baroness of the Sea, Jeff went to the balcony to see if he could get a better view of what was going on. He could see that the crew of the NATGAS 2 had put fenders all the way along the bow and side of the NATGAS 2 and had then cast lines to the deck of the Baroness of the Sea. However, instead of the crew of the Baroness of the Sea securing the ropes it was the Sheik's bodyguards who were lashing the two ships together as if they were taking the NATGAS 2 in tow.

"You're up early, what's going on?" Karen's sleepy voice suddenly asked from the bed.

"I don't know yet but I don't think I like it" Jeff answered looking worried then as things started to slip into place in his mind an announcement was heard over the cruise ship's PA system ordering all passengers to stay in their cabins until further notice and if they obeyed they would come to no harm.

Jeff did not like the suspicions that were forming in his mind and the realisation he was coming to. His fears were that the NATGAS 2 had been hijacked and that the pirates were also at the same time hijacking the Baroness of the Sea which meant an estimated 3,000 plus passengers and 1,500 crew could all be in danger.

He went back inside the cabin. "I think we are being hijacked by pirates and I believe we are going to be used as a human shield" Jeff said "I believe they are attempting to tow a gas tanker behind us and will threaten to blow it up if there is a rescue attempt".

"What? How can they do that?" Karen asked, coming awake instantly, "this is a British cruise ship. They can't rob a ship on the high seas. Passengers don't carry large amounts of cash, it's all booked to your debit or your credit card and you pay at the end. People will only have travelling cash. Nobody is going to pay a ransom for you, you're not that popular!"

"Thanks" Jeff replied wryly.

Just then, someone called his name from the adjoining balcony. Jeff went back out onto the balcony to see who it was, and it was John. He explained to Jeff that he had just been ushered back to his cabin from the gym at gun point. It appeared that the boarders were Middle Eastern terrorists.

"Do you have any idea what they want?" Jeff asked.

"From what I can gather, they want to take their fight to America" John answered "by sailing both ships tied together to an American port and then blowing both ships up in the port, killing everybody in the area plus nearly 5,000 passengers and crew from both ships".

"You and I both know the Americans won't stand for that" Jeff stated promptly "they will blow us out of the water long before that happens".

"Surely" John continued "it would take a massive amount of explosives to blow up a ship of this size. How did they get it aboard the NATGAS 2, or come to that, aboard the Baroness of the Sea?".

"They don't have to have a large amount of explosives" Jeff replied "the gas aboard the NATGAS 2 would do the job for them. We need to find out what the manifest of the NATGAS 2 is".

"A gas ship is a gas ship" John said "the gas ignites when you set light to it".

"It's not that simple" Jeff explained "if it's LPG (Liquid Petroleum Gas) it's stored under pressure so as to reduce the gas to a liquid state for easier transportation and storage. It's very nasty stuff in a fire as it often explodes. If it's Liquid Natural Gas (LNG—known as Methane Gas) it is reduced down 620 times its size from a gas to a liquid and transported and stored at cryogenically low temperatures of below minus 280 degrees Fahrenheit. If that is released it will expand 620 times from liquid to gas. Everything in its path will be freeze dried, and it burns at a temperature three hundred degrees hotter than burning petrol".

Jeff thought back to "YOU HU MAROO" incident this had been a gas ship that was involved in a collision in Tokyo bay, with a loss of all lives the Japanese had to torpedo and bomb the gas ship to the bottom of Tokyo bay otherwise the gas onboard would have burned for five months

"The Americans won't let it get into their territorial waters, they will bomb both ships to the bottom of the sea first" John responded then added "if they do that, they'll kill the passengers and crew on both ships, and then the Americans will do the terrorist's job for them".

"The terrorists don't care if they die. They've said their goodbyes to the world long ago" Jeff said grimly "if they can force the Americans' hand they would have scored points and this would be an advantage in their political game of chess. We have just become the pawns in that game and we will be the ones sacrificed unless we do something about it before we hit landfall".

John retorted "Don't tell me you want to do something about it?" Then with a dawning realisation answered his own question "What! You want to take on a bunch of highly trained armed terrorists, take back two ships that are lashed together with ropes, all with pampered civilians that have a job doing up their shoe laces in the morning and who know nothing about sailing cruise ships or tankers, all before the Americans decide to blow us out of the water. You're off your trolley mate, we'll be slaughtered".

"We're going to be dead anyway if we don't do anything" Jeff replied "so why not go down fighting for what we believe in by saying no! Say no to going quietly in the night to suit the political ideal of a fanatic or say no to being the pawns in this worldwide chess game. May I remind you that pawns may be small but if they co-ordinate their moves together they can be a powerful force and can take down a queen, so we need to do something to change this game of chess to our advantage. We already have four in our little army, there's Cyril, Derek, you and myself, that's four people I would not upset, especially now they have ruined our wives' holiday cruise. Derek's wife Sandra was in the Army until recently, and even I would not upset Jen, she can be quite a formidable force, and believe me when you piss off a woman big time you have a tiger by the tail. All we have to do is to find likeminded passengers and crew members".

"You make it sound like something out of the 'Roy of the Rovers' comic book. You can't create an army out of strangers who have just met, it takes time and training" John exclaimed exasperatedly.

"No it doesn't" Jeff replied calmly "all it takes is enough people to say no! Bind them together, and then think of ways of stopping these maniacs. As soon as the passengers on board realise nobody is going to rescue us, they'll want to fight. The authorities will not send in the SAS or the SEALS as we are politically expendable. It is up to us to survive and if it means taking on the terrorists then that's what needs to be done. I don't know about you but I do not intend to go quietly".

"Do you remember our conversations when we first met?" John asked.

CHAPTER 8

Jeff let his mind drift back to the conversations in question. It was during the Estuary incident, after he had left the first aid unit. He had walked down the road and had come across a makeshift sign on a building saying Temporary Police Station. He had climbed the steps to the building's door and had entered into a large reception room.

He had been greeted with what appeared to be utter chaos. People had been shouting and screaming, demanding to know what had happened. Some had been in tears, some had been pleading and begging, some had been angry and demanding to be told what had happened to their families and friends and what the authorities had been prepared to do to sort things.

The desk sergeant had finally stood on a chair, withdrawn a whistle from his crumpled tunic pocket and had blown on it loudly. The shrill noise had pierced right through Jeff's head, but it had also had the desired effect as everybody had quietened down to listen to what he had had to say.

The Sergeant had said "Don't ask me any details because I don't know any. All I know is that there has been a very large explosion in the Estuary area and we have been informed that martial law will be imposed in the whole of this area whilst the emergency services do their job".

Jeff's heart had sunk. He had edged his way towards the desk sergeant who had looked at him and had stated nonchalantly "It looks like you've been through the wars".

Jeff had said "Sergeant, you said the Estuary area?"

The Sergeant had looked at him and had asked "Do have you have any family there?"

Jeff had nodded "I came from there this morning".

The Sergeant had replied "I'm sorry" and then he had looked at Jeff quizzically and asked "what's your name?"

Jeff had told him. The Sergeant's face had stiffened "Take a seat" he had said quite tersely "and I'll see what I can find out".

The Sergeant had left his position behind the long desk and had exited through another door behind him into what Jeff had thought must be other offices or rooms.

After about 10 minutes the Sergeant had returned and had asked Jeff to follow him through into the office area. Jeff had obliged, following the Sergeant into a further room where he had been told to take a seat. "Someone will have a word with you" the Sergeant had said very curtly and then had left the room to return to the crowded front desk.

A few moments later, a man in a pin-striped suit had entered through another door and had promptly asked him to confirm his name and address. Jeff had complied.

The man had then commenced an interview by saying in a matter of fact fashion "You don't need to know my name, all you need to know is that I work for a Government department that you won't know exists. It's lucky I was in the area. The Sergeant recognised you from the television programme you featured in last week in which you were talking about a high profile meeting you were supposed to be attending in the Estuary area. The Sergeant has a daughter and her family who live there so takes a close interest on what happens there. Now what I want to know is why you are here? Why were you not at that meeting?

Where is Bob? Where is his attaché case? What do you know? How is it you are involved this explosion?"

The man's tone tone had then changed to one of cold menace "You people will go to any lengths to highlight your cause, but this is a step too far. Until I get some answers you won't be leaving here. Tell me what I need to know or I could let the Sergeant in here for a while and as his granddaughter is the apple of his eye . . ." and he left the sentence hanging inferring that Jeff would be in trouble at the Sergeant's hands if left alone with him.

Jeff had swiftly turned on the man "Whoa pal, pull your neck back in and let me answer for God's sake! Draw yourself some breathe before you die of oxygen deprivation".

The two men had eyeballed each other intently and silently for some moments, like two circling gladiators, and then the man had asked "Well what have you got to say?"

Jeff had finally explained reluctantly what had happened and that Bob had died in his arms in the collapsed building.

"Don't lie to me. Nobody managed to get out of that building alive" the man had scoffed "we searched it thoroughly".

"I did and you can ask a soldier I met by the name of John" Jeff had responded "he sent me to the new first aid centre and a nurse by the name of Mary gave me first aid. Then I came here to find out what's happened. And your sergeant put me in here. I didn't know until 10 pm last night that the meeting had been changed by Bob. He said he had to meet someone very important here as soon as the meeting was over and rather than cancel, he asked if I could make the journey to here and he would be able to kill two birds with one stone. So, is there anything else you would like to know or do you get the thumbscrews out now?" By this time, Jeff's tone had become very belligerent.

For a little while, it had become very quiet. Jeff's thoughts went back to what his friend had said about him ending up in a slab of concrete propping up a motorway.

Jeff's head had still be throbbing, his mind had been doing overtime attempting to make some sort of sense out of the situation he had found himself in. He asked himself how come this man knew about Bob, their meeting, and that Bob had had an attaché case? Jeff had had a wild idea and had asked "As you have asked, was that person Bob was supposed to meet with you?"

"That is none of your business, keep your nose out of it" the man had replied dismissively.

Jeff had realised straightaway that he had guessed right and that he had also touched a very raw nerve. This had puzzled him as he had believed that Bob was what he had seemed, a concerned environmentalist with legal knowledge who wanted to do something for the good of the community, not spy for what was some sort of secret service.

"What do you know about the explosion? And how were you involved?" the man had asked.

Jeff had become angry again. He had been tired, his head had hurt, he had been heart sick and he had wanted answers.

"I know as much as you do about this explosion, that's nothing, and if I'm here how can I be involved?" Jeff had snapped "I have family and friends in the Estuary and I want to know what's happened to them. I've had a good friend die in my arms, I've nearly been crushed to death in the last few hours and I've lost contact with my wife and family, so, have you got any more shit you want to throw at me because if you have, feel free, and let's get it over and done with, then you can get someone of importance in. They might have something intelligent to say, and then I can talk to the organ grinder not the monkey?"

The man had chosen to ignore the sarcastic, angry retort and had said "We have to know what happened because we might need to take necessary and irrevocable action against the terrorist bastards who did this and you may be able to tell us who that might be".

"How would I know whether or not this was an act of terrorism?" Jeff had asked, his voice rising "in the past, I've been a victim myself of a London terrorist bombing and I don't want to repeat the pleasure, thank you very much". Jeff had paused, and then in an exasperated tone of voice, had said "anyway, this is too big to be a terrorist bomb unless it's nuclear".

"What else could it have been other than a terrorist attack to create this sort of devastation?" the man had asked.

"Have you thought it might be an industrial accident?" Jeff had asked.

The man had looked incredulous "Don't be a prat, the Government controls the industrial world and they wouldn't be allowed to be such idiots as to let something like that happen. Apart from that Health & Safety keep an eye on things and they wouldn't let them get away with anything that would be that unsafe. So I reckon this has to be terrorism and you will tell me what you know or you'll not see daylight for years".

"Oh please, use your loaf" Jeff had spat angrily "just over two years ago, they had a near miss at the gas terminal but that was covered up by your Whitehall mandarins in the so called national interest, and no terrorist group has the capability to make a non-nuclear bomb that could create this sort of devastation without you people knowing about it. Maybe the Americans have that sort of power at their fingertips but the last time I looked we were at peace with the United States".

The man had looked at him and had raised an eyebrow.

This had started Jeff thinking and thinking fast. He was being held for a reason, and the reason was buried back in that large pile of masonry in Bob's briefcase and until he could convince this man that that was the case, he was going nowhere, and it could get very painful. And the joke about him propping up some motorway had started to appear very real.

"Ok" Jeff had said as calm as he could "let's assume, hypothetically mind, that you knew Bob and you knew what he was doing, and that the meeting was with you".

The man's face had stiffened, but he remained silent.

Jeff had continued "Bob spoke to me of this very important meeting he had to go to. He didn't say with whom, only that what I was confirming in my investigations, if it proved his suspicions correct, could open a can of worms. But, he needed to confirm it with the paperwork he had, the results of my investigation and this meeting he was having. All I know is that Bob seemed very concerned and that was unusual for him, because he was quite laid back and a change of venue at the last minute was not his style".

The man had stayed silent for a few moments as though thinking and then had asked "What was the information you were bringing Bob?" and then he quickly added "I'm not saying I knew Bob you understand, or that we were due to meet yesterday, but I must know what you both discussed".

Jeff had thought "Yesterday?" He must have lain unconscious in that alcove for over 24 hours, no wonder he was feeling hungry.

Jeff had eventually stated "This is going to be a long story, can I have a cup of tea and something to eat as I haven't eaten or drunk since yesterday morning?"

The man had gone to the door, called the Sergeant and requested that he rustle up some tea and sandwiches. He also requested that someone have another look for Bob's case in amongst the rubble near to where the meeting area had been inside the main hall.

The Sergeant had looked very sourly in Jeff's through the door.

"We might be barking up the wrong tree with this one Sergeant. I will let you know one way or another. If I'm wrong, as I promised our mum, I'll turn a blind eye and let you at him first, before he goes to the cells. I think the same way as you do about his kind" he affirmed to the Sergeant as the latter went to get some tea and something to eat.

Jeff had not liked this generalisation about himself. This was why he had respected Bob, as at least Bob had seemed to realise and respect what he stood for.

Jeff had snapped at the man "Do you think I'm some sort of swampy, political agitator, or part of the great unwashed brigade that wants to create anarchy, just for anarchy's sake?"

"Well aren't you?" the man had asked quite vehemently.

"No I'm not" Jeff had replied, trying to stay calm "I, and I believe Bob, came to realise that there was more to this campaign then met the eye as there was too much money involved".

The man had stiffened at this and inclined his head, as if listening "Carry on, I'm listening and don't forget I've checked up on you and your history. For example, I know you've got a reputation as a successful environmental fighter. I can tell you that that didn't go down too well with my boss".

"Who is your boss?" Jeff had asked curiously.

"I've told you that's none of your business. All you need to know is it's higher up the ladder then you think".

"I can think of some very tall ladders" Jeff had retorted.

The man had ignored this remark and continued "Tell me everything you know from the very beginning and don't leave anything out, even a small detail might help to throw some light on this incident. This situation seems to go back a long way".

The Sergeant, at that moment, returned with a plate of sandwiches and a mug of tea, put them on the table and said "I hope for your sake he's right about you because if not your life won't be worth a plugged nickel" he had said.

"That's enough" the man had said "if what I suspect is true, he might not be the villain of the piece".

The Sergeant had looked surprised.

"Leave us, I need to get to the bottom of this and I need his co-operation. He might not know it but he could be the key to all this".

Jeff had felt relieved that he wasn't on a one way ticket to the secret camp of no return he had heard about. Once there you were forgotten about and your existence denied.

"Right, let's hear it from the beginning and don't leave anything out. I'll determine if it's of any consequence" the man had said and pushed the plate of sandwiches towards Jeff and waited.

Jeff had picked up a sandwich, realising how famished he was, and had bit into it. Before long he had cleared the plate and then was sipping his tea whilst the man had waited patiently.

CHAPTER 9

It had all started more years ago then Jeff cared to remember and he had been so naive then. When he looked back, he mused that he hadn't even known how to form a committee let alone a pressure group in those days.

Jeff had moved into the area with his first wife in 1964 from south London. He had taken advantage of the cheap mortgage that was available from the bank and bought a bungalow. They had had two sons which he thought the world of.

It had been an ordinary working day. Jeff had gone to the bus stop in the morning to go to work.

As he had waited for the bus he had looked out over the fields by the main road and had seen lots of stakes dotted all over the field. He had wondered what they were. His bus had come along then and he had gotten onto it and sat down next to his neighbour, Fred.

"Good morning Fred" Jeff had said "how come you didn't get on at the same stop as usual?"

"Dropped my car in for its MOT" Fred had replied.

As the bus pulled away from the bus stop, Jeff had asked "What are all those markers over there?"

"They want to build an oil refinery at that location I hear". Fred had replied.

"You must be joking" Jeff had exclaimed.

"Apparently there's an inquiry going on now in the Community Centre on the mainland" Fred had explained.

Jeff thought about what Fred had said all morning and had decided to take the afternoon off to attend the inquiry. He had kept asking himself how he could have been so wrapped up in his own little world and not have known what had been going on around him and on his own doorstep.

He had telephoned his wife at the time, advised her about it and explained that he was going to the Community Centre that afternoon straight from work. She said she would ask around to see if what Jeff had found out was true.

When Jeff arrived at the Community Centre on the mainland, it was a hive of activity. There had been a large table with a map of the area on it and all the land near where he lived was marked out in black lines.

"What's that represent" he had asked the man standing nearby.

"That's where we'll build our oil refinery" the man had replied.

"You can't do that" Jeff had answered "I live right next door to it and it's too close to where people live. You can't put an oil refinery next door to where people live".

"I represent one of the oil refineries and my colleague here represents the other one" the man had said.

"You want to site two oil refineries on this land? This represents a large part of the Estuary area, you just can't do that" Jeff had stated in an outraged tone.

The man had looked at Jeff with contempt and said "Hey little man. Go away, you're not big enough, you can't and you won't stop us".

This had angered Jeff. How dare this person be so arrogant! "You think you're too big and powerful to stop? Watch this space" he had replied emphatically.

Unbeknown to Jeff, two local press reporters had been standing nearby taking notes of what was being said, in particular, his threat to take the oil companies on. Jeff had turned away from the oil company representatives with a parting shot "You have not seen the last of me".

Jeff had gone into the Inquiry, registered his name, address and objections and asked to speak at the Inquiry (Jeff had not known at the time that this had been the last day of the Public Inquiry). He had been granted a few minutes to address the Inspector.

He had then proceeded to speak passionately about how he felt about a refinery being sited on his doorstep.

The two reporters had come up to him, had asked his name and where he lived and how he felt about the prospect of having two oil refineries sited next door to where he lived.

Jeff had gone home feeling that at least he had said his piece even though it might not turn out to be important in the big scheme of things (he did not know it then but he was to be dubbed the 'Oil War Leader' by the media).

The following evening, the local evening newspaper had printed what he had said at the Inquiry on the front page and they had played it as a David and Goliath fight.

Jeff had realised that having the media on his side was a weapon the oil companies could not combat provided he could create or provide a story that the newspapers could use that would be of interest to their readers.

How many times could you say 'I don't care if it's made of solid gold and built by the Red Cross' before that was old news and was not printed. He would have to come up with different angles and different stories to keep people's interest and concerns in the cause and the press publicising the plight of the local area.

He had proceeded to speak to three other friends and neighbours and they had decided that they would meet at his bungalow that evening and discuss what could be done.

From that meeting of four people had been formed one of the most successful non-violent, non-political environmental pressure groups called Stop the Oil Refineries Resistance Group which was to go on after 14 years of campaigning to stop two oil refineries being built, which was the first time in Europe that oil companies had ever been beaten (what happened during that campaign could be the subject for a whole book).

Jeff had realised that violence solved nothing, and in actual fact lost you support, and you had to use the political party's framework for your cause and not let the political party take over your cause for their own ends, a very delicate balancing act, as political groups were for the most part very blinkered to their own political views and eye someone with different political views from theirs as an enemy.

Jeff had realised that whilst there were people that went into politics on a grass root level and did a lot for the community, at the top echelon there were political statesmen.

During those 14 years there had been some highs and lows in the campaign and some highs and lows in his personal life which had hardened him.

One of those lows he nearly did not get through. This had been when his first wife had left him to go off with his friend and fellow campaigner and took his boys with her. He had come very close to suicide then and it was 5 years before he had come to terms with it. It had been very hard to carry on as he had felt that the loss had been total.

He had had to take the loss, the pain, and the rejection even though it ripped him apart inside. It had been worse than any physical hurt he had ever experienced. It had been a pain that had only dulled with time and it had left him a bit cynical and slow to ever trust anybody again. He had felt that the treachery had gone against all the principles he lived by. For this reason, it had stuck in his craw, but he had had to let it go eventually or it would have twisted and poisoned his way of life, and then the Devil's disciples would have won and the code that he lived and would die by would have been destroyed and at the end of the day that was all he had.

After five lonely years he had met Karen at a party at his brother's house. She had had two daughters, one who lived in Scotland and the other who lived in Surrey.

For him, it had been like finding a valuable diamond in the dustbin of life after going through a lot of rubbish and pieces of coloured glass.

The 14 year refinery fight had been coming to its climax at the time. They had forced the oil refinery fight to a number of inquiries with the help of their MP and some of the local councillors and eventually had held up the building of the refineries for so long that it had become a non-viable financial project for the two oil companies and they had scrapped their projects. The people had, therefore, been victorious.

It had been the first time in the history of Europe that oil companies had been beaten and Jeff had felt very proud that he had been part of something that had changed the course of planning history. To him it had proved that if people bound themselves together like a bundle of twigs no matter how strong or powerful the companies were, they could never break the people and the Devil's disciples wouldn't win.

CHAPTER 10

"Well, what have you got to say about today?" the man had shouted, bringing Jeff out of his reverie and back to the room he was in. This man was playing for keeps.

"Ok. Do you believe Bob knew more than he let on?" Jeff had asked the man.

"Maybe" the man had replied.

Jeff had asked forcefully "Did you know that there were certain Whitehall mandarins involved in the acquiring of permission to build gas and oil installations for their own profit, and they used their position to get the installations built, no matter what the danger posed to the community they were putting them in?".

"Have you run through the stupid forest and kissed every tree?" the man had asked sarcastically.

Jeff had sighed realising that he had to take a gamble with this man "How far can I trust you? I don't know your name, I don't know who you work for, all I can go on is that Bob appeared to have trusted you and I trusted Bob".

After a few moments of contemplation, the man had said "Ok. My name is John and I work for an agency that does not exist and only answers to the Prime Minister directly. It's an organisation that is set up for every Prime Minister and answers only to the current Prime Minister of the time. The organisation was set up after a well-known past Prime Minister's phone was bugged and he was spied on by unscrupulous Whitehall mandarins as you call them. I am aware that Bob trusted you and by the way, the Sergeant really is my brother and he has got a granddaughter who is living in the Estuary area and he is concerned about her, does that help? Is that enough trust for now? Now tell me all you know whilst we wait to see if the man I sent can find Bob's attaché case and hopefully the important papers you spoke of that were in it?"

There was a short silence then John started to question him again about his involvement in environmental issues.

After a while, a man, much resembling a weasel, had put his head round the door, had nodded to John and had said "It's gone, and the body's been moved recently. It must have taken some effort to move that masonry to get to his case. By the way, we did find what we believe to be our friend's bag".

Jeff had gone to grab for his bag, but John had snatched it from the man and said "I'll have that".

"Christ! That was quick" Jeff had thought "unless they knew about the papers in Bob's case beforehand".

John had said "When you and Bob were spotted going into that building, our people put two and two together and our man let us know and he followed you in and never came out".

"He was probably crushed under all that masonry" Jeff had replied "when the world fell in".

"The last time I looked, masonry did not carry a knife and put it into people's backs, also cut people's throats with it" the weasel-looking man had retorted sarcastically.

Jeff had looked astounded "What!" he had exclaimed "he was murdered?"

The weasel-looking man had then quickly thrown Jeff a biscuit from the plate.

Jeff had caught it one handed and had said sarcastically "Are we having a food fight now?"

"You're lucky you're right handed". The
observed which hand Jeff had caught the
"Our man was killed by a southpaw. He wa
the back and then his throat was cut by a left
was then thrown into a corner, and by the looks of it by a professional. As clever as you think you are, even you can't do that. So for my money you're off the hook".

The weasel-looking man had then added "So, I reckon your life could be at risk now, big time, as it seems they were after you".

"Thanks" John had said to the man "make a report and I'll see it later". The other man had nodded and had left the room.

Jeff had promptly stammered "What did he mean my life could be at risk now?"

John had said "Before, you might not have realised because of being so well known and the publicity you created, that you tended to be a bit untouchable because the press and people would have asked where you were. And questions would have been asked if you suddenly went missing? Well, not now! At the moment your best way to stay alive is to stay dead and you need to stay dead under that rubble until this is sorted out".

Jeff had felt a chill run down up spine. "This is not real" he had thought and "it's like something out of a novel".

"Now tell me what you know" John had said, noticing the fear and horror on Jeff's face "perhaps we can get round this. Tell me anything that Bob might have said. Any papers you know of that might help. I need to know so I can get to the bottom of this mystery of why my agent was murdered".

Jeff had not believed what he was hearing—murder, spies, Government secret agents—what the hell was going on and how was he being drawn into all this intrigue?

It was then that Jeff had remembered the papers in his inside coat pocket which Bob had asked him to look at, and he had inadvertently slipped them into his inside pocket as he had got out of his car and was walking to the meeting hall with Bob.

"Are these of any help?" Jeff had asked, pulling them out of his pocket. He had handed them over to John. John had glanced at the papers noting that it was a list of names, dates, and numbers. Some of the names he had recognised, others he had not known. What he had known was that the names were amongst the top echelon in the world of industry and politics. "You got these from Bob?" John had asked.

"He gave them to me as he met me from my car, why?" Jeff had replied.

"Have you looked at this list?" John had asked.

"I was looking at it as I went to get a cup of coffee at the meeting when the world fell in on me, why, are they important?"

"Do you know anybody on this list?" John had asked another question.

"There are two names I've heard of plus another one of them I've met. Why?" Jeff had asked again.

"It's only a list of who's who in the energy world. The question is, what was Bob doing with this list? Why was Bob giving you this list? And what relevance did it have to your meeting?"

"That's easy" Jeff had replied "we were cross-checking my list of names of people I was suspicious of against a list of names he had of people he was not sure about himself".

"This is supposed to be a list of suspicious people? Huh! You're talking about the untouchables of this world" John had scoffed.

"I know, and that's why we were cross-checking our lists to prove or disprove that the risk to our community was from greedy speculators and not from some foreign power or terrorist group" Jeff had explained further.

Jeff relayed what he had always suspected "Look, imagine the hue and cry if the people of this country suspected, or it was proved that certain powerful people manipulated the planning system for their own ends, and, if there was a very big accident in the gas or oil industry which caused a lot of deaths? The ramifications would be worldwide and it would totally destroy them and their empire. But, if it was proved that there had been a terrorist attack on these installations that killed hundreds of people then that would be an act of war and no blame would pass to the gas and oil moguls and their regime would stay intact".

John had whistled "You spin a good yarn, I'll give you that" he had said "can any of this be proved?"

"Well" Jeff had replied cautiously "in my bag are another list, and those two lists need matching up with the right people. My list should work upwards in importance, and Bob's list should work downwards in importance and if I'm right somewhere in the middle they should meet up at the same name or names, and then the trail to the top person or persons involved. Together the lists tell a story, but apart they are just lists of people's names. Bob knew or knew of most of the people on his list. Unfortunately, I don't know who they are, or what they do. I only know the people on my own list, what, or who they represent".

"Ok" John had said "let's marry them up and see what we come up with, if you are to be believed that is". John had gotten both lists and put them on the table together, spreading them out to look at them side by side.

After some time, John had said exasperated "See, nothing! On your list there are the names of local councillors, county councillors, health and safety advisors and Government researchers and Environmental Agency officials. On Bob's list there is the who's who of the gas and oil industry, some members of Parliament and two opposition Government ministers, so nothing suspicious there. All you've got is a lot of red herrings and nothing more". Then the expression on John's face suddenly changed. "Wait a minute. This man named Ray Wilson—his name appears on both lists, how come? He's a henchman and an advisor to Sir William Waite, the President of UK United Gas and Sir William is on the list also".

CHAPTER 11

John had continued "I met this Ray Wilson when he attended an annual meeting with the PM and some energy barons as I call them, nasty little maggot. I know the PM didn't like him or what was said by his boss Sir William. They had quite strong words at the time. I thought he was trying to intimidate the PM. I was going to step in but the PM said that he would deal with it".

"That's the link then" Jeff had said, feeling vindicated "I knew there was a link and Bob proved it. Unfortunately he died in the process of trying to prove it".

John had then said "If what you and Bob suspected is true then this involves collusion between multi-billion pound conglomerates and central and local planners and it involves them right down to the grass roots planning. That is unbelievable!"

Jeff had added "If it was proved there was collusion and that corners in safety were cut for the profit of UK United Gas, also, if there was an accident resulting from those safety cuts, the whole pack of rotten cards would collapse and the top people and all their cronies would be held on corporate manslaughter charges. It would be the biggest scandal ever. No wonder in the past they tried to put a D Notice on what we had to say and to brand us as some sort of anarchists or worse. All so nobody in authority would listen to what we had to say or what we could prove".

"If what you say is true, you're between a rock and a hard place" John had mused.

Jeff had replied "I stopped worrying long ago about what people think of me. They'll believe what they want to believe because they're not prepared to listen to the truth, and I'm not going to waste my life worrying or trying to tell people what to think of me as a person. I'm not important. The issue at hand is".

"No" John had said "I meant with all the media attention on this catastrophic event that's just happened, the attention the papers gave to you every week or so will disappear and that makes you very vulnerable to these people".

"I've heard pigs fart before" Jeff had replied scornfully.

"Hey! Wake up and smell the roses. I told you, this Ray Wilson is a nasty little maggot" John had said.

"Are you telling me I'm being threatened by you and this Sir William?" Jeff scoffed "when are you bringing on the goons to take me to a cell, kick me to death, and then my body disappears into an unmarked grave?"

John had ignored this retort. "You're not being threatened by me or the Prime Minister's team. In actual fact the PM admires what you do privately but he can't say or even show it publicly. There is no threat to you from me or my team, not after listening to what you have to say and what these papers from Bob prove".

"Are you telling me my life is in danger" Jeff had asked.

"If Sir William or this Ray Wilson think you're alive, with this sort of information, it could be" John had replied. He started thinking out loud. "For now, let's say you died under the rubble of that building in the middle of that meeting, and you did not wander in here, and we have not spoken. Where could you be safe? And where could you do the most good?"

"I'm not being a pawn in your political game of chess" Jeff had snapped, cutting the other man off.

"Face reality Jeff" John had hissed "these people play for keeps and so does Sir William. As I've said, this Ray Wilson is a nasty kettle of fish and is capable of doing anything underhand. The last I heard they had some people in powerful places and you've probably come across one or two without realising it. You need to find a bolt hole to either hide in, or do what you do best. Use the media to expose what you know to your advantage and become untouchable to the Wilsons of this world because they can't be seen to be involved.

There has to be a paper trail of some sort. They can't be this organised without it. The second option will be the hardest, to get media attention now with all this going on, and everybody being told its terrorists. They would probably try to engineer it so you are in the frame as well. As I said, you are between a rock and a hard place. Until there's proof of some sort like papers or information linking them all together, all there are, are theories and a few suppositions made up by anarchists and trouble makers to create instability in the country, and that's the smoke screen they will use to get away with their power struggle to control the country.

In this political arena we're in at the moment, the PM is being attacked from all sides and he is fighting for survival. His hands are tied and his power is being eroded by the likes of Sir William who thinks the country should be run as one of their companies and if people don't do as they say they should be, shall we say, sacked permanently".

"There are quite a lot of us who don't believe in a total right wing society believe it or not" Jeff had stated.

"Yeah, yeah" John had retorted "I know, poli is many, tics are parasites. I heard you the first time, and you don't do politics. But you could help to be the lynchpin in all this if you wanted to be. Also, to get to the heart of the matter and the people that seem to be behind all what you're trying to resolve. What do you think? Make a difference?"

Jeff had said "I have been making a difference for more years than you can remember so don't tell me I need to do my bit. I'm not one of your raw recruits to be indoctrinated and manipulated to suit your purpose and then put back in the cupboard when finished with and denied they exist".

"Whoa! Whoa" John had said "I'm not asking you to do anything. You can find whatever stone you crawled out from under and go back in there and pull the lid closed for all I care, but if these people find out you're alive outside the protection of your area where you are well known, they can make you disappear. Even in the Estuary area you won't be totally safe until the facts can be proved and this is resolved, and that's the reality of the situation. So what's it to be—put you away in a cell for your own safety and with some of the inmates who might be able to control and get to you? That might not be too safe either. Or somehow get you to the Estuary without anybody knowing, see what you can find out, also where you can do the most good? Now that is not going to be easy".

"Why can't you fly me in by helicopter or get me in by road?" Jeff had asked.

"Have you had your brain removed?" John had enquired sarcastically "haven't you heard anything I've said? Everything is locked down. Even I can't protect you without compromising the Prime Minister at the moment, and hell will freeze over before that happens".

"Typical. So you hang me out to dry?" Jeff had retorted "so much for all your fine words and pontificating. What am I, another piece of cannon fodder for your political guns?"

"Come down off your high horse" John had placated "I didn't say I wouldn't help you. All I'm saying is that it won't be easy. At this moment, if it was discovered you were alive by certain parties and you could point the finger even in a small way at them, your feet would not touch. At the moment, you're a loose cannon they can't control, and a cannon that is capable, with the right ammunition, of bringing down their pack of cards. Look. At the moment only three people know you are not brown bread and lying under a pile of rubble either here or in the Estuary area. Those people are me, my man you saw and my brother out there. It's not in my interests to say anything and he won't say anything and they'll help cover your back if I ask them. Does that tell you where I stand?" John had asked, then added "at this moment in time, the only thing that stops you from being in the place of no return is that you're more important to me alive and as a loose cannon then being in a cell, and if what you and Bob suspected is true, I want to put these bastards away for a long time.

It won't be long before all this area will be under military control and our little friends control certain ministerial positions that control the military, so they could be controlling the military without the military realising it and that worries me. So before everything locks down, we need to try to put you in the Estuary area without drawing attention to you. If we can get you inside the cordon they are setting up to stop anybody going into the area, you will be able to move around within the cordon freely, but, if we leave it any longer, everything locks down and nobody gets in until the area is sieved clean by them, so they're not implicated in any way. They will use this as a cover and say it's for a Government investigation, all to cover their own backs.

Are you prepared to put your money where your mouth is? Or are you all talk?" spoken in a taunting manner "I can't give you any guarantees, but you still have a lot of respect amongst the survivors, and before you say anything there are always survivors. You can move around better than anyone from the outside and have more contacts then any plod trying to get information, so you have a much better chance than most of us getting the information to hang these bastards. What do you say?"

Jeff had thought about what had been said. He had liked the thought of the challenge, the chance to get even for himself, his family and everyone else, to prove that they had been right to oppose the siting of high fire risk industry close to any residential area, and it was all for the profit of the few, and not in the interest of the people.

"Ok, what backup do I get?" Jeff had finally asked.

"At the moment very little" John had replied apologetically "as no-one outside the cordon needs to know you are alive except my boss, my brother, and a few of my need to know trusted friends. We need to get you out of here this evening under cover of darkness".

"But there's a curfew due to be put on the streets from tonight" Jeff had warned.

"No-one will question a police sergeant escorting someone after dark" John had explained and smiled wickedly "he will take you to a house so you can wash up and get a change of clothing and be fed then we'll see about getting you moved inside the cordon if that's ok with you. In the meantime get some rest, you're going to need it. You'll be travelling later tonight and we will get you as far as we can without compromising the situation".

Then he had added "We must get you inside the cordon before its set up properly. They will set up the main roads first and then the back roads. Once they are set up no-one gets in or out without their names being checked and logged, a report being made on them and then put on the central computer, and that's when our nasty mates do their dirty work. They can find out your movements and track you down.

But if we can get you within the cordon before it's set up and later lightens, you can move around within it, do what you need to do for a short time without them knowing you are there. By then I can try to stabilise what I can from outside here. So far they haven't got the power to touch me yet, but if we don't do something soon they could sterilise me completely and we don't want that, do we?"

John had left Jeff to get some rest saying "Nobody will disturb you as nobody except we three know who you are and that you are here".

Jeff had lain back on the camp bed that he had been supplied with. His headache had eased to a dull ache but his head was still in a spin with regard to what had transpired in the last hour or so. He had thought to himself that unfortunately this man John, whoever he was, was right. There was a lot more to this then met the eye and the ringleaders who he suspected and he knew of, if they survived, were going to be very busy covering their own backs.

As Jeff had lain there, his mind had wandered back to some of the incidents that had transpired since he had been involved in this campaign, some minor, some quite serious but they had all centred around a few well-known local public figures who had always seemed to benefit in some way or another either at the time or later when planning decisions were made or being made but there was nothing that could be proved.

He had worried how badly it had gone wrong and how and if Karen and the rest of his family were safe. But it would be no use worrying until he could get there and see for himself, and this gave him that opportunity. His mind had wandered back to the time he had met Karen after 6 long lonely years of being on his own.

Oh, he had gone out and had relationships with many women that had been single or divorced during that time. He had never been unfaithful to anybody but he had not met that special person until then. In this melancholy state and being very tired Jeff had fallen into a deep sleep.

CHAPTER 12

Jeff had awoken with a start when he had been shaken awake.

"You could snore for England" the Sergeant had said "here's a cup of tea, drink that and then we can go".

"Ok, I'm with you" Jeff had replied and had taken the chipped mug of steaming hot tea. The first gulp had burned the inside of his mouth and tongue but it had also gone some way to clearing the sloth from his head and bring him back to reality. He had also taken a couple of pain killers to get rid of the residue of the headache.

The Sergeant had led him via the back door out onto the street. It had been getting dark. "We won't be seen this way" the Sergeant had said "but keep quiet".

They had walked quietly for quite a while, past damaged buildings and had come to a sheltered quiet area with a house nestled at the end of a terrace. "Right, round the back and make it quick".

Jeff had gone round to back of the house and into a kitchen where a nicely rounded middle-aged lady had greeted him in a friendly warm manner. "I'm Jane" she had said "my Sergeant Dick told me you would be coming".

"Her Sergeant and his name was Dick!" Jeff had thought.

"I'm sorry to put you and your husband to any sort of bother" Jeff had said.

"Oh, we're not married. Dick's wife is in a nursing home, been there for years. He can't get a divorce so we've had this arrangement ever since my husband died when he tried to stop a hit and run driver. He was Dick's Inspector at the time. They never found the driver or the car. Big green Jag it was, they say, all they could get was part of the number plate, W something. They're still looking today but haven't seen hide or hair of it, but they'll keep looking until they find it" she added confidently.

Jane had studied Jeff for a few minutes then had said "The water is hot for a bath if you want one and I've laid out some of my husband's old clothes. See if they fit. I've got dinner on, sausage toad alright? It will be on the table as soon as you freshen up".

As Jeff had sunk into the hot water of the bath he could hear the murmuring of voices. He had felt the hot water gradually easing away his aches and pains. He had eventually gone downstairs dressed in the clothes she had laid out, feeling all at once more alert and refreshed—and clean.

"You look almost human" Dick had said with a small smile.

"They appear to fit you quite well" Jane had said "now sit down and eat you two. I've got a food parcel to make up for this young man" she had pointed at Jeff "and Dick has some information to help you".

Jeff and Dick had started eating and both had remained silent and occupied until the plates had been completely cleaned.

"Right" Dick had said "push bike is the best way, and you can use the one in the shed. Tracks and country lanes are best without raising any suspicion, but we must leave before the curfew kicks in and the cordons are not fully in place. I can only go so far with you without raising suspicion and then you make your own way after that.

There are a few things in the panniers of the bike you might need, if things get sticky, you never know".

Dick had added "There's a mobile phone. If you find out anything about my granddaughter let me know please. I've put the name and number on a pad in there as well as John's number. Don't let anyone see those numbers, it could make things difficult this end as the mobile phone is tuned in to a 10 to 15 frequency so it's not blocked by COBRA in an emergency situation like all other civilian mobile phones which have a frequency of 1 to 9".

Jane had said "I've put a flask of tea in the bag on the bike as well as some food and some spare teabags that should keep you going for a while. There's also one of my husband's warm coats in the shed he used to use for gardening. I always said he was the smartest gardener in the street".

Jeff had thanked her for the lovely meal and the clothes and said "I almost feel human again".

"We had better get going whilst we have the darkness" Dick had said.

They had made their way to the shed, obtained the bikes and had made their way down the road without incident.

After a few miles Dick had said quietly "This is where I leave you, you're on your own now so take care. I don't want to hear you've been picked up. Sorry I gave you a rough time back there, but I didn't realise what you had been trying to do all these years. Like the rest I believed the propaganda put out about you, I know different now, no hard feelings?"

"No hard feelings" Jeff had replied "I understand that you're concerned about your granddaughter, thanks for your help and I hope I can find enough information to put these bastards away for a very long time". They had shaken hands in the dark and Jeff had made his way towards the Estuary and what was left of his home.

There had been a little used road which could be used by emergency vehicles in the event of an emergency. The road had led to the Estuary area. This was the route Jeff had taken to avoid being stopped or seen from the hill that overlooked the Estuary and where a survivor's camp was growing in size.

He had only been stopped once and with the heavy bandage on his head he had pretended to be wandering lost and dazed. He had been told to go to an emergency centre set up along the road in the same direction he was travelling, by a sentry in a black military-type uniform on duty near the gateway to a large house. Little did Jeff know that this large house was to be the central command post set up by Wilson, the professional killer that was to hunt him down and try to kill him.

When Jeff had rounded the bend in the road, he had gone through a field to avoid the emergency centre and then on to the road that had led to the Estuary area.

Jeff had snapped back from his memories to the situation he was now in. Now John had realised that what Jeff was saying was true about the situation he said "If we are to get organised, it means we need to be talking to the other passengers and getting their support. We can't do that cooped up in our cabins. I can use my lap-top to communicate with number 10 via satellite link so we can use that as a link to the PM direct. We must inform him of what's going on. By the way, I can get our location via the same satellite".

"What else can you do with your box of tricks and when were you going to tell me about it?" Jeff asked suspiciously "before or after you reported to the Prime Minister and how did you get that box of tricks through the security check when we boarded?"

"Let's say the officer in charge of security and I go back a way's" John said.

"Your coat buttons up over more areas then I care to imagine" Jeff said wryly "is that more from your cloak and dagger background that you're not going to tell me about?"

John ignored the terse remark and said "We need to use all the tools we have in the box, this one gives us an advantage, so whoever is responsible for this hijack must not know we have a link to the outside world".

As they were speaking, there was a further announcement over the ship's PA system advising everybody that they would be able to leave their cabins soon but would not be allowed on the outside decks. The voice emphasised that any attempt to go outside on the rear of Deck 5 by any passenger where the gas ship was lashed to would be shot.

"What do you make of that?" Cyril asked as he came out onto the adjoining balcony of the other adjoining cabin. On the other side of Cyril's cabin, Derek also came out onto his balcony "Jen wants to rip somebody's head off for trying to ruin her holiday".

"Calm her down and tell her we are going to make plans to rectify the situation" Jeff replied "but we have to wait until we can get more passengers involved and we can't do that holed up in our cabins".

The PA system burst into life once again, this time advising passengers that they were to make their way to the Restaurant Deck where they would be fed and that there would be an announcement. All passengers were to be on the Restaurant Deck by 0800. Those passengers who did not comply would be forced to walk the plank.

"Walk the plank!" Cyril exclaimed "that went out with Blackbeard the pirate. Well, it looks like we now have his great grandson to deal with. I heard what you were saying to John, I'm in so is Derek. He and Sandra are in the next cabin to ours".

"I suggest we all get up to that deck as soon as possible to see what's going on" John said "it's 0715 now. See you outside your cabins at 0745 then we can go in numbers. We stand a better chance that way by sticking together".

"Right" they all agreed together.

They all hurriedly got dressed and met outside their cabins. They made their way to the Restaurant Deck with trepidation but also with solidarity and determination, not to be bullied by some jumped up pirate terrorist.

CHAPTER 13

The Restaurant Deck was filling up as they made their way to the middle of the crowd of passengers and waited by a pillar to hear what was going to happen.

By the doors, were men dressed in black uniforms holding guns and looking very sinister. Jeff recognised the men as they were the same men who had been serving them at the Sheik's reception the previous night.

There was a loud buzz of noise as the passengers on the deck were herded towards a small stage area that was acting as a platform.

One of the guards fired some shots into the air and the hubbub stopped immediately.

Mustafa stepped up onto the stage whilst everybody stood in sullen silence.

Mustafa spoke "I introduce our leader Sheik Ali Mustafa who will tell you what is going to happen".

The Sheik stepped up onto the small stage and waved his hands as if he were their saviour and said, with a beaming smile on his features "We are here to remove the yoke of the West from your shoulders, the yoke of oppression which has strangled you and my people for decades. Do not be frightened. We are your fellow passengers in the struggle against oppression. We are here to liberate you. Do as my men ask and you will come to no harm but, if you not to do as we ask, you will face the consequences like the men who were told not to go out on the rear of Deck 5, see for yourself from the viewpoints".

Quite a number of passengers moved to the side of the Restaurant floor to look out over the lower deck. Lined up at the side of the ship were a number of crew and a few passengers. They were being herded towards a plank that had been lashed to and was hanging over the side of the cruise liner.

The Sheik continued "These people are an example to you that we mean business and you are to do as you are told". With that, he raised his hand then dropped it.

The hapless people were pushed towards the plank. Their screams of fear could be heard even through the toughened glass of the viewpoints by those within the Restaurant. The passengers within the Restaurant reacted by shouting "You can't do that, it's inhuman" and the noise of horror and anger began to rise in volume.

The guards, at a signal from the Sheik, reacted to this noise by opening fire with a volley just above everyone's heads.

"The next volley will be lower" the Sheik shouted. There was a mad look in his eyes. "They disobeyed me" pointing to the people on Deck 5 "and will walk the plank or be shot and then tossed over the side. They are already dead. It is their time to meet Allah".

The guards pushing the people towards the plank separated two Filipino crew members from the other passengers. The guards then pushed the two crew members towards one side of the plank and the others to the other side of the plank. Parvis was on the gas tanker watching with a sick eagerness through his binoculars. He had recently done this same thing to the crew of the gas tanker and had enjoyed it.

The first Filipino rushed the guards and tried vainly to get passed them and away from the edge of the ship. He was beaten to the ground with the butt end of a gun and lay where he fell in a pool of blood.

The other crew member was pushed towards the edge of the plank by a ring of bayonets from the guards. He was screaming and pleading with the guards to let him live.

A guard stepped forward, a man who was later to be known as Abdul. He looked up to where the Sheik was standing. The Sheik moved his hand across his throat in a cutting motion.

Abdul pushed the hapless man to the end of the plank with the point of his bayonet, digging the bayonet into the man's stomach.

The man fell from the end of the plank but managed to grab onto its end in desperation and cling to it like a vice. Abdul moved to the end of the plank and stabbed at the man's fingers. The man let out a piercing scream and tumbled into the sea, his screams diminishing and then cutting off abruptly.

The guards grabbed the other Filipino up from the deck. He was unconscious and they threw him over the side like a sack of meat.

The guards then approached the other prisoners and surrounded them. Abdul looked up at the Sheik who held up his hand in a stop sign and signalled to the guards to bring the prisoners inside.

A passenger in the Restaurant shouted "You evil bastard" another shouted "bloody murderer". The guards moved in on the two men and hit them in the faces with the butts of their guns.

"Enough" the Sheik said to the guards who promptly backed off.

The Sheik continued "The two crew members who have just left the ship are an example for you to see that I will be obeyed in all things".

Just then, there was a scuffle at the back of the Restaurant and guards entered with the Captain of the ship under escort.

The Captain shouted at the Sheik "You have just murdered two of my crew, what have you got to say for yourself".

"You can join them if you wish" the Sheik replied with a shrug "or better still, you can choose which of your crew goes next or you can shut up and sail this ship to where I want you to go".

"This ship goes nowhere" the Captain said "you can't hijack a British ship and get away with it. You'll hang for piracy".

"Captain!" the Sheik exclaimed "I can do what I wish. I have the NATGAS 2 which is a ship with a cargo of Liquid Natural Gas being towed by the Baroness of the Sea. Any interference by you or your crew, or any attempt to rescue you, your crew or your passengers by outsiders, will be met by my men on board the NATGAS 2 using the valves to release the cargo of cryogenically cold Liquid Natural Gas". The Sheik then addressed everybody and said "For those of you who do not know what Liquid Natural Gas is, it is Liquid Methane. I do have to tell you that once my men operate the valves on that gas ship there is no going back. We will all meet Allah together. Everyone on board both ships will be freeze dried before they are incinerated. There will be a fireball at least ten miles across when it ignites, so, as you say in your country, I hold all the aces in the pack of cards".

Then the Sheik addressed the Captain with maniacal glee in his eyes "You called me a pirate, so I act like a pirate, by putting over the side people who I feel are mutineers because they did not do as I say and argue with my orders. So from now on, you will obey my orders and if I feel you need persuasion you and I will pick out the next people to walk the plank, so, whoever dies will be your choice, do you understand my meaning? You and your passengers must know by me setting the example that I mean what I say".

The Sheik then noticed Jeff and pointed to him. "Mr Jeff is known for being a man of his word in his country, so am

I a man of my word and I will keep my word and it will be up to your Captain who dies if I am not obeyed. Do I make myself very clear?"

The Sheik seemed to then mentally steady himself, to bring himself under control and to calm down. He continued with his speech in a pleasant tone. "To show you all that I am not a cruel man Captain, your passengers can enjoy their cruise and I want everybody to act as normal, however, let me make it quite clear that nobody goes outside onto Deck 5 without my permission. Is this clear?" and he left the platform surrounded by guards.

There was a hubbub of noise as the passengers realised they were being held prisoners even though they were on a luxury cruise liner. The realisation and the resultant indignation that their lives were at risk if they interfered with anybody on Deck 5 started to dawn on them. Some passengers surrounded the Captain as he was flanked by the Sheik's guards and asked him to intercede on their behalf. The Captain advised them that his hands were tied and he could not intercede at this moment as his officers had been locked in the forward hold.

It was then that someone pointed at Jeff and said "Why did he refer to you and pick you out as his hero?"

Jeff retorted "Did you see the look in his eyes? The man has got a screw loose".

"He might have but he admires you" the man said "so you speak for us. Tell him to let us go, we don't want to be part of this hijack. I am an important business man, I have important friends in the American Senate".

Jeff said "Don't let the Sheik hear that, he hates America with a vengeance, so your American friends could get you killed just by you knowing them. I would keep quiet about them if I were you. I suggest you think of ways of resolving the situation as we are on our own here, because no-one is going to rescue us".

"You mean, take on the terrorists?" the man asked with disbelief "but they control both ships. It would mean taking control of both ships at the same time, stopping them operating the valves on the gas ship, plus taking on armed guards. May I remind you that we are unarmed civilians. It can't be done, not even by the SAS".

"So, are you going to lie down and let him kill you and your loved ones?" Jeff asked "without you saying no and meaning it".

As they were discussing the situation, the Captain was escorted away by the guards who seemed oblivious to what was being said.

"Well" the man said "I'd like to do something but I'm only one person and I don't know what to do".

"Well" Jeff said "firstly, I suggest you find out who is willing to do something, and then we can work out if we can do something. If so, what to do, and when we do it because if you lie down and accept your fate without doing something about it and you live through it, you will always live to regret it. What is needed, is to find out who can, and how they can help. We all have our own skills so we need to find out who has any skills, then we have to work with the tools we have in the box".

"But they have guns" the man said "also, they are killers. We don't have any guns and most of us have never used a gun".

"Then it's time to learn or die, or watch your families die" Jeff said abruptly.

"You're a cruel bastard" the man said "you know we can't fight back".

"Yes you can" Jeff said "say no. It's either that, or you die whimpering. I'll try to have a word with the Captain somehow and find out how many of the crew are not locked up who we can count on. You can help by finding out how many men you have met so far on this cruise that we can rely on. Let them know we will be fighting back at some time in the near future but above all, keep it quiet so that the terrorists don't get wind of it because if they do we'll all be for the plank. So far, it looks like most of the guards don't understand English. That will be an advantage".

Just at that moment, a group of guards came towards them with Mustafa in their middle.

"Mr Jeff" Mustafa called "you will come with me to see the Sheik now".

Derek moved to stand in front of Jeff. "You aren't going to kill him, not while I breathe" he said, glaring at Mustafa menacingly.

"He is not going to die yet" Mustafa said "the Sheik only wishes to speak with him on his own. If you do not move aside you will be shot dead where you stand".

"I'll break you in half before you do" Derek said, his voice quiet but firm and convincing.

"Leave it Derek" Jeff said calmly, knowing that the terrorists would shoot Derek out of hand. For them all to do as they were ordered would go some way to appeasing Mustafa's pride.

Jeff murmured under his breath to Derek "If I don't come back then you can kill him".

CHAPTER 14

Jeff remembered back to when he had first met Derek and Jen.

When Jeff had got to the Estuary, on approaching a corner of a street, a group of three men had stepped out in front of him. One was built like a scrum half and looked a nasty piece of work, the other two had just looked mean.

"Right sunshine, who are you? And where are you off to on such a lovely night?" the man who looked like a scrum half had asked in a very surly manner "and what have you got in there?" pointing to the panniers and looking expectant.

Jeff had thought to himself how stupid he had been to walk right into a trap, but before he could answer one of the other men had spoke up.

"Hang on a minute Dave" the man had said as he looked closely at Jeff "don't I know you?" He had shone torchlight into Jeff's face studying him more closely and had said "You're Jeff Baker, the bloke who's always banging on about the gas and oil people not caring about us people, aren't you? We heard you were dead. Take a look around you. Unfortunately you were proved right about them not caring about us. It's cost me everything I hold dear, my wife and kid and his also" pointing to the other man "and also Dave's wife".

"I don't know how my family is or whether they've survived either" Jeff had replied. For a moment, the group of men stood in silence, united in their sorrow.

"Do you know what happened?" Jeff had asked eventually.

"We were all together working away, all three of us, when it happened. We came home as soon as we heard about it. We caught two looters by the public house. They won't be able to fix their teeth with broken fingers, or pick anything up for a long time will they Harry" Dave had replied laughing a little.

"That's why we're here now" the man Harry had added "making sure they, or their friends don't come back".

"How come you're coming onto the Estuary at this time of night and via the emergency road?"

"I've seen you before" Jeff had replied, pointing at the third man "how far can I trust you three?"

The third man had spoken up "My name's Tom, this is Dave" pointing at the big man "and this is Harry. We've been friends since school. I've been to a few of your public meetings about the dangers of putting this lot" pointing in the general area of where the installations were "next to us and you were right. As far as I'm concerned you can't do anything wrong. You can trust me and I can vouch for these two. Why?"

Jeff had explained why he had come to the Estuary in secret and what he was trying to do. He had also emphasised that if they ratted on him not only would he not be able to find out what had really happened, but the culprits would be able to cover their tracks and get away with it. And nobody would be any the wiser.

"If I had heard this story a few days ago I would not have given you house room" Harry had said "but after this you have my total support. If you can prove what you say is true, I'll help you bury the bastards."

"I never did believe that old bollocks about terrorists. They couldn't get that far up the Thames without someone knowing about it" Tom had said "that would mean they could get lost in a broom cupboard, and I'm certain our intelligence people are not that stupid. Right. How can we help?"

"I'd like to check up on my family to see if any of them are alive but I can't be seen, not yet anyway. Also I need a base to operate from, and trusted people to work with for starters" Jeff had replied.

"I'll check up about on your family. One of your boys went to school with my son, I can say I'm their Uncle" Harry had said.

"We can use the back of the pub. It has a cellar we can get to and we won't be seen. People looking for family survivors go backwards and forwards from there all the time, so it won't raise suspicions if we come and go from there" Dave had said.

"Good thinking Batman" Tom had retorted with a wry smile, and getting into the spirit of the challenge "that's probably the best place and we'll be able to recognise or know who goes in or out of the area from there as well".

The big man Dave had turned to Jeff, coloured up and said, "I've not said this to many men but thanks" and he took him in a big bear hug and spoke surprisingly softly "you've given me something to hope and fight for, instead of hanging around useless. It also gives me a chance to help get the bastards who did this".

Jeff had thought "I'm glad I'm on his side. He could be a handful if you got on the wrong side of him on a dark night".

"Let's get you bedded down in the cellars" Harry had said "that's what we've called what's left of the pub".

Dave had said "I'll stay here and keep watch. Nobody will get past me".

Harry and Tom had helped Jeff to the Cellars. When they got there, they knocked on the beam by the door.

A pickaxe handle had come round the door frame followed by a gorilla of a man "Who's this?" the man had asked of Harry and Tom.

"He's all right Derek" Harry had said soothingly.

"As long as you say so" Derek had said "you can't be too careful now-a-days. We've taken over the cellars. We swap the beer and spirits for food from the soldiers up the road. They like a drink and we can get some of their rations, straight swap like, you understand?" He had looked at Jeff adding "You know what I mean. We have to survive and it's up to us. Did you know they evacuated a lot of the surviving councillors and council officers from the Council Offices almost straightaway so they would be safe from looters and mob rule? But as usual we have to fend for ourselves. Bloody typical of politicians, pull up the ladder Jack, I'm alright".

He continued his tirade about the situation "They really don't give a shit about the people they're supposed to represent. Oh, they'll bleat on, as how come they survived and it was a shame that quite a few of their colleagues and their families died trying to help the people, but they were in the bloody safety bunker in the Council Chamber when it all kicked off. Talk about them not digging in the same ditch as the rest of us. Oh! They've been on the news saying how terrible it was and how it should never ever happen again.

But like you said it right at that public meeting that time, they could have stopped it. But they were too busy looking out for themselves—by going to all the bun fights put up by the gas and oil companies and only paying lip service to the people that elected them. You haven't seen a poor councillor in the district since the gas companies got their planning permission. Elect them—I'd hang them if I had my way. They are as much use as a balsa wood anchor".

A woman had put her head round the door and said to Derek "Derek, I thought I heard your dulcet tones. I've not heard you say more than ten words in one day and here you are on a soap box, that's a first".

"Well they deserve to hang" Derek had snapped angrily.

She had turned to Jeff and said nastily "I know. You're that Jeff Baker who stood up against all this and said it could happen. Well, you got proved right! Are you happy now?"

"Hey this isn't my fault" Jeff had responded defensively to her "at least I tried to stop it, that's more than some did".

"I'm sorry" she had immediately apologised "I'm so angry and frustrated at what's happened. As you said, this could have been avoided but they got on the gravy train and all lined their own pockets, and I shouldn't take it out on the one person, who tried to do something about it. My name's Jenny, Jen to my friends and that does include you. Sorry about my outburst but I get so angry with all this greed that's gone on and I do know you put a lot of dedication into trying to get the right things done and at least tried to do something to stop them".

Jen was a medium-built woman with a warm nature. She was a very friendly person, but there was a hidden hardness that had come with life.

"You make a friend of Jen you got a friend for life. Even I don't upset Jen" Derek had said laughingly then added "she has a fearsome temper".

It had seemed so strange that this big powerful gorilla of a man was frightened of this woman's temper, but you could see he had a very soft spot for her.

"Come and get a cup of tea, not that there's much of that left" Jen had ordered in a far more friendly manner.

"I'll have a look to see what's been packed in here" Jeff had said and had reached inside the panniers from the bicycle that he had detached when he had left it by the bunker at the corner before he had run into the others and he had brought it with him. He started sorting through it.

He had found a large pack of teabags which Jane had put there. "She thinks of everything" he had thought as he gave them to Jen.

Jen had said "Hey, don't give us all your supplies, tea and coffee is currency here now. Keep some in case you need them, but thanks for the offer".

He gave her a big handful.

"Thanks" she had said "I'll be able to make them stretch a long way. The troops will be pleased. We can have a decent cup of tea tonight".

As Jeff had put the rest of the teabags back into the pannier, at the bottom of the bag he felt something metal wrapped in a cloth. "I'll have a look at that later" he had thought.

He had picked up the panniers and had followed Jen into the building which looked as if it had been shelled. "You said troops?" He had directed the question at Jen's back.

"Well. You'd call them survivors that don't want to be away from their homes or what's left of them. We all use this place as a centre to meet and find out anything that's happening on and off of the Estuary. All we've seen is one helicopter and that flew over the Gas Terminal, looked as though they took some photos and flew off. We've been left pretty much to fend for ourselves. What with the councillors being rescued and deserting us and one helicopter only looking out for the Gas Terminal, we've become the poor Cinderella that no-one cares about".

"This helicopter" Jeff had queried "did anybody see it land?"

"No. Apparently it tried to land on the Terminal Control Room roof. Mind you, it's the only part of the Terminal that stood up to the blast, so whatever is in there they couldn't get at it by air just yet or maybe they were having a good look round. They might have to come in by road and that's going to be difficult with all the debris on the road and the cordons being put in place.

Here! I'm surprised you got here, how come they let you through the main road cordon?"

Jeff had answered casually "I didn't come though the main road cordon I came via the emergency road. They haven't set up road blocks there yet, unless they're locals they might not know of that route in or out".

He had continued "It's better that I am honest with you as to why I'm here as well. Apart from finding out how my family is and if any of them survived . . ." He had gone on to tell her about trying to find a connection between the Terminal, UK United Gas in the Estuary, certain councillors, and Sir William Waite. He also told her he believed that if these people found out he was still alive then certain people would try to change that very quickly.

"Bastards" Jen had spat vehemently "if what you say is true I'm glad you told me first, because I know who to trust and who not to trust, and if I tell them not to say anything they won't, not if they know what's good for them".

Jeff had felt glad he had confided in her. He felt that this was one person to have in your corner when all hell broke loose.

"In that case" Jen had said "you're my cousin who was staying with me and we were shopping in the retail park at the time when all this happened, and the people you met in the area so far will confirm that, after I've had a word with them. You had better keep your first name, but you're too well known by your surname so use mine, its Jones. I'll put the word out to look for any activity at the Terminal and I'll get young Michael to find out about your family. If you let me have any details that would help, Michael can be very discreet when he wants to be.

Now, get that tea down you. And get some sleep, you're going to need it" she had said "you can kip over there in the corner. I'll see to it that no-one disturbs you and I guarantee you'll be safe all the time you're here".

Jeff had hunched down in the corner and had drunk his tea. He hadn't realised how tired he was until he had sat down and then everything had hit him all at once. His emotions washed over him and he found tears pouring down his face which he could not control. It seemed that all the time he had been doing something positive his emotions had been held in check but now he had stopped and felt reasonably safe he had had time to think of his own feelings and it all flooded in on him.

Jeff had felt an arm around him and a voice saying "Let it out, come on, and let the hurt out". With his vision blurred by tears Jeff had just made out the shape of Jen and he felt her strong arms around him.

"I'm sorry" he had said "it's just everything hitting me all at once".

"I've been there and got the t-shirt" Jen had said "so don't apologise. By the sound of it you're the one person we have to protect".

Jeff had reached for the panniers and using them as a pillow he had laid himself down and had immediately fallen asleep exhausted.

CHAPTER 15

Back on board the Baroness of the Sea, Derek tried to hide his grin at the thought of tearing these terrorists apart piece by piece if they harmed his friend.

Karen looked worried as Jeff walked off with Mustafa.

Jen put her arm around Karen, attempting to calm her down and said "He knows what he's doing".

As they were leaving the Restaurant, Jeff was telling Mustafa that Derek was not very clever and was hot headed and protective where he was concerned, hoping Mustafa would believe him so as to keep Derek from being shot. "He's harmless as he only has the mentality of a child. He's totally a gentle giant and would not hurt a fly".

Mustafa and the guards escorted Jeff to the Sheik's cabin. On the way, Mustafa seemed anxious to convince Jeff that the Sheik was not the megalomaniac he appeared to be and all he wanted was for people to respect and obey him.

"You tell that to the two unfortunate crew he chucked over the side of the ship" Jeff retorted "that was plain murder and murderers might be obeyed by fear for a short time but they don't get respect. That you have to earn".

"I have known the Sheik all my life. We grew up together, my father is his father's personal bodyguard" Mustafa said apologetically "though I have not seen him for 5 years as our lives went different ways. He called me and tells me in our friendship's name as we are also blood brothers that he wants me to help him make a name for himself so he will be respected by his elders back home. He has always been seeking approval of them. I did not know what he had planned and I do not agree with his new found friends. You must believe me" Mustafa said pleadingly "you are his hero, he admires you for what you did, how in your country you always took on the establishment against impossible odds and won through, never compromising your code of ethics that you live and will die by. He has read every article written about you and wants to emulate you. He wants to be the people's champion like you are. He read how Wilson hunted you and shot you and nearly killed you but you lived. How you stopped a powerful man like Sir William Waite from taking over your country, and in gratitude your country raised you from the ranks of the poor to the position of power you have today".

"I am not a hero" Jeff exclaimed "I only stood and was counted. I was prepared to fight for what I believe in like many others. You have it wrong. I don't have any power as an individual, I have been entrusted to do a job that I believe needs to be done, that's all. Now I am on holiday with my wife and friends".

"Do you know" Mustafa said "that the Sheik and his new found friends have had this hijack planned for a long time. I did not find out about it until I was on board, so when he found out you were on board as a passenger he went into ecstasies. He reread all the articles written about you".

"Some of those articles are totally fictitious" Jeff snorted.

"He believes that every word written about you is true" Mustafa said "you are what he wants to be, a people's champion, a modern day Robin Hood".

"He has a screw loose if he thinks that" Jeff stated flatly.

"Please do not say that in front of him, please do not disillusion him" Mustafa begged "many lives on board this ship depend on it. He is not the man I used to know as a boy. He is, how shall I say, changed. He flips mentally at the slightest thing to which he feels is an affront to his principles. I am sure he is being used to further the ends of political anarchists or by unscrupulous people in my country using his family name for their own ends. At the moment he still trusts me as his blood brother".

The Sheik was waiting for them as they got to the Sheik's cabin. He said to Jeff "Welcome my friend. We are the same you and I. We are men of our word, are we not?" He looked as though he was seeking approval from Jeff.

"Look at him being modest as usual" the Sheik said, turning to Mustafa, and then turning back to Jeff "do you know that I have read every article they have printed about you?"

"Don't believe everything you read about me" Jeff said "to read what someone has written is to borrow that person's thoughts". This was stated in a philosophical tone.

"See how deep he thinks" the Sheik said to Mustafa, looking proud that he had met his hero and was not disappointed in him.

"We must discuss the virtues of life and how you and I think the same. Please sit. I am humbled by your presence" the Sheik said, inclining his head slightly and pointing towards a table and chairs "do you require refreshment?"

Jeff nodded, having accepted the hospitality and guest rights of the Sheik's dwelling. He sat down, trying to get his thoughts in order and attempting not to alienate this obviously mentally disturbed man. He felt he was mentally walking on eggshells.

"Refreshments for my revered guest" the Sheik said to a man standing in the corner. The man left the cabin immediately to get refreshments leaving Mustafa and the Sheik and Jeff in the cabin.

The Sheik sat down with Jeff. With his eyes looking at some distant object in his mind he said "I will be the hero of my people just like you are to yours".

Then he started blurting out all the plans he had made, how he and his six tactical advisor friends had secretly arranged the hijack of the loaded NATGAS 2 a day after it left its harbour. How his men had used a motor launch and boarded the gas tanker and hijacked it at sea just like they were trained to do by Somalian pirates. How he had arranged for a May Day distress call to be sent to the Baroness of the Sea when it was the nearest ship and would respond straight away and then how they rendezvoused with the Baroness of the Sea.

The Sheik laughed when he said that by the time the Captain of the Baroness of the Sea realised that it was a hoax May Day call it had been too late and his men had captured the Baroness of the Sea by taking over the Bridge whilst the NATGAS 2 was put in tow. The officers had been locked in the forward hold and the Captain was now confined to his cabin under guard. The vessel and all the passengers were now the Sheik's human shield and the key that would open the gates to the American ports where he, the Sheik, would make the Americans listen to his demands.

"I will be a hero to my people just like you are a hero to your people" the Sheik reiterated "the Americans will not attack us or try to recapture this ship as I will give a message to my men on board the NATGAS 2 to open the valves and release the cargo in the hold. You know what would happen if that is done".

"Yes" Jeff exclaimed horror struck "I know what would happen. Everyone within an 8 to 10 mile radius would die".

"Exactly" the Sheik said "and I have made plans that it will. They will not try to bomb us as that also would mean the deaths of all the passengers and crew and they would have that on their political conscience. So as you see, I hold all the aces in the deck of cards and the Americans will do as I say. I am on a winning formula and I cannot lose".

The Sheik then seemed to withdraw into himself once again and after a few moments of silence, suddenly jerked and said "They will know I am a man of my word, as they know you are, and I will be the hero of my people as you are a hero to yours".

"What happens if the Americans refuse you entry into America?" Jeff asked.

"Then I will get as close as I can to America and release the cargo then we will all die martyred to a cause for freedom from oppression". He suddenly looked very resigned "we have already made our peace with Allah".

Jeff realised that he was dealing with a very dangerous megalomaniac and the trouble was that this maniac seemed to hero worship him, and that worried him.

He was also worried about the people who were apparently backing the Sheik. They were hidden in the background and someone would have had to finance an operation as big as this. It was obvious from what Cyril had said that the jewels in the dagger were fakes and therefore he felt that the Sheik was not as rich as he gave the impression he was.

Mustafa had said that Mustafa's father was the Sheik's father's bodyguard so he must be descended from a sheik. Perhaps the father was still alive so he might only be a sheik in title and not in wealth yet and therefore was being manipulated by more powerful people with a hidden agenda like The Senate. They had been behind the incident in the Estuary. Until he knew more about the Sheik and his friends he had to play along with this insane man.

"How many men did it take to take over the two ships?" Jeff asked, pretending that he was asking out of an awed interest.

"Why do you wish to know?" the Sheik responded suspiciously.

"I was only admiring what you did, and how simple you make it sound. I am impressed with what you have achieved in such a short time?" Jeff lied hastily and he hoped, convincingly.

The Sheik puffed out his chest like a parrot and replied "You were impressed? That is praise indeed coming from you". He looked cunningly at Jeff and continued "I used the men from my household bodyguard that are sworn to me. There are six munitions advisors from a friend of mine, Mustafa, his wife, myself and four of my wives. We do not need many to hold the West to ransom. Are you suitably impressed my friend?"

"Very" Jeff answered, injecting as much enthusiasm and admiration as he could "you seem to have thought of everything. When this is over you will be renowned and respected throughout your country".

The Sheik suddenly stood up. The audience was obviously over and he stated "We will speak again soon. I do so enjoy your company. Men like you and I are men of their word and should meet more often".

Jeff then left, once again under escort from Mustafa.

On the way back, Mustafa talked to him again, telling him how sorry he was for the men that had died so horridly.

"Don't be sorry to me" Jeff said "be sorry for their families, you killed them".

"I did not kill them, or condone their killing "Mustafa said, horror struck "the Sheik wanted to set an example to make sure everybody obeyed him. He had them killed. He let loose that maniac Abdul to carry out that execution. He and Parvis who is on the NATGAS 2 are a matching pair. He also did the same to the crew of the NATGAS 2 and he enjoyed it like Abdul. They are both nasty sick minded animals".

"You did nothing to stop your friend from killing them so in my eyes you're as guilty as he is" Jeff said "he set an example alright. By killing those men in that way, he proved to everyone on board that he will stop at nothing to further his cause. He is a dangerous ally to have as a friend and I believe he is seriously mentally ill. If he were my friend I would disown him or try to change what he is trying to do".

"You do not understand" Mustafa said "our families go back generations. My ancestors have always been bodyguards to his family. I am the first eldest son in my family not to be a bodyguard to his family. I disappointed my father very much when I said I did not want to carry on the tradition".

"How can you protect him when you see what he is doing?" Jeff asked.

"He does not keep me as informed as he used to" Mustafa admitted "he spends more time with Abdul who is one of the six advisors he spoke of. As I said, he is a cruel man and I do not like the influence he seems to have over the Sheik. It is as if he is being led by him. When I told him so yesterday he dismissed me out of hand. He told me I had been out of touch and did not know what the real situation was with the Western world. He never used to be like that when we were boys. Yes, he always wanted to be the knight in shining armour, and I was his faithful trusted servant, but he has changed and is not like he was.

I have known him all my life, but he frightens me now and I do not know what to do for the best. Please do not tell him we have spoken like this, he might not understand. The guards do not speak English so they cannot repeat what we have said. The only ones who speak English, apart from the Sheik and I, are the six advisors.

I have loved him as a brother all my life but I am worried that he is out of his depth and has gone too far and cannot find his way back. I tell you this because I respect you and your principles and I hope that you can understand that he is not a bad person, he is only misguided and I believe being led by Abdul and the other five advisors he surrounds himself with at all times".

As they parted company Mustafa said "We will talk again" and left Jeff to find Karen and the others.

CHAPTER 16

Jeff found Karen in their cabin with Jen and Cyril. When Karen saw him she rushed over to him and hugged him, crying with relief.

"You had us worried sick. We thought he would hold you hostage or something" she said, a frantic tone in her voice.

"Derek wanted to rip some heads off, but we calmed him down" Cyril said "the guards treated the big man as though he was a 5 year old wayward child. We didn't know why until I realised what you had said to that Mustafa about him being a gentle giant. Mustafa spoke to the guards in what sounded like Arabic and it was then that they started to treat Derek very gently".

"If they realise how powerful and intelligent he is they will fear him, and quite rightly so" Jeff explained "that means he becomes their first target. By him playing weak minded he lulls them into a false sense of security. I understand they treat the less fortunate with reverence because they believe they are closer to Allah".

"Very clever, remind me never to play chess with you" Cyril said.

"Where are the others?" Jeff asked.

"They should be here any minute" Jen replied "they went to see the guards to find out if they could get the First Officer or if someone was available to see us. I flooded your bathroom as an excuse to get them here so act indignant about the mess when they get here. We have to use it as a cover to talk to a member of the crew. John suspected you had been given guest rights by the Sheik so the guards would not want you upset otherwise it would reflect badly on the Sheik's integrity".

"It seems John judged it right" Jeff said, as they were waiting "it was an interesting meeting". Jeff had learned a lot from his encounter with the Sheik and Mustafa, particularly that only the advisors spoke any English and that the guards didn't speak any English and that was worth knowing. He was however considerably concerned that the Sheik's mind could be unstable.

As they were talking about Jeff's meeting with the Sheik, John and Derek arrived back together with the First Officer and two members of the crew.

Jeff stepped in straight away and said in English "I am speaking to you as if I am very annoyed over the flooding of the bathroom. It is only a cover so we make contact" then he pointed at the bathroom and gestured throwing up his hands in mock horror.

It seemed to work as the two armed guards at the end of the corridor looked at one another and laughed at the embarrassing situation the First Officer was being put in.

Quickly Jeff said to the First Officer "We are prepared to go down fighting. We know that they intend to blow up the gas ship with us alongside it and they want to do it in an American port if they can. We also know that there will be no rescue attempt as America will not be held to ransom, so if anything is done we have to do it ourselves".

"I am afraid what you say is true" the First Officer replied "the Captain would like to do something but they hold the passengers and the crew as a human shield and he is very concerned about his crew members who are locked away in the forward hold".

"We can organise the passengers. Are you able to organise any of the crew who are left?" Jeff asked.

"They are watching the few remaining officers closely. They only let us come to you because that bloke Mustafa said to let us come to you as you had some sort of guest rights. Mustafa seems to hold you in high regard and seems quite decent. The others are fanatics" the First Officer answered.

"How about the catering staff?" Jeff enquired.

"The other terrorists treat them with contempt" the First Officer replied "and they don't like it".

"What if we use the catering and cleaning staff as couriers? Would they help us get organised?"

"It was their friends and colleagues who were made to walk the plank, they will not forget that. I believe they would love an opportunity to strike back in some way".

"Good" said Jeff "at least we can communicate. Can you find out how long it will take us to reach 75 miles off of the American coastline?"

"Why 75 miles?" the First Officer asked.

"After that the Americans will not let the gas ship get any closer to their coastline because of the damage it could do when it blows up. They will have no choice but to blow us out of the water before then, so that is the deadline we have in which to do something" Jeff responded.

"Having the NATGAS 2 strapped to us on a tow line will slow us down as we will lose a lot of trim and have to keep matching speed with it. I will get the Navigator to work it out and let you know via your table waiter".

"Now to put on a show for the monkeys otherwise they might get suspicious" Jeff said, nodding. As he stood by the door, he began to rant and rave loudly, gesturing at the bathroom. The guards started to laugh again at the First Officer's predicament.

The First Officer shook his hand and said very sincerely "Good luck. We are going to need it" and left with one of the people he had brought with him, leaving the other one behind to clear up the mess Cyril had made.

Whilst the crew member cleared up the water in the bathroom which had been caused by Jen stuffing a towel down the waste outlet, Cyril said "A good idea using the catering staff as they can mingle with everybody without raising suspicions, as long as the Sheik does not find out".

"Don't forget his advisors. They are the real problem in this poisonous brew" Jeff said "apparently he really is the son of a sheik. That makes him a royal prince. But, he is a royal prince with a very serious mental problem and I believe he is being used".

"And I thought it might be something simple like we had been hijacked by some Middle Eastern terrorist organisation who want payback for some insult" Cyril said wryly "but if I read between the lines what you're saying is that we are being held hostage by some spoiled brat of a boy prince who has lost his marbles and wants to prove himself in the eyes of his elders and is being helped by some right wing advisors of a political wing of some Muslim organisation. Why does that sound familiar?"

"I believe that behind all this could be a splinter group of the same fascist organisation we ran into who were involved in the Estuary incident called the The Senate" Jeff said "if it is the The Senate who has raised its ugly head again we have a bigger problem than we had first thought. There was no reasoning with them at that time and I don't suppose that has changed now"

"Wasn't Sir William Waite the head of that organisation?" Cyril asked "and isn't he still serving a 50 year life sentence in a maximum security prison?"

"He was head of the British connection of The Senate" Jeff replied "but we always knew there were other splinter groups throughout the world even though there was a big manhunt worldwide to eradicate the organisation, but it went to ground somewhere on the American/Canadian border the cell that was under suspicion suddenly splintered and no trace was found, 3 suspects turned up dead from some mystery illness, so whatever the outcome of these issues that we are involved in now is only a small part of a much bigger picture".

"It does not come any bigger than the hijack of a gas tanker and the threat to the passengers on a cruise liner" Cyril said.

"How about the enemy of my enemy is my friend until I get what I want philosophy?" Jeff mused.

"You talk in riddles" Cyril said "what do you mean?"

"What if The Senate is a bigger and more secret organisation than we first thought? What if The Senate is playing the Middle East against the West?"

"The two areas have been at each other's throats for years, and you and I know it does not take much to stir up that cauldron?" Cyril mused.

Keeping on the same train of thought, Jeff said "What if a very influential Sheik's over-indulged son is killed by the West in some incident? It could destabilise the support that comes from the Middle Eastern very powerful oil sheiks and cripple relationships between the West and the Middle East during this unrest. The Senate then takes over the destabilised areas as they tried to do in England and very nearly succeeded".

"Jesus Christ! You are a cynical bastard" Cyril said "where did you think that one up?"

"From trying to reason out what is happening and why" Jeff replied "because for every action there is a reaction. There has to be a reason for the action in the first place and I think this is the action that will create the chain reaction that will ricochet throughout the Middle East and destabilise the newly found peace in the Arab States that is held together by the powerful oil sheiks".

"So all of this hijacking is nothing to do with an insurgence from a Muslim faction at all" Cyril said "it's a very unstable sick man being led around by a splinter group of The Senate. If that is the case how many of The Senate are on board?"

"My guess is the six armoury advisers" Jeff said "the rest are just the Sheik's personal bodyguard".

"Where does Mustafa stand in all this?" Cyril asked "I understand those two have been friends from childhood".

"At this moment in time I don't know" Jeff responded "but I will find out. First we have to find out how much time we have before we get near American territorial waters. Once there the Americans will bomb us out of the water before we can get anywhere near their coastline to be able to do any damage. If they are aware of the situation, which by now I am sure they will be, they will tell all shipping to avoid us like the plague. They might shadow us with a sub if they can get one to us in time, but I am sure any sub will have orders to sink us as soon as we near American landfall".

"Can't we signal the sub and ask them to pull alongside and board us, tell them we will help take over the ship" Cyril asked.

"Firstly, we have to know if there is a sub out there" Jeff replied "where it is, find out if it is friendly, and get a signal to it, then get them to believe we are who we say we are and not luring them into a trap so the terrorists then get hold of a nuclear sub as well to add to the party. No submarine commander would endanger his ship, not even for all the passengers and crew. I think the first you will know when there is a sub out there, is when its torpedoes slam into the side of us or the NATGAS 2.

I believe that all the time the NATGAS 2 is tied to the Baroness of the Sea we are cannon fodder" Jeff continued "so we have to do what has to be done but until we know how long it's going to take us to get near the American coast we can't do anything because that is the deadline. Once we pass the point of no return, sure as eggs are eggs we will be attacked and we will be destroyed by the American Forces".

"What about Michael?" Cyril asked "perhaps we can get a message to him and he can let his cousin in the American Intelligence know what's going on. I have a contact number for him and you could use John's lap-top to get in touch with him".

"How do you know about John's lap-top?" Jeff asked.

"You forget, I'm a tea-leaf and a good one" Cyril replied grinning "I even know he has a mobile phone that can get a signal anywhere in the world, and if I was to guess he did not tell you about either of them until he had to. As I've always said, that John has more tricks then a clown's pocket and probably always will be a very dark horse".

"Let's meet up with the others over lunch, and we can find out what our options are?" Jeff said to Cyril.

Jeff's memory swung back to the incident in the Estuary when he first took on The Senate and the events leading up to it.

CHAPTER 17

Jeff had woken up hearing a throbbing sound pounding in his head which gradually faded. He had realised that it had come from outside so he had got up to go outside to look.

Jen had stood in the doorway and said "It's not safe for you out there at the moment. That's the third helicopter this morning that's gone to the Terminal. That one landed inside and I hope they didn't catch Cyril".

She had looked at him and said "Cyril and I go back a long way. We had a thing between us that didn't work out then, and he still holds a torch for me. He's the best professional tea leaf you will find. There isn't a lock he can't get passed, that's why he's nicknamed 'the Squirrel'. He can squirrel his way in anywhere.

Whatever is in that Terminal must be important because they've ignored people asking for help and only wanted to get to the Control Room of the place. Knowing the situation with you I asked Cyril to have a look around and find out why the Control Room is so important. He's due back any minute, have a cup of tea and some food while we sit and wait. We got the rations from the soldiers".

They had finished drinking their second cup of tea and were chatting quietly when there had been a scuffling noise and a head had popped around the corner and said "Hi darling, it's all kicking off over there, is this the bloke you told me about?"

Jen had introduced Jeff to Cyril, who was slightly built but looked very wiry and strong "So you're what it's all about" Cyril had said with understanding.

Jen had said "Come on, what did you find out?"

"Well" Cyril had replied "I got inside with no problem but whilst I was there a helicopter turned up and I had to hide behind an inspection panel when they came into the Control Room".

"You got into the Control Room?" Jeff had asked, disbelievingly.

"Easy" Cyril had replied "I could see through the grill of the panel at who was saying what to whom. There was a man called Ray Wilson having a go at a man he called David about how stupid it had been to put the fireproof filing cabinets in the Control Room whilst the room outside was decorated and wanted the cabinets moved back into the adjoining room, left on their side, emptied and the papers inside them taken away off site and burned as he didn't want any evidence found on site that could be linked with the new President of the United Kingdom.

When this David bloke said he had no transport to move that amount of papers this Ray bloke said for him to go to County Councillor Rodger Randle's house and at the back of the rear garden in what looked like a big hump in the garden was an old large underground World War II Anderson shelter that had been covered in soil and grassed over which was used as a garage. In this garage he would find a Jag covered by an old tarpaulin. He was to use Sir William Waite's written authority which he gave him, use the Jag as transport, take all the files to the local tip and burn them there and then get rid of the Jag.

Then this Dave asked why not take the papers outside and burn them?

This Wilson character seems to have more tricks than a clown's pocket. He said to this Dave bloke that he was a can short of a six pack. If he burned the papers outside it would create smoke and would advertise that they were there. He said they weren't supposed to be there. And if the Prime Minister or his cronies were to find out they would all hang.

When this Dave asked Ray Wilson why wouldn't Councillor Randle mind, Wilson said that Councillor Randle was dead and that he must have had his neck broken defending his home against looters. I have to say this Dave looked terrified of this Ray Wilson.

I had to wait for them to leave before I could come out from behind the panel, is that of any use?"

"If what you say is true, it's vital information that can link Wilson with Councillor Randle" and Jeff had tangled with Councillor Randle in public on more than one occasion over the siting of high fire risk industry so close to residential areas. At one time, Councillor Randle had threatened him with a writ if Jeff did not stop involving him in his remarks. Jeff had told Councillor Randle "if I am not telling the truth serve the writ". Needless to say they had clashed many times.

Jeff had mused "Now we know Randle is linked to Wilson and Wilson is linked to Sir William Waite. Sir William Waite wants to bring down the Prime Minister and the Government so he can be President, it's incredible".

Jeff had to find the proof needed to confirm this, plus he had to get it exposed, both not easy tasks. Jeff had posed a question to Cyril "Could you get me any of these papers or files so I can see what's in them?"

"Later maybe" Cyril had said "why is it so important? By the way, why would they break the clocks and dials and alter the hands on them by a few minutes?"

"What?" Jeff had snapped back, stunned.

"Yeah, this Ray bloke smashed the dials and altered the clock times by a few minutes. He also tore up the printouts from the machines. He didn't move any of the bodies which looked like they'd died from a lack of oxygen in the meeting room, but he took all their papers away with him".

"That was strange" Jeff had thought.

"There's more to this than meets the eye" he had said aloud.

Jen had interrupted at that point and had told Cyril what was going on and who Jeff was and what Jeff was trying to prove. Cyril had whistled and said "The bastards and they call me a tea leaf. At least I'm an honest tea leaf. I'll see what I can do. We need to stop these bastards" and then he had slid out the door and was gone.

"Seems what you suspected is true" Jen had said musingly.

"Yeah" Jeff had said "but don't forget these people are professionals, don't underestimate them. What I can't fathom out though is why smash the clocks and dials and alter the time? I need to get a look at the site from the sea wall, can I get there without being seen?"

"You would have to be very careful" she had said "and you can take Derek with you in case of trouble".

She had called Derek and said "Go with him and make sure nothing happens to him".

"You know I'd do anything for you Jen" the massive man had said, blushing "you can rely on me".

CHAPTER 18

Jeff and Derek had made their way slowly through the rubble and broken houses towards the sea wall and to the ruin that had, at one time been a 400 year old public house. When they had arrived at the sea wall, the full extent of the damage could be seen, it resembled something out of a disaster movie.

The surprising thing was that the sea wall had still been intact although had been damaged in places with large chunks of concrete missing at the top of the wall. It had looked as though a giant had taken chunks out of the iron grey stone.

There had been scorch marks on the inside of the wall all the way along the area of the Terminal. Where the jetty had been there were twisted metal and pipes, the burned out hulk of a large gas ship was at the end of the jetty. Just inside the jetty between the gas ship and the jetty had been the hull of another small coaster that had jammed under the jetty and burned out. The oil refinery sited up river had still had pockets of flames burning, scattered here and there within its devastated site. The refineries across the river had still been burning and wreathed in dark ominous clouds of smoke. The Gas Terminal on the opposite side of the Estuary had looked as though it had been flattened as had the coast. It had been like a scene out of some sort of horror movie.

In the middle of the river had been the burned out hulk of another gas ship and this had drifted aimlessly in the oily debris-laden water of the Estuary.

Rubble had still been smoking and there had been pockets of burning buildings all the way up and down the river as far as the eye could see.

As Jeff and Derek had made their way towards what was left of the Gas Terminal, both of them had not been able to comprehend the extent of the loss of life and damage caused by this incident.

Derek had suddenly said "Get down someone's coming".

Jeff had ducked down behind the sea wall just as a man in a black uniform turned the corner and shouted "Hey you! This is off limits, what are you doing here?"

Derek had reciprocated harshly "What's it to you?"

The man on seeing Derek's build and hearing his belligerent tone of voice had spoken again, this time in a more courteous tone of voice. "I have to keep everyone away from this site until the experts have investigated it" he had explained.

"I only wanted to find out if I could fish from here" Derek had offered smoothly.

"Fish up the other end and not here" the man had shouted, pulling out a gun "now clear off".

"Ok, no need to be nasty".

The man had snarled "You heard what I said, now clear off or I'll shoot you and say you were looting to the officials and the police".

Derek had turned around and had walked away along the sea wall path towards what was left of the public house.

Jeff had also walked towards the public house but on the seaward side of the wall so that he could not be seen by the security guard. When he was out of sight of the Terminal he had joined Derek.

Derek had said "Bumptious little bastard. That man and I are going to have a reckoning. He doesn't remember me but I remember him. He was on a site in London I worked on and he stole a lorry load of timber and tried to blame me and my crew. I'll do for him you mark my words. What are they trying to hide I wonder".

"Let's look at the situation from here, what do you see?" Jeff had begun.

"A bloody mess caused by that ship out there blowing up and setting light to everything else, right?" Derek had replied.

Jeff's mind had started doing overtime. He had started to mull the situation over to try and make sense of it all.

"If that ship out there caused this, the burn marks from the explosion would be on the seaward side of the sea wall, correct?" Jeff asked "as you look at it, you only get that stress and burn mark from the landward side and jetty area on the seaward side, the worst scorching is all along the landward side of the sea wall right up to here. So the explosion came from the Terminal and then went outwards, and what caused the Terminal to go up was an explosion during a ship to shore transfer at the jetty and the explosion that was started at the jetty created a domino effect that went right up and across the Estuary.

What we have been saying in the past and which was a possible worst case scenario caused this accident and it was not caused by terrorism as put out by the media. So, why go to all this trouble to hide it?

Why smash the dials and clocks? Unless you don't want anyone to know what time factor was involved or you wanted to alter the appearance of the time factor to make it look as though the ship exploded first.

What was that other gas ship doing on the river at that spot when the regulations state there should not be another gas ship moving in that part of the river whilst another gas ship is unloading?

That gas ship should not be there. Unless, they were trying to cut corners and do a quick turnaround on the jetty. And also try it on the same tide. But that would be so stupid. That gives a good possible theory as to why they smashed the clocks and dials because of the time factor. If they are trying to say the gas ship on the river exploded first, it would show an earlier time on the broken dials and clocks on board the gas ship than at the Terminal.

But if the Terminal exploded first, the dials and clocks at the Terminal would show an earlier time then the clocks on board ship. It seems they couldn't get onto the ship and alter any dials or clocks so they tampered with the dials and clocks at the Terminal.

So they wanted it to appear the ship exploded first causing the conflagration. Not the Terminal exploding causing the conflagration. It would therefore leave them and the operators of the Terminal blameless.

They also need a reason as to why the other gas ship was out there and what better way than to say they had no control over the ship as it had been hijacked by suicide terrorists but they had all died in the explosion. If that theory is proved, the story about terrorism is a load of crap to create political unrest and bring down the Government and install a dictator. All this is a smoke screen to hide their profit and greed and use the situation to create political unrest in this country.

It's well known that the Prime Minister favoured talking to terrorists first from a strong position to hear their points than having the dictatorial attitude that Sir William Waite had. Sir William Waite's attitude is, if you don't agree with me, you're my enemy, and need putting down". Jeff was convinced Waite wanted a dictatorship "no wonder they don't want anyone near that Terminal, and want me dead. Proving any or all of this is not going to be easy".

They had made their way back to the Cellars.

CHAPTER 19

On their arrival back, Jen had asked "Did you find out what you wanted to?"

"I found out plenty" Jeff had replied.

Jen had added "It's just been on the news, Sir William Waite has said that the Prime Minister should resign for allowing the situation to get to this stage. Martial law should be declared and there should be retaliation for the hijacking of a gas ship that created the terrorist attack in the Estuary area straightaway".

"Well, he certainly didn't waste time trying to usurp the Prime Minister" Jeff had remarked.

"Why? Isn't this a terrorist attack?" Jen had asked "like Sir William Waite said".

"Not from what I found just looking at the area" Jeff had replied. He went on to explain his interpretation of what he had seen to her, also what it had meant, and how he had felt that there was a cover up going on.

Derek had jumped in, saying "That little shit down there. I'll do for him. No jumped up little maggot is going to pull a gun on me and get away with it".

"He did what?" Jen had asked.

"Don't worry" Derek had replied "I can crush little maggots like him with no problem".

"You try to be careful" Jen had warned "I know you, when you lose your temper. I've lost enough loved ones without losing you".

On hearing this, Derek had gone red and had suddenly looked very shy, but he had had a beaming smile on his face.

"Do you know anyone with a camera as I need to get some photographs of what's down there whilst it's still in that state, and before they destroy the evidence" Jeff had asked.

"We'll find one from somewhere" Jen had answered.

"I picked up these when I went down there last time" Derek had said, holding out some little sealed units "are these any good?"

Jeff had looked at them.

"Look, some are still working" Derek had said as he had turned them over "I found them near the pipes that came from the jetty".

Jeff had hoped that these units were what he thought they were. The units monitored and recorded any dramatic change in pressure in a pipe and activated a shut-off valve. Of the four units two had still been working. The other two had looked as though they had never worked.

There had also been some pieces of triangular shaped metal that were twisted at different angles.

"Keep them somewhere safe" Jeff had said to Derek "they could be important".

"Shall I throw the broken ones away?" Derek had asked.

"No" Jeff had replied "the broken ones could be more important than the ones that are still working".

"How can something that's broken be more important than something that's not broken?" Derek had asked.

"Because, if it broke at the time of the explosion, you can get the time of the explosion exactly, and probably the events that led to the explosion, and that could be an important factor" Jeff had explained.

"You can tell all that just from these little units?" Derek had asked turning one over in his hands.

"I can't, but an expert could" Jeff had answered "and if those triangular shaped pieces are what I think they are that will prove what caused the accident, and I believe they could be the inner part of a bursting disc, which is a device that is set to blow at a pressure just below the stress break factor of a tank or pipe therefore releasing the LNG before the whole tank or pipe breaks into atmosphere at a controlled point".

Turning to Jen, Jeff had asked "Can Cyril get some photographs of the inside of that Control Room? Pictures of dials, clocks, or get any papers or printouts that can tell us more of what happened? Because Ray Wilson and his cronies are trying to cover everything up very fast and soon there'll be nothing left to prove they caused this".

"You don't think this was a terrorist attack do you?" Jen had asked.

"I think it's more sinister then that" Jeff had answered "much more sinister".

"They wouldn't deliberately cover up an accident would they?" Jen had asked disbelievingly "what on earth for?"

"It's a long story but I believe it to be true" Jeff had replied.

"We've got time until Cyril gets here and the kettle's on", Jen had said "Derek will keep an eye out".

"Well" Jeff had begun "it all started when I got involved in a situation when UK United applied for planning permission to store Liquid Natural Gas (LNG) at the Terminal.

I already had this reputation for fighting the energy companies as I had been involved in the oil refinery fight a few years back".

"Involved? Is that how you describe it? From what I remember you were the lynchpin in that fight" Jen had interrupted.

"Hey! I was only part of a great organisation, not the main stay" Jeff had retorted.

"You never did take the praise for what you did" Jen had said "I remember the words that Inspector at that public inquiry said after you gave your evidence, 'if nothing else comes out of that inquiry the people of the area owe you a debt that could not be repaid'.

Everybody knows it was you and not the councillors that stopped them building their oil refineries. The councillors only stepped in and tried to take all the credit after you had won, up until then they were in the oil companies' pockets. Didn't some of them go to America with their families to look at a working refinery for 10 days, all expenses paid?" Jen had continued contemptuously "and then they came back and said how wonderful it was that foreign oil companies wanted to invest in the community. If they wanted to see a refinery they could have gone across the creek to see a working refinery at no cost at all. If I remember they said at the time that it was a fact finding tour that had to be done. I wouldn't trust them as far as the end of my nose" this had been added scornfully "no matter what party they stand for, they're only in it for their own ends".

"Well, there was no mention of terrorist activity anywhere near here until after the explosion" Jeff had explained "and if they had hijacked a gas ship everyone would have known about it. It was only brought to the Government's attention by a UK United source that the gas ship that was drifting in the Estuary had been hijacked by terrorists and blown up and that caused the disaster. Sir William Waite soon after that demanded the resignation of the Government and that marshal law be put in place until the terrorists were brought to heel stating this as a failure of the Government to stop this so called hijack. I believe Sir William Waite is using this as a way to get control of the country and put it and the people under his dictatorship".

"Perhaps I'm being thick" Jen had said "but you've not explained to me why you think it wasn't terrorists and if not, what caused all this and why?"

"Those sealed units and bits from a bursting disc that Derek found may be a clue to what happened" Jeff had said "I believe those sealed units and the bursting disc were attached to the pipeline valves. The bursting discs are designed to blow just below the fracture stress point of the pipe work. In the event of a fracture of the pipeline the units operate a shut off valve that is supposed to operate instantly and shut off in the event of pipeline failure. These units and valves as well as other high level alarms in tanks have to be maintained on a frequent basis, failure to do so can result in heavy fines or even shutting down of the Terminal. The trouble for the operators is that to maintain or replace these units takes operating down time and sections have to be closed and that eats into their profits. With the breaking of the pipeline, those sealed units should have operated and shut the pipeline down therefore isolating the section of the break but if those units failed the pipeline would have been exposed to catastrophic failure which would have meant the LNG would have been released from the pipeline in a massive amount.

That sudden release of LNG onto water would have set off a chain of events. That chain of events could have been an explosion damaging the integrity of the hull of the gas ship unloading its cargo which in turn vented part of its cargo.

This in turn created a domino effect of explosions all the way across the Estuary mouth and all the way up the river. All because of cutting corners on inspections and safety precautions to save time and money.

If Sir William Waite and UK United Gas can convince the country the accident was caused by terrorists and not by them cutting corners for profit they're off the hook and Sir William can try to use the chaos as a smoke screen".

"Proving that is not going to be easy at all" Jen had said worriedly.

"But if we can expose them for what they are then Sir William and UK United will have to answer to the country and the surviving families of all the thousands of people who have been killed" Jeff had continued explaining and then said "getting back to some semblance of order will take some time.

If you remember, it took 3 to 4 years before the families affected by the Buncefield incident could get back into their homes and businesses but the companies that caused the problem were up and running and making a profit in a matter of months".

At that moment, a man of about 35 years of age and of stocky build had popped his head around the door and had said "Jen, I got your message. I started checking up on . . . ." The man had stopped in mid-sentence when he saw Jeff "who's this?"

"This is the man whose family you have been trying to find out about" Jen had answered.

She had then caught sight of the bruises on the side of his face "Who did this to you?" she had demanded.

"They wanted information about him" the man had said, pointing at Jeff "pretty badly".

"Who do Michael?" Jen had asked.

"The suits at the cordon" Michael had replied.

"Tell us what happened" then she had added "get over here and I'll put a cold compress on your bruises".

"Oh don't fuss" Michael had said, raising a hand as if to ward off an irritating fly "I've had a lot worse".

"Tell us what happened then".

"Well" he had said "I got jumped by these three blokes when I was checking his bungalow. Apparently I disturbed them checking through his computer files. They said even though the computer was badly damaged they could still retrieve a lot of the data and took it away.

They took me to a hall in back of the pub on the mainland then questioned me as to why I was there. Then they asked me how did I know you? And did I know if you was alive, if so of your whereabouts? They were about as bright as Alaska in December. As you can see, they tried to be very persuasive, but as you know I've had worse in the ring. They let me go on the proviso that if I heard anything I would let them know".

The man had turned to Jeff and had said "This suit named Wilson must want you pretty badly".

"Was Karen there?" Jeff had asked.

"No. Wilson asked me if I knew where she was".

"Did you tell him anything?" Jeff had asked

"What do you take me for?" Michael had snapped obviously much offended by the question.

"Neutral corner you" Jen had said to Michael "we all have a lot to lose in this. Let's not clash over others otherwise they succeed and divide and rule".

"I'm sorry" Jeff had apologised "I was ungrateful and I apologise for my outburst".

"If I was in your boots" Michael had said "I'd probably do the same. No hard feelings" and he had leaned across and shaken Jeff's hand.

Jeff had been surprised at the powerful grip Michael had for such a stockily built man.

"Look, I'm sorry about your wife and family" Michael had announced "like everyone else they didn't stand a chance. These terrorists are going to pay big time".

"What if I told you it wasn't terrorists" Jeff had said to Michael.

"What?" Michael had exclaimed.

"What if I told you this was an industrial accident that could have been prevented but greed and political machinations are being manipulated to hide the facts and create a political coup and the people you met are the henchmen of Sir William Waite who wants to be the new dictator of this country".

"Then they would want you dead yesterday" Michael had replied "they would want try to persuade people to help find out if you were alive. But from what I gathered from them you were at a meeting in the area at the time and didn't survive. How did you survive, no-one lived when the Hall the meeting was in caught it?"

"I wasn't at that meeting, the meeting I went to was changed to the mainland at the last minute".

"That was lucky for you" Michael had said "but if what you say is true they want you dead big time so you can't nail them for this. I asked around for Jen's sake, just because she asked me, but now I know this is maybe because of them I'm right behind you and so will all the other survivors. How can I be of help?"

"I need people to be my eyes and ears out there until I get enough information to go to my press contacts to expose this, and get the takeover stopped" Jeff had said.

"According to the latest news, the Middle East is up in arms about these accusations and are threatening a Holy war" Michael had said.

"Then we need to work fast" Jeff had said "before all this blows up into a world war and we are governed by a dictator who has the reputation of being a warmonger and who is stirring it up at the slightest opportunity. When you're out and about see if you can find anything out about the family Smith who lived in No 5 by the turning next to the Town Centre. Man, woman, little girl. If you find anything let me know" Jeff had asked.

"Are they family or friends?" Michael had asked.

"Neither but I would like to know if you can find anything out" Jeff had answered.

CHAPTER 20

Just then Cyril had come in.
"Hi, you want some snaps taken then?" he had asked Jeff.
"Yes, but be careful, those bastards don't take no prisoners" Jeff had replied.
"Right, what do you want?"
"Shots of the smashed dials and clocks in the Control Room, any papers from that meeting room, shots of the jetty, the sea wall, and the drifting tanker, but don't get caught. There have been enough people killed already" Jeff had said.
"I haven't been caught yet" Cyril had rejoined confidently then had added "I'm not knitting with one needle you know!" then he had ducked back out of the door.
"I'll check on that address" Michael had said and he had followed Cyril out of the door.
Jen had sat down beside Jeff and had said "The damage is pretty bad and there have been a lot of people killed. What I can't forgive are those poor children in the schools that were killed.
They didn't stand a chance without an evacuation plan, but the authorities didn't care enough to do something about it, it's all too late now, thousands of people are dead.

I wonder how they'll justify the decision to pass that planning application. They'll probably come out with some bullshit about it was in the national interest, and they didn't know or they weren't given the full information". Jen had paused then "did you want to look around? It's not a pretty sight. They haven't been to the Estuary yet to help us, they've been too busy evacuating councillors, dignitaries and their families from here and the outlying areas and putting them up in luxurious hotels to worry about us".

Jeff had said he would have a look round.

They had gone out and had walked towards the centre of what was once a vibrant community. On coming to an infant and junior school, Jeff had not prepared for what he had seen.

As Jeff had entered the school he had crossed the playground. He had been able to see into the collapsed building and had seen that there were parts of the roof lying at a drunken awkward angle. The windows and doors had looked as though a giant hand had angrily smashed them. Paint had been blistered and blackened, and there had been the cloying stench of burned flesh and death.

With a morbid dread, Jeff had forced himself to approach the building, stealing himself for what he had been going to see and what he had been about to witness, but nothing had prepared him for the horror that was there. Only his anger of what had happened to the innocent children had driven him on as he felt someone had to be a witness to the nightmare.

He had felt his stomach start to reject what was in it as he looked around at the twisted, burned shrivelled bodies. They had looked like sausages that had been thrown in a pan and seared in the heat, the little bodies had been huddled together. At one point a teacher had tried to protect some of them with her body but to no avail, the heat of the igniting gas had done its damage. The massive loss of innocent life had been seared into his brain forever. All he had seen was blackened and scorched and then the smell had hit him. He had immediately vomited and had staggered back out of the building retching. He had never forgotten that smell.

He had insisted to Jen that he look in the school on his own, he had not wanted her to see what he had seen. When she had seen him come out and how it had affected him she had asked in a tremulous voice "Is it that bad?"

"My god yes, worse than your worst nightmare" Jeff had answered in a voice that was hoarse and shook with emotion "and you're not going in there".

They had walked around for an hour or more getting some air and looking at the devastation. Jeff had been trying to rid his mind of what he had seen within the school but it had been like a repetitive nightmare that he had not been able to wake up from.

As they had passed what had been a grocer's shop the basement was open. Jen had slipped in to pick up some tins of food.

As she had gone into the building, Jeff had heard a helicopter approaching them.

Jeff had dived for cover, hoping that he had not been seen. The helicopter had circled once and then had flown on to the Gas Terminal building.

Jeff had called out to Jen "We had better get going before that helicopter comes back".

They had just arrived back at the Cellars when they had heard the helicopter engine again. This time it had circled round where they had been. It had looked as though it had landed for a few minutes, then it had taken off again, circled around once more and had flown off.

"That was close" Jen had said relieved "we'll have to be more careful in future. If they'd caught you it would all be over for all of us".

They had sat talking about what they had seen for some time over a cup of tea. It had seemed that talking about it had helped ease the nightmare. As it had started to get dark they had heard a scraping sound.

They had gone out to investigate and had found Cyril staggering into the doorway with blood running down his chest and arm.

"Bastard got me" he had gasped.

"What happened?" Jeff had asked, helping the man into the room.

"Got what you wanted but the bastard saw me. Must be slipping in my old age" he had grimaced "mind you he only saw me after I'd been inside and was making my way back".

"Who saw you?"

"The bloke in the helicopter" Cyril had replied "as he landed there I took a photo of him and that's when he chased me. He told me to stop and hand over the camera or he would shoot me.

I didn't believe someone would shoot me for taking their picture so I told him to go to hell, or words to that effect. He chased me, and during that chase he shot at me, but I managed to dodge him. I took the chip out of the camera and dropped the camera deliberately to let him pick it up. I dodged back and made my way back here".

"Let's have a look at you" Jen had said firmly.

"First things first" Cyril had said warding her off as he had handed Jeff the chip from the camera "this is what you needed".

"But not at the expense of getting you shot for Christ's sake" Jeff had responded.

"It looks worse than what it is" Cyril had said "you just get the bastards that's all I want. Right, you can nurse me now Jen".

"Nurse you! I'll knuckle you" Jen had said angrily but with great concern "now come on over here, and stop bleeding all over the place. I've just cleaned up". They had both looked at the state of their makeshift shelter and smiled.

Jen had very gently washed his wound, clucking over him like a mother hen. "Macho men" she had said, affectionately "thank God it's only a flesh wound but you're going to be sore for a few days".

"That bloke in the helicopter didn't want to be seen anywhere near here by the looks of it. I wonder why? And how come he didn't look in the camera for the chip?" Jeff had asked.

"He did and he would have found one. I swapped an old one for the one I used so he wouldn't know and would just think I dropped the camera as I ran. As soon as he picked the camera up he stopped chasing me, checked the camera had the chip in it and flew off" Cyril had replied chuckling "good thinking huh?"

"You sail too close to the wind for your own good, you do" Jen had replied "now will you let me see to this wound?" and she had continued to fuss over him and dress his wound.

Derek had put his head round the corner and had said "I heard what happened. This proves that what you've been saying all along is true, otherwise why would they shoot Cyril?"

Derek had continued "Was it that little ginger haired shit at the Terminal? Because I have a score to settle with him and I want him first".

"No" Cyril had said "this one had black hair, the one at the Terminal has blonde hair. This one was the one called Wilson. I saw him earlier when I was there before. Looks like an evil piece of work and I've met some nasty people and I'd put him in the top three".

CHAPTER 21

"The sooner we get copies of these photographs the better" Jeff had said.

"Michael knows of a computer shop on the mainland that his brother owned where he stored computers in the basement" Jen had said "I wonder if any are still intact. I'll ask him".

"I know it's important to get these films developed but not if people are going to get hurt. There has been enough death as we saw today" Jeff had intervened.

"Where's all this fighting spirit we heard you had?" Jen had asked putting her hands on her hips.

"It's alright if I take the risk, I'm the one that pays the price" Jeff had said "but I can't ask anyone else to pay the price for taking the risk".

Jen had turned on him with her eyes flashing very angrily "Who the hell do you think you are, telling us we can't take risks. As far as someone paying the price, don't you think those kids you saw in that school today didn't pay the price? Now it's payback time and I for one will die before those bastards you are after win". She had checked herself "Sorry, but you men make me so angry when you only want to be the hero on your own, without letting anyone else take some of the strain".

Derek had nudged Jeff and had said "I told you not to upset her and that she had a temper".

"Michael's quite capable of looking after himself" Derek had added "he can use his loaf as well, that's more than can be said for most boxers".

"Ok then" Jeff had submitted "I stand reprimanded. If he can get to his brother's shop, copy the photographs, and then perhaps he can send copies and attach a message via email to contacts I still have in the media. But if he's caught it will go badly for him. He has to know the risks".

"He'll be thinking of those kids who didn't stand a chance, not of his own skin, but I will tell him" Jen had said.

Cyril had interceded and said to Jeff "Don't you want to see what present daddy brought you?" Handing over a small bundle of papers to Jeff he had added "I thought they might be important".

"Where did you get them?" Jeff had asked.

"Well. You know I told you Wilson took all those papers off the dead bodies in the Control Room, well, he missed the ones under the body of the bloke that sat in the chair at the top of the table, and these are them".

"Brilliant" Jeff had said "I need to study these".

He had taken the papers into a corner, sat down and had started reading them.

There had been a list of very urgent outstanding maintenance and repair work that had been overdue to be done which had been recommended to be deferred until the following year's budget due to the time required getting them repaired and the down time that would incur. The rest of the papers had read like a who's who of the gas industry world. One separate document had spoken of a deal supplying gas at a cheaper rate with an organisation called The Senate and how UK United Gas had aligned themselves with The Senate and also how any companies or countries that did not align with The Senate would be brought to its knees and the companies forced out of business.

It had also explained how The Senate was going to commandeer all the gas fields under its worldwide organisation and control the flow of gas throughout the world so that they could control countries and their way of life.

For giving The Senate support Sir William Waite and UK United Gas would get control of all the energy markets within the UK and Sir William would become the President of the United Kingdom.

The papers had been dynamite with a short fuse and Jeff had had to keep them safe and get them to John as soon as possible without being caught or the papers found, but how?

He had thought of the little safe in his bungalow but Wilson's people had been there already so how safe was that? However, if they had already searched his place recently, they were not likely to search it again very soon so they should be safe there for a while until he could get them to John.

"I need to put these somewhere safe" Jeff had said to Jen "these papers are important, nobody must know where they are, in case they're caught. What they don't know won't hurt them and I don't trust that Wilson to play by the rules, so I need to go out for a while if you can cover for me?"

"If it was anybody else I'd say go hang" Jen had said "I won't ask what's in the papers but they do seem important to you. If you assure me they're that important then ok".

Jeff had said "What Cyril got was probably one of the most important documents we need to prove treachery and treason by this Sir William Waite and UK United Gas and the papers need to be kept safe and the least amount of people that know that we have them and where they are the better for now ok. Do you have a camera that takes the same chip as this one? I want to photograph these papers so I can send them on via the net and keep the originals for safe keeping".

"There's one in that cupboard" Derek had said when Jen had asked for a camera "we all had a scratch around and we got three altogether". He got the camera checked there was a chip in it and had given it to Jeff.

Jeff had photographed the papers page by page then had said "We need to send this on with the photos. Later on I will have to go out for a while but I won't be long".

"Do you need somebody to go with you?" Jen had asked.

"Better not, the least known the better" Jeff had replied and had settled down to re-read the papers Cyril had managed to find.

He had waited until much later when it was quiet before he had ventured out.

Jen had said "I gave that chip from the camera to Michael and he's gone to get the prints done and also to send them off in your name to your press contacts and that address you spoke of, if he can. He said it had to be in your name because they know you, but not him, and you have a reputation for telling the truth to the press".

Jeff had thanked Jen and then had said "I hope he keeps himself safe? He's taking an awful risk for me".

"Hey it's not just for you, it's for those dead kids" Jen had retorted "so rest up before you go".

She had left the room and had started fussing over Cyril.

In the other room Cyril had said to Jen "What makes a man like him tick? He takes on the impossible odds for what? What does he get out of it? What's in it for him financially?"

Jen had responded "He'll get nothing out of this financially, you can bet on that".

"What does he do it for then?"

"Principles, moral justice" Jen had answered. She continued "I love you for what you are Cyril. I know you're an old tea leaf and a very good one, but even you would not take an old lady's handbag, you like a much more principled challenge like today that not many other tea leafs could do, right? You wouldn't take an old lady's handbag but you would take gems and paintings from the very rich because you have the ability and principles to achieve it. Well, he has the same sort of principles but in his case he's much too honest to be a tea leaf and he lives by an old fashion code of principles that you don't see much of now, integrity, honesty, a gentleman in the right sense of the word and a man of his word, and above all he'll die by his principles and that is a rare trait today".

Jen had continued "If he believes something is fundamentally wrong he will oppose it and stand up against anyone no matter how much money they have or how powerful they are to protect the less fortunate".

"What! Like some knight in shining armour like Don Quixote?" Cyril had scoffed.

"I love you Cyril. I just admire what he does and why he does it".

Cyril had looked at Jen and realised that what she had just admitted to was that she loved him still and he had warmed towards her.

Jen had continued "He's just cut from a different cloth that's all, and he's fighting for you, me and what happened to those kids and all those families.

We did not ask him, he does it because he believes someone should do something and stand and be counted, not sit back and just let it happen and then say someone should have done something. Like you're a very good tea leaf, probably the best, he's good at what he does, being a loose cannon. He's that good that UK United Gas has put a price for information on his whereabouts of £1million".

"A million pounds cash, just for saying where he is?" Cyril had stammered, astounded "he must be able to seriously hurt those bastards for them to offer that sort of money".

"The help he needs to expose these bastards, he won't ask for" Jen had said angrily "it has to be offered and given freely with no strings. He has a code of ethics that is rare today, and principles we have lost in this world of today that is full of greed.

He is old fashioned but I wish there were a lot more like him then this world would be a better place to live without the constant attitude of what's in it for me?"

CHAPTER 22

Jeff had retrieved the gun from the cycle pannier and had hid it in the waistband at the back of his trousers feeling a lot safer with it.

He had made his way towards the area where he had lived, picking his way over broken buildings and the grotesque horrors that were inside them and lying around outside.

He had just arrived without incident when he had heard the throb of the rotors of a helicopter and he had dived for cover in a doorway, hoping he had not been seen.

The helicopter had circled around once and then had passed overhead and had headed toward the Terminal.

Jeff had made his way to what was left of his bungalow dreading what he was going to see. He had made his way inside the charred remains of the place he had once lived in and had learned to love over many years, bracing himself for the worst. Everything had been scattered about, all his personal possessions that had survived the colossal fire were thrown around as Wilson's henchmen had left them. With trepidation Jeff had searched for any sign of Karen but could not find her or her remains.

He had gone straight to the floor safe. It had been open and papers such as his passport and other documents that had been inside had gone. He had taken the papers and had put them in the safe and had set the combination and locked it.

He had felt that if they had looked here once they were not likely to look again in the same place. If they had already taken his papers that had been inside they wouldn't be expecting more to be put back in, so therefore they should be safe for now until he could get them to John. He then had made his way out of the bungalow and back to the Cellars. As he got near the junction that led him to the pub he heard someone call his name softly and it made him jump.

He had looked around and had spotted Michael making his way towards him. As Michael had approached closer, Jeff had seen that he had been in a fight. There had been a cut and bruising around his eyes and he had a swollen lip.

"What happened to you?" Jeff had asked in a quiet voice.

Michael had explained. "After I sent your photos and emails I was coming back when these two goons jumped me. They started asking questions about you and if I had seen you. They had a real bullying attitude. I don't like bullies. So they tried being Mr Nice Guy and when that didn't work they started the rough stuff. I let them think they had softened me up and they then untied me. That was their mistake.

They didn't know that have I never lost a fight in the ring, now they'll be eating out of a straw for months. As I told them and their boss who I also put to sleep when he came in at the end, I don't like bullies".

"I'm sorry I got you into this" Jeff had said.

"Hey, I got myself into this. All I needed was a prod from you and I'm glad I'm in it. I'm big enough and ugly enough to look after myself as those three found out the hard way, so that's enough from you, right!"

"Thanks anyway" Jeff had said.

Michael had smiled "Let's get back to the others and bring them up to speed".

As they had made their way back, Jeff had told Michael about the papers that Cyril had found and what they proved.

Michael had whistled "Those bastards want to cover up all these deaths they've caused to further their own ends, it's inhuman. I'm glad I had the chance to get a few blows in for us. If I'd known then what you just told me, they would have been dead by now".

They had arrived at the Cellars just as the helicopter had started to take off from the Terminal so they had hurried inside before they had been seen.

There had been a crowd of people inside, all of them eager to see him and ask questions, such as, was it true that this was an industrial accident being covered up by UK United Gas also, if it was true, how they could help?

Jeff had said "I need proof of what is going on and I need to stay alive long enough to expose the truth through the media which at the moment is the only weapon we have".

Michael had said "There's a price on his head by UK United Gas and anybody thinking of trying to get that price answers to me understand?"

"And me and Jen" Derek had stated from the back of the room.

Someone had also said from the back "Everybody thinks you died at the Community Hall, well that's what the news has been saying",

"My death seems to have been much exaggerated" Jeff had said laughing.

Michael had butted in "As far as we're concerned he is dead and that's the only way he's going to be able to stay alive, understand? Because if they find out he's alive before he exposes what's going on we are all in big trouble.

Make no mistake, they'll take no prisoners. If they find out there's any evidence to expose them they'll crush it, and they'll crush the people who they think will do them the most harm. You only have to look at what they did to Cyril because they thought he took a photo of one of them and what they did to Michael when they wanted information.

If they can do that and get away with it, they can do anything".

The people had murmured and then had talked amongst themselves and then a woman had spoken up saying "I don't know about the others here but I'm with Jeff. He's always tried to look after the area and its people and that's good enough for me".

Then she had continued "Where are the few of our so called elected councillors who survived? Nowhere to be seen that's where. Oh, we've heard them from the comfort of the radio station, trying to say the best plaudits of how terrible it is, but none of them are here to help us. They're all too busy looking after themselves and their own families".

Then another man had shouted "All we ask for is help to get our lives back in some sort of order, and what do we get? We get treated as though we're criminals, the only helicopters that could bring us help have only gone to the Terminal and back and how do they treat us?"

Just then, the sound of the helicopter had started to get closer. They had all looked concerned so Jeff had put his head round the door frame to see if he could see what was going on. Just at that moment the helicopter had made a pass overhead.

Above the noise of the rotor blades Jeff heard the sound of small arms gunfire and a man and a young woman near a burned out car which had been across the road fell to the road, shot.

The passenger in the helicopter had been laughing as he had taken pot shots at the rest of the people in the group that were trying to hide from the bullets he had been spraying at them.

"You sick bastard" Jeff had yelled and had drawn his gun. He had aimed quickly at the helicopter and had fired two shots, one after another at the man in the helicopter.

Two things had happened very quickly.

More by luck than judgment the passenger had fallen out of the helicopter bleeding from a chest wound and had screamed all the way to the ground where he had crashed in a heap and thereafter had not moved.

The helicopter had started smoking, the rotors juddering and the engine coughing. It had started pitching and yawing then the pilot had managed to regain some control and had flown the helicopter away. It had managed to stay in flight a short distance before it had plunged into the ground, bursting into flames on impact.

"Good shooting" Derek had said "where did you learn to shoot like that?"

"We had a gun range in the bank where I worked and they had a gun club which I belonged to" Jeff had replied.

"But they were good shots" Derek had insisted.

"More by luck than judgment" Jeff had said "now let's see if those people survived he was shooting at".

When they had reached the burned out car they saw a young man and a young girl, no more than 14-15 years old, dead in a pool of blood. They hadn't stood a chance. They had been shot down for sport.

"Bastards" Derek had said, hate in his voice "see what identity the bloke from the helicopter has on him".

Derek had kicked the body of the passenger from the helicopter and the man had moaned. Jeff had run over to examine his injuries.

"Who sent you?" Jeff had asked angrily.

"Wilson" the man had replied weakly before he had hitched in a final breath and dying.

"What identity has he got on him?" Jeff had asked.

"A set of keys to a car, a security door pass card, a driving licence, a wad of money, a gun and two spare clips and a letter of authorisation to shoot looters on sight signed by none other than Sir William Waite Derek had said "we get hunted down and shot at for wanting to survive. To them we're sport and a bullet is a lot cheaper than the cost of supporting survivors".

"What gives Sir William the right to authorise men to shoot looters on sight unless he has taken over the country already?" Jeff had thought "or he's confident that he will very soon. If that is the case, John and the PM were in trouble and so was he and he had to work fast and get back. He had to use the mobile phone to contact John or Sergeant Dick to see how the situation overall was".

"Let's have that stuff it might be useful" Jeff had said to Derek.

When they got back, Jeff had gone into a quiet corner and used the mobile phone, calling the number that Sergeant Dick had given him, whilst Derek had told everybody what had happened down by the car.

A voice at the other end of the phone had asked "Who is this?"

Without giving his name Jeff had asked for John. The voice on the other end had repeated the question "Who is this and how did you get this number?" Jeff had asked for John again and added that if he wasn't there he would speak to Sergeant Dick instead.

It had gone quiet at the other end of the phone then a voice which he recognised as John's said "Yes, who is this? And how did you get this number?"

"It's Jeff" Jeff had said "I need to let you know what's happening".

John had said "Dad, how many times have I told you not to call me at work, you know I'm busy".

Jeff had said "It's not your dad it's me, Jeff".

John had said "Yes dad, I did tell you to let me know if there was any change in mum's condition but I only gave you this number for emergencies only".

Jeff had said "You can't talk very much can you because someone's there?"

"That's right dad" John had answered "now you're on the phone how can I help you?"

Jeff had briefly explained to him what he had found out so far and about the shootings.

"Ok" John had said "thanks dad for letting me know how mum is. I'll certainly try to see you and mum at the weekend but I have to go now. I have to fly to investigate a helicopter crash in a couple of hours. I know you were into aeroplane crash investigations before you retired, you would find it interesting if you could have been there. We could have had a drink in the Cellars if it was still standing. And by the way, I will pick you up your favourite tobacco at the same time on my way back, so don't worry, bye for now and I will see you and mum soon, alright?"

Before John had rung off Jeff could hear him talk to someone at the other end of the phone. "Sorry about that PM but my dad worries about mum a lot and he thinks I should be informed every time she has a bad turn" then the phone had clicked off.

Jeff had thought "Boy that was cryptic. So he's coming here and he's already heard about the helicopter crash that has just happened, that was fast. He needs to see me but how? How can that happen without breaking cover, and if he is coming to the Cellars he needs to get everyone clear of it".

He had turned to Cyril but before he could say anything further Cyril had said "I see you got one of the bastards from the helicopter. They'll think twice before messing with us again".

"They already know what happened" Jeff had said.

"What" Cyril had said "they can't have, it's only just happened".

"Not only that but they're going to come and investigate the crash within the next couple of hours. We need to make sure this place looks unoccupied and I need to meet this person that is coming and he will help us get these bastards for good".

"You move in strange circles Jeff" Cyril had said "if it was anyone else I wouldn't trust them, but after what you did for those young kids who were just trying to survive, you got my support in whatever you decide".

Cyril had continued "That bastard shot those kids for sport and deserved to die, unfortunately he died too quickly for my liking. All I hope is that the pilot dies and if he does he dies slowly and in agony. Bloody sick bastards. What they did out there shows what they think of us and how we can't trust them. I thought we got rid of the Hitler and fascists of this world, but it looks like we still need to exterminate a few more that have just crawled out of the woodwork".

Jen had said "I heard what you said to Cyril about visitors and I agree with you, we need to get these people out of here or they could get hurt and I'll have a word with them because if they talk it would blow your cover and probably get them killed as well".

"How's your arm?" Jen had then asked Cyril.

"Stop fussing woman" Cyril had said "I'll live, that's more than those poor bastards out there will, sick bastards. They never stood a chance".

"Right, let's get things moving" Jen had said and went to organise the people, where they were to go for now and also to make the area look as though it had not been lived in.

The people had drifted off in ones and twos and gradually there was only Jeff, Derek, Jen and Cyril remaining in the building.

Derek had said "I'll be in that house over there watching in case you need help".

Jen had said to Cyril "You need some TLC and I know the place for that, so come on wounded hero".

"Now don't you embarrass me woman" Cyril had responded "I might have to spank you".

"When you're a big enough boy you might try" Jen had answered Cyril smartly with a twinkle in her eye "come on, we don't want to be seen by Jeff's visitor and Derek will make sure Jeff is safe, come on you need nursing" and she had grabbed his hand and they had left and Derek went with them.

Jeff had been left alone with his thoughts of how it had all come to this situation of violence and the deaths of thousands of innocent people, all caught up in the machinations of a megalomaniac like Sir William Waite who wanted to be a dictator and did not care how he achieved his aim or who died so he could totally dominate the country.

Jeff had thought back to what had started it all and why he had picked up the banner again so long after being very much involved in stopping the two oil refineries from being built in the 1970s and 1980s.

CHAPTER 23

After a while, Jeff had heard the sound of a helicopter drawing nearer he had an uneasy thought. "What had happened to the body of the man who he had shot and who had fallen out of the helicopter? They surely must see it unless Derek had moved it".

The sound of the helicopter had gotten much louder and dust had started to blow around from the downward wash of the rotor blades. The engine of the helicopter had slowed and the rotors whirled slowly to a stop.

Jeff had heard a muffled voice which seemed to be giving instructions. After a while, there had been the sound of rubble being disturbed by the door. Jeff had peered through the dust to see John standing by the doorway.

"Can I get any tobacco here?" John had whispered.

Jeff had slid out from the alcove holding the gun "Are you alone?" Jeff had asked equally quietly.

"Just me and the pilot of the helicopter" John had said "and he's under instructions not to leave the helicopter for any reason. If something happens to me he is to take off straightaway and detonate a device over this area then return back and report what has happened".

"You're expendable as well then?" Jeff had exclaimed "that's a bluff".

"No it isn't. Either you have something for me or I leave now" John had said "the situation is poised on a knife edge and could go either way".

"Ok" Jeff had said "that helicopter crash, did the pilot survive?"

"No he didn't! What do you know about that?" John had asked suspiciously "this is a restricted area. There have been no authorised flights near this area since the incident".

"Well those bastards were taking pot shots at a couple of kids for fun. I got a couple of lucky shots in that put the passenger out of his misery and hit something in the engine. Then the pilot crashed over there and I had hoped that he had died too. And as far as there being no authorised flights in this area, they have landed in the Terminal or on the roof of the Terminal at least a dozen times and they have somebody within the Terminal site threatening to shoot anyone who goes near it".

"They are not my people". Then John had added "I thought you were going to be discreet in finding out information, not advertise to all and sundry you were here? I've had a hell of a job to keep that crash quiet for now. I've not got long, as far as the pilot knows I am reminiscing about having a good time with my dad here years ago, so what have you found out so far?"

Jeff had told him about the visits to the Terminal by Wilson and a few others.

"Wilson came here? He wouldn't dare, unless they were very desperate!" John had said "But I'll have to take your word for it as you obviously can't prove it".

"But I can!" Jeff had replied heatedly "there is a clear photograph taken of him by the Terminal in his helicopter, and Wilson shot at the person who took the photograph. It's on the email attachment we sent to your email address which you gave me, along with a photograph of the papers seized by us that were at the Terminal in the Board Room".

"Wilson would shoot anyone who saw him" John had said "he can't be seen anywhere near here as that links him directly with UK United Gas and Sir William Waite. If he thinks you have a photograph of him here he will kill you for it".

Jeff had explained the circumstances of how the picture was taken and how Wilson believed he had the camera and the chip, also about the papers and what was in them and the fact that he had hidden them for safe keeping, how Wilson had destroyed all the meeting papers and broken the dials and clocks in the Control Room of the Terminal and how he thought the incident happened by the scorch marks on the seawall.

John had said "I need those documents to link it all together, where are they?"

"They're safe" Jeff had said "but you have the photographs of them to prove they exist".

"Don't you trust me?" John had asked, forcing a note of quite childish hurt into his voice.

"Those papers are the people's safe ticket, and I'm not going to give that away" Jeff had answered firmly.

"Don't play hard ball with me, matey, I invented the game" John had warned.

"I need guarantees for the people here. And all the time I hold those papers no more people are going to be shot as sport" Jeff had said "and they also get the help they need".

"The emergency forces are stretched to breaking point and working their way towards you as we speak but there is a lot of devastation and victims to clear away first. Now I can't give any guarantees" John had said.

"You can make things happen, I know you can" Jeff had said "you or the PM can make sure Sir William Waite guarantees their safety and gets Wilson and his cronies to wind in their necks".

"Sir William and his cronies are trying to take control of this country and if they succeed you'll have a jack boot on your neck" John had replied coolly "and there's nothing I can do to stop that".

"Whose side are you on anyway?" Jeff had asked sarcastically "Sir William's people are trying to clear away any evidence of their involvement as fast as possible and your people do nothing but work slowly from the outside inwards clearing the ground as you go. By the time you do get around to doing something here he will have wiped away any sign of it being an accident, and he will have made political gains and blamed terrorists and got control of this country. When that happens, the last one leaving the country should switch the lights off because this will not be Great Britain anymore but a fascist state".

"What do you see being done then?" John had asked.

"Get some support to these people and stop Sir William's men tampering with the evidence at the Terminal" Jeff had answered.

"I need evidence of this tampering before I can confront them" John had said.

"I sent you copies of the papers and Wilson's photograph to that email address you gave me, those papers should condemn him on their own" Jeff had urged.

"Ok, I accept that" John had said "now where are those papers?"

"Safe" Jeff had reiterated again, not giving an inch.

"Did I tell you we found your wife Karen and your daughter Joan alive at a health farm?" John had suddenly volunteered this startling piece of information as though it was some kind of carrot being dangled in front of a donkey.

"Are they alright and safe?" Jeff had asked quickly, automatically pulling a mask of careful blankness over his features.

"They are as safe as those papers are" John had replied. His meaning was very clear.

"How come Karen and Joan were not at home when everything went up?" Jeff had asked suddenly.

"Apparently they were at a health spa. Joan had got a last minute cancellation that morning and had taken Karen with her" John had answered "but, as I said, they are safe for now. But no-one must know they are alive otherwise they can be used to get to you. They are safe, that I can guarantee, as you guarantee those papers are safe. Do we understand one another?"

It was then that Jeff had remembered that Karen had said something about Joan trying to get a cancellation at a local spa but he had been on the phone at the time and engrossed in the paperwork he was doing and had not listened to all what Karen had said. He felt overwhelming relief and happiness for himself and terrible sadness for the families of the loved ones that had not escaped the terrible chain of events that had led to so many deaths. "As long as my family is safe those papers are safe" Jeff had said "and I know how bad you need those papers, so, if anything happens to my family those papers will be destroyed, that I can also guarantee. So, we do understand one another".

"You still don't trust anybody do you?" John had commented "ok, well you can trust me".

"We'll see" Jeff had said then he had gone on to tell John about the conversation between Wilson and the other man at the Terminal in reference to the green Jaguar car at the councillor's house.

"My brother is going to be very interested in that information. Look. Things are not quite in place at the moment to act on and stop our friends, but they will be soon" John had said "I must go now if I'm not to make the pilot suspicious. I'll send some parcels for you all, that's the best I can do for now, but I will give your regards to Karen and Joan in the meantime. The mobile you have, destroy it".

He had handed Jeff a new mobile phone and said "Use this one, but only use it once, and only once, using the number pre-set into it and then destroy it so you can't be traced. I'll send you another one with the parcels. Do exactly the same with that one. Sorry about the cloak and dagger attitude but at the moment it's for the best". Then John had added "You can trust me Jeff, you really can. Now I must go" and he left.

Jeff had heard the helicopter's engine fade into the distance and he had been left alone with his mind in a spin.

He had been elated that Karen was alive but then as the reality had hit him he had been suddenly overwhelmed with depression, sadness and grief for those who had lost everything. Mixed in with those feelings had been an element of hope for the others and himself and the desperate situation that he was in and also the situation he was putting others in. He had shaken himself out of his depression and had mentally told himself off for feeling sorry for himself as there were other people considerably worse off than himself. Clearing his mind of personal matters, he had sat back and analysed his situation and what he had to do from here.

CHAPTER 24

It had been dark by the time Jen and Cyril had arrived back at the building and they had both had a twinkle in their eyes. Jeff had smiled at them thinking that at least out of all this chaos somebody had found happiness even if only for a short time.

"Well, what did your friend have to say?" Jen had asked.

Jeff had felt that he could not tell them about Karen being alive yet, not with all the loss and sadness they were holding inside, plus all the death and destruction around them. He had felt it was the wrong time. He had told them of the parcel drop that was due and what he had told John.

"At least we will get some decent food and the threat of us being eliminated for fun will stop" Cyril had commented.

"Oh, we'll probably get the food but don't relax against the threat from Wilson and his cronies" Jeff had said "I don't trust that one as far as the end of my nose".

"What do we do now?" Jen had asked.

"Take photographs of everything you can and try to record details so it can be used as evidence later" Jeff had replied.

"Won't the forensic people do that?" Jen had queried.

Jeff had replied "They'll only be able to study what they see when they get here, and if Wilson and his mob alter the evidence, then that's the evidence they will investigate and then reach the conclusion that Wilson wants them to come to, so it will be one giant cover-up and that's what they're doing at the Terminal now, altering the evidence to suit themselves and trying to get themselves off the hook".

"That's criminal" Jen had snapped, horrified.

"Not if you don't get caught doing it" Jeff had said "so we have to catch them and record it in any way we can so as to make them pay for all these deaths. But make no mistake, it will not be easy and it could be very dangerous if they find out what we are doing, so if anybody wants to say no I will understand. All I ask is that you just accept that I'm going to do what it takes to put these bastards away forever".

"And you think you can do it on your own?" Jen had retorted, raising an eyebrow.

"If that's what it takes, then yes" Jeff had answered.

"Typical male" Jen had scoffed "I told you before, if you think you can do this on your own you've got another thing coming. Who gave birth to those kids who are dead in the schools? Who watched over them through their illnesses? Who has had to watch them die horribly? Us women that's who. Do you have any idea what it's like to see your child die and not be able to do anything about it? So don't tell me or any other mother she can't help put these bastards in hell, and whether you like it or not, women are a match for any man, you male chauvinistic pig".

"Whoa! I didn't say you couldn't help lady, all I said was it would be dangerous for you" Jeff had said placatingly, holding up his hands in submission.

"And women can't face danger?" Jen had queried angrily.

"Back off you two" Cyril had said "you know you'll both do what it takes to nail these bastards as will the rest of us, so don't ruffle each other's feathers. The enemy is out there not inside here right?"

"Yes" Jen and Jeff had said together and had smiled sheepishly at one another feeling rather foolish. They both had voiced apologies at the same time and then had laughed again.

"Now what's to be done? And what's the best way of doing it?" Cyril had asked.

"Well, we need to get as many trusted people together as possible" Jeff had replied "and find out who will, or can do what. We must know our limitations or we'll overstretch ourselves and get caught. If that happens there will be no mercy because these animals play for keeps. We might also have to find another safe place to meet if they find out that we operate from here."

"Leave that to me" Cyril had said "I'll hunt around".

"We need to make a list of the types of things that will be of importance such as photographs of any alterations carried out by them, or any papers that might be of importance, and photographs or descriptions of any of the people attending the site before the investigation team arrives and if someone has the stomach for it, possible photographs of the inside of the schools and the surrounding areas but above all nobody must be caught doing it".

Cyril had said "I might have a list of safe places soon but to let you know they are safe when you approach them, how's this for an idea? You will see the moving feature that is the sign of a windmill. They are so well known nobody takes any notice of them (there are lots of them on the Estuary, in gardens, on churches, on the apex of houses). If the vanes of the windmill are in the shape of a kiss it's safe, if in the shape of a cross it's not safe".

"What a brilliant idea" Jeff had said.

"It's so obvious it's fool proof and it's right under their noses" Cyril had continued "I read it in a book once. It was a system adopted by an underground movement during World War II in Holland".

"Ok. In the morning we get going, but don't get caught" Jeff had said and they settled down for the night.

Jeff had sat in the corner, his mind in a spin. Karen was safe, thank God. He had wanted to be with her but there was a price on his head and until this was over he and she were expendable so instead he had concentrated on trying to put everything in order of priority. The more information he received the better, but at the same time he had to keep that information safe and then send it to John and hope John's side won. If not, he was dead and buried but he already knew he had made the choice of whose side he was on.

He had eventually drifted off to sleep mulling these things over.

CHAPTER 25

Jeff had been shaken awake by Derek whilst it had still been dark.

"What's the matter?" Jeff had asked, as he became instantly alert.

"There's troops moving around up the road and they're not the usual pickets stationed near here, we need to be out of here in case they come here" Derek had replied.

"What time is it?" Jeff had asked.

"Just gone 6 am" Derek had replied "come on move, if you don't want to be caught".

They had made their way past the squad of troops that were dressed in black uniforms. They seemed to be looking for survivors and taking them away in trucks to what had been the Sports Centre.

Jeff and Derek had made their way slowly along the ditches, using the hedgerows, towards the Sports Centre making sure they had not been seen. When they had arrived at the derelict building that had once been the swimming pool, they had crept to the corner of the building and from there they had been able to see and hear what was going on. Jeff had heard his name mentioned and something about a reward then a couple of the troopers had started slapping some of the women around. Just at that moment a young man had run from the group towards where they had lain hidden. Bullets had promptly impacted around his legs and the man had stopped dead in his tracks and had put his hands up.

What appeared to be an officer of some kind had shouted to two troopers "Teach him a lesson not to mess with us".

Two troopers had broken away from the group and had walked over to the man. They had started pushing and punching him and when he had fallen to the ground, had commenced kicking him in the ribs and legs. The man had managed to scramble to his feet and limping slightly, had managed to break free and had run directly to where Jeff and Derek had lain hidden.

The man had run around the corner of the building into Jeff's arms with the two troopers hard on his heels.

As Jeff had placed the palm of his hand over the man's mouth to prevent him from calling out in startled surprise, he had heard two grunts as the two troopers ran into Derek and were knocked to the ground by two hard and fast punches. Derek had stood over them ready to hit them again.

"Quickly, get their guns and grenades" Derek had ordered Jeff in a whisper, at the same time motioning the man to stay quiet.

Jeff had cautiously put his head around the corner to see if anyone had heard them. What he had seen had shocked him. The people had been lined up and the officer was questioning them and violently pushing his gun into their bodies in a very threatening manner, obviously indicating that if they did not tell him what he wanted to know he would shoot them. Jeff had also seen a lorry loaded with ammunition pull up facing them.

The driver had climbed out of the lorry and had joined the other man in the back of the lorry where they had uncovered a machine gun and had pointed it at the people.

"We have to do something fast, he's going to kill them all" Jeff had whispered urgently to Derek "follow my lead" and he had grabbed a rifle and some grenades from one of the unconscious troopers and had run towards the truck.

He had made it to the truck without being seen with Derek close behind him. He had signalled to Derek that they needed to get the two troopers off of the truck and disarmed.

Derek had climbed onto the truck from the driver's side, slid up behind the two troopers who had been busy being very graphic on what they wanted to do to two of the young girls amongst the crowd of people.

The troopers had not heard Derek until the last moment. He had hit them with the butt of his gun and they had instantly slumped to the floor of the truck. Derek had then rolled each one out of the back of the truck and onto the ground unconscious.

The noise of the two troopers hitting the ground had startled the officer. He had instantly run towards them with his gun raised and had snarled "Who the hell are you? Wait a minute, you're the man I'm looking for" gesturing towards Jeff.

"Well you found me and if you don't lay down your arms I'll drop these armed grenades into this ammunition truck" Jeff had said.

"I can shoot and kill you from here very easily" the officer had said lightly.

"Then I drop the grenades anyway and take you and your squad with me, that seems a fair exchange" Jeff had returned, equally lightly.

The officer's face had been a picture of uncertainty. Finally he had said to his men over his shoulder "Put down your guns, now".

Jeff had then said to the men in the group of people "Disarm them and you don't have to be gentle".

When the troopers had been disarmed and rounded up along with the officer, the officer had said "You can't kill us, I was only following orders from Sir William Waite the new President elect to apprehend you at any cost and these people might have known where you were".

"So you were going to kill them if they didn't tell you what they didn't know?" Jeff had said.

"I was only following orders as were my men" the officer had explained in a surly manner.

"In the Second World War the guards said the same about the death camps" Jeff had stated "right, now order your men to drop their trousers round their ankles but not to take them off".

The officer had looked at him strangely, but surprisingly volunteered no argument and had given the order.

"Your men can't run anywhere or go after these people with their pants down and their hands tied behind their backs" Jeff had explained.

When the two troopers who had been on the truck had come too, they had been ordered to carry out the same and then had their hands tied behind their backs.

The two young girls who had been the recipients of the two troopers' leering remarks had ventured over to their verbal assailants and had kicked them in their crotches very hard. The troopers had doubled over in agony.

"Animals!" the girls had said and had spat on the troopers viciously.

"Did you see what those two girls did to my men" the officer had asked Jeff.

"No, I didn't see anything" Jeff had answered "the same as you obviously didn't see anything when you controlled your troopers".

Realising he was not going to die there, the officer had started feeling brave again and had said to Jeff "You'll get yours when Wilson finds out what you've done".

Derek had stepped in and had hit the officer in the face with a punch that had laid him flat on his back then had said to Jeff "If his brain was taxed he would get a rebate" then looking down on the man had said "well, you've got yours now for being a bully and that's what Wilson will get if I catch up with him".

Jeff had turned to the people and had said "You need to get out of here. You'd better use the trucks and head to a safer area and try to avoid any men in black".

"What about them?" a man had asked from the rear of the group.

"Were they going to show you any mercy?" Jeff had asked.

"No" the man had replied.

"Well then, I suggest we leave them as they are and let their people find them but make sure you take a note of all their names and keep that information safe, so that it can be used at a later date if there is a crimes tribunal. Now we have to go" Jeff had said.

"Thank you two for doing what you did" a man had said "we won't forget it. I'm sure they would have killed us men and done God knows what to the women and those two made their intentions known" the same man had said pointing to the two men rolling on the ground in agony. They had that uncontrolled animal look about them. He had added "Don't worry, we'll deal with these scum in our own way" pointing to the sorry sight of troopers huddled together trying not to look sheepish, silly and undignified with their trousers around their ankles.

"If the rule of law has broken down, avoid the black troopers, and look for our soldiers, you should be safer with them" Jeff had said "good luck. Come on you ugly brute" jokingly to Derek" they don't need us anymore".

"Ok" Derek had said slapping him on the back and sending him flying "we make a good team you and me, a dynamic duo, eh?"

"More like beauty and the beast, and you're no beauty" Jeff had rejoined smirking.

Derek had laughed heartily, slapped Jeff on the back again and had said "I like you, let's go, and by the way where are we going?"

"Councillor Randle's house" Jeff had answered.

"What! That means we have to pass the picket line" Derek had exclaimed.

"Not if we go via the seaward side of the barrier" Jeff had replied "and with them looking after the trucks of people that are going there now, they won't see us".

CHAPTER 26

Jeff and Derek had made their way to Councillor Randle's house without incident. As they had passed on the seaward side of the Barrier from a distance they had seen the soldiers stopping the trucks then escorting their passengers away. Jeff had had the feeling that the people would now be safe.

They had found a way into the back garden and had made their way to the concealed garage to find it empty. The green Jaguar that Cyril had spoken of was gone, so they made their way into the house.

The place looked as though it had been turned over by professional people looking for something important. They had gone into another room to see a safe fixed to the wall open and the contents riffled through completely and scattered on the floor. The body of Councillor Randle had lain twisted in a grotesque heap his neck obviously snapped as his head lay at a peculiar angle.

"Looks like there's no honour amongst thieves" Jeff had retorted.

Derek went over to the safe "Bloody empty" he had stated in a disgusted tone.

Jeff had looked at him and said "Strange that, he has the same type of safe I have, but his is a much more sophisticated model. I couldn't afford this type, it was too expensive, no difference in looks from the outside, but I believe this one had an extra compartment at the back". Jeff had put his hand inside the safe and had felt around. He had then pushed the back of the safe and something had clicked inside. The back wall of the safe and slid across revealing another compartment in which Jeff had found hidden papers and passports under different names but with Councillor Randle's picture on them and numerous different currencies and a bag of gold sovereigns. "I bet whoever rifled this safe didn't know about this compartment. The only reason I know about it is because at the time when I had my one put in I could not afford this model, it was a hell of a lot dearer but the salesman showed it to me to try to get me to buy it. Here, you can have the sovereigns if you want" Jeff had said, tossing the bag of coins to Derek "he's past caring" pointing to the body of Councillor Randle. "I need to see what's in this paperwork".

Jeff had taken out the papers and had started to study them closely.

After a while, Jeff had paused and whistled "Jesus Christ!"

What he had found would open a can of worms for sure. The papers had named names and linked all the conniving lot together. No wonder they wanted Randle dead. He had held them all to ransom all the way up to Sir William Wait and more. The papers had tied in nicely with the papers that he had given to John when he had first met him in the police station.

"This is dynamite" Jeff had said "we need to copy these and send them to John".

"Who's John?" Derek had asked.

"The Government man who visited me in the helicopter" Jeff had responded.

"Are you playing me for a sucker?" Derek had said to Jeff very menacingly.

"No" Jeff had said and sat down and went through all that had happened to him up until the time they had met.

"Now you see why they want me dead and anyone who knows as much as I do along with me".

"So I'm on their hit list as well" Derek had said "nice to be popular". He broke into a great big beaming smile.

"We have to send these papers on and then keep the papers safe for our own protection" Jeff had said.

"I do believe you don't trust anybody in high office, not even this John bloke, do you?" Derek had mused.

"My old man always said to me 'walk gentle in this world son, but carry a big stick just in case'" Jeff had replied "I trust these people about as far as the end of my nose and at this moment in time no further, but of all the options I have, John is the better one, and is at least trying to stop Sir William and his sidekick Wilson taking over the country and covering up mass murder".

"Let's make our way to Michael's brother's computer place and see if we can copy these documents" Derek had suggested "then we can send them off to this bloke John. I know the way it's not very far".

They had made their way there without incident by using the back roads and hedgerows as cover. Just as they had neared Michael's brother's computer shop, they had heard a scraping noise and immediately both men had ducked down. They had crept forward and had entered the basement of the building.

"God, you two scared the life out of me" Michael had said as he appeared from behind a cabinet.

Both Jeff and Derek had also been startled and Derek had said "What are you doing here?"

"I was checking to see if the fax machine and the copier were still working knowing you were going to need them at some point" Michael had replied.

"Well are they?" Jeff had asked.

"Yes" Michael had replied.

"Good, we need to send some stuff right now, it was lucky you were here" Jeff had said.

Jeff had produced the papers and had passed them to Michael to fax off to a number which he had given him.

Michael had looked at some of the pages as he was copying them and said "Christ on a crutch! Did you get this information from Councillor Randle's safe? Tell me this is a joke. This information will have repercussions right across the political arena, it names who's involved right up the political ladder and right into Whitehall. If this gets out these people on this list will be destroyed, and Randle was murdered because of these documents? You know, if they find you have them they will want your head on a pole, no wonder there's a price on your head, and now ours, now we know why".

As they had been finishing and getting to the last page they had heard a noise outside the front of the building. Men had been shouting and there had been the stamping of boots.

Michael had looked out through the basement skylight and had said "We had better move, and now. There's a squad of troopers outside dressed in black, and they look as though they're coming in here, leave everything and run".

Jeff had grabbed the papers and had joined Derek at the basement door closely followed by Michael just as the front door had come crashing in.

The three of them had run out of the building and along the hedgerow so as not to be seen from the building and had slowly made their way back to the lower part of the Barrier where they had hoped to cross the creek.

"Did you get those papers sent off?" Jeff had asked Michael when they had recovered from their mad dash away from the basement of the building "at least we were not seen otherwise there would have been a hue and cry".

"All except the last pages. As they came in the door upstairs I grabbed the documents and disconnected the call" Michael had answered.

"Hopefully they won't think of tracing who we made the connection to" Derek had remarked hopefully.

"They can't, it's on a loop, it would take a computer buff to track that connection" Michael had explained.

"What do you mean?" Derek had asked.

"Well, when the fax lines were connected, it was done on a secure scrambled line. I don't know how my cousin did it, so providing the connection was terminated before they got to the fax machine it can't be tracked or traced. The only thing is, Jeff and I might have missed faxing the last few pages but we have the original documents with us".

They had made their way slowly back towards the Estuary. There had seemed to be more activity about but not enough to stop them slipping through the picket lines.

"I need to put these papers away somewhere safe" Jeff had said "wait for me near the Cellars" and he had left to make his way to the safe in the floor in the ruins of his bungalow. As he had approached the building he had kept a wary eye out but there had been nobody around and nothing untoward going on and it all looked as though it was the same as he had left it. He had opened his floor safe, put the papers in the safe, closed it then sprinkled some dust and small bits of rubble over the safe to make it look as though it had not been disturbed. Then he had gone back to the Cellars.

As he had approached the Cellars, the massive outline of Derek had sprung up from nowhere and had suddenly pushed Jeff to the ground.

"What the hell was that for?" Jeff had asked in a decidedly put out voice.

"Look at the windmills in the gardens" Derek had whispered hastily. Sure enough they were in the shape of a cross.

"Christ, I nearly walked into that" Jeff had hissed.

"So did I" Derek had replied "but the neighbours are noisy and restless" pointing to a faint movement near the wall approaching the Cellars. "Michael has gone to another area to suss out the situation there".

Just then there had been an explosion near the Cellars and a few troopers rushed forward out of hiding.

"It's a bloody fox you got, stupid" one of the troopers had crowed "so much for getting them with your booby trap. Wilson will do his nut getting him out on a wild goose chase just because you insist on using your poaching skills to catch our friends".

As Jeff and Derek had hunkered down they had heard the engine of a jeep approaching. It pulled up and out had jumped Wilson.

"Well what happened here?" he had demanded. It had been the first time that Jeff had seen the man who had been hunting him.

Wilson was about 5ft 10ins, very stocky with cropped hair.

"Jones set up a booby trap to catch the rebels" the Sergeant in charge of the troops had said to Wilson "all he got was a fox for his efforts".

Wilson went to Jones and had said "Have you got an infinite space between the ears? I need them unharmed for questioning. They now have important papers from Councillor Randle's place and I need to find those papers. Whilst I don't care what you do to them or their women I need to be able to question them, not pick up their pieces from the surrounding trees because you want to play poacher. You're not mentally qualified for handicap parking, get out of my sight".

A second jeep had then pulled up and the officer who they had seen at the Sports Centre had jumped out.

"Not a very good day for you is it? It looks like the lights are on but no-one's at home" Wilson had said to him "firstly, you let a small number of civilians overwhelm you, leave you tied up with your trousers round your ankles, they take your guns and escape to the police authorities. Then we find that Councillor Randle's house who your squad was supposed to be guarding was broken into and papers we needed to keep secret were taken. Then quite by chance on a raid I carried out in a computer shop I find some copies of the original pages of these documents we are looking for left on a copier. Now I leave you and your men on stake out duty to see if we can catch any of them if they come back and you advertise you're here by letting off a grenade. Is there anymore stupidity in your family or is it that God has a sense of humour and you're the proof? Is all the stupidity here in one box?

Now you've destroyed the element of surprise you better get your men to stand down and tell them to make safe any booby traps in case they blow themselves up and advertise this covert operation to police and army authorities".

"Aren't we under martial law orders from the Government? And don't the police authorities take orders from us? So why is this operation covert?" the officer had asked.

"You ask too many questions. You take your orders from me, and if you don't like it I can remove you from command now" Wilson had stated, drawing a gun and pointing it at the officer "and you and your family will go to the camps, is that understood? Now get your men squared away or do I relieve you of your command?"

"Sir!" the officer had responded hastily then had added "I will get the men squared away now Sir". Then he had barked "Jones! Front and centre. Get these men squared away and if you so much as breathe wrong I'll nail you to the wall, understand?"

Derek had whispered "That was close. We need to find a safe place to bed down".

"Wait a minute, let's see what Wilson does" Jeff had whispered and had placed a restraining hand on Derek's shoulder.

"I'm off" Wilson had said "and don't disturb me unless you have any of them in custody". He had climbed back into the jeep and had driven off.

"Nasty bastard Colin" a sergeant had said to the officer "when I signed up for this lot, it was to protect the country from terrorists, not to beat up and bully my own people. I can't say I'm happy about that, also, how come we've never received written orders confirming Wilson's authority. We only have his word for it, and have you thought from what we hear that that Jeff bloke might be right and if that's the case we're in deep shit and those people that humiliated us, they would have killed us all if it wasn't for him. And, we would have deserved it for the way the men acted until you and I stopped them. Those girls were right, they acted like animals".

"That's enough Sergeant Bates, we agreed to the money we are paid to do this job, so don't question orders, we have to obey them until we know otherwise, understood?"

"Yes, but not to the point of being robots for some megalomaniac" Sergeant Bates had said "that's how Hitler started".

"That's enough I said. You don't want me to tell Wilson you now want out because you think the going is getting tough and you are now having second thoughts?"

With that remark the colour had drained from Sergeant Bates' face and the fear had showed. He knew how nasty Wilson could be.

"By the way, don't call me by my first name, it's sir to you, understand."

"That sounds like dissention in the ranks" Derek had whispered to Jeff "let's go, we need to get to another area to see if Michael found out if there is anyone around?"

They had carefully made their way there keeping alert for any small units like the one they had nearly stumbled across by looking out for windmill vanes in the shape of a kiss instead of a cross.

"Over here it's safe" they had heard Michael call softly as they had approached the area and what had been left of another public house. It was then that Jeff had noticed one or two windmills in gardens or on houses with the vanes in the shape of a kiss.

"See it works" Cyril had said as he had greeted them "how did you get on? We had fun whilst you were away with Wilson's troops. There's not many of them by the looks of it. We think there's only one small squad on the Estuary, and they look reluctant to carry out the orders Wilson is giving them".

"We ran into them twice" Derek had said and told them of the incident with the trucks and how they thought they were going to shoot all the civilians and how they had humiliated the troops by disarming them and getting them to drop their trousers earlier in the day, and the recent run in at the Cellars.

"No wonder Wilson is pissed off big time" Cyril had said "things don't seem to be going his way."

Good" Jen had said with a saucy smile on her face as she had come out of the shadows. She had given all three of them a hug "take a load off your feet, and rest up. We have more recruits to keep an eye open for trouble. And by the way did you notice you had a hard job getting around the debris? That's been put there to delay any troops in case they accidently find out where we are? That was my idea".

Then she had said proudly "You walked past five of the new recruits without seeing them. Michael did better than you two. He spotted them after he passed the first two. We told the pickets to keep an eye open for you.

Now we'll let the other safe areas know that you're with us and safe".

"There are other safe areas?" Jeff had queried.

"Yes" Jen had replied "we haven't sat on our hands whilst you've been off gallivanting. We located a few structurally safe places that can house families, appointed someone to take control, as smaller units of people can move faster than large ones, shared out our rations with them, so at least they can eat for a few days until we can decide what our best course of action is.

We can send runners to the other safe locations in no time at all. Come on, you must be hungry, we'll talk about this over something to eat and a cup of tea".

"You're well sorted out" Derek had said admiringly.

"It takes a woman to get you men organised" Jen had retorted laughingly.

"I'm not going down that road again" Jeff had said "the last time I had this type of conversation with you I took a good hiding".

Jen had laughed.

They had sat down, ate a warm meal of rabbit stew and then had drunk the hot tea with no milk.

CHAPTER 27

"So, what have you been up to?" Jen had asked when they were alone "and what did you find?"

Jeff had told her about the papers they had found in Councillor Randle's house and had passed her the copies he had taken for her to read adding "I haven't had time to read and digest them properly yet myself, but from the initial reading it opens a can of worms and Sir William and this Wilson bloke are in it, right up to their necks, as are other Government officials who have had their pockets lined and these papers prove it.

Randle names the people that are involved in those documents. They cover the junkets they got invited to, deals that they got a backhander from, free holidays for themselves and their families, cars, and other gifts. All are listed. It runs into millions and once in they stayed in, or they had a visit from Wilson. Apparently, at one time there were four people who wanted out, but after a visit from Wilson one changed his mind, two had fatal accidents, and one apparently committed suicide.

It's all there and it was Randle's guarantee of safety, but he obviously did not take into consideration that Wilson is a megalomaniac and he wanted those papers and snapped Randle's neck to get them and made it look like a break in by looters. What Wilson didn't know was that there was another compartment to the safe with access by a hidden lever at the back of the safe. He did not know they were there, he only got what was in the front of the safe".

"These are copies, where are the originals?" Jen had asked.

"As I said to our Government friend John, safe" Jeff had answered.

"You don't trust anybody do you?" Jen had asked.

"It's not that I don't trust you, it's more a case of if you don't know you can't get killed for not knowing and I trust you with my life and the copies of these papers but I don't want to see you be heroes where Wilson is concerned. He's a killer with no scruples, that's why Sir William chose him.

So what's been happening with you lot today? Jeff had asked just as Cyril came in the door.

"Cyril just missed being seen by a maniac driving a green Jag going towards the Terminal" Jen had replied.

"I thought you weren't going to take risks after the last episode" Jeff had said turning to Cyril.

"There's more than one way into that Terminal without being seen, besides, what I learned from Wilson's henchmen I think is important".

"And if you'd got caught, I would have lost a friend, and Jen would have lost someone she loves dearly. Don't you think there's been enough killing? Remember these bastards play for keeps. Promise me you won't risk your life unnecessarily".

Resignedly he had looked at Cyril and said "So consider yourself told off because I care ok?" and he had smiled.

Cyril had given him a look as if to say I hear what you say but I am not listening then Cyril had given him a mock rude sign.

"Did you see what he just did" Jeff had said to Jen pointing at Cyril "I'm mortified".

"Pack it in you two, you're worse than a couple of kids".

"Well, what did you learn?" Jeff had asked.

Cyril looked at him like a little boy who had been told off and praised at the same time "Well, I overheard them saying that they're moving the papers from the Terminal. To avoid any suspicion, they are burning them at the tip as smoke coming from the Terminal would cause raised eyebrows but smoke coming from the tip would look natural".

"Who's taking these papers to the tip and when are they doing it?" Jeff had asked.

"Well, I understand Wilson's second in command (weasel of a man) was getting transport from the mainland, a Jag I think. I didn't hear that bit clearly" Cyril had replied.

Derek who had been standing by the door had said "There was the green Jag missing from Councillor Randle's underground car parking place in his back garden".

"If they use that Jag and the police pull them up and tie it in with the hit and run that killed that police inspector the police will show them no mercy" Jeff had said.

"What police inspector?" Cyril had asked.

"It's a long story and I'll tell you about it later" Jeff had replied.

Cyril had added "That's not all I heard. I overheard them boasting about the massive bonus they were going to receive after tomorrow. That's when Sir William takes over the country with his vote of no confidence in the Prime Minister, after which he'll install martial law using the units he has in place in strategic places now, all ready to take control. I also took some photos of who was there and of them destroying evidence. Plus, they were also making a recording that sounded like a terrorist threat that they were going to say they had received".

"Well, it looks like events are overtaking us" Jeff had said "there's not a lot of time left to get the people that are left on the Estuary safe and the papers we have sent to the media before they are taken over by Sir William. Also, we must get a message out to John as soon as possible so he can nail them at his end".

"Drink your tea first and then get in touch" Jen had said "you've been at it all day. We'll give you privacy if that's what you want".

"It's too late for secrets between us" Jeff had said "we've been through too much now to have secrets from one another".

He had picked up the mobile phone and had rung the number John had given him. He had heard John's voice at the other end of the phone. Jeff had told him what they had found out between them all and about the coup that was set for tomorrow, then had asked him if he had received the fax which had been sent of the papers from Councillor Randle's house.

"Do you want me to pick your people up tonight?" John had asked "if so, how many are there?"

"First thing in the morning, about 8 am" Jeff had replied "I'll need to get them all together. I'm not sure how many at this moment in time but we'll be at the side of the Golf Course".

"Bring the original papers with you, so we can study them", John had ordered.

As John had rung off, Jeff had heard him say to someone "Yes, we have them all at last".

Jeff had had a nagging feeling of doubt in the back of his mind to which he could not put his finger on but he put it down to nerves.

"What's up?" Jen had asked him.

Jeff had told them about the conversation he had had and then added "I'm not sure. Things just don't ring true, but perhaps it's just me and I'm just getting nervous".

They had all sat around a makeshift table, drinking tea and discussing their options and how to avoid Wilson's men or if necessary take them on.

A man had come in who Jeff had not seen before, it was obvious he had been listening to the conversation. The man had said "It's not up to us to take on the professionals, we're not trained for it. We're better off out of it". Then he had added "If they said they would pick up our people at 8 am in the morning then that's great, we can consider it's all over and that's got to be good. All this ducking and diving will be over and we can rebuild our lives".

"This is my nephew Alan" Cyril had said "he's come in this morning to help us. He works at Scotland Yard".

Jeff had eyed the man up and down. For some reason he did not trust the man but he could not put his finger on the reason why.

"I see you're a doubting Thomas?" Alan had said "you don't want to believe this is over do you?" Then he had added "You've been fighting the establishment for so long you don't know how to stop. You want it to carry on, don't you?"

Jeff had just raised an eyebrow, he had heard pigs fart before, but he had said nothing.

Then very rudely Alan had said "I believe it's your only purpose in life, there's nothing else for you".

Then because he had not received any reaction from Jeff, he had accusingly said "You have to have a reason for your ego trip, so you can be the people's hero. I for one will be glad to help clear this mess up and build us back up to a normal life and get my uncle back with his sister, she needs him and he's suffered enough".

Jeff had seen red and could not control his temper anymore. He flew for the man. Derek had grabbed him and had held him back.

"You consider that I'm on some ego trip and what's happened here can be returned to normal?" Jeff had snapped furiously.

"We have to rebuild and rise like a phoenix out of the ashes" Alan had taunted.

"The ashes of those hundreds of children, families, and all that devastation, that's a price too high for me, and I believe someone should pay for that" Jeff had said "we should fight until the end".

"What is the end, everybody killed?" Alan had asked "you said, according to the phone call you just had with your mysterious contact whoever they are, that according to you we have to trust them, that they'll take us safely out of here, therefore we should go".

"Let's see what the others think first shall we?" Jeff had asked, ignoring the retort and starting to calm down.

"Well, we need to let them know about tomorrow at the Golf Club and the meeting at 0800 hours" Alan had said, and then he added "so if you like I'll go to the other locations with my uncle and tell them about the meeting. By the way, are you bringing any papers with you? If there are a lot I can help you with them".

"No need, I can get them from their safe hiding place on my own when they're required" Jeff had replied warily.

"Don't be so touchy, I was only trying to help, that's all" Alan had said, holding his hands up in mock surrender, then he had turned to Cyril "if you show me on the map where all the other groups are, we can start out now as soon as I get my stuff".

The two of them had huddled together over a map of the Estuary for a while and then Alan had got up and left.

"Who is he?" Jeff had asked Cyril, once they were alone.

"He's my sister's boy. He asked her if he could help us and she sent him over to us" Cyril had explained "he might be a bit hot headed but I'll vouch for him."

"Are you sure?" Jeff had asked.

"You doubt him, you doubt me" Cyril had spat and then had stormed out in a huff.

"Ok, you win" Jeff had shouted after him "I'm sorry".

They had drunk their tea in silence, then after a while Jen had said "You don't seem convinced? Cyril's been with us from the start, he was shot defending what we all believe in".

"It's not that I don't trust Cyril, it's his nephew that I'm not so sure of. Perhaps I'm being a cynical old bastard" Jeff had replied wryly.

"Well, you spoke to that bloke John on the phone and he's arranging it all so what are you worried about?" Jen had enquired.

"Yeah, but I am worried. He forgot to call me dad in our conversation or refer to any tobacco which was our password" Jeff had answered.

"Well, call him back using a different number if you're so worried" Jen had urged cynically "you've upset Cyril to let him think you don't trust him after all we've been through but if you feel you need to check up on your information, use one of the numbers you had before to contact this John bloke".

"Why is it women always use common sense in these situations?" Jeff had mused smiling at her and had taken out the mobile phone. He had dialled a previous number knowing he was taking a chance on being tracked and traced to his location.

After a while, John's voice had answered the phone saying "It's for me, it's my dad. I'm sorry, I told him not to call me here, I'll take it in the other room" and then Jeff had heard a door close.

"What the hell are you doing calling me on this phone for?" John's voice had snapped "I thought I gave you a different number to ring".

"You did, and I just phoned you on it and you said you were going to pick us all up at 0800 hours tomorrow with all the paperwork that you wanted".

"What, I said that? When did I say that?" John had asked instantly, his tone alert.

"An hour and half an hour ago. It was your voice on the phone I'll swear to it" Jeff had replied.

"It wasn't me. Whoever it was might have used a voice replication machine. I've been in this meeting for over two hours" John had explained "did I mention our password, tobacco or my dad?"

"No" Jeff had replied "but it sounded so like you".

Then the realisation had suddenly struck him "So, you have a traitor in your organisation" he had said.

"That's what this meeting has been about" John had replied "we caught a traitor who has been a leak in our organisation for years, and he was copying those papers you sent and was sending them on to Wilson, but Sir William denies any involvement.

The man died sending the last message and we can't prove a direct link to Sir William yet, but we're working on it. My people are studying those copies you sent and we believe there's a link that proves that Sir William is in it right up to his neck but we need the originals to prove it, so I hope you have them somewhere safe".

"I have, but don't take too long proving that link. We're out on a limb here" Jeff had said "also I think we also might have a traitor in our midst as well".

"If the shit hits the fan make your way to any Army post outside the direct perimeter as I don't think the inner ones are safe" John had said.

"Now you tell me. When all these people are going right near one of them at 0800 hours ready to be rescued" Jeff had said.

"What stupid person thought that one up?" John had asked "they must think electricity bill is a rock star."

"You did in your last conversation with me" Jeff had said "which I was stupid enough to tell everybody here about".

"Then Sir William and Wilson are getting desperate and you're hurting them big time, and like you I believe it's a trap they've set for you" John had finally concluded "remember, Sir William at the moment only has small private troop units with which to operate with. He uses Wilson and pressurises the local Army pickets into doing what he wants. If they catch everybody there now with those small units they can nip any local opposition in the bud, also, it stops you getting any more information on them, and then they can cover everything up and tip the delicate balance in their favour. Added to that, they count on you being soft enough and giving them that paperwork if they torture or threaten to kill your new found friends. If they get that paperwork they've won. So they mustn't get their hands on it no matter what it costs, also the people they intend to trap have to be warned. I'll do what I can at my end but it will be a close run thing. I must go now or Sir William will get suspicious and if that happens he'll cover up everything he is doing up. Everything is very finely balanced on a knife edge at the moment.

Jeff had gone to find Jen and had asked her where Cyril and his nephew were. She told him that they'd gone to the other safe houses to get the people to meet tomorrow morning at 8 am by the Golf Course.

Jeff had told her about the conversation he had just had with John.

Jen had replied "How can you trust this second person called John that you spoke to. Cyril's nephew is an officer stationed at Scotland Yard and is on compassionate leave, as his mum, who is Cyril's sister is seriously ill. He seems well informed and certain it's over, and that the relief forces will be here tomorrow. Cyril swears by what his nephew says".

"I don't know why, but I have this feeling about tomorrow morning, that it's a trap" Jeff had said "but I can't prove it".

"Well there's not a lot you can do tonight as we don't know which way they went. Besides, we can intercept them in the morning before they get to the Golf Course" Jen had said "now tell me how you got on today? I gather you had some fun, safe breaking and nearly being caught sending copies of papers to your contact and then being chased back here, by the way, where are those original documents? You didn't have them on you and I heard Cyril's nephew asking Derek and Michael about them. He seemed anxious to see them. When they told him you had gone off on your own to hide them, he wanted to know where, but they couldn't or wouldn't tell him".

"I believe the fewer people that know where they are the fewer people can get hurt. It's not that I don't trust you it's because I think too highly of you to get you hurt unnecessarily" Jeff had answered "but I will tell you what's in them and how it opens up a whole can of worms and it names the people involved".

He had explained to her the names of the people named in the documents and how they were involved.

"That's a bundle of dynamite, no wonder they want you dead" Jen had said.

"Well" Jeff had continued "apparently Councillor Randle was responsible for co-ordinating all the safety issues involving any Top Tier COMAH sites in the area and the relative agencies such as the Health & Safety and the Environmental Agencies and the Emergency services.

His reports were supposed to make sure all safety aspects had been taken into consideration appertaining to the surrounding community and including them in the land use planning, bearing in mind the totality of effect of a worst case scenario at the planning permission stage.

If he hid any of the dangers reported, or failed to add them into his report, or did not let one agency know there was a problem that might affect their individual reports then on reading those reports the councillors and planning officials would be getting false information when making their decision, so then the planning permission would go through relatively smoothly.

The documents not only list the names of the people involved, but the reports that were covered up, by whom, and when. It was an accident waiting to happen and it puts Sir William Waite right in the frame as there are receipts of monies paid by him to Randle and records of other payments to other officials. Randle knew he was being investigated by some of his fellow councillors who had had him under suspicion for some time and he had told Wilson that he had this documentation to safeguard himself, but I think Wilson killed him to shut him up. It takes a professional to break a neck like that".

Jen had said "Do you mean to say that in the grand scheme of things there is a process that safeguards communities from too much conflagration of high fire risk industry being sited close to them?"

"Yes" Jeff had replied "it came about at a meeting I attended with County councillors. At that meeting I was insisting that the County Council Emergency Co-ordinating Committee use its powers that it held under the Civil Contingencies Act, to safeguard against a worst case scenario disaster, as the Government does not have a safe siting policy for Top Tier COMAH sites. The County Council are ultimately responsible for search and rescue after a major incident involving massive amounts of deaths, injuries, and areas requiring evacuation in that emergency".

"So what went wrong here?" Jen had asked.

"Councillor Randle hid the evidence of the worst case scenario reports from the councillors and officers so when they went to a public inquiry to oppose the plans they did not have the damning reports that would have won them the case, so Sir William Waite used Councillor Randle and bent all the rules and got his planning permission".

"So if Wilson or Sir William get to you with all this information and quietly dispose of you, it stifles the information, he covers his tracks and wins, then takes over the country" Jen had said "how come he hasn't taken you out earlier?"

"Because first he thought I had died in the explosion that took out the Estuary area, and then he found out somehow about my cancelled meeting that was transferred to the mainland, then he thought I was killed in the building collapse now he knows otherwise. All the time I could keep the issues in the public media he would not attack me physically. All he did was to try to discredit me, and make me out to be some sort of anarchist. But now the media attention has been focused on terrorism that has all changed. He can attack me, and accuse me of terrorism. He wants me dead any way he can get me. All the time he believed I was dead, I was safe, as soon as he finds out I'm alive and with enough evidence to hang him, my life won't be worth a plugged nickel and he will do anything or use anybody to get to me. The meeting at the Golf Course worries me. It's too slick and I think it's a trap".

"Well we can't do anything tonight" Jen had said soothingly "you get some sleep, there are enough people on watch out there that you did not see on your way in that will warn us. I will try to intercept the others and warn them in the morning".

"You believe it's a trap as well?" Jeff had asked.

"I'm not sure, but like you say something doesn't ring true, but I don't know what it is, so I will give it the benefit of the doubt for now. Have some bread and cheese, cup of tea and sleep on it, and sort it out in the morning" Jen had said.

Jeff had taken a chunk of cheese, a doorstep of bread, and a mug of tea and had found himself a corner to settle down in to where he could contemplate what to make of all that had happened in the last few days and how desperate their situation was getting. He had eventually fallen asleep mulling over the problems.

CHAPTER 28

Back on board the Baroness of the Sea, they entered the Restaurant area where the Sheik's bodyguards were searching everybody as they entered the Restaurant. One particular guard was freer with his hands than was absolutely necessary and was taking his time frisking the women intensively. This resulted in reactions from the women and their partners and a rebuff from the guards.

"This should be interesting" Cyril said.

"Don't you do anything" Jen warned him "I can deal with it in my own way".

As the guard started to frisk Jen, he put his hand on her chest and took his time feeling her breasts. Jen promptly placed her hand over his and held it to her chest between her breasts, gripping very tightly. She leaned forward, pinning the guard's hand against her chest.

The guard could not remove his hand which was flat against Jen's chest because of Jen's vice-like grip. As Jen bowed the guard's fingers and wrist were bent backwards and the more Jen bowed forward the more the guard's fingers and wrist were bent backwards. The guard went down on his knees, leaning backwards as he desperately tried to avoid more pain from his trapped hand, hoping his wrist did not snap. The leering grin he had had on his face faded to one of surprise and then agony as he tried to remove his hand but Jen would not let go.

The two other guards who had been laughing at first at their friend's predicament, now started to react to their friend's screams.

Things happened very quickly. Cyril stepped behind one guard and with his thumbs extended jammed both hands together either side of the guard's head in the area just below the ears. The guard sank to the ground. The other guard was trying to raise his gun to open fire but he found himself held in a vice-like grip by Derek who had put him in a bear hug and was crushing his ribs.

Mustafa came running up with more guards and ordered them to fire into the ceiling above everyone's heads.

Derek dropped the unconscious guard to the floor. Jen released the other guard who was screaming in agony and holding his hand because with the resultant increase of pressure, two of his fingers had snapped.

"What is going on here" Mustafa asked loudly.

Jen smiled and said "Your man was not treating us women as ladies and was pawing all the women when searching them" pointing at the unfortunate guard holding his hand. "He wanted to put his hands on my chest so I let him then held his hand there and bowed to him".

Mustafa questioned the injured guard harshly.

When he had received the answers he wanted he kicked the crestfallen guard then turned towards Jen trying hard to hide the grin on his face and said "He will think twice before manhandling the Sheik's guest. The Sheik will hear of this. You are shall we say, a guest in his tent and as such his staff must accord you guest rights".

Turning to Jeff Mustafa said "You and all your party will be treated with respect at all times. All I can do is apologise for this fool's behaviour and he will be dealt with accordingly".

"The other guards reacted to his pain and were going to attack me" Jen said "my husband protected me as any man of honour would do, as did this poor unfortunate friend of ours" pointing to Derek who immediately adopted the look of an unfortunate idiot.

Mustafa looked at Jen wryly and said "I will guarantee you your safety all the time you have guest rights, and no women will be molested. We are not animals. Anyway I do not think any guards will manhandle anymore women on board this ship especially after this last demonstration. He will be taking a lot of insults from his fellow guards as he deserved what he received. All I can do is to apologise on behalf of the Sheik". To the other men he said amusingly "remind me not to upset you" then he left three guards on guard duty by the door and carried away the unconscious and injured guards.

"I could have told him not to upset Jen" Cyril said as Mustafa left.

"How did you do that?" Karen said to Jen admiringly "all I saw you do was lean forward and then he was screaming in agony".

Jen said "I had older brothers who taught me self-defence. I'll teach you what I know, it might come in handy".

"How did you do that trick?" Karen asked.

"When he had his hand on my chest with his fingers pointing upwards" Jen explained and she demonstrated "as I held his hand in place so he could not remove it, I then bowed forward trapping his hand. The more I leant forward the more I bent his fingers backward therefore snapping his wrist and fingers".

"We need these to protect us" Derek said, pointing at Karen and Jen "all we have to do is organise them into an army".

As they sat down to lunch, Jeff said to John and Cyril "Derek may have a point there about organising the women as a fighting team".

"What!" Cyril exclaimed "Jen might be capable of handling herself, but not every woman can".

"Whoa, back tiger" Jeff said "think about it. We need to communicate with other passengers freely and co-ordinate any action we will have to take later. What better way than using the women to spread what we are doing to the other passengers in secret".

"That puts the women in danger and no-one is going to let that happen especially me as far as Jen is concerned" Cyril said very arrogantly.

"You what?" Jen exclaimed.

"Neutral corners you two" Jeff said "before we have a domestic in front of all the passengers. Listen to what I have to say first then let me have your opinion.

Have you noticed, women always seem to go to the Ladies' Restroom in twos and threes, unlike men. Men normally go on their own".

"We taught you little boys how to do that when you were very small" Jen joked "then we let you do it on your own, at least that was something you learned" she continued sarcastically.

"What I am talking about is, as women meet in the toilets more times than men and in greater numbers we can let the women be our secret communication system between one another and as the guards wont disturb the women not after today's incident all the guards will do is stand outside the toilets. The women can communicate inside and pass on information without the guards finding out. It's not unusual for two women to go to the toilet together whereas it is unusual for men to do it and it will allay any suspicion being aroused by the guards".

Just then a waiter came to their table and addressing Jeff said "Your tea, Sir" and placed a tray of tea in front of him.

"I don't remember ordering tea" Jeff said as he lifted the napkin. The napkin was covering a plate of small pancakes on the tray. As he looked at the pancakes he realised that there was finely piped wording written on the pancakes '1000 hours, 7th'.

"We have less than two days before the deadline is reached" Jeff said, handing round the small pancakes showing what was written on them. After everybody had read the message, the pancakes were consumed.

"I knew you would have to eat your own words someday. Now that's a first" Cyril joked.

"You can eat the next communication" Jeff said to Cyril "this will create havoc with my figure if I carry on like this".

"What figure?" Cyril bantered, and they both laughed.

"Well, it seems to work" Jeff said "now let's get organised and plan what we can do and when we can do it".

They settled down into a huddle.

"Somehow we need to knock out the guards on both ships at the same time. That's going to be very hard to do and will need some organising".

"We will need to speak to that First Officer again" John said.

Derek's wife Sandra spoke up and said "I wonder if they have any Tamasipan on board in the Medical Centre".

"What's Tamasipan? Derek asked.

"It's a bitter tasting substance that is misused as a date rape drug" Sandra replied "it can knock a horse out. Also, it's a medicine that should be carried by all medical centres. If you can get the guards on both ships to take some it would put them out for quite some time. We could get it injected into sweet chocolates by the Chef, or sprinkled onto a strong curry. I understand Middle Eastern people have a very sweet tooth and like spicy food".

"Brilliant" Derek said "you're not just a pretty face but intelligent as well" and he turned to her and hugged her.

"There are intelligent women as well you know" Sandra said from within the circle of his arms.

"Hey big boy" Jen said, slapping Derek on the back in a friendly way "don't think you men have all the brains. It's men's thinking that gets us into the problems we have today".

"Ok, let's get back to the matter in hand" John said "what Sandra suggested is a brilliant idea. We need to put that to the First Officer to see if it can be arranged. What we have to work to is a timeframe of at least half an hour before the deadline, that's 0930 hours the day after tomorrow".

Just at that moment, Jen spotted a female Entertainments Officer by the door near the Ladies' Restroom. She said to the others "No time like the present, nature calls" and hurried to the Ladies' Restroom, passing one of the guards who followed her towards the toilets. Jen spoke to the Entertainments Officer and they both went into the toilet together. The guard hesitated about following them inside appeared to make up his mind and stayed outside waiting for them to reappear.

Just as they were discussing ways to administer the drug to the guards, Mustafa came into the room and approached them.

"You look agitated" he said to Jeff "what are you up to?" Then turning to Cyril he asked "is there a problem?"

"My wife has just gone to the Ladies' Restroom and your guard was going to go in as well" Cyril said "if he does go in I don't rate his chances".

"You could not reach him before he put a bullet in you" Mustafa said "I will go and have a word with him".

Mustafa went over to the guard and spoke to him in Arabic.

Cyril said to the others "I wasn't worried for myself or Jen, it would be the guard that would have come off worse".

They all smiled and Derek said "She has a fearsome temper".

Mustafa returned and said "There is no need to worry. I have reminded the guard that you are the Sheik's guests and as such you are to be treated with the greatest respect as will your women".

Then Mustafa added "The Sheik is concerned that a plot is being hatched by a few officers to free everybody, but I advised him that that was impossible as there were not enough of them and they would have to co-ordinate a plan that would mean taking over both ships simultaneously. He also feared the women were part of that plot, that is why he was going to follow them into the toilet".

"He would not have come out of there a whole man if he had done that" Cyril said.

"As I said" Mustafa said "you would not have reached him and unfortunately would have been shot in the process and we would have breached guest rights as you are under our protection as our guests. Don't worry your head about your women. I have left instructions that the guards will not molest or follow empty headed, chattering women into toilets. That would serve no purpose, and it would only unnecessarily inflame the men on board and could cause unrest. We in our country don't allow women to be part of any decision making as women are put on this earth to please their men, but we will discourage any group meetings of any of the men, excluding meal times of course, because that is when you will be under scrutiny by the guards.

I came to tell you that the Sheik would like a word with you after you have had your lunch" Mustafa said "he would value your opinion on a little matter that affects you all, shall we say 1400 hours?" He then turned on his heels and walked away.

"What an arrogant person" Rose said "doesn't he know women stopped being chattels for men over a hundred years ago?"

"It is the way they think in his country" John said.

"That could be to our advantage" Jeff said "by leading them into a false sense of security. As you know I led them to believe Derek is a harmless nit-wit, but we know that he is very powerful and very intelligent.

If we can make them believe we treat our women as chattels and don't take any heed to anything they say, they will think that is normal. We can then use that as an advantage, and the women can carry out the vital role of communications right under their noses in secret. It can all be done in all the Ladies' Restrooms throughout the ship".

Just then, Jen returned and Cyril explained to her what had happened whilst she was in the Ladies' Restroom.

"He would have been singing soprano if he had come in" Jen said.

"See, I told you she had a fearsome temper" Derek said "even I avoid upsetting her, and she would have crucified that guard had he entered the Restroom wouldn't she?" Turning to Cyril.

Cyril answered "And then some. When I said to Mustafa I was concerned over the situation he thought I was going to attack his guard to protect Jen, it would have been the guard who needed protection from Jen".

"Well enough of that" Jen said "that female Entertainments Officer I have just met is going to help by being a go-between between the officers and passengers but it has to be co-ordinated and before 10 am tomorrow, that is the deadline, so we have to have a co-ordinated plan of attack by then.

But according to her there is still one other major problem. They have placed explosives against the bulkheads of the Baroness of the Sea which can be detonated by a plunger near the explosives. Apparently we are lucky they are not remotely controlled".

John said "Our biggest problem is the crew on the NATGAS 2 tanker. If they get wind of anything amiss they will use the gas valves on the tanker. We need to silence them first and the only way to get to the NATGAS 2 is via Deck 5 and that is guarded".

"We need to find and disarm the explosives on board this ship" Cyril said.

"Then we need to cut free the Baroness of the Sea from the NATGAS 2 and get the two ships at least ten miles apart" Jeff said "whoever takes on the NATGAS 2 will be on a suicide mission".

At the same time all the guards have to be disabled on board this ship, all in the space of 36 hours by ordinary people and a few cruise ship staff" Derek said "no pressure then. What bright bastard thought that one up for us?"

"We also need to get a message to the Americans, hopefully before they blow us out of the water" Jen said "tell them what we are planning to do without the Sheik or any of his cronies finding out".

"How are we going to co-ordinate all this if you men aren't allowed to talk to the male members of the crew" Jeff's wife asked.

"We need to see the Captain and find out if he can get a message out to the Americans from his Radio Room and help organise his crew".

"There is another complication" Jen said "according to Mary that female Officer I spoke to, the Captain is kept locked in his cabin with two guards outside when he is not on the Bridge".

"Then I will visit him in his cabin" Cyril said "and have a word with him to find out what can be done".

"How are you going to get to him?" John asked "he is guarded at all times".

"If I know Cyril he'll find a way" Jeff said.

"Is there something I don't know?" John asked.

"Let me introduce you to the now retired Squirrel" pointing at Cyril "and he can get in anywhere if he wants to. He does not have that nickname Squirrel for nothing" Jeff said.

"Your reputation precedes you" John said "I never knew it was you, I have heard of you under that name, but only by the reputation of being one of the best tea-leafs in the world".

"How do you think we got that information about Sir William Waite out of the Terminal and to you, right from under their noses?"

"I never knew" John said "what a dark horse you are".

"Never mind, that I will go and have a chat with the Captain" Cyril said.

"Be careful dear" Jen said "I don't want to lose you now I have found you".

"There's no fear of that you sexy thing" Cyril said.

"Cyril!" Jen said "you'll make me blush".

"I'll be a little while, you keep everything warm till I get back" and he kissed her and slipped away.

Jen coloured up embarrassingly, and then lovingly said "I will sort you out later" as he walked off.

"I will have a wander around to see if I can find out where these explosive devices have been put" John said "and before you say anything" he interjected "I used to be a demolitions expert for the Army before I worked for the PM so I do know what I am doing. I will know the best places where to put explosive devices. If I can, I'll disable them without being discovered, but I'll have to find them first and I don't know how many there are".

Before he left, Rose said "Please take care of yourself". John squeezed her hand lovingly as he left.

"I have to go and see the Sheik" Jeff said "what about, I do not know, but Mustafa said the Sheik wants a word with me. Perhaps I can find out what he intends to do, knowing your enemy is half the battle".

"You'd better be careful as well" Karen said "I don't trust that Sheik".

"Neither do I" Jeff said "but it would help us if we know what he has planned and when he plans to do it. I will see you back in the cabin. Derek will see you are safe".

"No-one will harm you while I live" Derek said to her "you are all safe with me".

Jeff walked away to find the Sheik whilst the women went back to their cabins escorted by Derek.

Jeff new that the ladies could be in no safer hands than Derek's as Derek had saved him at the Estuary

CHAPTER 29

Jeff had woken with a start. It had still been dark outside but dawn had just been starting to break. He had been instantly alert to his surroundings seeing men, women and children sleeping all around him. He had assumed that all of them had come into the shelter overnight but none of them had disturbed him.

A little boy had been looking at Jeff wide-eyed from behind his sleeping mother and had whispered "You're our leader aren't you. You're going to save us all from the bad men. My mum said I wasn't to wake you up. I didn't, did I?"

"No" Jeff had replied soothingly to the little boy.

At that moment, the little boy's mother had woken up and had told the little boy off for disturbing Jeff in harsh whispers.

"He didn't, I was awake anyway" Jeff had said, attempting to stop the child from being reprimanded any further.

The boy had looked pleased with himself that he had been vindicated and had said "Did you really shoot that helicopter down, and shoot the man who killed my sister?"

"Jason" his mother had warned "you must not ask such rude questions of the nice man like that".

"Well did you?" the boy had asked, looking at him from wide and beguiling eyes.

"Well, if you mean the man who was in the helicopter who shot a young lady who was with a young man near the Cellars, then yes I did".

"I hope he died horribly" the little boy had said, the words shocking from such a young mouth.

"Jason" his mother had said again and then she had turned to Jeff "I'm sorry" she had said to him "we've been through a lot just lately and we'll be glad for it all to be over, but let me thank you for putting that animal away for good. We won't forget it and if it's any consolation my husband would have done the same if he had lived. He worked at the Terminal and died in the explosion. Even though he worked there he admired what you did and the principles that you stood by, not many men have those principles today".

Jeff had felt embarrassed by her praise, knowing that she had lost everything and would have to struggle to bring up her child, and he had said he was sorry for her loss and that he had to get things sorted and had hurried outside to look around.

"You're an early bird" a voice had announced behind him.

It was Cyril. "Sorry I went off in a huff last night, damned pride" he had said "Alan and I have always been close, but he gets headstrong sometimes and can only think of what suits him like most youngsters today. But I put him straight.

I sent him off to bring in the out-posts so we can all get everyone together and all meet up at the same time at the Golf Course but I understand from Jen you have reservations about your first message and about us all going there. You think it's a trap".

"Yes" Jeff had answered "but I can't put my finger on it, but things just don't ring true".

"Well, I'll take the people there and if it is a trap we'll be prepared for it" Cyril had replied, then said "you do what you do best, that's follow the evidence.

By the way, I heard that the papers that were in the Terminal Control Room are being moved to the tip this morning for burning by Wilson's second in command in that green Jag. You can cut him off if you go via the Creek crossing to the tip. He has to go all the way round via the mainland as he can only use the main road and he has to go through all the road blocks. You can get there before him if you use the pushbike you used to get here on the day we met. It's still by the old concrete bunker. I think there are a couple more there as well. I'll get Derek to go with you, he's a good man to have in a tight corner. By the way, I know how important this information is so I hope all this paperwork nails those bastards once and for all".

"How did you know about those papers being moved this morning?" Jeff had asked curiously.

"Alan said he overheard it when we went back to the Cellars to pick up any stragglers" Cyril had replied "he said Wilson had instructed the man to burn the papers at the tip as a fire there would raise less suspicion than a fire at the Terminal, which makes sense. Alan also said Wilson had mentioned that he would give the man the authorisation for him to get through the road blocks and to use the Jag to take it there as it would be easier to get a car through the picket lines than a lorry. When he got to the tip he was to burn the whole lot, Jag as well".

"Well, you're right. We must stop those papers from being burned if we can as they might be the final nail in those bastards' coffin" Jeff had said "I'll see Derek and see when we can get moving".

Jeff had turned to Cyril and said "I might not see you until later, so good luck. And I hope you, Jen and the people make it safely out of here. Don't forget to stay together as a group. Don't let them split any of you up as you have strength in numbers. Let everybody know what's happened here so as many people know as possible so it can't be covered up. It might be a good idea to share out the copies of some of the documents that I gave to Jen so everybody can have one page to hide. Carried that way, at least some copies might be saved". Then he had left.

Jeff had found Derek packing supplies in a knapsack. "I'm ready when you are" he had said to him.

"I want to say my goodbyes to Jen first" Derek had said "before we go. I'll catch you up, where will you be?"

"I'll make my way via the Cellars passing near to where I lived" Jeff had replied "I'll pick up something from there on my way past. I'll see you on the way".

Jeff had started to make his way to his bungalow, making use of the natural cover, glancing behind him as all the people started gathering together to make their way to the Golf Course.

He had made his way to his bungalow. It was as it had been since he had last been there. He had made his way over to his safe, opened it, retrieved the papers he had put in the safe and had checked to see if they were all there. He had then put them inside his jacket pocket and had started to leave.

A voice had suddenly said "I'll have those".

Jeff had spun round to face Alan, Cyril's nephew, who had been holding a gun in his left hand. It had been aimed at Jeff's chest.

"Very clever, hiding the documents in a place we have already searched. We never thought of that" Alan had said.

"I never trusted you, but Cyril will kill you for betraying everyone like this" Jeff had said, raising his hands slowly.

"He'll never find out. He and the rest of them pilgrims are being rounded up as we speak and they'll be in a concentration camp for many years as suspected terrorists. Anyway, if he did find out it was me, I'll be long gone, and spending the £2million pounds I get for you and these papers from Sir William" Alan had replied.

Alan had moved towards Jeff in a threatening manner and had said "I've been itching to take you out ever since you got me demoted a few years ago when one of your swampy mates had an accident and got killed in my custody. They didn't believe he fell down the stairs trying to escape".

Jeff had remembered the death in custody of his friend Doug only too well, and the hue and cry that had resulted at the time.

"Those stairs you mention only led down to the cells, so how could he have been escaping and in handcuffs?" Jeff had retorted.

"I can tell you now as you won't be around to repeat it" Alan had explained "he had the IQ of an ice cube, and he wouldn't tell me what I wanted to know about who was going to be at that demonstration? So, maybe I did hit him harder then I should have, it was his fault. If he had listened in the first place and told me who the others were, he wouldn't have died. You've been very elusive. I tried to get you and missed you when that building collapsed. I was spotted by that Government agent. He thought I was on his side until he stepped in front of me. His death was very quick. He didn't know I was trying to get those papers from you way back then. We knew if you and Bob married up the names on those lists it was only a matter of time before we would have been exposed and we could not risk that".

Jeff had looked at Alan. He had been holding the gun in his left hand. He had suddenly remembered that John's man was looking for a left hander or as he had said a 'southpaw'.

Alan had continued saying "Now it's going to be chalked up to terrorists and Sir William gets control of the country and I retire in luxury".

"So, if people don't do what you want, they die?" Jeff had asked "then you, Wilson and Sir William make good bed fellows. Your Uncle Cyril would kill you if he knew what you were really like".

"He's not likely to find out with you dead, him interned and me living the life of luxury I've always dreamed of" Alan had said confidently "Sir William helped me out when your friend Doug died. He covered for me then, and paid for an expensive Brief so no charges were brought, but I still got demoted and that you will pay for, and with the reward on your head, dead or alive, I can retire to a villa in Spain". Then he had added "I always believed revenge is best served cold, it's so much sweeter. And boy is this going to be sweet".

Jeff's mind had been racing. What could he do against what appeared to be a professional killer? Then he had an idea and on a wild guess had asked "Your last name is Wild isn't it? I read that name recently. I know, it's in some of those documents that Sir William wants so badly. Now I'm curious as to what you're going to do with the documents".

"What documents name me? And where are they?" Alan had asked suddenly uncertain.

"Some of these documents" Jeff had said pointing to the safe "or are you going to let Sir William have them? Then he can have a bigger hold over you then he has now".

Alan had looked confused as to what to do at that moment, and then he had said "I don't have time to look through all those papers and pick out the ones that affect me, so if you show me the right papers I'll make your death clean, if not, it's going to be very painful. Remember, I've killed before so no funny stuff.

Remember, I know where to hurt with or without it showing and don't forget you've been registered as dying in the explosion so you've been living on borrowed time, and that time has now run out".

Alan had moved slowly towards Jeff still holding the gun levelled at Jeff's chest "Let me have the relevant documents".

"I need to find them first" Jeff had said, making out that he was rummaging around in the safe, playing for time.

"Come on" Alan had said impatiently "don't mess me about". He fired a shot at Jeff. It ricocheted off of the ground near to where Jeff was standing.

"Ok, give me a chance to find the right pages" Jeff had said hurriedly "you want all of them don't you?"

"Yes, but be quick about it and stop stalling for time" Alan had ordered.

Jeff's mind had been doing overtime, trying to figure out how he could jump Alan and catch him unawares but Alan had been keeping a safe distance away from him. He would have to get him closer to stand a fighting chance of surprising him.

"Here are two of them" Jeff had said, holding up two pages "and there are some more pages with your name on them".

"Let's have them then" Alan had said.

Jeff had moved towards him, ready to spring at him when he had had the chance.

"That's far enough" Alan had said "you can put them down on the ground where you are and move back to the safe and carry on looking for more documents with my name on them".

Alan had picked up the papers and had started reading whilst keeping a watchful eye on Jeff and on what he was doing.

Alan had whistled and said "Councillor Randle had us all by the short and curlies. Anymore like these there?"

"I think so" Jeff had replied "I'll look".

After a few minutes, Alan had begun to get impatient "I am not waiting much longer, come on get a move on. Are there anymore or not?"

"Yes, here" Jeff had said, holding out a bundle of papers.

"Let's have them now" Alan had said, moving towards him.

Jeff had held out the papers, had pretended to stumble on the rubble, then had leapt at Alan throwing the papers in his face, and grabbing for the gun as it went off.

Jeff had felt a burning sensation in his ribs, but had managed to hold on to the hand holding the gun as he had struggled with Alan.

CHAPTER 30

Alan had been much younger and much fitter than Jeff was. All Jeff had was the distant memories of when he had done judo many years before when he had been a member of the Bank's judo team, so he had tried a judo throw in the hope that it would come off, and to his surprise it had.

Alan had been shocked as he went tumbling through the air and had landed heavily, the gun flying out of his hand. He had got up on his knees and had said "I didn't expect that from an old fart like you".

The gun had lain on the ground near Jeff but as he had reached for it Alan had grabbed a rock and had thrown it at Jeff, hitting him on the head. Jeff had gone down stunned.

As his head had cleared, Jeff had just make out Alan standing near him pointing the gun at him saying "I won't underestimate you again. It's time to meet your maker". As Alan had pointed the gun at him, Jeff had heard a salvo of shots but there was no pain.

Alan had collapsed in a heap.

Jeff had struggled to his feet and had been stunned to see Derek holding a smoking gun. "I didn't trust him either" Derek had said.

Jeff had said "Thank Christ you turned up when you did, I thought I was a goner".

"Jen told me to look after you. I promised her I would and I don't break my promises" the big man had smiled "the only thing is he got me too" and Derek had collapsed with blood pumping from a wound in his shoulder.

Jeff had ripped off his own shirt and had wrapped it around the wound in Derek's shoulder.

"That smarts" Derek had murmured as Jeff had used Derek's coat as a sling.

Derek had asked "How is our friend?"

"He's gone off" Jeff had replied.

"He was gone off years ago from what I hear" Derek had remarked.

"How are you feeling now?" Jeff had asked "and by the way what made you follow me here?"

"It was Michael's idea. He's got a lot more upstairs then people give him credit for.

If you think no-one knew where you were hiding your paperwork, he knew from day one, but he didn't tell anyone and he told me to check here first. Just as well. When I heard that first shot I thought I was too late, but I think I just made it, that little shit had it in for you".

"All I can say is thanks" Jeff had said "I owe you my life and I won't forget it".

"Well it's no good sitting here, we must get those other papers from Wilson's second in command at the tip if we are going to nail them all.

It's too late to warn Jen and Cyril, all we can hope for is if they heard those shots and that might alert them".

"Before you go anywhere" Jeff had said "I need to see that wound. It looks clean, and I think it missed the bone". Then Jeff jokingly had said "We don't need you bleeding all over creation just to get some sympathy from Jen".

Derek had blushed and said "Does it show that I think a lot of that girl".

"Just a bit" Jeff had replied "but I won't tell anybody" and then winced as he moved because his ribs were starting to hurt. He had looked down at his ribs to see a large bruise forming and a wound in his side.

"Not a very good shot was he?" Derek had said "you're not exactly a small target are you?" looking at Jeff' wound.

"Look who's talking you great lummox" Jeff had replied.

They had both started laughing at each other.

"Ouch, that smarts" they had both said together, then had laughed again.

"He couldn't hit a barn door at ten paces" Derek had said "I winged him with the first shot, now that got his attention. Then he fired at me, hit me in the shoulder at the same time as I got him again with the second shot. This time he went down for good.

Bloody amateurs, they pay peanuts they get monkeys. Fancy sending a boy to do a man's job, what do they expect".

Derek's shoulder had been a clean flesh wound and not as serious as it had first looked.

Jeff's wound had looked ugly but not life threatening. He thought he had a few broken ribs where the bullet had impacted them.

They had patched one another up with the cloth left from their shirts, put their jumpers back on and then their coats.

"Come on, we have a few things to do and places to be" Derek had said "can't sit here all day sunning ourselves".

Pulling Jeff to his feet gently Derek had said "We need to find those bikes, I hope some tea leaf hasn't nicked them".

They had both laughed.

Jeff had winced and had said "Stop making me laugh, it hurts my ribs".

"What do we do with him?" Derek had asked, pointing at the crumpled body of Cyril's nephew.

"Let him rot. Worms have got to eat" Jeff had replied callously "he would have let you rot if he'd had his way. I tell you what, if we see Cyril we'll let him know and then if he wants to he can claim the body".

They had made their way to the corner to find the bikes so they could cycle to the tip via the Barrier then onto the tip.

They had found the bikes hidden behind the concrete bunker and had made their way down to the Barrier.

"I'll go ahead" Jeff had said "just in case, it might be safer".

He had cycled along silently and arrived at the Barrier. It had seemed as though nobody was around. Then he had spotted a very young policeman lying dozing in the morning sun.

As he had approached, the young policeman had awakened startled.

"Who are you? And where did you come from? Are you my relief? I've been here since yesterday with no break." Then the policeman had spotted Jeff's wounds. "Hey, you're wounded, how did that happen?"

Jeff had pretended to be very hurt and had staggered off his bike towards the young policeman.

"You look bad" the policeman had said, just as Jeff sprang into action and hit him hard. The policeman went down, out cold.

"Not a bad right hook" Derek had praised as he had approached, and then had added "I must remember that".

They had made their way across the Barrier, and then on towards the tip without incident or being seen. They had managed to dodge two of Wilson's trooper patrols on the way by ducking down behind a hedge.

They had eventually arrived at the tip but it had seemed to be closed and the gates had looked locked.

As they had waited by a closed gate for the green Jag to turn up they looked at each other's wounds, checking to see if they had become worse.

They had heard a car engine being gunned, and sure enough the green Jag was seen approaching.

"Leave this to me" Derek had said "he knows you. Hide behind the concrete pillar so you're not seen".

The Jag had pulled up and a man had got out and had started opening the gate. As he was doing so he had spotted Derek.

"What are you doing here?" the man had asked in a tense voice.

"Finding bits for a shelter" Derek had replied.

"Well clear off, you're not allowed near here" the man had said.

"I got family, we've got to survive" Derek had said, trying to look destitute with a pleading look "and anyway, who says I'm not allowed here".

"Find bits for your shelter somewhere else" the man had ordered harshly.

"All right mister. Just trying to survive" Derek had snapped, edging his way closer to the man.

"That's far enough" the man had said then he had pulled out a gun and had pointed it at Derek.

Then seeing Derek's bleeding wound he had said "You've been shot. You're wanted by the troopers, move away from me or I'll give you another bullet, this time where it hurts".

It was then that Jeff had moved out from behind the pillar pointing his gun at the man and had said "Put your gun down nice and slowly".

The man had spun round to face Jeff.

"You, I was told you were dead" the man had said, recognising Jeff straight away.

Then Jeff had added "Look, we're not after you, just the papers in the car, so don't be a hero for a shit like Wilson, he's not worth it".

The man had appeared to think about it, and then had handed the gun to Derek.

"What am I going to say to Wilson?" the man had asked.

"Tell him we jumped you, knocked you out, and stole the car" Jeff had said.

"And how and when did this happen?" the man had queried.

"Just now, like this" Derek had said, landing the man a roundhouse that pole-axed him and laid him flat.

Derek had then said "He was in two minds simple and dim and he talked too much. Ouch, that smarts "holding his shoulder.

"If you've opened that wound again, I'll have words with you" Jeff had joked. He had then approached Derek and had checked his shoulder, looking quite concerned. "You're bleeding like a stuck pig, why did you have to hit him so hard?"

"I only tapped him" Derek had said, putting on an innocent expression.

"Well I don't want one of your taps" Jeff had said looking concerned then had added "we need to get you medical attention urgently, you're losing a lot of blood".

Derek had answered "No. You'll get caught then all this will have been for nothing, and besides, I promised Jen I would look out for you".

"You have and you are" Jeff had said trying to appease the big man "but even massive tanks like you run out of petrol sometimes. Come on, we'll use the car to get you to a medical unit".

They had climbed into the Jaguar, turned it around and with Jeff driving, had driven back in the direction the man had just come from.

Jeff had spotted a wrench that was tucked down beside the seat.

After a mile or two they had come across a sentry post. Jeff had reached for the wrench that he had found.

They had approached the sentry post slowly. As they drawn up level with the hut, the trooper had come out looking very bored "You weren't long" he had commented.

He had then quickly realised that it was a different person driving the car than the one he had been instructed to let into the tip.

Jeff had swung the wrench, hitting the trooper on the side of the head. He had collapsed in a heap and they had driven off before anyone could react.

After a short while, they had turned a corner and there in front of them in the distance was a road block with troopers stationed at strategic points along it.

"Let me drive and you make a run for it" Derek had said.

"They've seen us. If we don't go towards them they'll open fire" Jeff had said "we'll try to bluff our way through".

"Let me drive" Derek had ordered again "if it comes to it, I can't run very far with this wound and you stand a better chance than I do of getting through. Also, I can draw them off using the car but we must get past this check point first".

As they swapped seats, Derek had asked "Have you got the most important papers on you?"

Jeff had tapped his inside pockets "Try to save this lot as well, if you can, you ready?"

"As ready as I'll ever be" Derek had answered, moving the car forward smoothly.

As they had approached the check point, a trooper lazily approached the car. By the time he had realised that it was not the driver he had let through a short while previously, it had been too late.

Derek had pushed his foot down hard on the accelerator and had gunned the Jaguar into the check point, barging his way past the trooper and bursting his way through the check point. They had gone speeding down the road with the troopers opening fire at them as they went round the corner.

"It was lucky they were fast asleep" Derek had said with some satisfaction.

"Not for long" Jeff had said as he had glanced into the wing mirror and seen troopers running for a jeep and starting to give chase.

"We won't be so lucky next time, not with them on our tail. It's time we split up, one or both of us must try to get through to your mate John with some of the papers we have between us" Derek had said "I suggest you bail out before the next road block and try to make it on foot. I'll lead them a merry dance away from you, which will give you a fighting chance".

"What about you?" Jeff had asked, not liking the idea at all.

"I can't move very fast with this" Derek had said pointing at his chest which had been starting to bleed profusely "I won't get very far on foot, I'll only hold you up.

It's a pity I didn't know you earlier, we could have been lifelong friends". With that Derek had slowed the car down just as they were turning a right hand corner and had pushed Jeff out of the car.

Jeff had rolled into some bushes, and the Jaguar with Derek in it had sped off leaving Jeff in a heap hidden from the road by the bushes. The Jeep with the troopers in came past at quite a speed but they had failed to see him and had carried on down the road after the Jaguar. All Jeff could do was to mentally wish the big man luck.

CHAPTER 31

Jeff had checked his surroundings. He had seen from where he had stood that on the hill in the distance there were makeshift tents and shelters and he had made his way towards them hoping to hide in amongst the refugees and the shanty type shelters that were being erected. Cutting across fields and hugging the hedgerows to avoid being seen by any patrols, he had made his way slowly towards the hill and towards the first group of tents.

He had been met with suspicion and resentment so he moved slowly on across the small encampment. The blood which had been running freely down his side from his wound had been receiving unwanted attention.

He had tried to make his way from one camp to another slowly and without drawing too much attention to himself, but unbeknown to him he had been watched by a trooper in an observation post who had phoned in to his section leader who in turn had contacted Wilson.

Wilson had mobilised two squads immediately to surround the area and carry out a search and a small fast response unit had been sent to the location indicated by the observation post. Then Wilson had ordered his helicopter to pick him up.

As Wilson had waited for the helicopter he had decided to phone Sir William Waite, but there had been no answer from Sir William's phone, so he had left a message telling Sir William that Jeff had been spotted near the make shift shelters and he had him cornered. He was going to capture him and enjoy questioning him intensively. Then he had boasted to Sir William in great detail how he was going kill to Jeff slowly and get any incriminating papers that Jeff had been carrying and destroy them. He had relished the telling as to how he was going to teach Jeff a lesson in how not to mess with him. Wilson had rung off quickly as his helicopter was ready. He had picked up his gun on the way out of the door, checking for the knife he had hidden in the sheath on his ankle.

Meanwhile, Jeff had been making his way from one small refugee camp to another. As he had got to the brow of the hill of a well-known landmark, it was then that he had spotted the first lot of troopers heading his way. In between the make-shift tents and shelters made from any scrap that could be scrounged or purloined with bare hands, the people had walked around this threadbare settlement looking dazed and desperate.

As the scene before him had unfolded, the higher he had climbed up the slope the more he had seen of the devastation to the surrounding area. Jeff had crumpled to his knees and had nearly broken down. "Why did they not listen?" he had cried to himself. He had sobbed bitterly and heartbrokenly with the loss and desperation of survival as the pain from his wound had threatened to overwhelm him.

He had staggered to his feet and had made his way from one pitiful, crowded refugee camp to another. The bare fact that he had survived was of no consolation as nearly everything had been wiped out, gone, no-more, in the total devastation which had occurred.

He had not wanted to be here, in this place, at this time, a mental and physical witness to the anguish, loss of hope and stunned disbelief which had permeated the air about him like a heavy veil of fog, but he had had to see it through. So many were now relying on him. With Alan dead he had known Wilson would not be far behind, so he was now being hunted by a desperate professional killer who would stop at nothing to see him dead.

As he had looked around at what had once been one of the most crowded and expensive areas to live in, this part of the Estuary had now been a wasteland as far as the eye could see. People who had survived, who had once been very wealthy, now stood with only rags on their backs, the only possessions they had left. Ironically, their money which had once bought nice houses, nice clothes, and holidays had not, when it comes down to it, bought life.

The devastation that had lain before and around him was unbelievable. From where he had stood he could see that the Hiroshima-type explosion had totally destroyed and wiped out the whole of the Estuary industry, killing thousands of people, crippling the country's economy and bringing down the Government to its knees. It had pushed the structure of life in this part of the country back to the dark ages. He had looked across at the devastating scene before him. It was like looking at a scene where someone had been allowed to go berserk with a giant blow torch. Many of the trees had had their branches shrivelled into charcoal, the bark of the trunks and large branches had been blackened and charred, in some places the ground had been seared black. A bitter acrid smell permeated the air. In other places it had looked as though the area had hardly been touched by the conflagration, some houses had still remained standing but there were no windows or doors. Some houses had looked as though a mighty foot had trodden on them, other buildings had been partially collapsed whilst others had been reduced to a pile of rubble.

Where there had once been a very busy, complex, thriving industry on the Estuary there was now a mangled mass of metal and twisted, drunken looking buildings. It had been a panoramic scene of unbelievable devastation that had seemed impossible for him to comprehend and it would be seared in his memory forever.

As Jeff had looked at what seemed to be a war-torn vista it seemed unbelievable that any life could and did exist within its vicinity. It had taken Jeff a few hours to arrive at where he was now standing. He had been getting weaker with the loss of blood and the pain from his wound. He had realised with a start that it had only been a few days since he had left the Police Sergeant who he only knew as Dick, and the Government man named John. Worst of all he now had to live with the fact that he had killed someone, though he felt that the man had more than deserved it.

He was now being hunted by Wilson and his men like some prize animal and all he wanted to do was survive long enough to reach the Government man named John and reveal the evidence he had had. He was being hunted by professional people who had no other intention but to kill him quietly at their first opportunity. According to them he had to be shut up at all costs and the evidence he had against them and their boss had to be destroyed.

His thoughts had been disrupted as he had heard the throb of a helicopter's rotor blades and had hoped that it wasn't getting too close.

Striding with a disguised, easy pace so as to show he was not wounded, hoping he would blend in, Jeff had passed by a large tent and had seen on the other side of the slope a group of men dressed in black military style uniform heading his way. He had promptly backtracked to the other side of the temporary refugee town only to see another group of men attired in the same type of uniform also heading his way, cutting off his retreat. He had seen that he was hemmed in on two sides. He had known without a doubt that the men were searching for him.

Just then a helicopter had flown high over the tree stumps and denuded vegetation and had swept down to where he had hastily hidden amongst a pile of blackened and splintered wreckage.

Out of desperation, Jeff had given one last effort rather than be caught like a rat in a trap and had made a dash for a small copse of trees. As he had run his side where he had been wounded began to cause him pain and he had realised that he was getting very short of breath. Out of the corner of his eye, he had seen puffs of ash and dust begin to spurt from the ground and round about his running feet and he had realised that it was caused by the ricocheting of bullets which were being spat at him from a high calibre gun set on automatic by a person in the helicopter.

Jeff had made it to the trees and had run straight into a group of soldiers who were brewing up tea. They had been a part of a much larger unit.

Jeff had been promptly and unceremoniously pinned to the ground by two soldiers whilst their colleagues had formed a group around them, and in turn started returning fire at the helicopter as did the rest of the squad.

Bullets had been heard ricocheting off the body of the helicopter, the rotor blades had stuttered and had attempted to carry on revolving. The engine had coughed and spluttered, and then the whole contraption had come down in a cloud of smoke and had impacted with the ground, hard.

As the helicopter had slammed to the ground the pilot and his two passengers had bailed out, rolling into a fighting stance. They had then approached the squad of soldiers with guns drawn and had pointed them menacingly at Jeff.

They had looked stunned that they had been shot down and a man who had seemed to be the leader was very angry as they had moved towards the squad of soldiers.

The squad of soldiers had closed ranks around Jeff with weapons aimed and pointing towards the crew of the helicopter. There had been a distinct clicking sound as the rest of the soldiers had come running up, releasing the safety catches on their weapons and faced the three men.

"Who is in charge here?" one of the three men from the helicopter had demanded as he had taken off his flying helmet and addressed the squad of soldiers. It was Wilson; he looked every inch the killer he had been told about

Jeff's heart had sunk. It had been Wilson who wanted him dead, and right now. He had seen that by the hate in the man's eyes. Wilson had the look of a hunter about to kill his prey

"I am, and who the hell are you? And what do you mean by firing on me and my men?" An officer had appeared it seemed out of nowhere and took a wary pace forward.

Wilson, with an attempt at a more conciliatory tone had replied "We're chasing a known leader of a terrorist organisation responsible for all this devastation and you have him there, pinned on the ground" pointing at Jeff "I want him, so hand him over, and hand him over now!"

"I said, who the hell do you think you are?" the officer had repeated "shooting up the area that I'm in charge of and endangering my men like you were a puny actor in some second rate movie".

"I want that man" Wilson had reiterated.

"I said who the hell are you?" the officer had repeated "and if you don't answer me now, you and your lot are under arrest until I can get to the bottom of this, so name and number young man, now!"

Wilson looked daggers at the Officer who was talking to him; Wilson was not used to being challenged

"Ray Wilson, Head of Security for Sir William Waite, and your new political head of the country" Wilson had explained diffidently.

"You are not my dictator! Or head of my country. I answer only to the military" the officer had said.

"You will hand over your prisoner to me" Wilson had demanded "he is a terrorist and a threat to the country. He has personally murdered at least once and caused thousands of deaths through his activities. I believe I outrank you" Wilson went on to say "so you will do as I tell you, and maybe I won't have you charged for shooting down my helicopter".

"Who the hell do you think you are?" the officer had asked "no civilian outranks me or my men when martial law has been declared. You might be some sort of detective but as far as I'm concerned you would need a search party to find your own backside, now what do you mean by attacking me and my squad, shooting at civilians and making demands from the military?"

"I want him, so hand him over now and remember I have people in powerful places so you better do as I say!" Wilson had said.

"You don't threaten the Queen's soldiers no matter who you are, or who you're supposed to know, if you want to stay in one piece" the officer had said "so put your guns down, you're being placed under arrest".

"I will have your rank and see you in the guardhouse for life for this" Wilson had said to the officer.

"Whatever, I've heard pigs fart before" the officer had replied to Wilson "now, I've had enough of this backwards and forwards riposte, you're under arrest until I get to the bottom of this".

Just then, there had been the sound of an engine and a small unit of troopers turned up in trucks. Two squads of men in black uniform had jumped off the trucks and had approached the group of soldiers with guns drawn.

"Now this might change things" Wilson had said to the officer "I think the boot is on the other foot now".

The officer had bellowed in a parade ground voice "Squad, fix bayonets, skirmishers ready!"

The soldiers had obeyed speedily and without question and fanned out into a skirmishing line.

"That's far enough" the officer had said to the men in black "if you come any nearer I will order my men to open fire and you'll have a bloodbath on your hands and they'll win as they are seasoned soldiers and you are not".

The men had looked fearfully to Wilson for instructions. It was very clear that they had had no stomach for a fight against seasoned troops.

"Alright men" Wilson had said "he's not going anywhere now" pointing to Jeff. "Go back to unit headquarters and by the time I finish with this officer he'll be peeling spuds for years".

"Take him away Corporal" the officer had said, pointing to Wilson "and Sergeant, have the rest disarmed and arrested".

"You can't do that" Wilson had said to the officer "I will have you nailed to the wall for this".

"Threatening an officer of the Queen's Forces will get you nowhere, now you have a choice, the easy way or the hard way, I don't mind which you choose. You can go very quietly with my men or you will be hog-tied and carried and if any of your men interfere they will be shot, do I make myself clear".

"Crystal" Wilson spat, resigning himself to the situation.

The soldiers had moved in and had taken Wilson away. The expression on Wilson's face had been a picture to Jeff and one that would remain in his memory offering a small sense of achievement and satisfaction for some time to come.

The men in the black uniforms had lain down their guns and had been rounded up and led away to the accompaniment of sullen mutterings and vindictive glances back at the soldiers.

"Right let him up" the officer had ordered to the two soldiers pinning Jeff to the ground.

"What's this all about?" he had asked Jeff, then saw he was wounded.

"How did you get that?" He had pointed to the bright red blood on Jeff's side.

"Him and his cronies" Jeff had replied wearily gesturing to Wilson as he was being led away arguing with the squad of soldiers.

Just then a Sergeant had stepped in front of Jeff and saluted the Officer.

"Yes Sergeant?" the Officer had said.

"I believe that man calling himself Wilson is not telling the truth, Sir" the Sergeant said.

"And what do you know about this Sergeant?"

"Quite a bit Sir".

"It comes to something when sergeants know more than their officers" then muttered "but there again, if the truth were known they always did".

"Well" the officer had added "you had better come to my quarters now and explain yourself, and bring him with you" pointing to Jeff "and by the way, you had better get the MO to fix him up, he's bleeding like a stuck pig. We can't have him making a mess and bleeding all over my nice quarters now can we?"

The officer had turned and marched off.

The Sergeant had turned to face Jeff, and Jeff recognised him straightaway as the soldier named John who had helped him out of the building after it had collapsed when this present pantomime of events had started.

"You're a sight for sore eyes, how come you're here and how's that nurse of yours?" Jeff had asked with a smile. He had been pleased to see John "she thinks a lot of you, you know".

"We're on picket duty for the area and are moving onto the Estuary later as part of some rescue package. Jane and I, well we're getting married when this is all over, now I got my promotion".

The Sergeant had pointed proudly to the three chevron strips on his sleeve.

"How come, you're here being shot at by that maniac?" the Sergeant had asked "the last time I saw you, you gave me a fright climbing out of that collapsed building covered in dust and dirt like a lost troll".

"I've been on walkabout since then" Jeff had said wryly.

The Sergeant continued "I know you're no more a terrorist than I am, and I know a bit more than you realise. You see my nurse and a particular police sergeant's lady friend are related, and sister's talk, small world isn't it" the Sergeant said knowingly.

Jeff's eyes had opened with surprise "Well you could knock me down with a feather, it certainly is a small world".

"My officer is of the old school, very fair but with discipline" the Sergeant had said "he'll get to the bottom of this, so let's not keep him or the Medical Officer waiting. You look as though you've been dragged through a hedge backwards".

As they got to the officer's quarters the Sergeant had said "At least I might be able to put a good word in for you, that Wilson bloke looks a nasty bit of work".

"He is" Jeff had agreed firmly "he's a professional killer".

"He's put my officer's back up and he don't like him so that's a plus".

The officer had called out "Sergeant! Bring in the prisoner and let's hear what he has to say for himself".

"Sir, I'm acquainted with this man and I do not believe him to be a terrorist of any kind" the Sergeant had interjected, once inside the large tent that was serving as the Officer's quarters.

"You'd better let me be the judge of that" the officer had said "we had better hear his story first and let that other bright monkey cool off for a while. I do hate to be threatened, especially by a jumped up civilian who thinks because they have a relation or friend in high office they can be above the law". He paused "Right, Sergeant. You say you can vouch for this man who is accused of being a terrorist?"

"Yes Sir" the Sergeant had answered confidently.

"You know you've not had those stripes long, do you want to risk them?" the officer had asked.

"If it's to get to the truth, Sir, then yes" the Sergeant said "I can't wear them without the pride and principles they mean".

"Good, I like my sergeants with integrity, you will go far in this Army and like you I'm not going to sell it short no matter what jumped up politician wants to pull strings. If you had said anything else, you would be a private and he would be on his way with this Wilson bloke" the officer had said.

Just then a Medical Officer had pushed his way through the tent entrance, saluted the Officer and had looked at

Jeff silently. He got out some field dressings, gave him an injection of something through the sleeve of his dirty shirt, and then started to dress the wound. He had then said briefly "the jab's for the pain" finished dressing the wound and left the tent just as silently.

"He doesn't say much" Jeff had said.

"Never does, but a good man to have in a tight spot" the officer had said "just like all my men, handpicked for their skills".

He had then eyed Jeff up and down and added "Right what's your story and it had better be the truth or you'll wish you had never been born".

Jeff had relayed his part in the events up to the present time whilst the officer had listened intently.

CHAPTER 32

The Officer had listened intently to what Jeff had had to say and had asked a few questions, particularly with regard to the shooting of the man in the helicopter. The officer had then made the comment "I wish some of our troops were as good a shot".

"Now, you are in all sorts of problems" the officer had said "on one side you could be genuine and be who you say you are, on the other hand you could be this very clever leader of a fifth columnist unit trying to overthrow the stability of the country, I have to determine which".

The officer had continued "Now we had better listen to what this Wilson bloke has to say now he's had time to cool his heels".

The Officer had shouted out to the corporal who was outside the office to fetch Wilson under escort, and then had said "Let's hear what he has to say and then we can decide who will go to the glasshouse because one of you will be locked up for good, that I promise you".

"Sir" the Sergeant had said to the officer "I wish to make a comment".

"Not until I've heard both sides, then I will hear what you have to say Sergeant".

The Sergeant insisted "But Sir it's very important to the facts in this case".

"Ok Sergeant, I will hear what you have to say whilst we wait for this Wilson character to be fetched".

The Sergeant had then started to relay what he knew "I first saw Jeff near our Headquarters the day after the explosion took place. He was covered in dust and was staggering out of a building. He had blood running down his head, and he looked awful, so I sent him to the First Aid Unit that had just been established.

Well Sir. You know I am due to get married soon?" the Sergeant had asked.

"What's that got to do with what's going on here?" the officer had stormed at him.

"Well Sir. My fiancée was the nurse who had attended to Jeff at the First Aid Unit. My fiancée has a sister, and sisters talk.

This sister has a boyfriend, who is a Police Sergeant, and that same Police Sergeant helped send Jeff on the mission he has been trying to tell you about, but he can't because they have been sworn to secrecy by the Police Sergeant's brother who works directly for the Prime Minister".

"Do you think I came over in the last banana boat?" the officer had said to the Sergeant "people like this Jeff character are not trained to be involved in espionage, now Wilson yes, you can see by just looking at him that he is a nasty piece of work. We will wait to see what pans out after we speak to Wilson. Until then I will keep an open mind".

They had waited in silence whilst Wilson had been escorted to the officer's tent. He had entered flanked by two soldiers and a corporal.

"Thank you" the officer had said to his men "stay in case you're needed". He had turned to Wilson "Right, let's hear your side of the story, starting with who you are and why you're hunting this man".

"I don't answer to you" Wilson had replied to the officer "and I'll have your head for this. I know some powerful people in powerful places that will bury you".

"Unless I get some civility out of you" the officer had returned "you'll be escorted back to where my men are holding you, and in a few days' time, if I see fit, I will ask you the same question again.

If I get the same answers as I've just had, you'll go back there for a month. Do I make myself clear? Because I don't give a pig's fart who you know or how powerful they are, you don't threaten me or my rank!"

Wilson had looked stunned. He had been used to giving orders, always using bullying tactics and thereby making others kowtow to his wishes, but here was someone that could not and would not be bullied.

"Very well, but I'll be making a report about this to Sir William" Wilson had snapped.

"You can make a report to the Queen" the officer had retorted "I don't care, but until I hear all about what is going on you're going nowhere and speaking to no-one. Also, I'll put you under arrest, do you understand me?" the Officer had shouted at him.

"I hear, but Sir William is going to hear about this" Wilson had said to the officer "this man you have here is a terrorist and you're harbouring him, so you can be charged with treason and are in as much trouble as he is".

"Corporal" the officer had said "escort this man back to where you had him, no-one is to see or speak to him or his men for seven days, they're to be kept in isolation until I say otherwise".

"You can't do that" Wilson had blustered "on what grounds?"

"I'll think of something. Perhaps you and your men went through a contaminated area and have to be isolated. Am I going to get the truth from you now without the threats, or do I have to lock you away for good?"

"Alright" Wilson had suddenly capitulated "but remember, he's considered to be a terrorist and you'll be held responsible for him".

"I'll be the judge of that, not you" the Officer had replied "so let's hear your version of events before I lose my patience".

"SAY NO"

Wilson had gone on to explain that he was Sir Williams' right-hand man. He had boasted that Sir William would be the next leader of the country and under his dictatorship only the pure bred people would rule. He went on to accuse Jeff of being the leader in a terrorist organisation. He told how Jeff had plotted the explosion in the Estuary area by using suicide terrorists to hijack a sea-going gas tanker using helicopters as it entered the outer reaches of the Estuary.

The terrorists had sent a message to Sir William Waite's offices demanding a ransom of £20million for the crew, the ship, and its cargo of liquid gas. If the ransom was not paid they would release the gas and blow up the ship. But before a rescue plan could be put into operation they had sailed up the river and had blown up the ship.

He added that Jeff was the leader of the terrorist cell and that Jeff was solely responsible.

At that point, Jeff had reached inside his coat pocket, withdrawn the papers which he had been carrying and put them on the table. "These will prove otherwise" he had said.

The look of horror on Wilson's face had been a picture as he saw the incriminating evidence he had been looking for on the table in front of him.

"Read those papers and the ones in the green Jag we stole from them that they were going to destroy. My friend is trying to get to one of your units as we speak with the papers that are in that green Jag"

The Officer had picked up the documents which Jeff had thrown on the table and had started to read them. He had then ordered the corporal to radio all units to look out for the Jag and for it to be stopped and brought to the camp. They were also to capture Derek but not to harm him but to tell him that the troops were being sent by Jeff for a safe passage for him.

The corporal had left to carry out his orders.

The Officer had then continued reading the papers and had then said to Wilson holding them up "This is very damning evidence for you and your people Wilson".

With that remark Wilson had reacted fast. He had bent over swiftly, reaching for his lower leg, had dropped his hand to his right ankle and had pulled out the knife he had hidden there. He had lunged towards Jeff shouting "You bastard! I said I'd have you".

Jeff had been slow to react to Wilson's lightning reactions and had not moved fast enough to avoid the knife completely. Wilson had managed to stab him in the stomach as the soldiers escorting Wilson had grabbed hold of him and had wrestled him to the ground very roughly and with great difficulty.

"Get the MO here fast" the Officer had shouted to the Sergeant and then had said to Wilson "you've just proved your own guilt" pointing at Jeff "and if he dies, you can add the charge of murder to your list of crimes. How the hell did he get that knife?" the Officer had shouted to the escort who were pinning Wilson down.

"Don't know, Sir" one of them had answered.

Jeff had felt a searing pain in his stomach and a warm sticky feeling oozing from the wound. The feeling had gone out of his legs and he had sunk to the ground. He had felt a sharp pain in his temple and everything went dark.

CHAPTER 33

Jeff had come to in a makeshift Army Medical Unit. He was being drip fed into his arm, his stomach had been very painful and sore and his head had hurt like hell.

"About time you joined us" a voice had said.

Jeff had turned his head and there had been Cyril and Jen looking down on him smiling. Cyril said "We only came to see the big man there" pointing at the next bed where Derek lay sleeping. He had been battered and bruised but patched up and wrapped in bandages "but you were here also, so we had to come and say hello to you as well".

Cyril's face had changed as he said "Wilson got away. He killed one of the soldiers, slightly wounded that officer, stole a jeep and crashed through a cordon. He must have left you for dead, and that sergeant is in a right mood over his men not searching Wilson properly. He said he was going to fry the balls off the man who was supposed to have searched him".

Jen had said "Your stomach wound isn't too bad, he missed any vital organs. You have three broken ribs, and that bash on your temple when you hit the table probably put you out. Maybe it knocked some sense into you, and by the way you have a flesh wound from a bullet. I can't leave you alone for 5 minutes without you getting into some sort of trouble".

"Sorry about Alan" Jeff had said to Cyril.

"He had it coming from what Derek told me. I didn't realise how selfish Alan had become and how money orientated he was. Derek made sure I knew before I saw you, which was before they operated on him to remove the two bullets Alan put into him".

"I knew he was hit once, I didn't know he was hit twice" Jeff had said "he never told me".

"He wouldn't, Jen asked him to look after you" Cyril had said "and he did. I know how he feels about Jen, but there's nothing I can do about that, and I wouldn't hurt him for the world. The man has a heart as big as he is, unfortunately for Derek, Jen loves me, she is very fond of Derek, but there could never be anything between them, and like me she would not hurt him. He'll take a while to heal but he will mend alright, you can't keep a man like him down for long" Cyril had added.

"So what's happening out there?" Jeff had asked "How did you get here? How did you get past the troopers? What happened to everybody? The last thing Alan told me was that you were all going to be rounded up and either shot or interned for good".

"One question at a time but slowly" Jen had replied "you've been out for nearly two days. You must have bumped your head pretty hard, so take it slow over a cup of tea".

"You and your tea" Jeff had teased "you would cure the world's ills over a cup of tea".

"Well it does help" Jen had answered "let's try to bring you up to speed, but I warn you I will stop if you get tired.

We made our way to the Golf Course, meeting the others as we went along. As we approached we heard shots being fired from the direction that you went in. This made us suspicious, so Cyril put out scouts and they spotted the ambush. The troopers started to open fire on us before we were in their trap.

As we returned fire two lorry loads of soldiers turned up. They were from your mate John. We spoke to the leader of the troopers and they laid down their weapons and then they were rounded up. The soldiers escorted us out of the area so the clean-up teams could go in. By the way, they talked of nobody being able to live there and the whole area being used as a memorial to the dead from this disaster".

Jen had looked at Jeff intently "You're getting tired, we'll go now, but bring you up-to-date later after you've had some rest. We met you're mate John on the way here. He said he will see you later after he's done some cleaning up".

When they'd both left a nurse had come in to fuss over Jeff and Derek. Jeff had then drifted off to sleep, his mind in a whirl, to piece together all that had happened in such a short space of time.

He had awoke much later with Karen sitting beside his bed and Joan was talking to Derek. They had both seen that he was awake at the same time and Karen had leant over to cuddle him hard. Both women had then said together "We are not letting you out of our sight ever again".

"Good job you decided to take your mum to the spa when you did" Jeff had said to Joan, holding her hand tightly.

Karen had replied "We've been under that John's protection ever since they picked us up from the spa. How he knew we were there I don't know, but we can't move without an escort of at least two armed men. I've been worried sick about you and this terrible accident. Why did it happen?" Then before he could reply "you were right. You said it was a disaster waiting to happen. Well it did. I hope they're happy now that they've destroyed a whole community. All those people dead and what for? Greed and profit! It's terrible".

Karen checked herself and apologised for rambling on but she had been so frightened. But worst of all she felt so guilty that they had survived when so many had died.

"What have you been up to?" Karen had then asked, and then she had promptly harped back to the issue at hand

and had added "It's terrible what's happened to Derek but I gather he will heal with that nurse looking after him. I'm sorry, I keep rambling on but I'm so relieved you're not dead". She had hugged him hard enough to make him wince.

Just then the door had opened and John had walked in "Sorry to break up the reunion but we need to talk urgently" he had announced abruptly.

"Can't you let him rest? Hasn't he done enough for you and country?" Karen had exclaimed angrily then had added "you won't be satisfied until he's dead, then what do I do?"

Then on seeing Jeff's face and knowing how strong his principles were, which was one of the reasons why she loved him so much, Karen had resigned herself to the inevitable "I'll be outside when you've finished. Try not to tire him too much".

"Well, what's the emergency?" Jeff had asked John once Karen and Joan had left the room.

"Well" John had replied "you know Wilson escaped, and we don't know where he is. He thought you were dead but he's found out you're still alive, and is trying to get to you anyway he can, so I've put a cordon around this place. We'll be moving Karen and Joan into safe custody and to a safe location as of now".

"Thank you for keeping your word and keeping them safe" Jeff had said.

"Like you I keep my word" John had acknowledged.

Jeff had said "Whilst you're here you might as well bring me up to speed with what's been happening with Sir William and his cronies. What's happened to all the documents I got for you? What's happened to everyone who was in the Estuary area? What's happening about Cyril, Jen, Derek, Michael and all the others that have helped get those documents you so desperately wanted? What's happening about the Terminal?"

"One question at a time" John stated "we had to stretch our resources pretty thinly to pull together all what we did in such a short time. The Prime Minister still has a few friends he can call on in a crisis.

The one lesson Sir William never learned was that you have to be careful of the toes you tread on the way up because they belong to the feet you have to kiss on the way down. In treading on those toes on the way up Sir William made a lot of enemies and they're having their day now, revenge is so sweet.

Sir William is under arrest and is being held in a secure location awaiting trial. Those documents are being studied as we speak and from the initial reading they will condemn Sir William, Wilson and a whole lot of councillors and planning officials. The implications in Whitehall will be far reaching and a lot of heads will roll.

People are being instantly replaced and the approaches to the whole of the Estuary on both sides have been sealed off and nobody is allowed into the area unless they have a written mandate from the PM and only then not until the Health and Safety and the Disaster Recovery Teams have done their investigation. All bodies are being removed and identified by the emergency services as best they can be, all of that will take some time. We are receiving a massive amount of aid from a lot of countries, especially America, and that aid is flooding in as we speak.

The PM has opened our borders to any humanitarian aid that has been offered. There is a hue and cry in every country in the world to crush The Senate. There is a massive response for all Top Tier COMAH sites to be relocated away from any population areas".

"It's a bit bloody late for that now" Jeff had said "it's bloody typical of politicians. They never listen to the peoples' concerns, because everyone wants to get on the gravy train of profit. They call people like me anarchists and trouble makers as an excuse so they don't have to listen to the truth. Then they wring their hands and cry 'we didn't know' when it all goes wrong.

It's not until thousands have to die, a Government has been brought to its knees and comes to the brink of collapse, a whole region has to be devastated, the country has been put back into the dark ages, all to prove that common sense was right and people come before profit. All the politicians are worried about is their political image to the world and not the views of the people who elected them into power. The only time they might listen to what people are saying is at election time when they are looking for that little cross that will give them a ticket to get them back onto the gravy train again. Once they have got that they put their feet back in the trough of profit".

"You're cynical about politicians and politics" John had said.

Jeff had replied "I've told you before, until they prove otherwise, I will always consider that politics and a lot of people that are involved in politics are what the word expresses—Poli-tics—Poli as in many and tics as in parasites, therefore there are mostly parasites in politics.

"What's happening to Cyril, Jen, Michael and all the others?" Jeff had asked, changing the subject.

"They're in a luxury hotel right now resting at our expense" John had replied "and they send their regards.

By the way, we had to move them from the first hotel we put them up in because some idiot put them in the same hotel as some of your local councillors who were boasting to the press over lunch how much they cared and how they were going to lead their community out of its crisis.

When they heard that, Cyril, Jen and Michael were baying for their blood and they created havoc. Our security people had to intervene. It's not done any of the councillor's images much good, and when Cyril told them and the press found out you were alive but injured, they've gone berserk and have been camping outside ever since waiting for a statement.

The Prime Minister will be coming to see you very soon so you can both talk about what you should say when you make a joint statement to the press, and then there could be an audience with the Queen in a few days' time".

"Are you and your political cronies trying to manipulate me?" Jeff had asked suspiciously.

"No" John had replied "but you must understand we are at a very delicate time politically, and we must be seen to be doing the right thing".

"I've never been a glory hunter so I'll pass on that, thank you very much" Jeff retorted dismissively.

"You are such a self-righteous bastard" John had snapped angrily "if you don't do it for yourself, do it for the people who believe in you. Do it for the Cyril's, Jens, and Derek's of this world. It's them that need something to believe in at this time of crisis and you're that something whether you want to be or not".

"Well ok" Jeff had finally agreed reluctantly "but if he's going to talk a load of politics I'll get up and walk out from the press conference. After what's happened, I want action not political promises that will be expediently withdrawn at the next political crisis".

"Be reasonable Jeff. You can't dictate to a Prime Minister what you want. Not when he's come to praise you in front of the world".

"Alright" Jeff had capitulated "but I don't have to like it. When is this conference going to take place? And will the others be there?"

"In a little while" John had replied "Derek will have to have his nurse with him but the others will be at the press conference and photo call as well as yourself and the Prime Minister".

"You don't give a man a lot of time to make himself good looking for the media?" Jeff had said jokingly.

"There's not that much time in the world to make you good looking" John had said laughingly then added "Cyril, Jen and Michael are already there, we have just enough time to get you and Derek spruced up" and he left.

CHAPTER 34

They had all been waiting in the wings, waiting for the signal to enter the forum.

Derek's nurse Sandra had been hovering over Derek like an angel and he had only eyes for her. It had been lovely to see a great big man reduced to jelly by the pretty nurse who had obviously liked him an awful lot.

"Do we hear wedding bells?" Jen had asked smiling and looking at Sandra and Derek.

"Aw Jen" Derek had replied very bashfully "you know I'll always have a soft spot for you".

"We know" Cyril had said "you can be best man at our wedding, unless you want to make it a double wedding or is it too soon?"

Derek had just coloured up and Sandra had kissed him and said "It's up to you big boy".

Just then, they had been advised to go on to the stage. They had entered from the left hand side, the Prime Minister had come on from the right hand side and had greeted them in the centre, shaking their hands one by one. They had then taken their seats.

The Prime Minister had opened the press conference by announcing the forthcoming trial of Sir William Waite and why he was being put on trial.

He had then fielded questions on what was happening in the disaster recovery area and how many estimated deaths there had been.

The Prime Minister had promised a full and frank investigation into the events and that the findings of that investigation would be made public and any recommendations carried out.

He had then told the press of the parts played by Cyril, Jen, Michael, Derek and mostly Jeff and then asked for questions from the reporters and television interviewers.

The Prime Minister had fielded most of the questions very well but one reporter had kept asking the same question "Will you change your energy policy to a safe siting policy for Top Tier COMAH sites?" But the Prime Minister had continued ignoring this question. The reporter had then asked the Prime Minister what lessons had been learned from all the devastation and massive loss of life.

The Prime Minister had replied that everything that was humanly possible was being done for the victims. Investigations were ongoing into the causes of the terrible disaster and life would be returned to order in the area as soon as possible.

The reporter had then repeated the same question "Yes Sir, but what lessons are being learned?"

Jeff had stood up "None" he answered for the Prime Minister.

The Prime Minister had looked embarrassed and shocked at the remark and Jeff's interruption.

The whole room had gone quiet for a few moments and John had looked on in horror from the wings. He had then indicated silently by putting his hand across his throat in a slicing motion that Jeff should shut up and not embarrass the PM.

There was then a buzz of voices from the reporters who had demanded to know what Jeff had meant by the remark.

The Prime Minister had seen that what had been billed as a hero's welcome celebration to gain him popularity was falling apart and was turning into a political nightmare in front of the press of the world.

The PM had turned to Jeff and had started to bluster about costs and time required to find causes and then time required to make the right recommendations.

Jeff had turned to the Prime Minister and had said coldly "There have been recommendations made in the past, but no-one wants to learn any lessons from all the accidents involving Top Tier COMAH sites and the recommendations from the investigations into those accidents. The reason is because it would affect the profits of the companies and the financial implications for the governments concerned and until there is a safe siting policy for Top Tier COMAH sites strictly adhered to, there will always be the threat of this sort of incident happening again".

"We will give assurances that everything that can be done will be done" the Prime Minister had said, trying to placate the press.

"That's not good enough" Jeff had said "I want you to guarantee to the media" pointing to the press "that you and the future governments of Great Britain will adopt a safe siting policy for all Top Tier COMAH site areas, starting now. Either move people away from within a cordon of safety surrounding these terminals or relocate these terminals to a safer location. Also, never allow any planning of any sort within a 4 mile radius of these terminals. You will openly encourage these companies to own the land within that cordon and for it to be kept as a safety buffer zone, plus encourage all other countries throughout the world to do the same".

The Prime Minister had looked at Jeff, smiled and whispered to him "I know now where you get your reputation. Thank god you're not in politics".

Jeff had ignored the soft soap remark that had obviously been meant to appease him.

"You must adopt this type of policy as of now", Jeff had continued "otherwise all these deaths have been for nothing and you'll be accused as being as bad as Sir William".

The Prime Minister had gauged the political situation instantly then had addressed the media, saying to Jeff "I'm willing to embrace all your suggestions and anymore safety recommendations that come out of the investigations into this incident in memory of those poor souls who have died".

"Your promise will be good enough for me. But remember, I will be looking over your shoulder to make sure you carry out that promise for the people and so will the worlds press" Jeff had replied.

The Prime Minister, not slow in using a political advantage had said to Jeff in front of the media "How about you putting your money where your mouth is and heading that team? This team will be funded by, but will be totally independent of Government intervention. You can even choose your own staff and teams to work with. What do you say?"

Jeff had been astounded and did not know what to say.

"Well?" the PM had prompted "will you do it? Or are you all talk?"

Jeff had known, whether he liked it or not, that he had been out-manoeuvred by the PM and he nodded, agreed and leaned across and shook the Prime Minister's hand.

The press and the media people had then cheered and there was a burst of pictures taken by the press and TV cameras.

As they were shaking hands, the Prime Minister had whispered to Jeff "I leave them to you" pointing to the media and left the press conference, leaving Jeff to face a lot of questions on how he was going to fulfil his new job and a barrage of photographs.

The PM had said to John as they had left the conference "I think I might just have contained our loose cannon by bringing him into the fold".

John had replied "If you want my advice, which you don't, if he does not get his own way on this, he could be a major problem to you politically".

"It's in our political interest at the moment to let the media and him believe what we have just said" the PM had remarked "the energy crisis that will be developing around the world will dictate the way we perceive the situation in ten years' time but for now I need to secure myself politically and then get this country back onto its feet. If playing lip service to this Jeff bloke and the media achieves that then that is to the good".

"You could be sowing dragon's teeth" John had said to the PM "just like out of that book 'Jason and the Argonauts'.

"Someone once said 'a week is a long time in politics'" the PM remarked "our main concern at the moment is keeping this Jeff bloke alive and not being killed by that killer Wilson, because if Wilson kills Jeff, or a member of his family dies, not of natural causes shall we say, the other papers that you did not find, will, I am assured, find their way to the press, and I don't want that to happen as that could be very embarrassing to me and the whole of the newly to be elected Government".

"Do you mean to say you're in on all this intrigue?" John had asked, slowing his steps.

"It's politics!" the PM had answered "you can't be totally blind in this game".

"A game, that's all it is to you. A bloody game. You know Jeff was right when he described politics as, Poli as in many and tics as in parasites. He described politicians as many parasites".

"That's a good analogy" the PM said totally unphased "I must remember to quote that sometime. You find those papers that this Jeff has squirreled away, and then we are off the hook, until then we play politics".

"I didn't know there were other incriminating papers" John had said, and then he asked "what do they contain? And where do I start looking?"

"I understand the papers we are talking about were in that Councillor Randle's safe" the PM replied "where they are now I don't know, but that Jeff was the last one to raid that safe so he must have them or know where they are.

At the moment he is untouchable because of the press interest in him and what he does, that's why I brought him into the fold where we might be able to keep an eye on him and have some control over him without him knowing".

"He's not likely to tell me where he's put them, or even if he has them" John had said "it could take some time to gain his confidence enough for him to trust me and then to tell me where these papers are?"

"That has to be your commission to carry out, and for it to be treated with priority" the PM had said "I will give you the written authority, and you'll only report directly to me is that clear?"

"Yes" John had said "well I'd better start now, and go back in there and rescue him from the press. You never know, he could get popular".

"That's my worry" the PM had said "I don't want him as popular as myself or my political party. At this stage we can't afford loose cannons flying around that we have no control over".

"The one thing I have learned about Jeff" John had said "is that he is someone you can't control. Oh, you can lead him around by a ring through his nose like a tame bull with the right kind of handling, but he is so stubborn. If you try to push him in a direction he does not want to go in you come up against a solid lump of granite that won't budge. He can be led but he cannot be driven and if he finds out you lie to him, he shuts up like a clam, and then you will never get anything out of him".

"A man of principles" the PM had said "that's rare today, but a man of principles must have a weakness somewhere. It's up to you to get on his good side and find it. Now I must go. I'm late for a meeting. Go and try to control our new loose cannon but above all at this moment in time keep him safe and don't forget that killer Wilson is still out there somewhere and he hates Jeff with a passion and will try to get to him by any means fair or foul".

Meanwhile, back at the press conference Jeff had deliberately taken a back seat. Jen, Cyril, Michael and

Derek were answering questions about their part in their survival and the incidents involving Sir William's men.

One of the reporters had said to Derek "So, it was you that was the hero who rescued those two girls we heard about, and the people at the Golf Course when they believed they were going to be lined up and shot".

Derek had replied "It wasn't only me. Jeff was there and did most of it".

Derek's nurse had snuggled up to him, indicating to everybody who was there that Derek belonged to her and she cared deeply for him, and Derek had said "he was a real hero".

They had all faced questions on all the various incidents which had transpired but the press had left Jeff until last and had started questioning him about what had happened leading up to, during, and after the accident.

All of the photographers had been lifting up their cameras to their faces to take their photos and then looking at their cameras then repeating the action to take another shot.

However, there was one cameraman during the interviews that kept his camera up hiding his face all the time, but he did not seem to be taking any pictures. He had slowly made his way to the front through the crowd of photographers who had been jostling one another for the best photographs.

Jeff had noticed this because he had not been fielding any questions at the time and he had thought this very strange as there was all the press and camera activity going on but this man had not been taking pictures.

It was then that Jeff had realised who the cameraman was. It was Wilson and he had been hiding a gun inside the camera and heading straight for them.

"That's Wilson" he had shouted, leaping to his feet "he has a gun" pointing in Wilson's direction. Jeff had then dived on top of Cyril, Michael, Derek and Jen, bringing them to the ground in a heap behind the desks.

Wilson's eyes held the gleam of a maniac and he was screaming "I thought you were dead, well you are now. And as for you bastards, you're dead too. I said I'd get you". Wilson had fired a number of shots from his camera gun.

Jeff had heard a fuselage of shots and had felt a searing pain in his side, leg and chest, all one after the other. He knew that he had been hit badly, and then everything started to fade. Shouted voices and screams sounded like that they were being heard in a tunnel, and then it all went dark.

Wilson was gunned down in a hail of bullets from the Secret Service gunmen who had appeared from nowhere. In the cross-fire three photographers had been wounded.

Behind the desk, Cyril, Michael, Derek, Jen and Jeff had lain tumbled together with blood all over them. People had swiftly rushed forward to help them.

"I'm alright" Jen had said, struggling to her feet.

"So am I" Michael had said "except for a nick in the arm". He held his arm out which was bleeding profusely.

"Well he didn't get me or Sandra" Derek also said, checking his little nurse to see if she was alright.

"He got me in the leg" Cyril had said holding his thigh.

Then Jen had said "So then where's all this blood from?"

It was then that they had seen Jeff sprawled unconscious in a heap on the floor bleeding from his leg, side and chest.

"Oh no" Jen had screamed, falling to her knees at Jeff's side. There had been screams requesting for an ambulance. The paramedics had arrived within minutes as they had been on standby wherever the PM was and they had gone to work on Jeff straightaway, ordering the security staff to move everybody out so they could do their job.

There had been a bevy of photographs being taken by photographers as they had been herded out of the room by the security staff.

The inquest on how Wilson had got past security with a camera gun would be held later by John.

In the meantime, John had had three wounded press photographers to get hospitalised in one hospital, he had had to get Derek and Sandra, Jen, Michael and Cyril into a more secure hospital. He had already notified that same hospital to clear the operating table for emergency gunshot wound surgery for Jeff in the hope that he would make it in time but from the look of it he had not held out much hope.

The paramedics however had been working hard to stabilise him so he could be moved to the hospital and an operating theatre.

"We can move him now" the paramedic had said "he's stable for now".

They had moved him to a waiting ambulance with Jen clucking over an unconscious Jeff like a mother hen, and woe be tide anyone who had got in her way.

CHAPTER 35

Everything had sounded muffled to Jeff as he had gradually come round. He had been able to see more clearly as each moment had passed. He had felt very restricted as though he had been confined in a straightjacket and had been run over by a steam roller.

As things had started to clear, he had seen Karen sitting by his bedside looking very worried. He had said in a croaking voice "Hi lovely".

Karen had burst into tears but at the same time she was smiling. She had said "You had me worried. I can't leave you alone for five minutes without you getting up to some sort of mischief". Then she had kissed and hugged him.

Karen had brought him up to speed with what had happened. She had said that some of the others had been hit but they were alright now, and they were up itching to see him.

She had told him that John had returned to the Press Conference Room just as Wilson had opened fire and how John had hit Wilson with three shots stopping him instantly.

She had also told him of some spectacular footage taken by a television crew of Jeff diving across the others when

Wilson had attacked and was being shown on the television throughout the world.

Jeff had started to get tired so she said she would let him get some sleep and be back later. He had already been drifting off into a peaceful sleep as she had been going out of the door.

Later, Jeff had been sitting up in his bed in the private ward he had been given. He had just had his dressings changed and the doctor had commented that he was doing very well and could have a few visitors.

John had come in and said "I can see you're on the mend at last. Well, I have some very good news for you. I've been trying to find out what happened to your boys and I've found your youngest one. He was on holiday with his family in Spain. You're eldest son was with his in-laws in Scotland, so they're all safe".

Jeff had thanked him for the news with eyes filled with emotion.

As John had been going out of the door, he had told Jeff that all the publicity that he had received had meant he could not do any of his undercover work and the PM had said that he was to be promoted and appointed to Jeff as his personal bodyguard.

Then saying he would see him very soon, just to bring him up to speed with everything, John had left and Jen, Michael with his arm in a bandage followed by Derek and Sandra who had never left his side and then Cyril who had been hobbling on a stick, had all tumbled into the room.

"You had us worried for a while there" Jen had said.

"I've never seen her in such a state as she was over you" Cyril had remarked "and that photographer who got in the way, and tried to stop the stretcher just so he could get a picture will be eating through a straw for a month. She gave him such a right hook when he would not get out of the paramedics' way so they could get you to hospital".

"Stupid man" Jen had said "fancy trying to stop someone getting life-saving attention just so they can get a picture for their paper".

"Remind me never to stand in your way when you're angry" Derek had said, smiling "I like my teeth too much".

Michael had said jokingly "Even I wouldn't upset her when she's angry".

"Hey, I'm not that bad" Jen had said defensively then burst out laughing.

"What do you mean"? Cyril had laughed at her and said "We're getting you a rematch with Tyson".

With that remark, Jen had whacked Cyril on the arm.

"See what I mean" Cyril had said in mock hurt.

"Shut up" Jen had said "we're here to see our blood brother".

"Who's you're blood brother?" Jeff had asked.

"You are" Jen had replied.

"When you needed a few pints of blood to stop you bleeding like a stuck pig it turned out Cyril and myself were the same blood type as you, so whether you like it or not you got our blood in you.

By the way, you also received some from that John bloke as well".

Derek had said "That John bloke gave you blood?" then added "do you know what his last name is?"

"No!" they all replied in unison.

It's Stone. So you actually got blood out of a stone".

They all laughed together.

"Stop making me laugh, you're making my stitches hurt" Jeff had gasped.

Cyril had said "The doc says you might be out of here soon, so when you're up and about, Jen and I would like you to be the best man at our wedding".

"You two are getting married" Jeff had said "that's great, when?"

"As soon as you're well enough" Jen had answered.

Derek had said "Can you make it to two weddings?" looking moonstruck at Sandra.

"Why not make it a double wedding?" Jen had suggested, looking at Sandra and then added "That's if you don't mind".

"That would be the icing on the cake for me if that happened" Sandra had said.

"Icing, wedding cake" Michael remarked "what a pun".

They had all laughed together.

CHAPTER 36

All that seemed a world away from what was happening now as Jeff was escorted to meet the Sheik near his suite of cabins. He was speaking to Abdul one of the English speaking advisors, and the Sheik had his usual amount of 4 bodyguards with him who kept their eyes on the Sheik at all times.

The Sheik greeted Jeff saying "It is my birthday today and I wanted to give you a present to celebrate my birthday" and he handed Jeff a jewel-encrusted dagger.

"This is a very expensive gift you give to a poor and humble man, I am overwhelmed" Jeff said, bowing. He did not want to make the Sheik suspicious by refusing the gift. He then added "surely it is for people to give you presents on your birthday? Not for you to give expensive presents to others. If I had known it was your birthday I would have arranged something for you".

"If you remember" the Sheik said "you said if a poor man gives someone a present it is a rich gift, if a rich man gives a rich present it is not a poor gift but its value is less because it costs the rich man less than it costs the poor man to give the gift".

"You know I respect you and the wise words you say" Jeff said to the Sheik, bowing. He was trying to hide the confusion as to what the Sheik meant but wanted to appease him as he had the look of a madman.

The Sheik's eyes lit up when Jeff said that he was wise and he respected him.

"That is praise indeed" the Sheik said to Jeff "coming from someone like yourself who I respect greatly, that really is praise indeed" and his chest seemed to puff out, then he added as he turned to Abdul "see, I knew he and his friends would join me in my struggle to prove I am worthy of respect. I told you so, he just said he admires me and my wise words. I told you mine and Jeff's lives are linked in the struggle of life".

Jeff's mind was doing overtime. It seemed the Sheik had flipped over the edge of reasoning and was in a world of his own. He expected him to turn at any moment into the dangerous megalomaniac he knew he was. It was then he had a wild idea.

"Will you permit me to arrange a small celebration for you and your party to celebrate your birthday?"

"You would do that for me?" the Sheik asked in surprise then added "it would have to be tomorrow night as I have to leave to see my father. You can come with me and tell him what you have said. There will be room for Jeff and his party won't there Abdul?"

"My friends and I would arrange a special birthday party for you if you will allow us access to the officers and catering staff so we can arrange a themed, formal surprise party for you" Jeff continued.

Abdul interjected and said "The Sheik is very busy and it's not advisable for you to mingle with the staff at this time. I don't condone it".

"The party will be for the Sheik, not for you" Jeff said to Abdul "anyway, who are you to tell me I can't arrange a party for someone I have come to respect and admire".

Abdul eyes flared. It was clear he was holding back his temper in front of the Sheik. Jeff thought he was going to attack him. He knew by his reaction that he had just made an enemy of someone that was a handful in a fight, and looked as though he had a very vicious killer streak about him. It was obvious the man was not used to his opinion being questioned and would find a way to make Jeff soundly aware of it if the moment arose.

It looked like there would be a standoff between Jeff and Abdul when the Sheik interjected and said to Abdul in Arabic "You are my paid advisor in military matters and I respect your opinion. I also have a great respect for Jeff and what he has achieved, but I would so like a party".

Then he looked into the distance and lost himself in another world of his own making. Then, almost physically jerking himself back into the present he said in English "I haven't had a surprise party done just for me in years". He then said to Abdul petulantly "I can't see why not".

"I still do not advise it" Abdul replied in Arabic "you don't know what they will get up to".

"What can they get up to?" the Sheik said to Abdul "they are surrounded by armed guards and we have the NATGAS 2 in tow with the Baroness of the Sea with your men ready to use the valves to make sure no-one attacks us by surprise from the sea. We have explosives in strategic places ready for someone to pull the pin, what more do you want, they can't do anything".

"I still do not trust them" Abdul repeated.

"You jump at shadows. I do not think you even trust your mother" the Sheik said to Abdul "and anyway, I would like a party for my birthday".

"Well! You had better watch them closely" Abdul said "I still do not trust them" and looked at Jeff with hatred.

"You are being paranoid" the Sheik said to Abdul, then turning to Jeff he said in perfect English "Would you and your friends do a party for me? I would love it. I am sure it would be so lovely".

"Leave it to me" Jeff said "I will give you a late night party you will never forget, but I will need time to get it done so I better start right away".

"I will get Mustafa to help you. We are blood brothers you know? He knows what I like" the Sheik said "that way we can appease Abdul here that you are being watched and not planning to kill all of my guards, and stop me blowing up the ship anytime if I wanted to".

The Sheik had a sly crazy look about him as if he was dreaming and was in his own world of make believe. Then his eyes cleared and it seemed sanity returned "I will look forward to it" the Sheik said as they parted.

Jeff headed back to the cabin with his ideas growing in his head as to what they could do. The timing however, had to be perfect otherwise they were all dead.

He explained to the others what had taken place at the meeting with the Sheik. He showed Karen the jewel-encrusted dagger.

Karen said that he could not accept such a gift from someone who was obviously mad.

Jeff replied "I had no choice. I had to appease his ego, it seems the only way to get through to him at the moment. It's Abdul that is the nasty one. That one is pure evil and looks as strong as an ox".

"You leave him to me" Derek said "he won't hurt anymore people after I have finished with him".

"I had this idea of throwing a late night party so we can get everyone together then we can take back the ship whilst the Sheik celebrates his birthday" Jeff explained.

"They don't drink alcohol, so how are you going to disable every one of the guards?" Rose asked.

"We have to find out if the Medical Centre on board has a supply of that Tamasipan, Sandra spoke about, and how much of it they have.

We lace the icing of the cake with enough Tamasipan to knock out a horse, as Sandra suggested. Tamasipan has a bitter taste, but if we put it in the icing we can disguise it. Also the Middle Eastern people have a very sweet tooth and love things like any icing on cakes or sweets and chocolates".

"The guards are not likely to refuse a piece of the Sheik's birthday cake" Jen said "those that do we can hit over the head, either way they finish up with a headache an aspirin won't cure".

"We then need to get the two ships parted at the same time as disabling the bombs on board this ship that is not going to be easy" Karen said.

"The only access to the tow ropes that bind the two ships together have to be accessed via Deck 5 and that is heavily guarded and those ropes are fastened in quite a few places" Derek said.

"It will take at least ten men to cut those ropes and the cutting of those ropes has to be co-ordinated as it has to be done at the same time as the swell of the two boats merge coincides" Jeff said "otherwise it will create a shudder through the ship that will alarm the Sheik and I don't know if he has a remote detonator that will blow up the NATGAS 2".

He then added "Whoever boards the NATGAS 2 will be on a suicide mission unless they find a way of getting off the ship before it is either blown out of the water by the Americans or it blows up on its own. That gas ship has to be ten miles away from us if we are to survive an explosion, even then it will be a close run thing. We have to have co-ordinated teams to find and disable the bombs on board this ship otherwise we will end up in Davy Jones Locker".

"All this whilst co-ordinating a party for a megalomaniac and his sidekick and it has to be done so he or his advisors are not suspicious" Karen said "have you got anymore rabbits to come out of this hat?" she added, turning to Jeff.

As they were discussing the issues, Cyril slid silently into the cabin and started to listen to what was being discussed then added "I got into the Captain's cabin and saw the Captain". He gave everyone a start as they did not hear him enter. "I gave him a bit of a start too just like you lot. He had not had anybody visit his cabin via the balcony before.

The guard came in during my visit but the Captain hid me in his shower until the guard went back on guard duty".

"How did you find out what cabin the Captain was in?" Karen asked.

"That's a trade secret" Cyril told her.

Jen said "My Cyril is the best tea-leaf in town" then added proudly "there is no-one he can't find and there is not a locked room he can't get into. I thought Jeff would have told you that".

Karen looked shocked.

Jeff turned to Karen and said "I will, and have always kept Cyril's secret and so must you dear. What the Sheik and Mustafa don't know gives us an advantage. Now what did the Captain have to say?"

"The First Officer is allowed to see him" Cyril explained "so he communicates to the First Officer in secret, right under their noses, and whilst the guards and one of the English speaking advisors are in the room, they do it via the signal flags that are surrounding the edge of a chart he has inlayed on his desk. Apparently each flag means a word or letter and they just point to it and they have a conversation in front of everyone without them realising it. It's brilliant".

"So what are they planning? Jeff asked.

"Well" Cyril replied "they have a specially equipped radio room that looks like an ordinary crew member's cabin and they are in touch via a special link with the British COBRA Incident Room and they in turn are in touch with the American equivalent.

You were right the Americans want to blow us out of the water but are being held in check for the time being until all the options are looked at and a plan of action takes shape. Mind you, they don't have many options.

I told the Captain what we were planning to do. He didn't like it, but it was better than he can do with his crew locked in the forward hold. This is not a military ship and it is fraught with danger. I also told him that we would muster the male passengers together and would communicate with one another via the women when they use the toilets. He thought that was a good idea. He also said he would communicate via the First Officer to let the Medical Officer give us all his supply of Tamasipan or any other sleeping draught he might have so we can put it into the guard's food when we have the Sheik's party".

Just then, John returned.

"What have you found out?" Jeff asked

"Well" John said "as far as I can make out there are 3 lots of explosives, one at the stern of the ship in the lower deck just below the water line, one in the middle of the ship on the port side at the same level and one in the bow of the ship. That one is above the waterline but I believe it's next to the bulkhead where the crew are being held. Each one has a guard within 20 to 30 feet of the detonating plungers, it will be a job to surprise them".

"Now we have to find out how many guards there are on board the NATGAS 2" Jeff said.

"How do we do that?" Jen asked.

"Well they have to eat" Cyril said "so the catering staff might be able to tell us".

"I can't see them putting up with Army rations if there is luxury food next door" John said "troops are the same worldwide. They march on their stomachs so someone is supplying them with food and that has got to come from the kitchens on board this ship. All we have to do is have a word with the Catering Manager to find out".

"That can be done when we meet up with them to organise the Sheik's surprise birthday party" Jeff said.

"What surprise birthday party?" John asked.

"The one I talked the Sheik into letting us organise for his birthday" Jeff replied.

"If he knows about it, how come it's a surprise?" Derek asked.

"If we use this as an opportunity to talk to the officers and willing passengers, when we organise the surprise it will be a birthday he will not forget" Jeff said.

"He let you talk him into doing a surprise birthday party for himself? John asked "when did this happen?"

"When he sent Mustafa to bring me to his cabin and presented me with this as a present to me on his birthday". Jeff showed John the jewel-encrusted dagger the Sheik had presented him with.

John whistled "That's a few bob. He must respect you to give you something like that".

"It was then I thought of doing a party for him as a cover to trying to take back the ship" Jeff said "but that advisor, Abdul, he does not leave his side. He is suspicious of my motives so we have to be careful".

"And I thought politicians were devious" John said "but you take the biscuit. If it works, I will take my hat off to you".

"We have permission to organise a party for the Sheik so let's go and organise one" Jen said "and boy, will there be a few surprises". She chuckled.

"Now see what you've started" Cyril said to Jeff "once she gets the bit between her teeth there will be no stopping her. This is what happens when someone upsets her and she plans retaliation".

"It will be fun" Jen said, slapping Cyril on the back "I think I might enjoy this, I like a challenge".

"This will be a job for the men" John said.

"Oops" said Cyril, as Jen rounded on John.

"You are not one of these men that think women are chattels and are meek little things that need protection all the time, are you?" Jen stormed at him "let me tell you, we are better adapted to protecting our loved ones than men, and don't you forget it".

"I did say not to upset her" Derek said to John.

John started to bluster "That's not what I meant "he said defensively.

Rose smiled knowingly at Jen and said to John "Darling, when in a deep hole stop digging, you'll only make it worse for yourself".

It all went quiet for a minute, and then they looked at each other and burst out laughing.

"On a more serious note" John said "what worries me is that we have not had the serious sabre rattling normally associated with a political hijack".

"What do you mean" Cyril asked.

"Well" John said "we have not had the usual call for worldwide media cover to highlight the plight of their cause. Also, they have not demanded the public killing of hostages in front of the media".

"What were the deaths of the two crew members about then?" Jen asked "that was an execution, making them walk the plank like that, it was horrible".

"That was a demonstration of what would happen if the crew and passengers did not toe the line" John said "it was a way to keep us all in check until they got within striking distance of America, where they could force America to do the killing blowing up the NATGAS 2 to stop it entering American waters".

"But what does the Sheik get out of this because he will die as well?" Jen asked.

"Notoriety" John said "I believe Osama bin Laden once said, we are in love with death, the West is in love with life, and that is the difference between us. It looks like this Sheik wants to make a name for himself by taking on the biggest country in the world alone, with only a handful of personal bodyguards in some macabre David and Goliath confrontation, and these 6 so called advisors are encouraging him for their own political ends".

"I believe there could be some truth in what you say" Jeff said "Mustafa hinted that the Sheik was out of favour with his father over him acting like an overindulged child and the Sheik took exception to it".

"That makes him even more of a dangerous nut case, as we don't know what he is going to do next" Cyril said "he is a time bomb waiting to go off".

"So, all this might not be a Middle Eastern confrontation with the West" Derek said "just a spoiled brat stamping his royal foot at his daddy".

"If that is the case" Jen said "how is he going to get off the ship before it blows up so he can tell his daddy I told you so. As I see it, any vessel that leaves this ship will be monitored closely and will be boarded".

John was thinking deeply "What if it was not a surface ship that takes the Sheik and his men off the ship. What if it's a fully equipped submarine. They could either blow holes in the Baroness of the Sea with the explosives they have put on board so she sinks therefore dragging down the NATGAS 2".

Jeff interjected by saying "Which in turn, when the liquefied gas comes into contact with the sea water will explode in a rapid phase transition and then boil off into an unconfined vapour cloud which also could explode. Or, if that did not happen as they wanted it to, they could always put a torpedo into the side of the NATGAS 2 to make sure".

"That is fiendish" Karen said "nobody in their right mind would do something like that".

"We are not talking of someone in their right mind" Jeff said "we are talking of someone who has lost the plot, but is also powerful enough to do a lot of damage. He could even wait until there was a rescue attempt as the Baroness of the Sea is sinking and then put the fish into the side of the gas ship taking out the rescue crews as well".

"That's horrible" Karen said "they would murder the thousands of people on board as well".

"That's why it makes it even more imperative that we carry out our takeover of the two ships as soon as possible" Cyril said "also we need to let the Captain know of our theories so he can contact the authorities so they can put in a co-ordinated plan of operation".

"Won't they sink us out of hand?" Sandra asked "because we are a threat to their territorial waters and coastline".

"I am sure they will wait until we are near their coast, in case there is a chance of a rescue attempt" John said "but not close enough so they are threatened, but there will be a point of no return when they will order us to be sunk out of hand".

"If we can let them find out if there is a submarine out there" Jeff said "then they might be able to find it and take it out before the Sheik gets off this ship and onto the submarine, then we get a small advantage".

"Are there any habited or uninhabited islands between where we are now and the North American coast?" Karen asked "if there are, we might be able to use the lifeboats to get people off the ship".

"Not in the middle of the Atlantic" Cyril said.

"That's not quite true" John interrupted.

"What do you mean, not quite true. I know the Atlantic is a vast ocean but I believe we are too far north to be near any of the Madeira Islands" Cyril said.

"But we do go within 50 to a 100 miles or so off of Sabre Island" John said "it's an island which lies about 150 miles off of Halifax, Nova Scotia and about 750 miles from New York. The island is about 22 miles long and about a mile wide at its widest point. It lies off the American/Canadian border. It has a Canadian research station on it, herds of wild horses and is a home for seals and not a lot else. The sea bed rises sharply about 25 miles from its coastline. Oh, I believe it is a hunting ground for the great white shark. It's a pretty bleak place. I believe there are half a dozen scientists living there at most".

"I've never heard of it" Cyril said "but it seems like hell's back yard".

"There have been 350 wrecks on or around Sabre Island with the loss of thousands of lives" John said "it has the reputation of being the Atlantic graveyard of ships".

"Not a popular holiday destination then" Cyril quipped.

"The Canadians are very particular about who actually lands on Sabre Island" John added "you also need special approval from the Canadian Government. It has quite often been mistaken for the coast at Nova Scotia because when you first see it from the sea it looks like a large piece of the main coastline. As I said, it is about 22 miles long and only 1 mile wide but it is surrounded by rocky outcrops and sandbars, that's why there have been so many wrecks on it.

The Island itself is long and narrow and slightly curved and is shaped like a long sabre hence its name. Nova

Scotia is just over half a day's sailing away and New York is still about one and a half a day's sailing away from Sabre Island. It does have a helicopter station and a small runway for small light aircraft on the beach".

"It seems better than nothing or Davey Jones's Locker" Cyril said "at least that could be our point of no return if we are to carry out our plans for taking over this ship".

"Well, if we are talking of doing something to rectify our situation then we'd better set up teams and get ourselves organised" John said.

"How many teams do you need?" Sandra asked.

"Well" John said "we need one team to liaise with the catering staff and to organise the party, get the cake made with the sleeping draft in it to knock out the guards and those on Deck 5 will have to be knocked out first.

Then we need another team to find out how to board the gas ship and disarm the guards on board and be ready to sail it away from us when the ropes are cut.

We then need another team to cut the cables between the two ships. It will take at least ten men to cut the cables at the same time.

Then we need another team to disarm the bombs on board which will also have to be done at the same time.

If there is a submarine out there we need to get the Americans or someone else to find it and knock that out before it can torpedo us".

"I doubt that it can be done" Sandra said "it will be like organising a military operation with civilians. They aren't disciplined enough so it will be a blood bath".

"What other options do we have, except to put our heads between our legs and kiss our backsides goodbye?" Jeff said "we must be under no illusion that these people play for keeps and the Americans will blow us out of the water rather than let us anywhere near their coastline, so we have to do something about the situation or die in the attempt. Look at it this way. If we do nothing we are dead, but by doing something we have a slim chance of living through it, and if we don't, at least we can say we said no and we had a go and did not give up and go quietly into the night with our tails between our legs. We stood and made a difference, that's the important bit".

"Right" Cyril said "I will pay the Captain a visit and let him know about our suspicions of there being a submarine out there to pick up the Sheik and his men. Maybe he can use that secret radio to alert the Americans. I will also tell him what we intend to do beforehand. He might have a member of his crew who knows about explosives".

"I will also contact our people in Whitehall via my lap-top" John said "and let them in on the act. They may be able to get some military support for what we are doing".

"Can I use your mobile phone to contact Michael?" Cyril asked "he might be able to get some pressure put on from his end via his cousin in the United States Naval Intelligence".

"How did you know about my mobile phone?" John asked, looking at Cyril suspiciously.

"You would be surprised at what I know" Cyril replied proudly.

"I know about explosives" John said changing the subject but still looking at Cyril with a suspicious look, then added "but we will need at least two more to help disarm the explosive devices if we are to do it at the same time.

Yes you can use my phone" John said, still shaking his head in disbelief that Cyril knew about his secret phone.

"Maybe some of the ships officers or crew might have knowledge of explosives" Cyril interjected.

"Don't forget to mention to the Captain when you see him that we need a volunteer crew to sail the NATGAS 2 and that will possibly be a suicide crew" Jeff added.

"If you ladies want to use the Ladies' Restrooms and spread the word to the other women on board make sure that they are aware that we need at least ten volunteers to cut those cables that tie us to the NATGAS 2 and we need women to help co-ordinate this, but above all it must be kept quiet" John said.

"Now we need to organise and dress the main dining room for the Sheik's surprise party" Jeff said.

"Leave that to us women, we are best suited for that job. We can do that without raising any suspicions" Jen said.

"Come on ladies, we have work to do" Karen said getting into the spirit of the challenge.

The women left the cabin to spread the word amongst the other passengers via the Ladies' Restrooms.

Cyril went to the balcony and just disappeared. Jeff did not see him leave.

John said "That was slick. I didn't see or hear him leave, no wonder he is good at what he does".

"What can I do to help?" Derek asked.

"Be my bodyguard. John is very fit and can look after himself. Cyril is as fit as a butcher's dog but I am still recovering from the injuries I got from Wilson" Jeff said "but you should carry on acting as though you are one can short of a six pack. It will lull them into a false sense of security. Anyway, I will feel safer with you looking after me than anybody else".

"Aw Jeff. You know I love you like a brother. We will be the dynamic duo again, or if you like beauty and the beast and you will be the ugly beast this time" Derek joked "and I will protect you with my life".

"I know you will" Jeff said "but don't forget to act stupid in front of the Sheik and his henchmen, and then when the time is right you can show them just how skilled you are".

"I did that in the ring sometimes, it always worked" Derek said "did you know I was a contender for the Olympics? But I had a bad fall which put me out of wrestling for months. By the time I recovered the Olympics were over. After that I never wrestled in the ring again".

"Cyril did mention it" Jeff said "have you thought of training young hopefuls in your art so they might be able to get to the Olympics?"

Derek looked as though someone had switched a light on "No, I never thought I was good enough to train anyone. Anyway, I understand Arabic if it helps".

"SAY NO"

"What" Jeff said "how come you can speak Arabic?"

"I can't speak it very well but I understand it. A friend of mine and the man who I trained with was an Arab. He was a good man. He taught me some great wrestling moves and some of his language".

"Well, from what Cyril tells me" Jeff said "you are more than qualified".

"If we get out of this alive, I think I might set up my own training school" then changing the subject Derek said "what are our chances of getting through this?"

"We have the element of surprise on our side and the Sheik thinks he has us at a disadvantage, but he has underestimated us and believes we will accept our fate, but he has forgotten the bulldog spirit of the British. I believe he wanted to lull me into a false sense of security with the presentation of that dagger but I had the feeling that he might want to take it back after I am dead. I got the impression he was an Indian giver".

"What's an Indian giver?" Derek asked.

"It's what the new early American settlers said about the Native American Indians when they traded goods as they always wanted something to their advantage in return. I hope what the Sheik wants is not going to be too expensive otherwise he is going to be very disappointed. I get the impression that if he gets disappointed he can turn very nasty. Now we need to wait to find out what Cyril finds out from the Captain".

CHAPTER 37

Cyril entered the Captain's cabin via his balcony after making sure he was alone. The Captain was startled but pleased to see him. "How did you do that? Appear from nowhere like that".

"I am not going to divulge my trade secrets" Cyril told the Captain "I am here on a mission to let you know what we are doing and also to ask you to let the Americans or whoever you are in contact with that we suspect there is a submarine out there ready to pick up the Sheik and his men, and we want it found and destroyed before we carry out our plan of attack otherwise it might be able to put a torpedo into us or the NATGAS 2 at any time".

Cyril went on to tell the Captain about the plans they constructed and asked if they could rely on the crew for help as this was going to happen with or without the help of his crew. He also asked if there were crew members that knew anything about explosives, and asked if he could get any volunteers to sail the NATGAS 2 away from the Baroness of the Sea once the tow rope cables were cut that bound the two ships together. He also asked if the Medical Officer would let them have the drugs to help knock out the guards by putting it in the cake for the Sheik's birthday.

The Captain said "You seem to have a plan that might work but there is a deadline which the Americans won't let you go beyond".

Cyril then asked him if the two ships would go anywhere near Sabre Island as he understood that that resembled the American coastline from a distance. He wanted that to be the point of no return and if the worst happened they might be able to evacuate some passengers there.

"That's not American that is Canadian territory. Although it is quite near to America it is closer to Nova Scotia in Canada but I understand where you are coming from. You do know it has the reputation of being the Atlantic graveyard for shipping, but you can rely on my crew to help where they can and I will get my First Officer to ask if we can get any volunteers from them and let you know".

Just then the door handled rattled and Cyril dived for the balcony and was gone. The Captain went to the door to slow down whoever was there to give Cyril time to get away.

Cyril managed to get back to the cabin unseen.

Meanwhile the women had set themselves up in parties of two and started visiting the entire Ladies' Restrooms on board to spread the word. As women entered the toilets, they were told to keep what they had heard a secret as their lives depended on it, and then they could let their men know what was planned. They wanted to know if they could rely on some of the women to help and make a difference.

It was all going to plan until one woman started to become hysterical. She started scream that they would all be killed. "We should do nothing then perhaps they might let us live" and she went on and on as to why the Americans would not kill them as they were British allies. She said she was going to tell the guards what they were doing then the Sheik would be pleased with her and let her and her family live if she said they were fellow Muslims.

Jen knew the noise the frightened woman was making would alert the guards so she had to react quickly.

Jen stopped her near the door, spun her round and swung a right hook which caught the woman on the nose. The woman went down as if she was pole axed, unconscious.

"Remind me not to argue with you" Karen said to Jen looking at the unconscious woman.

"That was close" Jen said "now quick, get a member of the crew. We need to get her to the Medical Centre and get her sedated. We can say that she tripped and fell and hit her face on the sink".

Karen summoned a female member of the crew, who in turn obtained a medical carrying chair and all three took the woman to the Medical Centre.

They explained what was going on to the Medical Officer who said he had already been informed of what was coming down the pipeline, and he was there getting the sleeping drafts ready.

"I hope we don't get too many panicking people otherwise it would jeopardise the whole plan" the Medical Officer said. He said he would keep the woman under sedation until this was over.

They both went back to spreading the word via the Ladies' Restrooms and in general after a few expletives about the Sheik, the response was overwhelmingly in favour of helping in any way they could and above all they knew secrecy was the watch word.

It would mean putting on a brave face at the party for the Sheik but it was the best smoke screen they could come up with and if it worked it was their only chance of survival.

Meanwhile, back at the cabin, as Derek and Jeff were talking there was a knock on the cabin door. Jeff opened it and there stood Mustafa with two guards.

"You are to come with me" Mustafa said "the Sheik has summoned you and wants to see you now". Derek moved forward and went into his role play of acting stupid, shaking his head and said "No".

"Easy Derek" Jeff said, taking Derek's lead in the role he was playing "he probably only wants to talk to me. I will be alright with Mustafa" and then turning to Mustafa said "he gets very clingy sometimes, can he come with us? I don't like to upset him".

"Very well, he seems harmless" Mustafa agreed.

"He is" Jeff said "he is a gentle giant and would not hurt a fly. He will be good". Turning to Derek Jeff said "Won't you Derek?"

Derek nodded, and adopted a very pleased child-like look about him.

As they made their way towards the Sheik's suite Mustafa said "We consider people like your friend Derek children of Allah as they are amongst the unfortunates of this world but we believe they have been touched by Allah".

Derek kept up the appearance of being a child out on a trip with his friend. He had found out from his experience in the ring that if you let people think you were stupid and harmless they let down their guard and talked as though you didn't exist, so that way you could learn more about your enemy by lulling them into a false sense of security. He also knew that they had limited resources and needed to find out as much as they could about the opposition. He knew it was a wise man that knew his limitations and played to his strengths and the weakness of his enemy.

When they got to the Sheik's cabin, Abdul was there as well. The Sheik greeted them and then asked "Who this is with you? I only sent for you so we could talk".

"This is a travelling companion of mine, he is one of life's unfortunates and he is totally harmless. His wife Sandra went off with my wife Karen to do some shopping in the on board store and I said I would keep an eye open for him whilst she was away. When you summoned me to your cabin I asked if he could come with me rather than keep you waiting whilst I found the women so they could keep an eye on him".

"Summoned to my cabin?" the Sheik said defensively "what gave you the idea I summoned you. I merely put out the invitation for you to join me to discuss a proposition I have for you".

Derek stood by the table near the other door looking at the bowl of differently coloured wrapped sweets.

"Help yourself" the Sheik said to Derek.

Derek looked at Jeff pleadingly. Jeff said "Alright but not too many you will spoil your lunch".

Derek sat down and gently picked a sweet from the pile and slowly unwrapped it, laying the sweet paper out and flattening it gently. He ate the sweet and did the same with the second sweet, making a pattern of the wrappers, trying to look totally harmless and in a world of his own.

"He likes the coloured wrappers to play with" Jeff said.

Just then, there came a knock on the cabin door and an advisor called Jake entered, looked at Abdul and said "We have a problem" and then suddenly Jake appeared to realise the Sheik had company and shut up.

The Sheik said to Jeff "Come with me onto the balcony, we can talk there in private". The Sheik stared angrily at Jake "your friend looks harmless and happy enough with the sweets. I will get him a bowlful to take away with him" and Jeff and the Sheik went out onto the balcony.

"What seems to be the problem that you have to burst in here at this time" Abdul asked in Arabic of the man that had just entered.

Jake replied "Sorry but it is urgent" then seeing Derek asked "what about him?"

"Don't worry about him he's a dummy and has a job understanding English. He won't understand what we are talking about but speak in Arabic to be on the safe side just in case the dummy repeats anything".

Derek carried on as if he was in his own little world, playing with the sweet wrappings and eating more sweets. He also developed a silly grin.

Abdul insulted Derek in Arabic, looked at Jake and stated "See, I told you he was a dummy. Now Jake, tell me what the problem is? But keep your voice down as our so-called Sheik is entertaining a guest".

"Well" Jake said "it's the 6 man crew on the gas tanker. They have had no sleep for over 48 hours and they are getting tired, and because of this they are making mistakes and at this stage that could be dangerous".

Abdul replied coldly "All the men have had virtually no sleep for 48 hours on board here and they are tired too. At first I was opposed to this party this Jeff person is throwing for the Sheik's birthday but now I might use it to our advantage. By the way I must say I admire those Somalian pirates, they certainly know how to board ships. We did it with steel wire ladders, they do it with long bamboo poles they hook over the railings then shin up the bamboo pole like a monkey up a tree. That reminds me. When you go back to the NATGAS 2 use one of the port-side lifeboats. You will be seen by the Bridge on the NATGAS 2 that way. The starboard ones can't be seen from the Bridge and you risk being shot at as they won't see you coming. Do not forget to pull up the lower ladder for the gang plank then you can't be boarded easily".

"How about the steel wire ladders hanging over the stern. Do you wish me to pull them up out of the way?" Jake asked.

"You won't have time" Abdul replied "anyway, do not worry about them. Nobody is going to board the tanker using them. It took us weeks to learn how to do that and we were taught by the best and we still lost two men".

"What will The Senate say if we deviate from the set plan?" Jake asked.

"The Senate taught us to think on our feet and adapt the situation to our advantage" Abdul answered and then he replied to Jake in a whisper "anyway, I was thinking of using this party the pilgrims are throwing for our so-called Sheik, to our advantage".

"How do you mean?" Jake asked.

"Well" Abdul whispered "we could use the time to try and get our men some much needed sleep. At the moment, I could not spare the men, but with a party going on I can put men on standby and use a skeleton crew, so if I let them rest now, then they can take over whilst the others put their heads down. You know, I was not sure about this party but on reflection it could be to our advantage, and to the advantage of The Senate. So, make up a skeleton crew, no more than ten men, plus two advisors. Use Parvis as one advisor for the NATGAS 2. We can keep that ship on auto pilot. Eight for this ship, two on the Bridge and two either end of Deck 5 as we cannot let anybody onto Deck 5 otherwise they might spot the submarine's signals and we don't want anyone on board knowing about The Senate's submarine just yet. Not even our so-called Sheik, as that is our escape route. They will know about the submarine after we are on board it and we put a fish in the side of the Baroness of the Sea and the NATGAS 2. They will be so busy trying an impossible rescue of the passengers that it will be then that we make a clean getaway.

Let us get down to details. We can then have one armed guard each end of the main dining room with you and I and two of the advisors as backup. That will leave one advisor to guard the explosives on this ship. It will also give the illusion that there are more guards. We can get that ten and the advisors to put their heads down now, tell the rest of the men to hang on for a few more hours until early evening, and then whilst the Sheik is celebrating his surprise birthday party, under cover of darkness we can put the gas ship on auto pilot and we can match that with this cruise ship. Tell the men they can get some sleep. We need them fresh for when we transfer to the submarine The Senate has supplied at dawn".

"What is going to happen about the Sheik and his friend Mustafa?" Jake asked "how do we get them to co-operate with the change in plans?"

"We do not tell them. They have been useful tools in The Senate's plan. They are expendable as are the rest of these pilgrims on board.

By the way, do not forget to tell them to switch over to the remote on the timers set on the explosives that are set in-between the inner and outer hull of the NATGAS 2. We do not want our men to be asleep and on board when it goes up and we do not want to be aboard this ship when those other explosives go off either".

Whilst this conversation was taking place, Derek was forcing himself to act as though he was mentally challenged and intent on making pretty patterns with the sweet wrappings and eating sweets.

"Are you sure about him?" Jake asked, pointing at Derek.

"Yes, don't worry" Abdul replied in Arabic "he ran through the stupid forest and kissed every tree" then turning to Derek smiled and said loudly "thick as two planks end on aren't you?"

Derek smiled at Abdul in a very harmless and friendly way.

"See, I told you he was not all there, so don't worry, and he certainly will not be able to understand Arabic so you just concentrate on getting the men rested so they are fit for tomorrow".

The conversation over, Jake left the cabin.

CHAPTER 38

In the meantime, out on the balcony the Sheik was talking to Jeff.

"You know how much I admire you and what you do" the Sheik began "you and I have so much in common. I believe you and your talents are totally wasted and not appreciated by your people so why not come with me and I can make you a very powerful and very rich man. This invitation does include you, your wife and your friends.

We will be leaving this ship soon. I have shown my father I am a man not to be messed with. I now hold that so-called great nation America to ransom and I have brought them to their knees. What do you think? We can rule the world you and I?"

Jeff realised that the Sheik had a serious mental problem and would need delicate handling. Jeff had to keep him sweet otherwise he could flip at any moment and order everyone killed out of hand.

"This is a great honour and major surprise" Jeff replied "I would have to talk it over with my wife and my friends".

"You will have to let me know before tomorrow morning" the Sheik said "after that it will be too late".

Jeff said "I will give you my decision at your surprise birthday party tonight, and then we can celebrate together".

"Does that mean you accept my proposal?" the Sheik asked looking excited.

"You will have to wait until your surprise party tonight" Jeff repeated.

"I want to know now" the Sheik demanded petulantly.

"All in good time" Jeff responded firmly "so don't spoil the surprise. You have been very generous to me, let me be equally generous to you. You will have to wait until tonight, and then we can all celebrate together".

The Sheik looked like a cat that had been given the cream jug and he sounded extremely excited when he said "I am really looking forward to tonight. I will wear my best robes in celebration". He escorted Jeff from the balcony and they joined Derek who was still playing with the sweet wrappings.

"Until tonight" the Sheik said then he turned to Derek and added "Allah has blessed you" as he handed Derek a large bowl of sweets for him to take away.

Derek looked at Jeff expectantly as though he was a child that had been given a Christmas present.

Jeff nodded "Don't forget to say thank you to the Sheik".

Derek said "Thank you" and they left the cabin and returned to Jeff's cabin.

When they got back to Jeff's cabin the women were there having a drink together. When the cabin door had been closed, Jen explained about the woman who had nearly let the cat out of the bag, and how Jen could pack a good right hook and how the woman would be sleeping off the rest of the trip.

"Don't you feel sorry for me?" Cyril asked, as he came in from the balcony "see what I have to put up with. She beats me terribly, you don't want to see the bruises".

"I wish you wouldn't do that" Jen said "spring out from no-where like that. You made me jump. So, let's find out what you know".

Cyril told them about the conversation with the Captain, and then said to Jeff "I understand you got summoned to the Sheik, and I gather you took Derek with you. Now that was sensible, he is a good man to have at your side in a tight corner".

Jeff told them about the conversation with the Sheik and all about his offer.

"I hope you told him to put it where the monkey puts his nuts" Cyril said.

"I told him he would have to wait until tonight's party where we were planning a surprise for him on his birthday, but I don't think he is going to like the surprise and I think it will be then we might have a few problems with his army of guards. The trouble is, we don't know how many he has and where they are".

"There are only going to be ten guards and four advisors on duty including Abdul and Jake" Derek said to Cyril "they were discussing it in front of me in Arabic in the Sheik's cabin".

"How do you know Arabic?" Cyril asked.

"I learned a bit of Arabic from my wrestling trainer" Derek replied "he was an Arab. I was able to understand most of what was said by Abdul and the man who burst into the Sheik's cabin. I believe his name was Jake".

Derek continued, pleased with himself that he had a very attentive audience who were hanging on his every word "Apparently the guards have been without sleep for over 48 hours and they are making mistakes because they are so tired. Abdul wants to use the party as a way of getting his men some sleep before tomorrow when they need to be very alert for when the submarine arrives to take them all off".

"John guessed right then about the submarine" Cyril interjected.

Derek continued "Abdul is going to install a skeleton crew of ten men whilst the party is on, then he has ordered the others to rest. I even know where he is going to put the ten guards".

"That's brilliant" John said from where he was sitting quietly in a corner of the cabin "where?"

"But there is a down side to this" Derek said "The Senate is involved and it's them that are sending the submarine".

"What?" John exclaimed "I thought we eradicated them after what they did in the Estuary area and when they tried to destroy the British Government".

"Apparently not" Derek said "according to Abdul The Senate are behind this".

"There had to be a reason why the Sheik seems frightened of Abdul and also seems to take his orders from Abdul" Jeff said.

"What else did you find out?" Cyril asked.

"There will only be two guards on the bridge of the NATGAS 2 plus that evil swine Parvis" Derek said "the NATGAS 2 is going to be put on automatic pilot which will be set on the same course as the Baroness of the Sea, with two guards on the Bridge. There will be two guards either end of Deck 5 to stop people from going out onto that deck and there will be one guard either end of the dining room. The Sheik will be at the party. The only other thing is we don't know where this Abdul or this Jake will be and those two I don't trust as far as I can throw them. They both look nasty pieces of work. If the other four advisors are like them two we could have a problem on our hands".

"Also, to add to the problem, Abdul has a remote he can activate the timers on the explosives on board the Baroness of the Sea and on board the NATGAS 2" John said "the fact that we now know for certain that they have a submarine on standby is important, but that is something we can't do anything about, all we can hope for is that the Americans can take it out before it can do any serious damage or it evacuates the Sheik and his men".

"They might not be evacuating the Sheik or Mustafa" Derek said "according to Abdul the Sheik is only on board to serve a purpose and then is expendable".

"I bet he and Mustafa don't know that they intend to abandon them, so they take the blame for the them and hide the fact that The Senate is involved right up to its neck".

Cyril turned to Derek "That was a wonderful idea letting them think you were a dummy who did not know Arabic. We can make good use of that".

"He's no dummy" Sandra remarked defensively turning to Cyril with her eyes flashing.

"Sorry if that came out wrong" Cyril said apologetically to Sandra "I did not mean he was a dummy. I was only saying that by him acting as a dummy he has been very clever".

All the women started laughing at Cyril as he slowly realised he was being wound up by Sandra.

"You got me fair and square" Cyril said, holding his hands up.

"Well" Jeff said "we know who is going to be where, apart from the advisors. Now all we have to do is to get ourselves organised. When we know that we can let the Captain know what we plan. The Captain can then get his officers to co-ordinate with us as to what they are going to do".

John said "The ten men who will be cutting the tow ropes will have to have very sharp knives, and don't forget they won't be able to take them into the party as they will be searched on the way in. So how do you suggest we get the knives to them without raising any suspicions?"

"How about using the waiters to bring the men the knives from the kitchens" Jeff suggested "nobody will suspect a waiter if he is carrying a tray with a cloth draped over it, and he can be circulating and handing out the knives to the chosen men".

"That's good, I like your thinking" John said "but how will the waiter know who to give the knives to amongst the men at the reception?"

Karen spoke up and said "How about the men who require knives wear a red carnation in their buttonhole. The carnations can be obtained from the flower shop, you could even use different coloured carnations for your different teams so as to identify one from the other without raising any suspicions by the Sheik and his men".

"That's an excellent idea" Cyril said "I wish I had thought of that".

They all nodded in approval.

Jeff said admiringly "Now I know why I married such a beautiful and clever woman".

"You men don't have a monopoly on brains you know" Jen said "we women can use our grey matter sometimes" and she gave Karen a hug.

"Now how do we find out who our volunteers are without putting them under suspicion?"

Jen said "Us women will have to go to the toilets again as we did ask the women we approached to let us know by mid-day one way or the other".

John's wife said "How about getting them to give us their cabin number and we can co-ordinate what we are doing by using the cabin phones between 2 and 3 pm then only the people that are directly involved will know what team they are on and who they will need to co-operate with and what coloured carnation to wear and what their task is".

"How will they know it's us talking to them over the phone and not the Sheik's men?" Sandra asked.

"We can use a password" Rose replied.

"Sounds good to me" said Jen "what will it be?"

"How about British Bulldog" Karen suggested.

"British Bulldog it is" they all agreed.

"They have this down to a fine art" John remarked "thank Christ they are on our side".

"Women are more dangerous than men when it comes to defending their loved ones" Jeff said "and I am glad I have these four ladies on my side, I am proud of them".

"Crawler" Cyril remarked jokingly to Jeff.

"I'll have you know that I can get under a snake's belly with a top hat on if need be" Jeff retorted.

They all laughed.

After a while, Jeff said "You four be careful out there, we care an awful lot about you".

"Come on ladies, let's take them on" Jen said, as the four women made their way out of the cabin.

Jeff said "What worries me is that right wing group The Senate are involved in this. They seem to be manipulating everything in the background with their usual cunning but not getting involved directly".

"There is not a lot we can do about The Senate at the moment" John said "we have enough troubles trying to get out of this situation as it is, so let's concentrate on what we can do and then let the governments deal with them afterwards. They will by this latest escapade of theirs piss off America big time, and they'll hunt them down".

"This will be the second time we have run across them" Cyril said "they seem to want world domination by playing both sides against the middle on a global scale. Next time I see the Captain I will tell him The Senate is involved and they are the ones supplying the submarine. Perhaps this submarine can be taken out of the equation earlier by the Americans now they know who is involved. By the way, can I use your phone now to call Michael?"

John handed Cyril his mobile phone. Cyril dialled a number he had remembered. There was a connection on the other end of the phone and he heard Michael's voice say "Hello".

They exchanged pleasantries then Cyril told Michael what was going on and asked him to intercede for them with his cousin in the American Naval Intelligence. He also outlined the plan they were going to adopt and how it all depended on The Senate submarine being taken out before they took on the terrorists on board the Baroness of the Sea. He also explained to him that if they managed to get off the Baroness of the Sea they would try to make for Sable Island.

Whilst this was going on Jeff said "What we need to discuss is who is heading which team and how we are going to approach the different obstacles we have to overcome.

"Firstly, under cover of darkness, we have to have a party of at least eight men to secure Deck 5, ideally knock out the guards and dress four of them in the guard's uniforms to ally suspicion.

Secondly, we need to get a small party on board the NATGAS 2 and take that over. Those men must have some idea of how to operate the ship. They take out the two skeleton crew plus Parvis. These men people must be volunteers as they might not make it back and if that tanker blows they will go up with it".

"How do we get them on board the NATGAS 2 without being seen?" John asked.

"The same way the terrorists took over the tanker in the first place" Derek replied.

"And how was that?" John asked.

"By the wire ladders trailing from the lower deck at the stern of the NATGAS 2" Derek replied.

John looked shocked.

"Apparently they left them there when they first boarded the NATGAS 2" Derek explained "they were taught by Somalian pirates on how to board vessels off Somalia as part of their training. If we can get one man on board that way he can get round the side and lower the steps of the gangplank where we can get a team on board. We need to use a starboard lifeboat as that can't be seen by the bridge of the tanker because of the angle we are at the moment. Well that's what Abdul was saying when he thought I was a dummy. By the way, did you know Somalian pirates use bamboo poles? They hook them over the bottom rail on the lower deck then shin up them in the dead of night and hijack any ship they want. We could take a leaf out of their book and board the NATGAS 2 the same way they hijacked it in the first place. Then as I see it we need a party of at least ten men to sever the tow ropes securing the two ships together.

We need a party to retake the Bridge and get the Captain back on the Bridge as he is the best one to sail the Baroness of the Sea.

We need a party to release the rest of the crew of the Baroness of the Sea held in the forward hold. We need another party of volunteers to find and disarm the explosives on board this vessel. That has to be done before we take back this ship.

We need another party to take out the guards at tonight's surprise reception and party for the Sheik. Abdul and that Jake I feel are going to be our biggest problems. They both look as though they can handle themselves.

We also need people to distribute the food with the sleeping medication in it. We need to speak to the First Officer to find out what help we are going to get from the crew. Have I missed anything out so far?"

"Timing is going to be critical" John said "and whatever happens you have to be at that reception otherwise the Sheik will get suspicious. It would be a good idea to take Derek with you, he will be able to handle anybody like Abdul if they get out of hand".

"Where are you going to be?" Jeff asked John.

"Disarming those explosives on board this ship and making them safe" John said "before they can be set off remotely".

"Why you?" Cyril asked "you could be blown to bits".

"Because I was in the bomb disposal service at one time" John said "and I know about timers and explosives and that makes me the best man for the job, and besides I know where they have put the explosives".

Jeff said "I will need to talk with the First Officer to find out if any of his crew will volunteer to sail the gas tanker".

"In that case I will take charge of the party that takes over Deck 5 and also the rope cutting crew".

"That just leaves the women to get the other women organised for the surprise party and get the drugged food to the guards" John said.

"That does not leave Derek and me a lot to do" Jeff said.

"You have to do the most dangerous job" John replied "actually be in the lion's den and bullshitting the Sheik. Above all Mustafa and the advisors must be made to believe that this surprise party is for real". John paused. "I mean this as a compliment" he continued "but you are the best bullshitter I know. I have seen a lot of politicians in action

"SAY NO"

but you take the biscuit for bullshitting and can run rings around most of them. We all will be relying on you to be convincing enough to allow us to do our part. If they for one minute suspect what we are doing, we are dead in the water. You will need Derek with you because with the Sheik on the cusp of sanity and the looks of Abdul and that Jake you will need instant backup if things turn nasty. The other two guards on that deck can be taken out by crew members, then all we have to deal with is the sleeping guards and that is the easy bit.

May I remind you it was your idea to throw this surprise party so we could retake this ship with the minimum loss of life. And it might work, therefore you have to be the best host there is to ally their suspicions".

"We will have to give the sleeping guards a chance to go right off to sleep before we get a party to round them up" Derek said "how about letting them have some drugged food before they bed down, they are bound to be hungry. Then all we have to do is go round and pick them and their guns up".

"That's a good idea" John agreed.

Derek pointed to his head then to his feet and said "Up here for thinking, down there for dancing".

All four of them smiled.

Cyril said "We now have to wait until the women get back then they can make the phone calls to the different cabins. They are the best at organising a party anyway".

"Cyril is going to see the Captain don't forget, and I will need to see the First Officer" Jeff said.

"When I see the Captain, I will get him to give a message to the First Officer to come to see you rather than risk you being caught in the act of something suspicious at this late stage" Cyril said.

"Now comes the hard part—waiting until we can put all this into action" Jeff said "I think it's going to be a long night and I suggest we get some rest".

CHAPTER 39

Jeff had had his lunch and was having a lay down in his cabin trying to catch up on some sleep whilst the women were in Cyril and Jen's cabin organising the different parties into colour coded operations by what carnation they were wearing, when there was a knock on his cabin door. He slid off the bed and opened the door and there was the First Officer standing before him.

"I understand you wish to make a formal complaint" the First Officer said loudly. The faint hubbub from Cyril's cabin stopped instantly, as the First Officer said "I am here to take your written statement so we are clear as to the nature of your complaint".

Jeff looked up the corridor to see two guards laughing and another guard trying to translate from English into Arabic what the First Officer had said.

As the third guard turned round he could see it was the man who had entered the Sheik's cabin unannounced who went by the name of Jake and he was translating what the First Officer had said to him.

It was obvious that the First Officer was using the embarrassment ploy to fool the two guards at the end of the corridor.

"You had better come in so we can get it written down" Jeff said.

The guards continued to laugh and seemed to take great delight at the First Officer's embarrassment.

After Jeff had closed the cabin door the First Officer said "We will have to continue that charade when I leave. I have a written false claim in my pocket. The Captain tells me you wanted to talk to me urgently".

Jeff explained what they had planned and when it was all going to take place and he then said that they needed a volunteer crew to sail the NATGAS 2 once it had been cut free from the Baroness of the Sea but it was a suicide mission.

The First Officer said "I will find you that crew" he then added "mind you, if we change the course of the NATGAS 2 we can leave it on automatic pilot for a short while, that will probably be long enough to get it clear of the Baroness of the Sea".

"How far away are we from Sable Island?" Jeff asked.

"We pass within 50 to a 100 miles of it between 5 to 6 am in the morning, why?" the First Officer asked.

"Well, I understand from the sea to a land lubber it looks like the American coastline" Jeff said.

"That is true" the First Officer said "but it is Canadian territory and it is not called the Atlantic graveyard for nothing. There have been hundreds of ships lost there on the deadly sandbanks that surround the Island".

"Well if things go belly up with what we plan" Jeff said "we might need to get any survivors off this ship and we are too far away from America or Canada for a rescue attempt for this amount of people, and besides they will sink us if they feel we are a threat to them, and all the time the NATGAS 2 is tied up to us we are".

"I can change our course slightly" the First Officer said "without raising any suspicions to enable us to veer nearer to Sable Island. By dawn you will then be able to see Sable Island on the horizon with the naked eye and at the angle you want, but as you say America or Canada won't let us get much closer to their coastline without reacting in a way we won't like".

"That's why our timing is crucial" Jeff said "we have to act at the end of the surprise party so we can take back this ship before the Americans decide we are too close to their territory for comfort".

"We do need the Americans to take out that submarine as soon as possible or at least before you change course, otherwise the submarine might give the game away to whoever is talking to them aboard this ship. If that happens we could get a torpedo in our side to add to our problems".

"What happens if the Americans can't find and disable that submarine?" the First Officer asked.

"Then it doesn't matter what we do" Jeff said "but at least we would have had the guts to say no and that's the important bit".

"Don't you fear these people and what they can do?" the First Officer asked.

"The only thing you need to fear is fear itself" Jeff answered "these people rely on the fear factor to make people do what they want. If you remove the fear factor then their control over you melts away".

"I never would have thought of it that way, but you are right" the First Officer said.

"By the way" Jeff said "so our people can recognise and tell which of your crew will be helping us, get the ones that are willing to do something to help to wear a carnation as a sign they can be trusted. Now we had better get on with the charade of my complaint so as to fool the guards".

The First Officer opened the door to the cabin and immediately went into a humble stance as he went out of the door "I will see that your complaint is addressed straight away" he said loud enough for the guards to hear "I have all the details, all I can do is to humbly apologise for any inconvenience caused".

The guards smiled at the First Officer's predicament as he left.

Jeff lay back on the bed trying to think if there was anything else he could do when Karen walked into the cabin.

"Hi lovely" Jeff said "how have you ladies done today?"

"Jen and Sandra are fantastic at organising" Karen said "it's all in place, and all we have to do is wait until tonight when it all slips into place just as you planned. By the way, we decided it is to be a formal dress party to help cover that a lot of people will be wearing carnation buttonholes".

"That won't please Cyril" Jeff said "he doesn't like dressing up as a penguin as he puts it".

"Can you pour me a drink?" Karen asked "I could do with one before we have to start getting ready for tonight's surprise show down".

Jeff said very lovingly as he handed her the drink he had poured out for her "I am very proud of you and the way you have supported me in this".

"I love you not only for you, but for what you stand for" Karen said "and if in my small way I can help and support the principles you live and die by then I am content".

"Now I know why I love you so much" Jeff said, as he hugged and kissed her.

"Enough of that" she said "if I am going to go, then I want to look stunning when I do go, and I don't want you looking scruffy either".

They both laughed.

CHAPTER 40

Jeff, Karen, Cyril, Jen, Derek, Sandra, John and Rose left their cabins together.

As all eight of them made their way to the cocktail lounge for drinks before dinner they were joined by Mustafa and Asar his wife.

"I hope this surprise party tonight is going to be successful" Mustafa said "the Sheik is looking forward to it. What surprises have you in store for him? He so does like surprises".

Jeff had come to like Mustafa and Asar and felt that the man was in deeper than he wanted to be and wanted to get out if he could, but his loyalty to the Sheik and the Sheik's family was very strong. His family had always been bodyguards to the Sheik's family for generations and he was the first one that had broken that tradition.

"It would not be a surprise if I told you what it was, would it?" Jeff said "the surprise you have to worry about is the surprise Abdul and Jake have in store".

"What do you know about Abdul and Jake?" Mustafa asked quizzically.

"Ask them if they are members of The Senate" Jeff said.

"Who and what is The Senate?" Mustafa asked.

"Ask them" Jeff reiterated "and if you get the answer I think you will get, come and find me at the party. As you ask them your questions think about the conversation you and I had about the Russian revolution, the Chinese uprising, and the German Nazis and the cost in millions of innocent lives, and all for a political cause".

Mustafa left with his wife to find Abdul and Jake whilst Jeff's party made its way to dinner.

"What was that all about?" Cyril asked "you're playing it close to your chest with him".

"Divide and rule" Jeff replied "it's about time we put some dissention in their ranks. If Mustafa wants out, as I think he does, but can't because of family loyalties to the Sheik, then if he thinks the Sheik is in danger, he becomes the enemy of my enemy that makes him my friend. We can tell him all we know but because of his family loyalty to the Sheik he won't believe us, and the only way he will find out the truth as to how him and the Sheik are being manipulated, is by him cross-questioning Abdul and Jake. All I have done is to sow the seeds of doubt in his head and now we let it grow".

"Remind me not to play poker with you" Cyril said "you are too devious for me".

"There is more than one way to skin a rabbit" Jeff said "now let's go and eat and you can order one of your lovely bottles of wine".

"You must have ice in your veins" Cyril said "what we are doing does not phase you does it? I believe you are enjoying the challenge of going up against impossible odds, with the hope of winning".

"We have nothing to lose and everything to gain" Jeff said "if we do nothing we are dead, if we all do something we might all live, and if we fail and die in the attempt, then we will have chosen the way of our death".

They went into the dining room and they were impressed by the amount of men wearing different coloured carnations, including a vast number of waiters and all of the senior catering staff who were dotted about in what seemed to be strategic positions.

The food was excellent as usual, and if you looked very closely as the plates were cleared you could see the men with carnations being given different sharp knives from the kitchen by the waiters.

The waiter serving them at their table gave them all a knife including one each for the four women, which they hid for safe keeping in case they were needed.

They had finished their meal and were making their way to the Reception area which was being used so the catering crew could prepare the dining area for the party. The area had already been dressed up and the final touches were being added.

There was an air of expectancy in the room. As they entered, they were handed a glass of champagne.

Mustafa spotted Jeff and his party and made his way towards them. He looked very worried and agitated and seemed as though he was having a hard time controlling himself. He blurted out "You were right, how did you know?"

"The Senate were behind the Estuary incident which very nearly brought down the British Government" Jeff explained "we thought we had rounded them all up, but it looks like they are trying to take over your country as well by getting the Americans to attack your country in retaliation for holding them to ransom over this hijack.

They are still stirring up bad blood between friends, tribes and nations for their own ends and they don't care who or how many people they have to kill to furnish their own ends. You, your wife and the Sheik's wives and his personal bodyguards will not be allowed to leave this ship when they transfer to the submarine as I believe there is only enough room on board the submarine for the six advisors and I also believe they are the only members of The Senate on board this ship and remember that the submarine belongs to The Senate.

By them using your lifelong friend and taking advantage of his sickness they are manipulating the situation for their own ends" Jeff finished.

"That is a farfetched story" Mustafa said "I don't believe you, by the way how did you know about the submarine?"

"Derek overheard Abdul and Jake talking about it in the Sheik's cabin" Jeff replied "he understands and speaks Arabic and he also heard what they were planning and how they intend to dump you and the Sheik at the first opportunity and leave you two to carry the can".

"But he is a dummy" Mustafa said, pointing to Derek.

"I have always found it is better to let someone think you are stupid than to open your mouth and prove them right, you then have the advantage" Jeff said "and by the way Derek is far from stupid because he fooled you and all the others into you letting down your guard".

Derek interjected and obliged Mustafa by speaking to him in Arabic.

Mustafa looked stunned and said "I do not believe it".

"I am good at reading someone's character" Jeff said "and I believe you don't want thousands or possibly millions of deaths on your conscience, and I also believe you are torn between your loyalty to your friend and his family and the realisation of being the instrument of those deaths, and that is tearing you apart".

"There is nothing I can do" Mustafa said "my family have always been bodyguards to his family, and the tradition goes back decades. I am the first eldest son in my family who did not follow that tradition".

"You and I know that the Sheik is not a well man" Jeff said "he needs protecting from himself and from The Senate and you are the best one to do it. You are his life-long friend, he will listen to you when he is more lucid".

"What are you going to do as a surprise for him at this party?" Mustafa asked.

"That is a surprise that we will enjoy giving Abdul and Jake also anyone else that stands in our way" Jeff replied.

"You can't, they will have you surrounded and out gunned" Mustafa said "besides they have explosive charges placed in strategic places on board both ships. Any attempt to take back this ship will be met with violence and those explosive charges will be detonated. Look around you. All you have are a few totally unarmed guests dressed up as dog's dinners waiting for free drinks and free food".

"Look more closely at them" Jeff said "every one of them is armed and they are not only fighting for their own lives but also the lives of their loved ones, and when that happens don't stand in their way because you will have to either stand with them or behind them. If you get in their way you will not survive. Have you ever seen a pack of hyenas take down their prey? It is not a pretty sight".

Mustafa looked shocked at what he was hearing and knew that the people he was looking at were not going to roll over and give up. They would die for what they believed in and that was the survival of their loved ones at any cost.

"You now have a choice" Jeff said "you are either with us or you are against us".

"What about Asar?" Mustafa asked "she has nothing to do with this".

"If you are with us I will put her under my protection, if you are not with us then I cannot help you if things get nasty, but one way or another we intend to take back this ship even if we die in the attempt. If that happens we will take a lot of them with us including the Sheik, so if you want to save him now's the time because here he comes with Abdul and he has Jake with him as well".

The Sheik was dressed in white robes. He looked stunningly handsome and proud. He had a very large jewelled broach pinned to his chest, he also had a matching dagger to the one he had given to Jeff tucked in his waistband.

"I am looking forward to my surprise party" the Sheik said "when do I get my surprise? I cannot wait".

"You would not like me to spoil the evening by giving you my surprise too early, would you?" Jeff said "we need to get everything ready. In the meantime, we can have the dancing girls on for your entertainment".

Jeff lifted his hand to signal the Entertainments Officer who was at the side of the stage and a troop of dancing girls appeared from off-stage and started dancing.

As the guests mingled, it was slowly becoming obvious that the longer the evening went on the more nervous and agitated they were becoming.

"What about my surprise?" the Sheik reminded Jeff "I have not had it yet, and you have not yet given me your answer concerning whether you are going to join me".

"Firstly, let me present your birthday cake" Jeff said.

An enormous, elaborate cake in the shape of a cruise ship was immediately rolled in on a trolley and positioned before the Sheik.

Jeff produced the ornate dagger the Sheik had given him and said to the Sheik "Shall we cut it together?" pointing to the Sheik's dagger.

The Sheik smiled and produced his dagger. They both sliced into the rich icing at the same time.

"Let everybody on board eat cake" the Sheik shouted benevolently "we must share it out with everyone".

Jeff's heart sank. He was relying on the drugged cake knocking out all the guards and with them asleep taking over the ship but if they all ate the drugged cake they would be knocked out also and their plans would go up in smoke.

The Sheik waited for Jeff as he hesitated to eat the piece of cake he had been given.

Karen said to Jeff "You will love it, it's your favourite cake and it was made especially for the Sheik. The other identical cakes are being cut up and circulated to everyone on board in honour of the Sheik's birthday".

Karen knew he was not a lover of cake, but what she was telling him was that this cake did not have any sleeping draught in it and was safe to eat.

The Sheik's birthday celebrations continued.

After an hour, the Sheik approached Jeff as he stood with his wife, Derek, Sandra, Jen and Asar.

The Sheik had Abdul and Jake with him and they both looked angry and concerned.

"When am I going to get my surprise you promised me?" the Sheik asked.

"Now if you like" Jeff replied.

"See, I told you he had a nice surprise for my birthday" the Sheik said turning to Abdul and Jake.

"It is not your birthday surprise we are concerned about, it is the fact that we have not heard from the submarine. They were supposed to have called us as we got near to the American coast" Abdul said.

"Check your radio again" the Sheik said "we have already been through this, and it is probably a delay in the signal or something" then turning to Jeff said "I have been very patient all evening, now where is my birthday surprise?"

"It will certainly be a surprise to you" Jeff said to the Sheik.

"Are you are going to join us" the Sheik asked expectantly "we can take on the world you and I, we will be unstoppable".

"No, you and Abdul surrender to me now" Jeff said.

"What?" the Sheik said, shocked.

Abdul interceded and said "You are joking. We outgun you, outnumber you, plus you have a torpedo aimed at you right now. All I have to do is snap my fingers and we all die".

"Now we know who is pulling the strings" Jeff stated "it's you and The Senate" Jeff said, looking at Abdul.

Abdul looked at Jeff with astonishment and blustered "What do you know about The Senate?"

"It was The Senate" Jeff said "who caused the mass murder in the Estuary. They tried to destabilise the British Government so they could take over the country and change it into a right wing state. They failed in their attempt and this attempt also is going to fail. Your submarine has been taken out of the equation by the Americans that is why you can't get a signal from it".

Abdul looked suspiciously at Jeff and said "How did you know its location?" he asked.

"We didn't" Jeff said "the Americans hunted for it and found it".

"How did they know there was a submarine out there?" Abdul asked.

"We told them after you let our friend Derek know".

"He's a stupid dummy" Abdul said "how would he find out?"

"You told him when I was talking to the Sheik on the balcony and Jake came in the room. Derek was sitting down pretending to play with the sweet wrappers. He was listening to your conversation".

"But we spoke in Arabic" Abdul said "he could not have understood".

"You overlooked one thing. You underestimated Derek" Jeff said "you treated him as a stupid backward foolish idiot. In fact he is perfectly able minded and he understands Arabic".

The realisation suddenly dawned on Abdul that he had been suckered and he stated furiously "You will die for that" and as he approached Jeff pushing the Sheik out of the way, he grabbed for the dagger in the Sheik's belt and slashed at Jeff.

Derek moved with lightning speed. He swung a punch at Abdul catching him squarely on the jaw. Abdul crashed to the floor unconscious whereupon Jake jumped onto Derek's back and held him in a wrestler's strangle hold.

Jeff held his dagger to the Sheik's throat and said "Let him go or the Sheik dies right now".

Jake scoffed "We don't care what happens to him. Kill him if you want to he means nothing to us, he never did. He is only a means to an end, and we used him to get what The Senate wanted".

As Jeff was distracting Jake, Derek suddenly spun round releasing the hold Jake had on him. At the same time Derek turned and put Jake into a spine lock. As Jake struggled in Derek's vice-like grip the people heard the clear snap of Jake's spine and Jake's body went loose.

There was a look of horror on the Sheik's face. He blurted out "He was one of our country's Olympic wrestlers and you snapped his spine just like that".

"I told you not to underestimate him" Jeff said, as Derek dropped the body of Jake and left it lying in a heap at his feet.

"Now where is that other toe-rag?" Derek asked.

Abdul was no-where to be seen. In the confusion he had regained consciousness and made his escape.

Whilst the scuffle was going on between Jake and Derek the guards on the door had been taken out by the people near the door.

CHAPTER 41

Whilst this was going on, on Deck 5, three guards had been taken out by the party headed by Cyril, but the fourth guard had got himself into a position whereby he could control the deck area and nobody could get to him without being killed.

Mustafa approached Cyril "I can get to him and take him out, give me one of the guns from the guards".

Cyril looked at him and said "I am not that stupid".

"It's the only way" Mustafa said.

"You can have the gun but it won't be loaded" Cyril said.

"Right, fire a few shots in the air" Mustafa said "and do a bit of dying or moaning if you get my drift".

Cyril fired a few shots in the air and Mustafa called out in Arabic to the guard that he had shot the insurgents and he was coming out to him as everything was alright now.

Mustafa slowly made his way toward the guard. The guard looked relieved to see Mustafa

"It is alright now" Mustafa said in Arabic "a small group decided to make a fight of it. We have just killed the last of them".

The guard looked relieved and as he relaxed and stepped in front of Mustafa, Mustafa hit him on the back of the neck with the butt of the gun Cyril had given him. The guard collapsed on the ground.

Mustafa waved to Cyril to come out onto the deck.

"Well done" Cyril said "now all we have to do is get our volunteers on board the NATGAS 2".

"I will have to go with them" Mustafa said.

"What, that is suicidal" Cyril said.

"No-one speaks Arabic" Mustafa said "and the sound of those shots might have alerted those two guards and Parvis the advisor on board the NATGAS 2. I don't need to remind you that they are armed and they can set off the charges at any time. I would not put that past Parvis, he is a nasty bit of work. You need someone who can speak Arabic to talk them out of setting off those charges. You also need to concentrate on getting those ropes cut and get these two ships separated otherwise if that gas ship is not clear of this cruise liner by dawn America will sink both ships. It will be false dawn in about 2 ½ hours' time, dawn will be a short time after that. It will be then that the Americans will be all over us like a rash".

"You can't do that on your own" Cyril said, handing Mustafa a loaded gun and a spare clip of ammunition showing him he trusted him.

"Look I admire what you are standing for, and I realise I have been on the wrong path. Jeff trusts me now, otherwise he would not have suggested I help" Mustafa said "he has guaranteed the safety of Asar who is with him now. We both know the Sheik is not a well man and he has been taken advantage of by The Senate. Jeff has said he will try to keep him out of harm's way until he can get some medical help for his condition".

Cyril could see Mustafa was having a job coming to terms with the fact that whilst he had been away pursuing his own way in life, his lifelong family friend the Sheik had become mentally ill and desperately needed help.

Mustafa seemed to check himself and said "Now let us get down to business because time is running out. Out of the ten volunteers we have chosen five and that includes me. I understand there is a fast motor boat on board the gas ship, they used it to hijack the NATGAS 2 in the first place. If we can launch that we might get a chance of getting away before it blows up if things go wrong".

"You know your chances are slim to none" Cyril said "so why are you doing this?"

"I don't expect you to understand" Mustafa said "but my family have been responsible and looked after the Sheik's family for decades. My father and his father and his father before him have been personal bodyguards to sheiks and it was to be my role in life, but I wanted a different way and left to find a different path.

The sadness and disappointment I caused in my family, I was not aware of until tonight. I now know I was wrong and even though I know the Sheik is not a well man, I will follow in my father's footsteps and try to prevent him coming to any harm, even though it might cost me my life, that is what it is to be a personal bodyguard".

Resolutely Mustafa turned to the four waiting men and waved them forward, and then he said to Cyril "Now let me get on board that tanker with my four volunteers. By the way, we took our guns from the rest of the sleeping guards, whatever you gave them knocked them out for the count. They are sleeping like babies. Give me a bit of time before you start cutting the tow ropes. I will try to give you a blast on the horn when to let you know when it will be the best time for you to cut them". With that parting remark, Mustafa disappeared into the gloom as he made his way towards where he was to get over onto the NATGAS 2 with his volunteers.

Mustafa and the four men launched one of the rear-most starboard lifeboats with the help of some of the crew, two of whom stayed with the lifeboat to help handle the lifeboat and bring it back to the Baroness of the Sea. The lifeboat swung out and circled round to come up behind the giant tanker. Cyril was relieved when he saw they had all made it to the launch without incident. He also knew that once Mustafa disappeared into the darkness he was on his own, creeping up behind the NATGAS 2 unseen.

Now would be the hardest part, waiting to give Mustafa time to get to the Bridge of the NATGAS 2 undetected before his crew cut all the tow ropes. At the same time he knew when that happened he would be leaving Mustafa and his four volunteers stranded.

Cyril gave the signal for all the men to stand by. They had allocated two men to each of the five tow ropes and they waited for the signal and were ready to cut frantically at his command. Cyril said "Pass the word along for them to lie down flat when you cut the rope, because if the rope is under strain when they are cut, the ropes will act like a bullwhip and could kill someone".

Mustafa asked the Coxswain to switch off all the lifeboat lights then circle as wide as he could so the lifeboat would not be seen from the bridge of the NATGAS 2. He then asked him to get as close to the stern of this leviathan of the sea as he could.

The Coxswain eased the lifeboat into the wash of the NATGAS 2. The closer they got to the giant tanker the more they bounced about in the tumbling cauldron of the wash. They could see the ends of the steel ladders dangling from the lower deck and bouncing around in the wake of the tanker.

The closer they got to the swinging steel ladders the more the lifeboat bounced about. The bottom rung of one of the ladders was bashing against the lifeboat and one of the crew members grabbed the ladder and swung out over the boiling water, his lower legs and feet dragging in the sea. Slowly the man climbed up the steel ladder, hand over hand knowing that if he lost his grip he would plunge to certain death.

Gradually he made it to the lower deck and swung himself over the guardrail. The crewman then made his way to the gangway ladders and lowered the lower steps of the gangway to sea level.

As Mustafa saw the crewman disappear over the lower deck railing he ordered the other crewman to bring the lifeboat round to the side of the tanker hugging the side of the Baroness of the Sea so as not to be seen from the bridge of the NATGAS 2 just to where the gangway steps were and as the lower steps were lowered he and the four chosen men sprang aboard the NATGAS 2 and made their way to the Bridge leaving the Coxswain and the lifeboat to fall back behind the NATGAS 2 then make its way back to the Baroness of the Sea as best as it could.

Mustafa and his small band of followers managed to get onto the lower deck of the NATGAS 2 without being seen. Mustafa knew that it was at that point that he and his volunteers would be at their most vulnerable. If they were spotted then they could be picked off like clay pipes in a fairground shooting gallery.

They made their way carefully to the gangway that would lead them to the Bridge. Mustafa knew that there were three heavily armed men on board the gas tanker and he had to either capture or kill them. Apart from a surprise attack the only other advantage he had was that he knew the terrorists were tired from lack of sleep.

He split his small attack force into two to approach the Bridge from both sides.

As he got halfway up the gangway steps that led to the Bridge he saw a shadow at the top of the gangway steps. He was caught out cold and expected bullets to rain down on him.

He decided he would try to bluff his way out of the situation he found himself in so he called out in Arabic "It's Mustafa. The Sheik sent me across to tell you we have put down their little rebellion so there is no need to worry".

"Come up here where I can see you" the voice said warily.

Mustafa raised one hand and used the other hand to hold onto the gangway railing as he mounted the steps to the top of the gangway. He stepped out on deck as he cleared the gangway steps. An evil looking Parvis stood facing him looking alert and ready for action.

"We had better tell the others" as Parvis waved his gun at Mustafa and pointed towards the door that led to the Bridge.

"How did you get on board?" Parvis asked.

"Up the gangway ladder" Mustafa replied "why do you ask?"

"I need to find out why they left the gangway ladder down and punish them as I ordered it pulled up" Parvis responded.

Whilst this was going on, the other volunteers had made their way around to the other side of the Bridge and had entered it from that side.

There was an exchange of gunfire on the Bridge as they got to the Bridge door and started to open it.

CHAPTER 42

After what Cyril thought was an eternity, he heard small arms fire coming from the Bridge of the NATGAS 2 and promptly gave the order for the ropes to be cut, knowing he would be condemning Mustafa to his fate.

The men frantically started cutting the ropes holding the NATGAS 2 alongside the Baroness of the Sea.

The last tow rope was taut and snapped when it was cut. Made weak by the strain on it, the rope parted with a resounding crack like a giant rifle shot. The last umbilical cord holding the two ships together was now strained to breaking point. It was like a giant tug of war between two leviathans of the sea. The rope at last parted and the two ships lurched violently as they parted. The two ships then slowly and almost imperceptibly began to pull away from each other.

As the two ships drifted apart, Cyril could just see by the lights on the Bridge of the NATGAS 2 a battle raging for the Bridge. After a flurry of shots all became quiet. After what seemed like a lifetime, the horn from the NATGAS 2 sounded. By the light of a false dawn that was rising in the east, the NATGAS 2 could be seen ploughing its way through the water, away from the Baroness of the Sea.

On the skyline, land could be seen and Cyril was relieved. He knew they had cut their timing very fine. He mentally wished Mustafa and his band of volunteers good luck as he knew they would need it.

On board the NATGAS 2, the loud cracking sound from the parting rope alerted Parvis on the Bridge and he turned around in surprise as Mustafa attacked him. They struggled together and then the NATGAS 2 lurched. Parvis was thrown off balance and at the same time Mustafa shoved Parvis. Parvis hit the railings and toppled over them. The man fell at least two decks before he hit a mooring cleat on the next deck with a sickening thud and thereafter did not move.

When Mustafa entered the Bridge there were four people lying in pools of blood, two volunteers and the last two guards.

Just then one of the injured guards reached for a device that had fallen out of his hands, grabbed it and activated it. He then succumbed to his wounds and died.

"What did he activate?" Mustafa asked "look around and see if you can see anything on the Bridge. We had better disconnect the autopilot and head away from the cruise ship and towards that spit of land on the horizon where there is a lighthouse light. You can just see it in the gloom. I am going to check on Parvis as he just took flying lessons".

Mustafa climbed down two decks and approached the man who lay still and twisted on the deck. As Mustafa approached him, Parvis moaned, calling out for water.

"What was the device they activated on the Bridge?" Mustafa asked the dying man.

"Water" Parvis moaned.

"What was the device they activated on the Bridge?" Mustafa asked more insistently.

"Auto destruct device" Parvis answered weakly "explosives have been set in between the inner and outer hulls, between the storage tanks and the ship's hull. There is a two hour delay before detonation".

"How do we deactivate it?" Mustafa asked.

"You can't. Once it is activated it stays that way. We were always going to blow the gas ship up no matter how much ransom was paid" Parvis explained weakly "if you have time to launch the speedboat and get clear, take me with you" and then he grimaced in pain and died.

"Great" Mustafa said to the heavens "we are sitting on a giant time bomb and the time is ticking away".

Mustafa made his way to the Bridge to tell the remaining two volunteers news that they did not want to hear. The only way off the floating time bomb was by the speed boat Fast Lady which had been used to hijack the NATGAS 2 in the first place. But before they could launch it and use it they had to get the NATGAS 2 as far away as possible from the Baroness of the Sea. They would still need time to get clear before the NATGAS 2 went up in a ball of flame.

As dawn started to break, the NATGAS 2 headed towards the Sable Island. With its many sandbars that surrounded the Island, Mustafa knew there was probably going to be another shipwreck taking its place in the Atlantic graveyard.

By using the Bridge binoculars, Mustafa could just make out the waves breaking over the sandbars at the end of the long narrow spit of land. He had cut the engines of the NATGAS 2 and using the momentum of the ship headed the ship towards the sandbars to beach it. He knew it could take up to two miles before this leviathan of the sea would stop. He could just make out the Baroness of the Sea in the distance and hoped they had changed course.

They were launching the Fast Lady but it seemed to be taking an eternity and the sandbars were getting nearer. Eventually the Fast Lady touched the sea and Mustafa gunned the engines into life. They sped away and when about a mile clear of the gas tanker there was a scraping sound of the big tanker running aground on the sandbar.

Mustafa gunned the engine of the highly powered Fast Lady and sped further away from the stricken gas tanker and out to sea towards the Baroness of the Sea where his wife was waiting for him under Jeff's protection.

As they were nearing the Baroness of the Sea, Mustafa could just make out that the cruise liner seemed to be listing slightly to one side.

Just as he was trying to make out why the Baroness of the Sea was listing, there was a violent explosion emanating from the stricken NATGAS 2 behind them.

Mustafa killed the speed of the power boat and let it drift round to point in the direction of the NATGAS 2.

The auto destruction device had done its job and the side of the gas tanker had split open like a tin can. Cryogenically cold liquid gas poured out into the sea and thereupon exploded into a fast expanding cloud of methane gas on contact with the water, spreading out at an alarming rate into a white fog of death.

The unstoppable chain reaction started. The liquid gas was expanding 620 times its size from liquid to gas instantly. There followed a large number of explosions called Rapid Phase Transitions that caused further damage to the ship's hull and released even more liquid gas from the other tanks on board the NATGAS 2.

Mustafa was witnessing the phenomenon at first hand and did not like what was unfolding before his eyes. He saw the deadly cargo of gas expanding and flowing towards him and the Baroness of the Sea. He knew that if the unconfined vapour cloud reached the Baroness of the Sea then any spark on board the liner would ignite it and envelope the ship in a fireball of temperatures hotter than burning petrol.

There were two options. He could hope the spreading gas cloud would dissipate into the air, or, the gas cloud had to be ignited before it reached the Baroness of the Sea.

He was hoping the first option of the gas dissipating would resolve the problem, but the gas cloud kept expanding at a phenomenal rate and was getting nearer. He gunned the speedboat to its top speed away from the stricken NATGAS 2 and towards Asar aboard the cruise liner but the boat seemed to be making heavy weather of it. Mustafa gradually came to the conclusion that the only option left open to him was to ignite the gas cloud before it got to him and to the Baroness of the Sea.

He said to the two men he had left with him "The only way is to ignite that cloud. When we do that our best protection is to go over the side and dive deep to avoid being burned. Hand me that Very pistol and get ready to go over the side. Dive as deep as you can when that cloud ignites".

Mustafa stopped the Fast Lady and turned her towards the expanding gas cloud. He extracted the Very pistol from its box which had been handed to him and pointed it high in the air towards the expanding cloud. He pulled the trigger.

A red star shell erupted from the pistol and arched its way towards the expanding gas cloud. The red light hung in the sky for what seemed an age then suddenly the gas cloud erupted into a fireball.

The three men dived into the sea and swum down as deep as they could. Above them the surface of the water sparkled brightly with the detonation and the resultant flames as they seared across the surface of the sea.

After what seemed an eternity, with bursting lungs, the men were forced to the surface only to find that the speed boat they had abandoned earlier was burning.

They swam to the Fast Lady and boarded her via the stern section. The front part was burning from the devastating heat sear of the exploding gas. Mustafa retrieved the fire extinguisher and proceeded to put out the fire on the bow of the boat.

He was surprised at how soon they managed to get the fire under control and he breathed a sigh of relief. "We should try the engine" he said.

One of the volunteers went to try and start the engine, it struggled to fire at first but eventually coughed into life.

"I didn't expect that" the man said to Mustafa "perhaps our luck has changed".

Mustafa looked in the direction of the Baroness of the Sea. He could see some structural damage on the upper decks from where he was but she was still afloat but she still appeared to be listing even more than the last time he looked.

Mustafa turned and looked in the direction of the NATGAS 2 but he could not see it. In the distance where the giant tanker had been there was a slowly increasing fireball like a new born sun rising out of the sea. The sea was also tilting at a strange angle.

As he watched the sea, he came to the realisation that a giant wave caused by the explosion on board the NATGAS 2 was heading their way. There was nowhere to go except to hope to ride out the wave.

He shouted to the two men "Strap yourselves down, that wave is going to hit us shortly and we need to turn into it. Give it full power, it's our only hope".

The wave was getting bigger and bigger as it headed towards them. All they could do was to keep the powerful engines of the Fast Lady at full throttle.

The giant wave came crashing towards them. It picked them up like a toy and the world tilted crazily out of kilter as the wave came crashing in. They seemed to be riding on a giant white knuckle ride as the powerful engines of the Fast Lady gave all the power they had as they attacked the wave head on.

It seemed as though they were climbing a giant hill of water. They crested the giant wave and teetered on the brink, the screws of the propellers screaming into empty air. The flow of the wave went under them and they crashed into the trough of the wave only to find another wave bearing down right on top of them.

Mustafa pushed the straining engines to their limit ready to attack the next wave with the battered Fast Lady. This time they almost got to the top of the wave when it crashed down on top of them and swamped them, burying them in a wall of water.

Water cascaded down onto them but the Fast Lady popped to the surface, only to face another wave heading towards them. All Mustafa could do was to steer the Fast

Lady towards the next wave. He felt like a cork in a washing machine being tumbled about as the Fast Lady started to disintegrate around him. All he could do was pray that she held together long enough for them to survive.

The next wave was not as powerful and they rose to the top of it and then pitched down into the trough of the next one and gradually the sea settled around them.

They were very battered and bruised but miraculously they had survived, but now they were drifting aimlessly on the ocean and at the mercy of the sea.

As Mustafa looked to where the Baroness of the Sea had last been seen, he saw the first of the giant waves that had battered them breaking over the Baroness of the Sea. The cruise liner tilted upward at what seemed an impossible angle with its bow pointing into and buried by the crest of the first giant wave. It looked as if the cruise liner would flounder, but by what seemed to be a miracle the Baroness of the Sea pushed its way through the crest of the first wave.

As the ship tilted towards the trough of the second wave, Mustafa could see the mighty propellers that were the powerhouse of this mighty floating luxury hotel come out of the water. He then lost sight of the vessel as the second wave crashed over it.

Suddenly Mustafa realised his own predicament and that the Fast Lady was swamped with water. He looked around for the other two men who had been with him but they were not to be seen. He was the only survivor. He looked around desperately to see if he could see them but to no avail. He then started bailing out the stricken Fast Lady and prayed that someone would see and help him before the Fast Lady sank. In the meantime, he would have a desperate battle against time to survive as the tide was slowly pushing him and the stricken Fast Lady towards the burning hulk of the NATGAS 2.

CHAPTER 43

Back on board the cruise liner, John had checked and made safe the explosive devices in the stern and the middle of the cruise ship and he was checking the last of the explosive devices by the forward locker and had just made them safe. He was then able to release the rest of the crew from the forward locker. An Officer who introduced himself as the Chief Engineer thanked him.

John said "You had better go to your Captain and take back your ship".

The Officer shook his hand and said to the other men "Come on, the Captain needs us".

John was making his way back to the middle of the deck he was on when he heard running footsteps on the grating above where he had finished making the devices safe. He looked up just in time to see Abdul making his way into a small cargo hold that John did not realise was there.

John followed Abdul to the hold and spotted Abdul over the far side. He was bending over with his back to John.

John's foot knocked against a small piece of metal lying on the floor and this made a scraping sound. Abdul spun round, saw John and said "You! You are the one that stopped me detonating the charges I laid. Now I know why my remote didn't work. Well, you will not stop me this time".

He then turned away from John, reached down and lit the fuse that was trailing from explosives that were pressed against the outer hull.

John rushed at Abdul, but Abdul was ready for him. They clashed together as they met in the middle of the hold.

Abdul was a highly experienced assassin. He had been picked out by The Senate for his skills.

John had been a member of the elite SAS and he had kept up with his training.

As soon as the two men clashed together, each knew from experience from the first holds that they had an experienced opponent that would take all their skills to overcome.

They crashed together smashing into stacks of metal racking that was in the hold. This racking started to tip over and as it toppled it crashed into other stacks of racking that also toppled over like tumbling dominoes. All this metal spilled into the emergency escape hatch blocking it. The only way out of the hold now was the way John and Abdul had come in.

John was trying to get to the explosives to defuse the detonator, and Abdul was trying to stop him at all costs. It was a clash of the titans and there seemed no impasse.

As the fight continued, the burning fuse to the explosives was decreasing in length.

John knew he had taken on a killer with a lot more experience than he himself had. It would only be a matter of time before Abdul got the upper hand and he could feel that Abdul knew it. As he looked over Abdul's shoulder and saw how short the burning fuse to the detonator had become, he gave one last mighty heave and pushed Abdul towards the explosives. He then turned and made a dash for the inward opening door.

Abdul smiled knowing he had beaten the Englishman and started to run after him.

John made it to the door and managed to get out of the room just as Abdul got to the metal door as John was closing it. Abdul pulled at the closing door, trying to free it from John's grasp and then the explosives detonated, blasting the door shut with Abdul inside the room. The concussion from the explosion killed him outright. John had the protection of the metal door from the blast but he was still thrown down the gangway with the force of the explosion.

Stunned and with his ears ringing, John made his way slowly back through the smoke to the Restaurant area where Rose was waiting.

CHAPTER 44

Whilst all this was going on, Cyril's team had cut the ropes securing the gas tanker to the cruise ship and Cyril had made his way to the Bridge. As he approached the Bridge, he heard small arms fire coming from that direction and noted that there was obviously a gun battle going on for the control of the Bridge.

Cyril went up the gangway on one side of the deck which would take him to the Bridge just as bullets were ricocheting off the guardrail of the ship. He could see the First Officer leading a team to take back the Bridge from the other side of the deck but he was pinned down by a fuselage of gun fire from the Bridge. Using the guns taken from the guards they had disabled, Cyril and the men who were with him opened fire from their position, catching the guards who were on the Bridge in a cross-fire. The guns on the Bridge went silent.

The two groups approached the Bridge from both sides very warily to find three men lying in a pool of blood, two seemed dead and one was badly wounded.

"Was I pleased to see you" the First Officer said "they had us pinned down and there was nothing we could do. They were first alerted by the gun fire on Deck 5, and then by the gun battle on board the NATGAS 2, so when we put our heads above the parapet so to speak they were taking pot shots at us and we could not return the complement. Good job you came at them from a different angle and caught them in a cross-fire otherwise they would have had us pinned down forever".

Now the First Officer said "We need to get this ship off of auto pilot and onto a different course away from the NATGAS 2. It looks like it is heading for the Atlantic graveyard off of Sabre Island and we don't want to be in the same graveyard".

As the First Officer took over the controls and took the ship off of automatic pilot there was a massive explosion and a black cloud and a massive spray of water emanated from the side of the Baroness of the Sea.

"Good God! What was that?" the First Officer said, as an acrid cloud of smoke bloomed from the side of the liner "we must have been hit by a torpedo or we have hit a mine".

Smoke was now billowing from the side of the cruise liner.

"See what damage there is" the First Officer ordered and a crew member dashed out of the Bridge to investigate.

The First Officer said "I don't know what damage has been done but she is starting to get sluggish". He then ordered another crew member to find the Captain and if he was alive to get him up to the Bridge quickly.

Just then the crew member he had sent to have a look at the damage to the ship returned and speaking breathlessly said "I don't think it's a torpedo or a mine. Looking at the way the plating is twisted, if it had been a mine or a torpedo the plating would have been bent and twisted inwardly, but by the looks of the damage it looks like it was made from inside the ship. The bad news is it looks like there is a large hole just on the waterline and we seem to be shipping water every time we roll with the swell of the sea".

"It looks like the only option we have now is to try and make it to Nova Scotia before we sink" the First Officer said.

"How about this Sable Island you spoke about" Cyril said "that's nearer and we can see it on the horizon. It looks a big enough piece of land from here".

"What you can see is what has made a fool of a lot of mariners over the last 300 years" the First Officer said "that land is very long and it is very narrow. It is shaped like a long curved sword blade surrounded by treacherous sandbanks, that is why it's called the Atlantic graveyard. Over 300 ships have been lost there. To beach a ship there has to be a last resort, our best bet is still Nova Scotia".

CHAPTER 45

As all of this was going on, what had been a reluctant birthday party reception had now turned into a survival party, with people congratulating one another and cheering as the NATGAS 2 had sailed away.

The body of Jake lay on the floor ignored. Derek took the Sheik back to his cabin for safe-keeping before the passengers had turned into an angry mob, seeking revenge against the Sheik for what they had been through. He left two passengers guarding the sheik

As the people calmed down and looked out at the NATGAS 2 in the distance they could feel the Baroness of the Sea starting to make heavy weather of the relatively calm seas.

Then from the doorway of the Restaurant came a blood curdling scream "You betrayed me!"

People screamed.

There in the doorway stood the Sheik, he had escaped from the cabin, He was armed with the jewelled dagger and looked as though he had finally flipped over into insanity. He had a crazy look in his eyes and was drooling. He was staring at Jeff.

"Why? I would have given you everything you ever wanted. Why did you turn on me? We are men of our word.

We could have ruled the world. Well nobody plays me for a fool, you will die for your insult to me". He then started stalking Jeff, slashing out at anybody who got near him but slowly making his way towards Jeff.

"I will cut out your heart" the Sheik said "and I will feed it to the fish. I will make you obey me".

The Sheik was shouting at the crowd of passengers who were trying to avoid him. "I am your ruler, I am your Sheik and I will be obeyed, or you will suffer. I will show you what I do to treacherous dogs like him" pointing at Jeff.

The Sheik circled Jeff, slashing out at him with the dagger.

Jeff backed away from the danger of the slashing blade and then dodged round a pillar, still facing the Sheik. It gave him a little ground in which to manoeuvre. He slid his right arm out of his coat and wrapped the rest of the coat around his left arm as a shield against the slashing blade of the Sheik.

The Sheik lunged at Jeff. Jeff caught the slashing blade on the coat wrapped around his arm. As he parried the lunge away he hit the Sheik with his fist, giving the Sheik a bloody nose. The Sheik backed away in shock, he had not expected to be attacked as he felt he had the upper hand.

This made the Sheik even angrier and he attacked with a new frenzy stabbing and slashing at Jeff.

As Jeff backed away from this latest onslaught he crashed backwards into a pillar.

The Sheik saw his opportunity and lunged forward at Jeff screaming in Arabic.

As the Sheik lunged forward Jeff again caught the blade of the dagger in the coat wrapped around his arm. He felt the blade bite into his arm. At the same time Jeff kicked out hard with his right foot at the Sheik catching the Sheik hard in the crotch.

The stunned look of shock and surprise on the Sheik's face was a picture. The Sheik went down gasping for air and curled up into a ball holding his crotch, dropping the jewelled blade in the process.

"Tie him up so he can't escape" Jeff ordered breathlessly to one of the men who were standing nearby. The man looked confused as to where he was going to get a rope from.

"Use the tie-backs from the curtains, but this time tie him to a pillar, and make sure he can't escape".

Derek came over to him holding the jewel encrusted dagger the Sheik had just used to good effect. Derek said "Yours now I believe?" as he handed Jeff the dagger "and where did you learn to fight like that, I'm impressed?"

"I grew up in the rough part of Tooting, South London during the Teddy boy days and there are some things you never forget, by the way where were you? You were supposed to act as my bodyguard" Jeff said smiling at the big man.

The big man looked hurt at first then realised Jeff was joking, then a big grin came over his face and he bear hugged Jeff and said "You know I would die for you".

Jeff looked down at the dagger and said "This will be a matching pair to the other one". As he said this, the coat he had wrapped around his arm dropped to the floor and there was a wound on his forearm where the blade of the dagger had caught him".

"You're bleeding" Karen said, looking stunned and seeing her husband in a light she had never seen him in before. She had never seen him in an actual fight and she was not sure it was a side of him she liked.

"It's only a scratch" Jeff said.

Karen grabbed a napkin from the table and wrapped it around his arm. She said "You frightened me. I've never seen you like that before, and it's not a side of you I like".

"It was me or him" Jeff said defensively to Karen "and don't forget he was armed with a knife. He's ruined my tuxedo, my tailor will go mad over this".

Karen laughed at his remark more out of relief than humour, and then she fussed over him for a short while as the hubbub of what had just happened died down.

As they were gathering themselves together, there was an almighty explosion and the ship shuddered. There was smoke starting to rise from the side of the cruise ship where the hull had been breached by the explosion.

What was a celebration had now turned in to a panicking mob of people screaming and wanting to know if they had been torpedoed.

Jeff grabbed a microphone from the stage area and asked people to calm down. He said "You are on the safest part of the ship so stay where you are until we find out what has happened".

Again, the ship's public address system burst into life.

"This is your Captain speaking. As you know, we were hijacked by pirates but that is all over now. There has been an explosion on one of the lower decks. Due to damage sustained we will be making for Nova Scotia in Canada where we will berth. The danger from the NATGAS 2 has passed as that is at least six miles away now thanks to the brave volunteers who sailed it away from us. We have sent out distress calls and help will arrive soon. In the meantime, please stay in the Restaurant area as this is the safest part of the ship".

Just then a bedraggled John came into the restaurant and said "It was Abdul. He set off an explosive device. I tried, but I could not stop him".

After what seemed an age, John got to Jeff's side. He appeared battered and bruised

"Where is he now?" Jeff asked.

"Scattered all over the cargo hold" John replied graphically.

"I see you've been having fun" John said, looking at the Sheik tied up against the pillar still bent double in agony and groaning.

He showed John the dagger the Sheik had attacked him with, and said "Now I have a matching pair".

John raised his eyebrows in surprise "I can see I will have to keep an eye on you if you show me anymore sides of yourself I did not know existed".

Jeff smiled.

As they talked about what had happened, Jeff pointed out the NATGAS 2 in the distance and told John how Mustafa had seen sense and helped take back the NATGAS 2, free it from the Baroness of the Sea and sail towards Sable Island and the Atlantic graveyard.

John said "Where is he now?"

Jeff said, pointing to the NATGAS 2 "Over there, making sure we are all safe".

"Rather him than me" John said.

Just then, there was a rumbling sound which came from the direction of the NATGAS 2. All eyes turned again in the direction of the giant gas ship. All could just see in the distance the side of the NATGAS 2 peel apart as though someone had used a mighty can opener then the tanker was shrouded in a giant white gas cloud that looked like sea mist drifting towards them. Jeff knew his greatest fears had been realised, and a catastrophe was playing out before his eyes that he had spoken of. He had been ridiculed that the scenario would never happen.

Then there was a deafening explosion emanating from the NATGAS 2 and the nightmare scenario unfolded as the white freezing cryogenically cold fog of boiling liquid natural gas started flowing from the NATGAS 2 reacting with sea water causing Rapid Phase Transition explosions. Jeff knew his worst nightmare was about to unfold before his eyes and there was nothing he could do about it.

Mustafa's wife Asar looked horrified at the explosions coming from the NATGAS 2. She put her hands to her face and screamed out "Mustafa".

Jeff then saw the Fast Lady powering her way away from the unfolding nightmare.

Jeff pointed the Fast Lady out to Asar and said "He might have made it". They watched as the Fast Lady turned to face the massive deadly gas cloud emerging from the NATGAS 2, then everything seemed to happen in slow motion as the nightmare unfolded in front of their eyes.

The cryogenically cold gas cloud was rapidly rolling towards them at a colossal rate. In between the Baroness of the Sea and the expanding deadly gas cloud emanating from the crippled NATGAS 2 was the lone Fast Lady waiting as if in defiance.

Jeff could tell by the way the gas cloud of methane was rolling towards them that they were going to be in its direct path and there was nothing they could do about it.

It would only be a matter of a short while before the crippled Baroness of the Sea with all its passengers and crew were engulfed in the deadly cryogenically cold expanding methane gas cloud and when that cloud was at the right mixture of gas and air, it would find an ignition source and would create a disaster of biblical proportions. They were trapped in its path with no way to avoid the unfolding scenario.

All they could do was watch as the ever expanding cloud of death rolled towards them from the crippled gas tanker. Their only hope was if the wind suddenly changed direction and blew the deadly gas cloud in another direction but that was very unlikely.

Jeff could just make out that the Fast Lady had stopped and was now facing the expanding gas cloud that was approaching it.

Then there appeared a red star shell from a Very pistol arcing its way towards the expanding gas cloud that had been fired from the speed boat.

The star shell seemed to hang in the air above the gas cloud for ages, and then with a devastating concussion the gas cloud ignited, firstly at the edges and then flashing back to the crippled gas ship almost instantly.

The searing heat of the ignited gas cloud spread out from the gas ship as the massive amount of released gas exploded into a fireball of horrendous temperatures.

The concussion from the exploding gas that followed this ignition was like an invisible wave of raw power slamming against everything in its path.

Forward panoramic windows in the dining room cracked with the concussion from the blast emanating from the now crippled NATGAS 2 and even at the distance they were they could feel the effects of the searing fireball of heat.

If the expanding gas cloud had been any closer to them or the person on the Fast Lady had ignited the gas cloud any later the Baroness of the Sea would have suffered more devastating damage from the heat sear of exploding gas than it did when the gas cloud exploded. It had been a very close run thing.

Jeff realised straight away that the person in the Fast Lady who had fired the star shell into the expanding gas cloud had sacrificed themselves so that those on board the Baroness of the Sea might stand a better chance of survival.

The chances of anyone surviving on the Fast Lady were virtually zero, so Jeff sent out a silent prayer of thanks to them, thanking them for their sacrifice.

CHAPTER 46

The events that started to unfold before Jeff now resembled something from a disaster movie.

There were further explosions from the crippled NATGAS 2. The fireball engulfing the NATGAS 2 streamed hundreds of feet into the sky and blotted out the horizon. It was as if a piece of the sun had landed in the sea and was boiling like a vast cauldron.

The resultant concussion on the seabed from the massive detonations began to create a tidal wave. It was as if some giant invisible monster had woken up and was rising from the bowels of the sea in vengeance for being woken up from its sleep. Pressure built up and the giant tidal wave was born.

Jeff could see the horizon starting to tilt. At first, he thought it was an optical illusion, but as the tidal wave built he could quite clearly see the wall of water bearing down on the ship.

He shouted out "Everyone, brace yourselves for impact. Hold on to something firm, there is a tidal wave on its way. It may swamp the ship".

Jeff thanked God that the sea was relevantly calm but the tidal wave that was heading for them continued to swell in the distance. The Captain was desperately trying to turn the bow of the crippled ship to head into the giant wave.

To add to the desperate plight they were in, the explosion in the cargo hold had been at the waterline. A hole had been blasted in the cruise liner's inner and outer hulls so every time the cruise ship rolled with the swell sea water poured in flooding the decks below the waterline.

The ship seemed to be getting heavier and more sluggish as she started to list.

For the passengers, what had started as a luxury holiday had turned into the worst nightmare imaginable.

They had been thrown into the middle of a political nightmare. They had been hijacked and forced to defend themselves against terrorists and now they were faced with the forces of nature at their worst. They had been pawns in a giant game of political chess and were to have been sacrificed so even more people did not die and political faces could be saved.

It had been up to them all, if they were to survive, too bind together, to fight against professional killers as there was not going be any outside help.

The passengers and most of the crew were huddled in the Restaurant and recreational areas on the upper decks except for the crew required in the Engine Room where they had all been until recently under guard by the fanatical terrorists who had hijacked the Baroness of the Sea.

The culmination of the scenario that was unfolding in front of Jeff was something out of bad dream.

The Captain of the cruise ship told the passengers he had sent out an international May Day so help would be on its way soon. He then explained to the passengers via the public address system that he could not use the lifeboats yet as he felt they would be swamped by the wave. Until they had ridden out the tidal wave caused by the explosions they were at the sea's mercy.

The wave was heading their way and he felt that everybody stood a better chance in a bigger vessel. Also he felt the wave would hit in the middle of launching the lifeboats and there would be more lives lost. He had hoped to keep passengers calm during this next crisis.

The Captain knew he could not outrun the wave and if he tried the wave would most probably swamp the ship from the stern. If the wave hit on either side it would probably roll the ship over. The only chance he had was to head into the wave bow first with the engines at full power and try to ride the wave and cut through it.

In the relatively calm sea, the tidal wave looked huge as it slowly made its way towards the ship, swelling massively as it got closer.

Over the PA system the First Officer was now instructing everyone on board that just before the wave hit everyone should hold on very tight and brace themselves for the impact. He said he would sound the ship's horn three times just before the wave hit.

Jeff could see the wall of water heading towards them through the windows at the side and front of the ship. The bow of the ship turned towards the wall of water slowly and was now pointing straight at the wave as it rushed towards them.

The ship's horn sounded. At the first long blast, Jeff finished tying Karen to a pillar with tablecloths from the table. He made sure she was facing the stern of the ship so any loose debris flying around would hit the pillar first and afford her a little protection and not pin her to the pillar. She also had a knife so she would be able to cut herself free afterwards.

It was the only protection he could find for them at short notice.

Jeff strapped himself to the binding that held Karen and they both held onto one another and prayed as the second blast sounded on the horn.

He could feel the tilt of the ship as the third horn sounded.

It felt as if he was on a fairground ride and was being tilted backwards, as everything twisted out of kilter. He could hear the thundering sound of the huge wave as it slammed into the Baroness of the Sea.

Lots of things happened as if in slow motion.

The ship felt as if it was climbing a giant hill as the Baroness of the Sea rose up the giant wave like a surf board. The water from the top of the wave crashed down onto the bow of the ship cascading over the deck and swamping the ship from bow to stern.

Tables and chairs were flung about like matchwood as was anything that was not nailed down. Debris flew around everywhere.

As the ship shuddered and ploughed through the crest of the wave the propellers could be heard screaming above the roar of the water as they were exposed.

It was then that Jeff felt a pain in his left arm and shoulder which was wrapped around Karen protecting her. Something that was flying loose had hit him. He looked at a terrified Karen to see that she was unharmed. He was relieved that whatever it was had only hit him and had missed her.

As the Baroness of the Sea crested the wave and slammed back down into the sea the second wave hit just after that but this wave was not as powerful as the first.

After the fourth wave the Baroness of the Sea had turned slightly sideways and now started to corkscrew and slowly settle. At least they were still afloat but the crippled ship had been severely damaged.

Jeff felt the pain that was coming from his arm and shoulder becoming more intense as they were flung from one side of the pillar to the other just like rag dolls. He felt as though he had been put through a tumble drier.

He knew that if he had not strapped himself to Karen he would have been unable to protect her during the violent tossing about.

Jeff could see that the brave Captain had headed the Baroness of the Sea to the shallows of the sandbars hoping to run the ship aground on a sandbar and in doing so, beach the ship before it sank.

As the Baroness of the Sea settled down from lurching to just swaying Jeff looked at a terrified Karen and they both thanked God that they had survived the explosions and waves created by the dying NATGAS 2.

Now their troubles would really start as they would have to try to survive the inevitable ship wreck of the Baroness of the Sea. Jeff believed that the ship had taken more punishment than it was originally designed for.

Using his right hand to cut the strapping he had used to bind them safely together, Jeff freed himself and Karen and they staggered as the ship swayed. Jeff fell into the pillar and in doing so landed on his injured shoulder which pained him greatly. Something hit him on the head hard and he passed out.

CHAPTER 47

Jeff came too, his head throbbing, his arm and shoulder very sore. Karen was bending over him. He was covered in dust and a few bits of ceiling. She was asking him if he was alright as she wiped away the blood from the wound on his head.

"How long have I been out of it?" Jeff said to Karen.

"A few moments" she replied "you were hit on the head by falling debris, you got the worst of it when you shielded me".

Jeff sat up his head thumping, but as it gradually eased to a dull ache, he could look at the damage done by the tidal waves that had hit the Baroness of the Sea. It looked as though someone had swung a wrecking ball though the Restaurant area. There were people moaning, some women were crying and some were rocking in silence, holding onto their pain.

As Jeff stood up, the world spun for a while and the throbbing in his head increased then died away slowly. Derek was supporting him in case he fell.

"thanks big feller" Jeff said to him.

"We need to see to the injured" Jen said, then she added "come on ladies, there's work to do" then turning to Jeff, Derek, and John said "you three make yourself busy and find my Cyril" then she turned to Asar and said comfortably "we all hope Mustafa makes it".

"Where's the Sheik?" Jeff asked "he's not where we left him. He must have broken free during all the chaos".

"Well he didn't go far" John said as he looked at the twisted body of the Sheik lying with a broken piece of handrail sticking out of his chest. It looked as though he had been speared by its jagged point as the cruise ship was tossed around like a cork in a washing machine.

"Hey you three! Go and find my Cyril" Jen ordered again "and don't come back without him". Pointing to the Sheik she added "he's not going to do anybody anymore harm, so go!"

They rushed off to find where Cyril was, like told off children trying to make amends for being naughty.

They took a deck each and searched amongst the debris and the smashed sun loungers, and then they met up and decided to split up again and do the same on the other decks.

They met up on one of the upper decks.

"He's nowhere to be seen" said John "I don't want to be the one to tell Jen we can't find him so we had better go on looking".

"Where can he be?" Derek asked, looking worried.

"The only place left he could be" Jeff said "is on the Bridge. We'd better go there and search. If he's not there then the only other thing that could have happened to him is that he could have been swept overboard. I really don't want to be the one to tell Jen that".

They approached the Bridge and as they got there a voice said "You're not allowed in there, that's for crew members only". This came from a crew member holding a gun captured from guards and that was pointing directly at Jeff's stomach.

On hearing the disturbance, the First Officer came out of the Bridge and asked what the fuss was all about. On seeing Jeff, Derek, and John, he said "You are a very welcome sight for sore eyes".

The crew member said "But Sir, you told me not to let anyone through and to shoot them if they did not obey".

"We will make an exception with these three" the First Officer" said "we have these to thank for the retaking of our ship. By the way" the First Officer added "we have a friend of the Captain's you should meet". He escorted them onto the Bridge.

Standing next to the Captain was Cyril.

Jeff let out a sigh of relief upon seeing his friend and said "Jen sent us out to look for you, when we couldn't find you we thought you might be feeding the fish my friend".

"The fish would have choked themselves and then spat him out" Derek said and laughed with relief at seeing that his friend was unharmed. He gave Cyril a massive bear hug "boy am I glad I don't have to tell Jen we thought we had lost you".

The Captain said "We are not out of the woods yet. The cruise ship is taking on water fast. I don't think we can make Nova Scotia with the hole we have in her side and the battering she has just taken. The only piece of land anywhere near here is Sable Island and we are already within the area known as the Atlantic graveyard, so Sable Island is the only chance we have. I need to beach her before she sinks, it's our only chance to save as many people as possible. It's going to be rough on them but of the two options it will give the rescue services a better chance of helping us and they will be able to save more people.

To add to our problems, I have to avoid the burning NATGAS 2. Luckily she has run aground on the far eastern tip of the sandbars.

We also need to put a patch over the breach in our hull. That would give me a bit more time to cover the distance between us and the crippled NATGAS 2 and allow us to make for the western end of the Island before this ship sinks. It's going to be a close run thing".

The First Officer interjected and said "The sandbar the burning NATGAS 2 has run aground on has to be avoided at all costs otherwise we will be going from the frying pan into the fire literally. We need to be able to avoid the other sandbars and make it to the beach at the western end of Sabre Island.

I don't want to add to the problems but unless we get a patch on that breach in the hull we are not going to make the beach at all. We will sink in the most awkward spot possible for a rescue attempt, so if we are to save as many people as possible we must make that beach. It's not going to be easy putting a plaster over that wound".

"How do you put a plaster over that sort of wound in a ship?" Jeff asked.

"We will use a massive canvas and slide it over the side of the ship above the hole. When we lower the canvas over the hole the pressure of the sea will suck the canvas towards the hole in the ship and hold the patch in place. This will slow down the massive amount of water that is pouring into the ship every time the ship rolls. The more the ship is wallowing the lower she settles in the water. Once the hole in the side of the ship gets to goes below the waterline the ship will go one way and that's straight down. The hardest part is keeping the canvas out square so that it covers the whole of the breach in the first attempt.

To do this we will need every able-bodied man to hold the canvas as we lower it as we don't have any cranes or jigs we can use as this is a passenger ship".

"I see the theory you are trying to put in place" Jeff said" but that will be very dangerous for the men holding the canvas if it goes wrong. They could be dragged over the side as the sea takes hold of the canvas and sucks it into place".

Jeff thought for a minute and then said "Why not use the jibs from two of the lifeboats to hang the canvas from whilst the canvas is lowered in place, then you can use one of the lifeboats to take the ropes from the bottom end of the canvas and help get those ends of the ropes to the other side of the ship so the bottom of the patch can be held in place using the other side of the ship to secure the ropes from. By going round the front of the ship the lifeboat can slide the rope under the hull until it is in the right position".

"That's an excellent idea, we have nothing to lose by trying it" the Captain said "see to it Number One. Take as many of the crew you need to get the job done. See that they wear fire suits as well in case we get too close to the gas ship. We might be sacrificing two lifeboats in the short term but in the long term it might make all the difference between being able to beach this ship and losing her and I would hate to lose my ship or get any of my crew or passengers roasted alive in an attempt to save her".

The officers departed and went to find the massive canvas required so they could put the patch in place. They knew it would be a race against time to get the job done and get to the beach in time before they sank.

"Now gentlemen" the Captain said "personally I would like to thank you all for your help and co-operation in taking back my ship. I will be forever grateful as will the owners.

Now, how is everything in the Restaurant area? It looks as though it took a battering, do you know what the extent of the casualties is?"

"I think it needs a fresh lick of paint" John said, wryly.

"A lick of paint! You must be joking" Derek said "It looks like a wrecking ball has been swung around by a petulant giant".

"Jen is organising the injured and she is quite a formidable force" Jeff said "there is a lot of help from your first aider's".

John then told the Captain his side of what had happened—as to how he had defused the explosives, and how Abdul had set fresh charges and what had happened to Abdul when the explosives had detonated.

Cyril told him his side of everything—of how his team had made sure the guards were put to sleep and how Mustafa had turned up trumps and had knocked out the last of the guards on Deck 5, then how Mustafa and his crew of volunteers had commandeered a lifeboat to take back the NATGAS 2 and the last he had seen of Mustafa disappearing into the gloom with the lifeboat.

They presumed that they had somehow made it onto the NATGAS 2 because when they had heard shots fired from the Bridge of the tanker that was when he, Cyril, had ordered the tow rope cut. Cyril told them that one of his men had broken his arm from the whiplash of the snapping rope. It was shortly after that, that he had heard the signal of a blast on the gas tanker's horn and the gas ship had veered away and had sailed off towards the eastern end of Sable Island.

The gas ship had eventually run aground and it had looked as though the explosives on board had detonated. This had released Liquid Natural Gas which had boiled out of the hull causing other detonations. They had seen a Very light igniting the gas cloud and the NATGAS 2 had then blown up.

Cyril added "That Mustafa was a very brave man. He saved us all and I want that on record. Without his change of heart and him helping us when he did we would all have been part of that fireball we just witnessed".

Derek told the Captain how he had understood Arabic and how he had let them think he was a dummy and because they thought that he was able to overhear what their plan had been which gave them the advantage they needed.

Derek bowed his head when he told the Captain how he had to snap Jake's neck "I did not know he was an Olympic champion. I did not want to kill him but if I had let him go he would have killed Jeff. His neck snapped in the struggle".

Jeff told him about his part and how he was concerned for Mustafa "If he was on that speed boat then he would have been the one to ignite that gas cloud. If he had not done that, that cloud would have reached us on this ship and ignited.

"I will put out an alert for Mustafa, which is the least we can do" the Captain said "if he is alive they might pick him up in a search and rescue operation whilst they are helping us. In the meantime" the Captain continued "you had better go and let your wives know you are safe. By the sounds of it they are very busy with the injured and could do with some help. I will need all my skill in saving my ship.

"What about helping your crew with that canvas?" John asked "it looks like they could do with a hand".

"Leave that to my Number one and the crew" the Captain replied "they know how to carry out emergency drills and they are the best people to deal with the operation.

You have done more than enough by helping to save my ship. It could not have been done without your assistance. You can best help by letting your wives know you are well and by helping with the injured if you can. My Medical Officer, the Nurses and all my first aiders are going to be stretched to their limits until help arrives from the rescue teams who are on their way as we speak.

The Captain turned to the crew member guarding the Bridge "if any of these four wish to see me for any reason they are the only passengers who are to be allowed on the Bridge. Now if you will excuse me gentlemen, my crew have a plaster to put over a wound on my ship. Everyone will be safer in the Restaurant area or in the inner areas of the ship as we get nearer the NATGAS 2. Anyone out on deck and exposed to the tanker fire will get badly burned".

All four men made their way back to the Restaurant, much to the delight of Jen who walked over to Cyril and hugged him as though she was never going to let him go. They all greeted their wives warmly. It was a sad sight to see Mustafa's wife Asar standing very proud and alone.

The four women quickly surrounded her and attempted to reassure her that Mustafa might still be alive and if he was he would be found by the rescue services.

The crew outside were making very good progress and fast work in getting the patch over the hole in the hull of the ship. They could hear the winches of the second lifeboat as it was being lowered with the end of a large sheet of canvas stretched out from stem to stern of the lifeboat.

The first lifeboat had already taken the ends of the ropes connected to the bottom of the canvas sheet had had gone around the bow of the Baroness of the Sea, trailing the ropes behind them. As the ropes tightened they slid under the hull and the ends of the ropes were passed up to the deck on the opposite side of the ship and connected to the lifeboat winch on that side.

As the second lifeboat was lowered, the winch on the other side of the ship lifted the ends of the ropes. The patch slid slowly down the side of the ship towards the gaping hole and was guided into place by the second lifeboat as it was lowered.

As the canvas slipped over the hole in the side of the Baroness of the Sea, there was a sucking noise as the pressure of the sea water flooding into the ship dragged the canvas over the hole was secured in place by ropes from both sides of the ship.

The Baroness of the Sea turned towards the burning NATGAS 2. The Captain knew that he had to get the Baroness of the Sea passed the NATGAS 2. It would be like running a gauntlet that was now a giant flaming beacon pouring out death and destruction for the unwary.

They had to sail as close to the inferno as they dared to save time and to avoid the hidden sandbars. They had to get passed it get as far away as possible to the other end of the Island.

The canvas patch had afforded them some time as it slowed down the rate at which the sea was flooding into the Baroness of the Sea, how much time nobody knew. All everybody could do was pray that the canvas patch held and that the pumps in the hold which were running at full capacity, could afford them enough time to make landfall and safety.

CHAPTER 48

The Captain could not increase the speed too much as he had to be very gentle with his crippled ship otherwise the canvas would be dragged from the hole and the sea would cascade into the hold of the ship and the Baroness of the Sea with its precious cargo would founder.

They had arrived at the point of no return. The Captain knew that he had to run the gauntlet of getting past the inferno of the burning gas tanker on one side and the deadly sandbanks on the other side.

He could not get too close to the sandbanks for fear of running aground in a slowly sinking ship. On the other side of the ship, he could see that they were getting nearer the burning gas tanker.

The heat was intensifying as they drew level with the NATGAS 2 and for what seemed an eternity they could feel the heat seer of the burning gas as they slowly passed by.

The paint on the cruise ship started to bubble and peel away and smoke appeared from smouldering light flammable materials dotted about the decks as the heat seer intensified. Wooden parts of the superstructure started to blacken as the searing heat scorched them.

For what seemed an eternity, the Baroness of the Sea slowly edged its way passed the crippled burning NATGAS 2.

Jeff, Cyril, Derek, and John had rejoined their wives in the Restaurant that was now serving as an emergency hospital. It was a hive of activity. There were many injuries consisting of mainly broken bones and severe bruising. There were three elderly people who had suffered heart attacks but all three were being treated by first aiders as the Medical Officer was seeing to other badly injured passengers. The ship's medical staff was stretched to breaking point. Everyone had been shaken up by the pounding the Baroness of the Sea had received.

Jeff said to Karen "Darling. We are not out of the woods yet. We have to get past the burning NATGAS 2 so the Captain can beach the ship at the other end of the Island. It is going to get awfully hot as we pass that burning gas ship".

Jeff went to the Medical Officer and said "We have to move these people by the walls to the middle of the Restaurant otherwise they might get severely burned when we pass the burning ship".

"We can't move all of them" the Medical Officer said "some have very serious injuries, we are lucky none have died so far. Some need urgent hospitalisation and medical help beyond what I can do for them".

"The only other way is to use the fire hoses and wet down that side of the ship as we sail past" Jeff said and as a second thought remarked "that's if they are working".

"The fire hoses are designed to work when everything around them has failed" the Medical Officer responded "if you want to put a water screen up covering that side of the ship, I will get the patients that can't be moved covered up so you don't drown them".

"Right, I need volunteers that are not injured" Jeff shouted above the hubbub of people talking and the moaning and crying of the injured passengers and crew "we need to wet the side of the ship as we pass the burning gas ship otherwise the heat seer will burn every one".

Cyril left Jen's side as she was organising medical supplies for those in pain and John left Rose tending a woman. Derek left Sandra helping splint a broken leg and they joined Jeff.

"What do you want us to do?" John asked.

"Find a member of staff to show you where all the fire hoses are on this deck then form crews of men, at least two to a hose, put the hoses on spray and dowse and soak the walls. As we pass the burning gas ship we make a water curtain of spray. We can't have any gaps in the water curtain so we need to work as a team".

There were a number of volunteers that helped form fire fighting crews. Some were still sporting bruises from the battering they had taken but they were determined to help in any way they could.

A crew member showed them where the wet risers were and explained how they worked. The wet risers were a system of fixed solid pipes that were full of pressurised water. The pipes covered the whole ship and had outlets at different staging points throughout. They were used to fight fires at any given point within the ship, so instead of trailing long lengths of fire fighting hoses all over each deck a fire could be fought from any part of the ship using shorter lengths of hoses connected to the wet risers. The lengths of hoses were stored in a compartment behind a panel next to the wet risers.

They opened the panel and connected the length of hose to the wet riser, broke the seal and turned the valve. Jeff felt the hose pressurise and was ready to deploy it as soon as he turned the hose nozzle on.

The crews manned the hoses and started wetting down the outer side of the Restaurant walls, soaking the beautiful drapes.

As the gas ship came into view, it started to get hotter in the room from the heat seer from the burning ship.

They formed a circle and within that circle they sprayed the hoses outward towards the damaged windows forming a giant curtain of water, cocooning everyone in the Restaurant within it and behind the wall of water.

Steam was forming as the water curtain was boiled by the intense heat but the water curtain held as the hoses replaced the heated water that was turning to steam with the heat from the heat seer with cold water from the wet risers.

There was the noise of hissing steam as a cloud formed from the water curtain as it boiled off and blew all along the ship and trailed behind the crippled Baroness of the Sea like a trailing fog.

It seemed to last forever but as the Baroness of the Sea slowly passed the inferno of the burning gas ship the room cooled down and Jeff ordered the hoses to be turned off.

"That was a close run thing" John said "where did you learn that trick from?"

"I used to be the fire manager of a building at one time and I had to go on a fire fighting course".

The heat seemed to ease the further away from the crippled NATGAS 2 they got. All of a sudden, there was an explosion that came from the bowels of the NATGAS 2 and like a searing sun spot a gigantic flame erupted from the gas ship. There was a mighty concussion that rocked the crippled Baroness of the Sea as a giant fireball exploded from the gas ship right where the cruise liner had just been, boiling the sea that they had just sailed through and the concussion from the explosion sent a giant wave towards them, chasing them down the coastline of Sable Island.

John looked in the direction of the NATGAS 2 then said "Oh no! Another tidal wave, get everyone to brace themselves for impact before that wave hits us".

The wave created by detonating gas also blew apart one of the giant gas domes. A giant fireball started to swell and tumble out behind them.

They knew that if the Captain had left it any later to run the gauntlet of fire they would have been hit by that expanding fireball of intense heat and would have certainly been incinerated.

It was now a race against time to reach the shoreline at the western end of Sabre Island. They had to make the beach before they sank and on the way they had to avoid any sandbars that were dotted about on the coast of the Island to give the rescue people the best chance of helping the passengers and crew to safety.

Sable Island looked bleak and windswept. The sand dunes that covered the island looked inhospitable, the sparse dwellings that dotted the island looked dated and the old ancient lighthouse looked tattered.

CHAPTER 49

They were limping along the coastline of the Island when they heard the roaring of the small tidal wave that had resulted from the last concussion of the death throes of the NATGAS 2. The wave was following them along the coast and was getting bigger as it approached them.

The Captain knew he could not manoeuvre the crippled Baroness of the Sea to face the wave before it hit them. He had to hope that it hit them on the stern and they could ride it out. He knew if it hit them to the side, they would roll sideways and with the damage they had already sustained, they could roll over completely.

It seemed ironic that they had fought so hard against impossible odds and had come so far only to have their hopes dashed at the last moment.

The Baroness of the Sea began to wallow like an old sea scow in the heavy seas created by the explosion from the dying NATGAS 2, the flames of which were now lighting up the sky like a giant burning beacon.

The crippled cruise liner started to flounder as they neared the coast. All on board had every faith in the Captain's ability to handle his crippled ship but they knew it was now a race against time and that timing was going to be crucial as the wave was bearing down on the Baroness of the Sea. There was no room for manoeuvring the big ship in the shallow water. All they could hope for was for the wave to lift them onto the sandbar near the beach to which they were heading.

The stern of the ship lifted as the swell of the wave hit them. The cruise liner gradually swung round to face the beach. There was a loud snapping sound like a rifle shot as the ropes holding the patch over the hole in the ship's side parted and the patch was swept away with the force of the impact of the wave. The Baroness of the Sea seemed to founder. The second wave swept the cruise liner toward the sandbar not far from the beach at the western tip of Sable Island.

The last of the big waves swept along the ship with such a force it turned the bow of the ship to face the sandy shore and the sand dunes. With one last effort, the Captain swung the bow of the ship round and headed the cruise liner for the shallow waters. The Captain shut off the mighty engines of the Baroness of the Sea and allowed the waves to take her. She was now at the mercy of the Atlantic graveyard. The Captain managed to beach the ship as the last wave washed over her, forcing it to a grinding halt on the sandbar near the beach and the sand dunes.

As the sea boiled around them and slowly settled, the cruise liner remained held fast on the sandbar and there she settled, tilted slightly at a drunken angle. With much grinding and groaning of deck and hull plates, the Baroness of the Sea eventually came to rest.

After the ordeal the Baroness of the Sea had not been constructed to go through, the fact that she had pulled through against all the odds was a testament to the builders who had constructed her and her Captain's skills in handling her and to a number of people who had said no to subjugation.

The wave and the pounding sea withdrew from the Baroness of the Sea. She was now left high and dry, stuck fast on the sandbar very close to the western tip of the

Sable Island shoreline and the Canadian territory of Halifax County.

Jeff looked out onto a bleak and desolate spit of barren land that was covered in sand dunes. They were at the end of a very long narrow stretch of land that was shaped like a long sabre that was bravely and defiantly sticking out into the edge of the Atlantic, curving away into the distant ocean, defying the sea to do its worse. On the high stretches of rough grassland horses grazed appearing quite unperturbed at the scene that was unfolding before them.

Jeff could see why the inhospitable coast of Sable Island was named the Atlantic graveyard and why over many years 350 ships had foundered on her coast with the loss of hundreds of lives.

But this time, this inhospitable coast, this Atlantic graveyard had been the saving grace of the souls aboard the Baroness of the Sea for without this stretch of coastline being strategically placed where it was, the Baroness of the Sea would have foundered and sunk in the unforgiving seas of the Atlantic Ocean with the loss of many lives.

In the Restaurant the atmosphere could have been cut with a knife. The silence was very eerie as the people realised they were stationary and safe. The deck tilted as the ship settled, and then the silence was broken with the sobs and cheers of the injured.

They started treating the injured and tried to make them as comfortable as they could until help arrived. Then the world's biggest ever sea rescue began and swung into action like a well-oiled machine.

Help arrived in the shape of throbbing helicopters that hovered over the stranded Baroness of the Sea, winch men and paramedics descended onto the sloping deck of the crippled cruise ship bringing much needed medical supplies and expertise in medical emergencies.

The paramedics quickly organised a triage system where the worst cases were evacuated first to the beach where makeshift hospitals were being quickly erected and then ferried onto hospitals in Nova Scotia, Canada.

Light aircraft were also brought in and the beach a little further down the coast was used as an emergency runway. These were used to ferry the injured.

The area was getting very busy with rescue ships from both Canada and America being used as staging vessels.

The lifeboats from the Baroness of the Sea together with lifeboats from other vessels that had responded to the May Day were used to ferry people to and fro from the cruise ship to the beach.

The helicopters in the sky around the area were like dragon flies hovering over a pond in the summer, sweeping to and fro on their urgent missions.

John later said that the logistical nightmare of moving so many people to safety was organised brilliantly.

Jeff, Karen, Derek, Sandra, Cyril, Jen, John and Rose together with Asar, Mustafa's wife were one of the last groups to leave the cruise liner. They were then transferred to the beach. It was getting dark now and they were tired as they had spent the day helping the injured. They themselves were checked out by a medic in the beach hospital and then they were flown in a private light aircraft to Nova Scotia in Canada where they were met by members of the Canadian Mounted Police who escorted them through a bevy of reporters at the airport.

The reporters were told there would be a press conference in the morning after everyone had all rested. They were then taken by cars under escort by the Canadian Mounted Police to a five star hotel.

As they arrived at the hotel, they had to run the gauntlet of the press and dodge the crowds milling outside the hotel and they were chaperoned through all the reporters waiting outside the airport. There were Canadian Mounted Police guarding the hotel where a very official reception committee was waiting for them in the foyer to greet them.

A man stepped forward and introduced himself as a Special Envoy of the Canadian Government who welcomed them to Canada. He asked if when rested, they could give a briefing so he could make a full report to his Government of what had happened.

Then the Government Envoy said "I understand one of your party lost something very dear to them". He beckoned and from behind a pillar came a very bedraggled Mustafa.

"We only just found him a short while ago" the Envoy said.

Asar rushed into his arms crying "I thought I had lost you".

They all crowded round Mustafa, telling him how pleased they were to see him.

"I must let you all rest. You all look exhausted. We can get the details in the morning when we will also get the Captain's report. A meal has been laid on for you if you are hungry and then you must rest. You all have a busy day tomorrow."

They were escorted to a private small restaurant area in the hotel where a light meal was laid out. They all wanted to know how Mustafa was and what had happened after he had left Cyril on the deck of the Baroness of the Sea and went aboard the NATGAS 2.

Asar never let him go. She clung to his side like a limpet as they all listened intently to every word he had to say, gasping when he told them about the shooting on the Bridge of the NATGAS 2. She looked apprehensive as he talked about the escape by the Fast Lady and told them about when he came to the realisation that the gas cloud had to be ignited or it would have spread to cover the Baroness of the Sea. He looked at Asar very lovingly and told her he knew that she was on that ship and he felt he had to save her and everyone on board before the gas cloud ignited killing everyone.

He said that he had had the idea of using a Very pistol just as James Bond did in one of his movies. He then fired the star shell from the Very pistol and dived into the water so the heat sear from the exploding gas would sweep over him. He said he did not expect the tidal wave that came from the crippled NATGAS 2. He then told them of his decision to try and outride the tidal waves, which he nearly did. He said it was the second one that caught them unprepared and swamped them. He felt that was when he lost the last two remaining volunteers. He was in the water for quite some time before a helicopter found him and brought him to the hotel.

"You're safe with me now" Asar said "I thought I had lost you and I am not letting you out of my sight ever". She clung to him afraid to let him go in case he was not real and he suddenly disappeared.

Jeff turned to Mustafa and said "Now we know you are safe we can all get some sleep. We will see you in the morning for breakfast".

They all went to their rooms for a well-earned rest.

CHAPTER 50

After all ten of them finished breakfast in the little private dining room within the hotel, they had all gone to the suite that had been reserved for them. It was then that the Canadian Ambassador entered the room. He had with him five men, two who he introduced as the American Ambassador and the British Ambassador and the other three men who were aides.

The American Ambassador said "We have had a short debriefing with the Captain and his First Officer and we wanted to hear your side of what happened. We would like to hear each individual report so we can report to our various governments as to the whole political mess and what we can do about it. We need to work out which Middle Eastern country was responsible and how we might be able to retaliate against the Arab country who trained the terrorists and sent them out to attack America and Canada".

"What do you mean by the whole political mess?" Jeff asked "may I remind you that we have just had to pull your political chestnuts out of the fire because you were going to do nothing about them".

"How can you say that?" the American Ambassador replied, slightly flustered "we carried out an act of aggression when we sank an old submarine, then we pulled your sorry arses out of the sea and put into operation the largest rescue operation ever mounted in full glare of the media. How can you say we did nothing".

"Apart from the sinking of the submarine which we told you was there and was threatening to blow us all up, the rest is a political smokescreen to save your sorry arses as you like to put it and to save political face".

"Gentlemen" the British Ambassador interjected calmly "let's not start out on the wrong foot" then holding his arms out in an all-encompassing gesture "you have all been through a terrible traumatic time and the shock of what has happened is taking its toll . . . ."

"Don't be so damn condescending" Jeff interrupted "we were the ones that stopped you having the biggest disaster in history on your doorstep". He then pointed to the American Ambassador and said "If we hadn't done what we did, you would have blown us out of the water as we got near the American coastline killing all of us".

"How can you say that?" the American Ambassador asked again.

"Quite easily" Jeff said "I open my mouth and the words come out. So what are you going to do about it, have us all bumped off so you can go back to your political world of lies?"

"Gentlemen, gentlemen" the Canadian Ambassador interjected soothingly "we cannot be seen to be at one another's throats in front of the media. You are all heroes. The press are waiting to see you, they are aware of the daring deeds you have done, and the impossible odds you have overcome. We just need to get the parts we played in this happy outcome right".

"Is this the royal we? Or is this a political we?" Jeff asked "we fought for our lives out there because we knew there would not be any help from any country. We were on our own and if we had not taken back that ship when we did, you would have sent out orders to blow us out of the water before we got within your territorial waters. Now you as politicians want to claim the glory for sitting on your hands and doing nothing hoping a miracle would happen. Let me tell you that the miracle happened when ordinary people decided to say no.

Jeff then pointedly addressed the American Ambassador "And that man there, who is proud to be an Arab, and I am privileged to call a friend" Jeff said pointing to Mustafa "saved everybody on board the Baroness of the Sea when he risked his own life by igniting that gas cloud before it reached the ship, because if that gas cloud had ignited any nearer we would have been brown bread".

"What do you mean by brown bread?" the American Ambassador queried.

The British Ambassador interjected and said to the American Ambassador "It's cockney rhyming slang, brown bread means dead". Then trying once again to placate the situation he turned to Jeff and said "The British Prime Minister warned me about your reputation for taking no prisoners when you are put out. He also told me that you are a reasonable man when common sense is brought to the table. I appeal to that common sense now as we need to have a dialog and a way forward must be found".

John interrupted "What Jeff is trying to say, if he" pointing to the American Ambassador "stops rubbing him up the wrong way, is that it was not Middle Eastern terrorists that carried this plot out but an organisation called The Senate.

"Who is The Senate?" the American and Canadian ambassadors asked together, looking very puzzled.

"They were responsible for the Estuary incident in England a little while ago" the British Ambassador answered "we thought we had eradicated them but if what John tells us is true they have come back to haunt us, this time operating globally and that is of grave concern to us all".

"I was told the Estuary incident was an industrial accident" the Canadian Ambassador said.

"It was, but it was orchestrated by The Senate" John said "which is a very right wing Nazi type organisation bent on world domination. They try to use divide and rule tactics and then undermine the established regime and take control, then they use a very right wing military rule to control the people".

Jeff added "Who and what is behind The Senate we have yet to find out. Going by what we have been told it looks like they have raised their heads again, this time they wanted to attack both your countries via the gas supply wells in the Arab States and also the terminals that store the Liquid Natural Gas in your country and cause dissent amongst yourselves and the Arab States".

"And they very nearly achieved that" John added.

"This Senate, where are they based?" the American Ambassador asked.

"They do not seem to have a base in any one country that we know of" John replied "but they are seriously organised".

"Well they were nearly successful in Great Britain and now they have tried to attack America and by the sounds of it they were nearly successful this time as well. If it had not been for you lot taking them on" the American Ambassador said "I would not like to have predicted the outcome".

At that moment, there was a knock on the door and a scuffle by the doorway. Michael pushed his way into the room followed by two security guards with guns drawn and pointing at Michael.

"Michael!" Jeff exclaimed "where the hell did you spring from?"

"Do you know this man?" one of the security guards asked.

"Yes" Cyril, Derek and Jeff replied together.

"I have been following your progress on the high seas" Michael blurted out "I can't leave you lot alone for a minute without you getting up to mischief without me".

"It's good to see you again" Jeff said "what have you been doing?"

"Having my holiday spoilt by mysterious phone calls" Michael answered "good job you did though. My cousin said the American submarine that took out The Senate submarine was going off station when you called. It only just made it to the rendezvous point. Lucky it spotted The Senate sub in time on its undersea radar just as it was surfacing to signal the Baroness of the Sea. They managed to jam the signal The Senate were putting out, and then they tried to board her. During the confrontation The Senate submarine fired a torpedo at the American submarine as she dived. The American submarine returned the compliment and The Senate sub sank with all hands. The captain of the American submarine said it was strange that The Senate sub seemed to dive for the sea bed instead of surfacing and she imploded when she hit the sea bed. It was as if they decided to commit suicide rather than be caught".

"I was not told of this incident that happened in our territorial waters" the Canadian Ambassador said in an annoyed tone.

"You are being told now" came a commanding female voice from the doorway.

They all turned to see that a stunningly beautiful brunette, dressed in an American naval uniform, had just entered the room.

Michael said "May I introduce my cousin. She is the one we have to thank for stopping The Senate sub from meeting the Baroness of the Sea. She is the one who convinced Naval Intelligence that the sub was a threat".

Those in the room all crowded around the Naval Officer, thanking her for getting the military involved.

Jeff's wife introduced everyone to her then the women seemed to take her under their wing.

Jeff said in an aside to Michael as the women were talking together on the other side of the room "Cyril said you were visiting a cousin in the Naval Intelligence but I didn't expect her to be that gorgeous and she has her head screwed on right".

"She is lovely" Michael agreed "technically we are third cousins and we have had a soft spot for one another for many years, but her career has always come first. I was hoping with this visit I might change all that. At the moment it seems to be going very well. She is here to get a report from you all as to what happened out there. By the sounds of it you had lots of fun and all without me to keep an eye out for you".

"You covered our backs" Jeff said "and without you and your lovely cousin intervening when you did it would have turned out very differently".

Just as they were speaking, there came a knock at the door and a man dressed in a high ranking Royal Mounted Police Uniform entered the room.

Michael responded by calling out "Laurence, where did you spring from?"

"Michael" he replied "I did not expect to find you here, and hey, is this Cousin Valerie as well over there? I have not seen you for years, how are you?"

"What are you doing here?" Michael asked.

"To report to the Canadian Ambassador that we have put the Captain of the cruise liner under close arrest as instructed".

"You what?" Jeff asked aggressively "on what charge?"

"And who the hell are you?" Laurence interjected without replying "to tell me what to do or what not to do as Chief of Police in my country?"

"Ease off Laurence" Michael said "I think we have some crossed wires here".

Michael explained to Laurence who was who and what had happened as far as he knew, the full details Jeff and the others could give later.

"Then why was I instructed to arrest the French Captain off of the cruise liner?" Laurence asked, confused.

"It might have been because he was French" Jeff replied.

"What do you mean by that remark?" Laurence asked.

"Well" Jeff explained "we are all British and Mustafa is an Arab. To arrest us would have created an international

"SAY NO"

incident and would have drawn attention to the incident that someone wants to cover up. Next, they will be saying the Captain endangered his ship and the passengers".

"How did you know the charge the Captain was being held on?" Laurence asked with disbelief.

"Who told you to arrest the Captain before he gave his statement to the press?" Jeff asked wryly.

Laurence looked at the Canadian Ambassador and said "I had written orders from your office".

As all this was going on, there was another interruption at the door. This time it was an elderly Arab Sheik with two bodyguards.

"What's going on?" Jeff asked "it's turning into Piccadilly Circus in here".

Mustafa raised his eyes in recognition of the Sheik and stepped forward. He bowed and said "Welcome Sheik Ali Ben Mustafa, may I introduce my friends".

Mustafa began introductions but the Sheik raised an elegant hand interrupting him and said in perfect English "I am here to bring to justice my son's killer, my son's death will be the cause of a holy war against the West that will have no end. You have failed to protect my son and brought shame and dishonour to your family".

CHAPTER 51

Jeff could not contain his anger at this remark. He shouted at the Sheik "Who the hell do you think you are going off half-cocked and putting two and two together and making six?"

"How dare you speak to the Sheik in this manner" the Sheik's bodyguard interrupted. He then pointed at Mustafa "and you my son, how could you have not tried to save the Sheik's son. He was your friend as well as your charge".

Jeff squared off to the Sheik's bodyguard and said "He saved all of us. If it wasn't for him we would all have perished". Then turning to the Sheik Jeff continued "if you want to blame anyone for your son's death you had better look at The Senate".

"And who are The Senate" the Sheik asked.

"We first came across them in the Estuary in England where they tried to destabilise the country. Sir William Waite owned the LNG terminal in the Estuary area".

Jeff went on to explain that he was an environmentalist who had campaigned against the lack of safety at the Terminal for many years. The Terminal had exploded in an accident when they cut too many corners with regard to safety. The resultant domino effect on all the gas and oil industry in the Estuary area created total devastation all the way along the Estuary. It put that part of the country back to the dark ages and financially crippled the country.

Sir William Waite tried to cover up the incident and blamed terrorists. He said Jeff was the leader of those terrorists. During the ensuing days Sir William used his contacts in a right wing organisation called The Senate and tried to destabilise the Government and take control of the military. He wanted to blame and attack the Middle East.

Jeff had gone back to the Estuary and found the incriminating evidence of corruption that was the downfall of Sir William Waite who had sent a professional killer named Wilson to hunt Jeff down. Wilson succeeded in hunting Jeff down and tried to recover the incriminating evidence but Wilson was killed by John the Prime Minister's special agent. Jeff took a long time to heal after the injuries he had sustained from the attack. After the arrest of Sir William Waite and his subsequent trial there was a massive shakeup in the Government.

Jeff had been charged with setting up the Safe Siting Policy of High Fire Risk Industry known as Top Tier COMAH (Control of Managing Accidental Hazards) sites by the Prime Minister. He also realised quite quickly that whilst the Whitehall mandarins had had their teeth pulled metaphorically after the Estuary incident, he knew he would have a target on his back. Also, he would have to live with the fact that he was going to be the political whipping boy so the Prime Minister could appear to keep his hands clean of any unpopular decisions.

Jeff did not mind that as he had been given the powers to get the issues resolved. He did not waste time as he still had the nightmare memory of the disaster in the Estuary that had claimed thousands of lives still ingrained on his mind. He felt very strongly that the issues would be painted over in time by greed and politics if they were not answered now.

It had been a very difficult time as the planning departments and councillors on those planning committees seemed to have their own agenda which seemed to be in line with their own ends and not necessarily for the benefit of the people who they represented.

He was not here for the popularity stakes. The ghost of the Estuary incident haunted him and even today he would suffer flashbacks of the horror that would remain with him forever. He was determined that there would be no more deaths due to bad planning.

Some bureaucrats were just totally incompetent. He felt that if they had had a brain they would be dangerous. All they had been interested in was the junkets that they attended and were full of their own importance.

He constantly reminded planners and always ended the argument at meetings with the statement that he was not prepared to pay the price in human lives ever again as that cost was too dear.

He had covered a lot of ground and had got into place a much stronger policy of Land Use Planning (LUP) that safeguarded populations who lived near these sites with a Cordon of Sanity. This meant no building was allowed on the buffer zone and neither could the sites be encroached upon by industry.

Above all, he was determined that the much wider corridors of safety around high fire risk and toxic industry would be a legacy of the future.

CHAPTER 52

"Who are you?" the Sheik asked of Jeff with respect. He appeared much calmer after Jeff's explanation.

Mustafa interjected and said "Let me re-introduce everyone". As he got to the Canadian Ambassador the Sheik said "Ambassador Thomas Waite and I are acquainted".

Jeff turned to the Canadian Ambassador and asked carefully "No relation to Sir William Waite I trust?"

The Canadian Ambassador suddenly and without warning pulled a gun from his suit pocket and pointed it at Jeff and the Sheik who was standing next to Jeff.

"He was my brother" Ambassador Waite stated "and you were the cause of his downfall".

Everything then happened swiftly. Mustafa reacted like lightning and dived into the path of the gun as Ambassador Waite rapidly fired three shots, one after another. Mustafa took the fusillade of shots with his body but managed to wrestle the gun from the Ambassador's grasp before collapsing to the floor.

Like a cornered rat, the Ambassador ran for the balcony followed by Laurence in close pursuit.

In his mad dash for freedom, the Ambassador tripped over a stool by the balcony door. The forward speed of his flight sent him tumbling onto the balcony where he overbalanced and went over the low railing. He fell screaming to the ground thirty stories below. The thud of his landing could be heard faintly in the room.

"Get a medic in here now" Laurence shouted to the guards by the door, seeing that Mustafa had been shot.

One of the Sheik's bodyguards reacted and shouted out "Son!" and fell down on his knees next to Mustafa.

The Sheik said incredulously "He stopped the bullet which was meant for me".

The medics arrived swiftly to attend Mustafa's wounds. Miraculously, he was only slightly wounded.

"We need to get him to the hospital" a Medic said.

"He goes under police escort and I want a 24 hour guard set up around his bed. He sees nobody except his wife unless I say so" the Sheik ordered then he said gently to Asar "you go with your man he needs you".

The medics took Mustafa away on a stretcher with Asar beside him and the Sheik's bodyguard looking on very anxiously.

"Seal this area and the hotel now" ordered Laurence and to the guards at the door "nobody is allowed in or out without my direct authority".

"But I have diplomatic schedules to keep" the American Ambassador said "you can't hold me as a prisoner".

"You are not a prisoner" Laurence answered "but as Chief of Police I can do whatever I want to do to safeguard my country and its diplomatic guests".

The American Ambassador blustered "The President of the United States will hear of this, this is an outrage".

Valerie spoke up "He will also get my report as well. Ambassador, why do you need to leave very suddenly? A little while ago we could not get you out of here with a tyre lever, now you suddenly have urgent business elsewhere".

"This is a conspiracy involving your family" the Ambassador said accusingly, pointing to Valerie and Laurence "you two are cousins and so is he a member of your family" pointing at Michael "you are all in this together. You are part of this Senate he spoke of" pointing at John "and they are going to kill us all".

"What do you know about us being killed?" Valerie asked the Ambassador very calmly.

"Now Waite is dead The Senate are going to kill us all" the Ambassador replied agitatedly, looking towards the window and the balcony expectantly.

"When is this going to happen?" Valerie asked, still being very calm.

"At any time now" the Ambassador said, becoming increasingly agitated and frightened.

"How is this going to be achieved?" Valerie asked, her tone of voice still soothingly calm, whilst the Ambassador was slowly becoming more and more anxious.

"Now Ambassador Waite will fail to give the safe signal because he is dead" the American Ambassador said "they have two rocket launchers trained on this hotel suite balcony from the two buildings across the street". He suddenly screamed "they will kill us all and I don't want to die".

"Hit the fire alarm and evacuate the hotel now" Laurence ordered, turning to the men stationed by the door "and find those rocket launchers".

Everybody scurried for the door of the hotel suite. They all made it to the landing and headed for the lift.

"Use the stairs" Laurence ordered "it will afford us more cover and it will give us more protection".

They just made it to the stairs.

As the fire door of the emergency stairs hissed shut behind them, there came an explosive concussion which threw them all off of their feet and they all fell into a heap on the stair landing.

"Is everyone alright?" Laurence shouted to make himself heard above the fire claxon which was now wailing loudly "and where is the American Ambassador?"

The American Ambassador was just getting clear of the landing and attempting to make a run for freedom but he had to pass Derek.

Derek let the Ambassador get almost past him before clamping his huge hand onto the back of the Ambassador's neck and pushing downwards and side-ways, propelling the unfortunate man into the wall head first with a sickening thud. He collapsed unconscious to the floor. Laurence promptly snapped a pair of handcuffs onto the unfortunate American Ambassador's wrists.

The group made their way down the emergency stairs to the lobby of the hotel with Derek carrying the American Ambassador across his broad shoulders. They were met with a wall of sound from the emergency sirens of the police cars and ambulances and fire trucks.

Laurence directed them into a reception room at the side of the main lobby where he ordered guards stationed at both doors. "This is for your safety and protection" he told everyone and then turning to the guards "Nobody comes in here without my say so". He then left the room and started organising his staff into investigating who had fired the rocket launchers.

The group all found seats and sat down to wait until emergency services had done their jobs and it was made safe for them to leave.

The Sheik was the first to speak. He said to his bodyguard "I cannot believe that after failing to save my son your son saved my life and took the bullets which were meant for me".

Jeff interrupted and said "Sheik Ali Ben Mustafa. You do Mustafa an injustice if you blame him for your son's death. He tried on many occasions to talk him out of his course of action, in fact, he was not on board when your son died, he was trying to save him and all the other passengers and crew". Jeff went on to explain how he had met Mustafa and what had transpired during the hijacking.

The Sheik listened intently to what Jeff had to say and then remarked "So my son died as a result of the tidal wave swamping the cruise liner when the NATGAS 2 exploded which was the ultimate doing of this group called The Senate who also just attempted to kill us all with rocket launchers, just so they can destabilise and take over the Middle Eastern countries and control the supply of Liquid Natural Gas for their own political ends. Well, I can assure you that it is not going to happen now we know they exist".

"Yes" Jeff said, and then added "I am so sorry about your son".

"I am a father who loved his son, I am also the father of my people" the Sheik said "but perhaps I indulged my son too much. He was also led astray by this group called The Senate and that will be investigated as to who was behind it in my country.

I have had my suspicions about my brother-in-law the Minister for Energy for a long time, and when I find out who else is involved, heads will roll, literally.

I am in your debt for exposing this plot to me and the danger it posed to my country".

"Well at the moment" Jeff said "not only are you going to be busy but it looks like America and Canada will be carrying out their own investigations as well".

"In the meanwhile you have had a spoilt holiday and that can be rectified" the Sheik said "therefore, I insist that you and all your friends be my guests on board my sea-going yacht. It will be yours to command for as long as you wish".

The Sheik then looked humbled "I have a very brave man to see. I have done Mustafa a grave injustice and that needs to be rectified now. I now have a debt of gratitude to fulfil with a person who has not only become your friend, he also fulfilled his family traditions with honour. His father will be proud of him, he will be honoured. You will be hearing from me as men like you are a rarity in my country. My debt to you and your friends will not be forgotten. Now I must act fast to clip the wings of my brother-in-law". With this final remark, the Sheik bowed and left the room with his bodyguards.

John said "Look, I have reports to write up so the British Ambassador can make his report to the British Government".

"You still work for the Prime Minister in secret then?" Jeff asked.

"After this little trip I will be resigning my commission" John replied.

"Well then" Jeff said "you and your lovely wife Rose will need a holiday with us on a luxury yacht".

EPILOGUE

At a secret meeting in a safe house on the borders of Canada and America, near Niagara Falls, two American senators together with two members of the Canadian Government met with their host who was a very powerful ex-Russian mafia leader boss called Val Voss. He was a stocky man with features that looked as though they had been carved from granite and hard eyes.

"I called this special meeting to discuss how the Waite brothers let the Senate down by being too greedy too soon, and nearly exposing what we are trying to achieve. We have progressed a lot further than mere drug and human trafficking, and we are legitimate now. We control the oil and gas fields in Russia and its pipelines to the west. Now that you in America and Canada are stockpiling all your gas and oil reserves you are controlling the gas fields in the West. By using up the Middle Eastern oil and gas it will start to run out in 20 years' time, it is then that we will be able to pool all our resources and have the power to control all the gas and oil sources and hold the world to ransom just as we control some of the African countries now because of the need for fossil fuel. As I have said before, he who controls the fuel lines controls the price of fuel, and in 20 years time we can demand any price we like and we will dominate the world.

As you are all aware the only other very large untapped major deposits of minerals, oil and gas is in the Weddell Sea area in the Antarctic and the British were allocated that area under the agreement back in the 1960s, when the Antarctic was divided up between nations.

The best and only jumping off point to the Weddell Sea area is the Falkland Islands. I still believe that's why the Argentineans invaded the Falkland Islands in the first place, so when they invade and take over the Falkland Islands again with our help, we will be able to control the massive mineral deposits and the oil and Liquid Natural Gas fields that are in the Weddell Sea, and in doing so we will be able to control the distribution of energy worldwide and therefore control the countries we want.

You know originally that is why we wanted to control the British Government by using the Waite brothers so we could get control of the Weddell Sea, but that failed because the Waite brothers were incompetent.

I have sent a visitor to Sir William Waite in prison by one of our friends. By now he has joined his brother and the both of them will now be dead, so our secret dies with them. Only the people in this room know of our plans for world domination by controlling the energy sources of the world.

Now, back to how we can redress our present situation. We need to keep a low profile and remain in the background and keep everything secret until we can manipulate the situation back to our advantage. We must keep a low profile and ensure that what we are planning is kept secret.

With a little patience we will be very rich, very soon, so until we meet again gentlemen I wish you good health".

All those present rose from their seats and shook hands and went on their various ways.

The seats that the American ambassadors and the Canadian diplomats sat on were laced with a slow reaction poisonous virus. Once they had sat on them, their fates were sealed and they would die of what would be deemed as natural causes within twelve hours.

As he left the room, the Russian let out an evil chuckle. "They were the only ones remaining who knew my mother was Hitler's love child, and she was sent to a Russian prison camp. I was born from her after being repeatedly raped in a prison in Siberia and she taught me how to hate.

Now is the time for revenge and that is best served cold, and I will enjoy dealing out that revenge. Who would suspect that under the smoke screen of a right wing Nazi group, named after an American Institution, The Senate was controlled by an ex member of the Russian mafia.